ARCTIC SEA

PREVIOUS BOOKS BY DAVID POYER

Tales of the Modern Navy

Violent Peace	*Korea Strait*
Overthrow	*The Threat*
Deep War	*The Command*
Hunter Killer	*Black Storm*
Onslaught	*China Sea*
Tipping Point	*Tomahawk*
The Cruiser	*The Passage*
The Towers	*The Circle*
The Crisis	*The Gulf*
The Weapon	*The Med*

Tiller Galloway

Down to a Sunless Sea	*Bahamas Blue*
Louisiana Blue	*Hatteras Blue*

The Civil War at Sea

That Anvil of Our Souls	*A Country of Our Own*
Fire on the Waters	

Hemlock County

Thunder on the Mountain	*Winter in the Heart*
As the Wolf Loves Winter	*The Dead of Winter*

Other Books

Heroes of Annapolis	*The Only Thing to Fear*
On War and Politics (with Arnold Punaro)	*Stepfather Bank*
The Whiteness of the Whale	*The Return of Philo T. McGiffin*
Happier Than This Day and Time	*Star Seed*
Ghosting	*The Shiloh Project*
	White Continent

ARCTIC SEA

A DAN LENSON NOVEL

David Poyer

ST. MARTIN'S PRESS
NEW YORK

First published in the United States by St. Martin's Press, an imprint of St. Martin's Publishing Group

ARCTIC SEA. Copyright © 2021 by David Poyer. All rights reserved. Printed in the United States of America. For information, address St. Martin's Publishing Group, 120 Broadway, New York, NY 10271.

www.stmartins.com

Library of Congress Cataloging-in-Publication Data

Names: Poyer, David, author.
Title: Arctic Sea : a Dan Lenson novel / David Poyer.
Description: First edition. | New York : St. Martin's Press, 2021. |
    Series: Dan Lenson novels ; 21
Identifiers: LCCN 2021027562 | ISBN 9781250273062 (hardcover) |
    ISBN 9781250273079 (ebook)
Subjects: GSAFD: Suspense fiction. | War stories.
Classification: LCC PS3566.O978 A88 2021 | DDC 813/.54—dc23
LC record available at https://lccn.loc.gov/2021027562

Our books may be purchased in bulk for promotional, educational, or business use. Please contact your local bookseller or the Macmillan Corporate and Premium Sales Department at 1-800-221-7945, extension 5442, or by email at MacmillanSpecialMarkets@macmillan.com.

First Edition: 2021

10 9 8 7 6 5 4 3 2 1

For George Witte

It is said that God left the northernmost point of the earth unfinished; for, He said, "Whosoever professes he is equal to Me, let him come and complete this land, which I have left unfinished; thus will all know he is My equal."

—The Talmud

I

POSTWAR

1

The Pentagon, Arlington, Virginia

The gray-eyed officer in khakis and leather jacket lifted his boot off the accelerator, slowing the car as it approached the first ring of security. AI-manned booths marked an outer perimeter of cameras, radioactivity monitors, razor wire, and concrete barriers. That cordon had grown outward like a coral accretion during the yearslong war that had just ended.

And there were no shouting, marching demonstrators. Anyone who opposed the government had been sentenced to the Zones long before.

A digital intelligence matched his features through a lens. A green light glowed, and a steel gate unlocked with a subdued *clank*.

Daniel V. Lenson steered cautiously through the zigzagged approach, then decelerated again as troops in black tactical gear, slung carbines, and the silver Liberty-head-in-a-wreath badges of Homeland Security waved him to a halt. The Blackies flashed lasers on his ID, scanned his face again, and gestured him out of the vehicle. As they wanded him a low-slung robot rolled beneath his car, searching the undercarriage with a subdued whine.

At last they saluted him—or more accurately, saluted the silver eagles of a captain on his collar. Two stars had glittered there before. But with the armistice, he'd reverted from admiral to his peacetime rank. "Forward as one, patriot," one guard muttered, waving him on.

As he drove the last few hundred yards the building coalesced out of the morning mists off the Potomac. Huge. Steel-patina'd. A limestone fortress.

In peacetime its sprawling lots had been filled with glittering chrome and glass, thousands of the latest sedans and pickups and SUVs. Today those acres of cracked asphalt stretched nearly tenantless, save for a few hundred rusty prewar vehicles near the entrances. Scraps of paper trash tumbled in a chilly autumn wind.

Despite himself, his gaze pulled north. Decades before, he'd been in the Navy Command Center when an airliner had plowed into it. He and Barry "Nick" Niles had crawled out together through burning fuel and collapsing ceilings.

And over torn-apart bodies . . .

He closed his eyes, unwilling to revisit that horror. Just as he wished he could forget many scenes of the war just past.

Peace. The very word sounded like paradise. But if it really was peace, it wouldn't be like anything America had known by that name before.

It was late fall, after a four-year conflict that had wrecked two continents. Both China and the United States had lost major cities—Honolulu, Seattle, Denver, Shanghai, Guangzhou, Ningbo, Haikou—and huge stretches of cropland, contaminated in the massive nuclear strikes that had ended the war. Both now struggled with riots, looting, disease, famine, and the revolt of whole states and provinces.

The Allies had declared victory. But neither side had truly won.

Like titanic, reeling boxers, they'd simply retired to their corners to pant and sprawl, trying to recover.

While new contestants took the ring for the next bout of the evening.

Dan mounted the steps slowly, pacing himself. He was still exhausted from five years of nearly continuous sea duty, first as commanding officer of USS *Savo Island,* then directing larger task forces as America rebuilt its fleet and smashed a Chinese submarine offensive. And at last, pushed forward again, island-hopping across the Pacific and China Seas until the final campaigns in North Korea, Taiwan, Hainan, and Hong Kong.

He was fighting radiation exposure, too, from a cross-country hunt for his daughter. Thank God, she'd surfaced again. Ill, nearly starved, but still among the living.

Though ten million other Americans weren't . . .

He flourished his ID one last time at the marines who flanked the massive doors, then trudged in.

The familiar corridors weren't exactly deserted, but they lacked the bustle he remembered from when he'd worked for the Joint Chiefs. He ambled up a ramp. Once these tiled decks had been lovingly waxed to a gleaming sheen. Now they were dirty and scuffed. Half the overhead lamps were burned out, and shadows gloomed the narrow side corridors.

"Admiral," said Donnie Wenck as Dan let himself into his closet of an office. The master chief stood by the coffee urn, holding a tablet computer. They'd been together since before the war. Wenck's blond hair was graying now, like Dan's, but his fierce blue eyes were as mad-looking as ever. "You're looking . . . better, I think."

Dan nodded. "The docs say the white count's trending up. And it's *Captain* again now, Master Chief. Not *Admiral*."

Wenck shrugged. "Whatever. That's good, right? New treatment's working?"

"Seems to be. What've we got today?"

Dan didn't expect much. He was on temporary limited duty with the staff of the chief of naval operations, assigned to help write a study on postwar force structure. The Joint Staff and Army Futures Command were planning war games, to revise contingency plans and redesign the force. *Regenerate the infrastructure* was the buzz phrase. His staff consisted of Wenck and two junior enlisted, but most of the actual research was being done by a think tank.

Also, as a self-assigned task, he'd advocated for the establishment of a small covert unit tasked to defuse emergent naval threats. Rather like the old Tactical Analysis Group, on which he'd served before the war. It was being stood up on the West Coast.

Wenck held up his tablet. "Just came in. You're needed on the E ring."

Dan examined the message. "The CNO."

"Maybe Nick's got something for you."

"Maybe. And you mean 'Admiral Niles,' not 'Nick,'" he muttered. Dan doubted there'd be anything important. He'd put in for his twilight tour, a favor retiring officers and senior enlisted were sometimes granted, but doubted he'd get it. With the signing of the Singapore Treaty, senior officers were in excess. The services were shedding anyone they didn't need to fight the rebellions.

Which meant next year's budget would prioritize the Army, Guard, and the new Homeland Security battalions. He'd probably end his career here in the Puzzle Palace, with a sheet cake from the cafeteria and a lunch-hour party before turning in his badge and walking out the door to retirement.

He read the rest of the email. 0800? He'd barely make it. Wenck handed him a paper cup so hot it scorched his fingers. He passed it from hand to hand and headed on out.

Dan had first worked for Niles at the Cruise Missiles Project Office in Crystal City. He'd disappointed his senior then, but as Niles had risen he'd given Dan another chance. Shuttled him to a stash billet after the assassination attempt in the West Wing. After becoming CNO a year into the war, Dan's reluctant rabbi had tasked him with Operation Recoil, a spoiling attack on north China. Hardly anyone had expected his force to survive. But against all expectations, Dan had managed to extract most of his ships safely after the raid.

Then, commanding a hunter-killer group, Dan had taken on a wolf pack in the Central Pacific. He hadn't exactly shone there, as he saw it, but had still been given bigger responsibilities.

Dan finished the coffee and flipped the cup into a recycle bin. He didn't miss his stars. Hell, he probably didn't even deserve being an O-6. It was time to hand things over to a new generation. To relax, get his sailboat back in the water, and spend some time at home with Blair and his library.

He hesitated at an imposing doorway. He hadn't been here in a while. Since before the war, actually, other than one brief meeting.

One that had left a bad taste in his mouth.

The CNO's flag secretary folded her hands behind her, glancing at the door to the inner office but not moving toward it. "He'll be with you shortly, Captain. You're looking so much better these days!"

"Thanks. How's he doing? Is the—" he didn't like to say *cancer*. Finished, awkwardly, "How's he holding up?"

Some unseen signal distracted her from answering. He got an impersonal smile instead. "He'll see you now, sir."

The office looked the same: expansive, light-filled, the windows giving a view out over Arlington National Cemetery. The only change was the GSA packing boxes stacked in a corner.

His old enemy, then reluctant sponsor again, had gone from robust to cadaverous. Niles half rose to acknowledge Dan's Medal of Honor, then sank back behind his desk. His skin looked like crumpled gray paper. Light gleamed from a bare scalp. His voice, too, was a memory of the old roar. "Lenson. A seat," he muttered, still keyboarding on a pad.

He finished, sighed, and swiveled toward Dan. Raised eyebrows that weren't there anymore. "You're looking better."

"Everybody says that, sir. So it must be true."

"Ha ha. Still riding that motorcycle?"

"No, sir. That was just a . . . convenience." Though it was still parked behind the house.

"Good job with Operation Rupture, Dan. If you hadn't stopped the clock, forced us to augment your ammo and fuel reserves . . . then kept shoving when things got gnarly . . . we'd have gotten our asses kicked back into the China Sea."

Dan debated how to answer. Nearly word for word, this was what Niles had told him when he'd first returned. He cleared his throat, trying to recall how he'd responded before. "The Chinese fought harder than we expected."

"Than Sea Eagle figured they would, anyway."

Sea Eagle was the expert-systems AI that had advised the commanders in the field. It took its direction from the overall artificial intelligence directing Allied strategy, Battle Eagle. "That took guts, to keep mushing when you were taking twenty, thirty percent losses," Niles added.

Dan nodded. After a moment the admiral said, "Of course, if that'd been the wrong call, we would've hung you by the balls . . . Blair all right? How's your daughter . . . Nancy?"

"Blair's working on the political side. Nan's fine too. Took radiation, but they think she'll make a full recovery."

"She's a . . . medical doctor?"

"Biochemist, with Archipelago during the war. She's with CDC now. What about your nephews, sir? Out west? Have you heard from them?"

"Heard from Dorus, but not Mack." A shade crossed Niles's face, but he just waved a big hand, signaling, apparently, that the courtesies were over. "And you're on that force structure assessment now. That keeping you busy?"

"I wouldn't say it's a full-time job, but—"

Niles rumbled, "As you've heard, I'm leaving the building. At last."

"Yes, sir."

The admiral glanced at the wall clock. "They kept me on because of the war. Horses in midstream. Anyway, you're still on the Senate list for confirmation of your wartime stars. I'll recommend you to my relief. No guarantees, but you understand that already."

"Appreciate it, sir."

"Anyway, we're coming up on Hlavna's hearing. Want to join us?"

This was unexpected, but Niles didn't make casual invitations. "Yes, sir. Certainly."

The CNO raised his voice. "Commander, let's adjourn to the VTC." Dan realized their conversation was being monitored, perhaps recorded.

Which led to another question. The last time he'd been here, Niles had emphasized how secure the Pentagon was, how they'd stonewalled Homeland Security's eavesdropping. He'd warned about one-party rule, and that the Joint Chiefs were determined to resist.

Had that changed? Had those intentions leaked? "Are the other chiefs being replaced too, Admiral?"

For answer he got only a hooded glance. Niles heaved to his feet. "Let's go next door," he said, his expression rough-cast of colorless concrete.

Seated with the rest of the CNO's staff, and some other invitees Dan sort of recognized from J3 and the SecNav's office, they watched the confirmation hearing on C-SPAN. Apparently all five of the chiefs were being replaced. A preemptive strike by the administration? Dan cut a look sidewise at Niles, whose compressed lips gave no clues.

The Navy nominee was Shaynelle Hlavna. A pale, stocky, blond-graying submariner, with five rows of ribbons on her service dress blues. A close-up showed the Navy Cross at the top of her ribbon rack, and the gold Combat Patrol insignia with four stars. So she'd fought the shadowy undersea war that had preceded the showier surface battles and amphibious landings the public heard about. Dan had listened to her present at a Naval Institute teleconference, but they'd never formally met.

The senators began by asking her what she thought the size and makeup of the postwar Navy ought to be. She responded animatedly, yet seemed to be speaking in code. "The force needs to road-map into a symbiotic fusion of autonomous technology and expert humans. Committed to equity and sustainability, we'll cooperate in real time to accelerate the flow of value in a high-velocity, high-tech ecosystem." She said investments were needed in the robotics and deep quantum AI both sides had relied on during the war, with limited but still sometimes impressive success.

"Sometimes it's the underdogs who've pushed the envelope the furthest, technologically, in wartime," she said at one point, which Dan found insightful. Could she have a background in history, wadded inside the MBA-speak? But each time she mentioned investments the senators leaned away in their leather chairs. Pretty obvious why. Half the states weren't paying federal taxes. Those that had stayed loyal were broke. In a reversal of World War II financing, the US had borrowed from Canada, Mexico, the UK, the Saudis, and the EU. Those debts had to be repaid.

Not only that, the Singapore Treaty—Blair had told him this—contained a secret codicil guaranteeing the Chinese war debt of nearly three trillion dollars.

War was expensive. But this peace would be nearly as costly.

When the hearing ended, the senators rising, shuffling papers, Niles stood too. His angry gaze passed over Dan, then snapped back to him. "Let's go offline," he muttered.

Back in the CNO's office a three-stripe commander in a medium blue, single-breasted dress uniform turned from the window as they came in. Dan noted her sleeve. Not the Navy star, the Coast Guard shield. "Dan, this is Sarabeth Blanco," Niles said.

Blanco extended a slim hand for a grip stronger than he'd expected.

She was nearly as tall as he, but shockingly young. *Damn*, he thought. Just looking at her made him feel grandfatherly. A glance at her hands revealed a heavy silver-toned ring. New London? He checked her ribbons, but except for a couple of Meritorious Services, they didn't track with DoD decorations. He lifted his gaze from her chest to see her checking him out as well. She narrowed her eyes as their gazes crossed. A glint of humor?

"Good to meet you, sir," Blanco said. "I've heard a lot about you from the admiral here. The two of you seem to go back a ways."

"Uh, you could say that," Dan muttered. Not liking the implication both he and Niles were getting long in the tooth.

The admiral glanced at the walls and lifted an eyebrow. "Let's take a walk."

In the corridors, the lunchtime crowd provided background noise. They turned several corners before the outgoing CNO cleared his throat. "Remember what we talked about before, Dan? About your twilight tour."

"Yes, sir."

"I said that, before that took place, I wanted you to do something for me. But it's all gotta happen behind the green door."

"Yes, sir," he said again. Blanco was on Niles's other side, listening intently. The sides of her head were buzzed close, but her hair, auburny but not quite red, was longer and streaked blond on top. He wondered again why a Coastie was involved in whatever this was. And what could be so sensitive Homeland Security, or maybe the White House Special Activities Division, shouldn't hear their discussion.

Niles muttered, "The administration just gave the Russians permission to clean up what they call 'space junk' from the war. You won't see this on Patriot News, but that includes our MOUSE nanosatellites."

Past the admiral, whose steps were slowing to a shamble, Dan and Blanco exchanged startled looks. "Our *recon* satellites?" Dan said. Too loudly; a passing sergeant glanced their way. He lowered his voice. "But how can we—?"

"The Russians say, just the older ones the Powers knocked out during the war. Yeah, they're toast. But as they recover those, our current microsats are in nearly the same orbits. Police a couple of those up along with the trash, they get our latest technology . . . Anyway, I need you to go to the Arctic," Niles muttered.

Dan flinched. "Excuse me?"

"To Alaska, sir," Blanco said. They turned a corner. This corridor was walled with portraits of past secretaries of defense. "You've done Arctic duty before, the admiral tells me."

Dan wanted to demur. His only experience north of the Circle had been aboard USS *Reynolds Ryan.* They'd operated north of the Gap, searching for the worst winter storm they could find, then trying desperately to stave off capsizing once they had. Oh—plus the time he'd nearly died in Canada, marooned with one of the prototype Tomahawks during the missile's development. Fun times.

Neither seemed to be a great recommendation. But he just muttered, "Uh-huh. A little," feeling stupid even as he said it.

They came to a café, actually just a side nook, a civilian concession with coffee and a few lonely looking, rationed buns. Niles pointed to a free table, but didn't sit. "I've got to get back. Commander Blanco'll get you up to speed."

"Uh, yes, sir. Are you going to—"

"We'll stay in touch." Niles knuckled his arm, an intimacy so unexpected Dan nearly gasped, then shuffled away.

Dan and Blanco regarded each other. After a moment he said, "Well, Commander? Apparently you're supposed to brief me."

"Sure." She looked over at the table. "As good a place as any, I guess. Want some coffee?"

* * *

They settled in a corner, far enough from the others to be out of earshot. She seemed as obsessed with the possibility of being overheard as Niles had, glancing around, keeping her voice low. Her posture was erect, her glance direct, her manner respectful but assertive.

"Okay," he opened, "what's this about?"

"Some background first," she said. "If you have a couple of minutes."

"At your disposal. It's not like I—well, never mind. Go on."

"Right now, Russia's making over twenty percent of its entire gross national product from extractive industries north of the Arctic Circle."

"Okay." This wasn't news, though he was surprised the figure was so high.

She unlimbered a tablet from a black briefcase. Masking it with a curled arm, she called up a photo. "Overhead of the Sabetta complex. A seaport-slash-airfield-slash-liquid-natural gas facility, powered by a new floating nuclear generation plant. The *Akademik Lysenko,* with three KLT-40D reactors. And this is only one installation out of many.

"Based on imagery from Planet, BlackSky, and Maxar, as well as NRO assets, and connecting the dots from a lot of data—intercepts, financials, social networks, shipping stats, weather information, energy futures, humint, open media—Battle Eagle concludes Moscow's accelerating a major push north. They're claiming huge areas of the continental shelf beneath the Arctic Sea. Up to, maybe even past the pole, toward Canada and Alaska."

Dan frowned. "They're sure there's oil there? Gas?"

"The US Geological Survey thinks between a quarter and a third of the world's remaining reserves are up there. The Arctic Research Council kept a study going on the sea ice melt all through the war. It's vanishing faster than anyone anticipated. The summer passage is ice-free, and Moscow's already tested a winter route, cleared by a nuclear icebreaker."

Blanco called up another screen. Shipping tonnages, by calendar year. "Cargo volume through the Northern Route will probably double next year. Transiting from Japan to Europe via the Arctic cuts days at sea in half over a voyage via Suez or the Cape of Good Hope.

"We have to start paying attention. Or we'll be left out of one of the major economic, and ultimately strategic, plays of the rest of the century."

Dan leaned back. Now he understood why the woman opposite wore a medium-blue uniform. Which, he could not help but notice, she filled out very nicely. He reeled his mind back. "So . . . Department of Transportation has the lead on Arctic issues?"

"Yeah, or sort of had it handed to us, while DoD was out winning the war."

Dan shrugged. "So how's the Navy involved? If this is a DoE, DoT issue. I'm not aware of any significant force structure there. I don't even think we have a port in the Arctic."

"We don't, at least not a deep-draft one. But let me continue to bring you up to date, sir. Because I'm leading up to that."

Dan was starting to pick up something else from her. He didn't consider himself particularly alert emotionally, but by the same token, if he was registering some hidden tension, it was probably really there. Blanco's hands showed a faint tremor. She sat forward, perched on the edge of her chair. Her smile was a quick stretching of the lips, accompanied by an intent stare that seemed too wide-eyed. Dilated pupils, almost as if she were on some performance- or alertness-enhancing drug. Though how could she be, given the services' testing regimen? A faint flush on her cheeks.

Dr. Dan diagnosed suppressed anxiety. Situational or personal? She couldn't be feeling uneasy about him, could she?

She called up another screen, this time a graphic. "You know Dr. Szerenci, I understand? The national security advisor?"

Dan nodded. He'd studied under Edward Szerenci years before, for his postgraduate degree. And Blair had kept him abreast of his former teacher's rise through the administration. "What's this?"

"Submarine incursion events. You know Russia's been making aggressive moves, claims, overflights, along her northwestern borders."

"Bullying Finland, Norway, and Sweden."

She nodded. "Focusing their attention on their borders, and pointing them away from investment in the far north. They're also clamping down on foreign passage through these new routes. Demanding that ships give advance notice, carry a Russian pilot, and submit to inspection."

Dan frowned. "What happened to freedom of navigation?"

"Right." She flicked. The chart of the polar regions was overlined in red and blue. The lines overlapped each other, making Venn diagrams of possible conflict. "With the ultimate goal, a National Defense University study suggests, of making it a Russian sea. The same way Beijing was trying to appropriate the South China Sea before the war."

Dan nodded and took a long swallow of tepid coffee. Chinese expansionism had turned former allies into first competitors, then opponents, and finally active enemies.

"Moscow seems to think this is the right time to move. You saw how the senators reacted when Hlavna proposed upping the defense budget. The war cost us over five trillion dollars. Maybe a lot more, depending on how you count."

"Uh-huh," Dan said. "While Russia's not just undamaged, it got that huge IMF/Qatari loan."

"Most of which is going to defense industries for a significant new buildup . . . again, mainly in the Arctic."

Another photo; another huge installation. Dan picked out piers, fuel tankage, blocks of housing, sprawling factory buildings, piles of cylinders that were probably gas piping." All right, so that's the background," he said quietly. Figuring, now, that he knew where this was going. But still, not grasping how he might be involved.

Then he wondered why he was wondering. It wasn't as if he had anything pressing to get back to. And having coffee with Commander Blanco wasn't exactly hardship duty.

Blanco seemed to pick up on his impatience. She put her tablet to sleep and folded her hands. "Okay, complications. The UN treaty governing Arctic issues, which is a subset of the UN Convention on the Law of the Sea, already pretty much grants Russia the seabed up to the pole, since they have the longest coastline on the Arctic."

"We don't recognize UNCLOS," Dan said, pronouncing it *unk-los*. "Or their claims under it. Right?"

"So friction, at some point, has always been inevitable. That's why Moscow's leaning on the other Arctic interests."

She took a sip of mocha latte and let her gaze drift away. Casually, but he could see she was checking the corners for cameras. She murmured, past the half mask of the paper cup, "Over the past year and a half, every Russian research submersible has been redeployed to the Arctic. DIA speculates about some kind of deep-ocean base. Seabed mining. Running mobile sensors, autonomous sampling, preparation for cutting internet cables . . . but no one's sure."

She lowered the cup, and he understood. No one around seemed interested in them, and they'd chosen this café at random, but there were apps that could lip-read.

"Let's walk some more," she suggested. "How far would it be if we walked all the way around the E ring? A full lap?"

"A mile, I think. Or a little under."

He trashed their cups and they headed out. Yeah, he needed the exercise. She had a long loping stride. "You walk like a runner," he said.

"I ski. And snowboard. When I can."

She picked up the pace a little, then even more, until he was pushing it to keep up. Just to pull her back, he said, "So what do the Chiefs want?"

"That's still being worked." The question didn't slow her down, unfortunately, and he reluctantly lagged back until she too had to slacken the pace so as to not leave him behind. She searched faces as they passed and kept her voice low. "We may have to set out with verbal orders. Written ones later, on arrival."

"Arrival. Where?"

"Kotzebue Coast Guard base, Alaska. Which actually is my command."

"You're the CO?"

"That's one of my hats. This assignment will be temporary additional duty. You'll be TAD too. We leave tomorrow."

That was sudden. He cleared his throat, glanced uneasily out the window at the towers of Rosslyn. Past and over the strange, curved benches and water hazards of the 9/11 Memorial. "You know, I'm still under medical supervision, Commander. Not that I'm unwilling, but I may not be up to anything too . . . physically demanding."

"I'll bear that in mind, sir. But my orders are clear. Pick you up here, brief you, proceed to Fairbanks, stand up a team."

"Okay, a team. To do exactly what? I'm still not getting my head around what our job is."

"We're going to do a survey, sir. On the North Slope," she said, and shut her mouth on that. And no matter what else he asked, the only response he got was, "It'll be in our orders."

He was still puzzled when he got home. The house in Arlington he'd missed so much during the war. It looked shabby now. Unkempt. He had work to do, on the roof, the gutters, spray washing, painting . . . Blair wasn't home, but Nan's old Subaru was parked in the driveway. He let himself in, carrying the groceries he'd picked up at the Fort Myer commissary. Still puzzling over Niles, and Blanco, and some kind of ad hoc, spur-of-the-moment jaunt to Alaska, which didn't sound so much shadowy as too-hastily thought out. Was Niles shunting him offline? Getting him out of the way, so he wouldn't be around for the promotion hearings?

No. Being buried in the Pentagon was like being entombed under the Pyramid of Cheops. No senator would call him over from there.

If they were interested in promoting him at all. Which he doubted, whatever Niles said. Retire as a captain, that would be great. He didn't admire the lot of too many of the retired admirals he'd run into. He didn't play golf, and with Blair in politics, he'd have to steer clear of any defense-related employment. Maybe a vacation? Mexico sounded good. Someplace warm . . .

"Someplace warm, what?" Nan echoed, turning from the stove as he set the bags on the counter. Dinner was already underway, to judge by the smells.

"Sorry, thinking out loud. Italian?"

"That's the basil and oregano, I think. I'm making lasagna with zucchini strips instead of pasta. Don't decide before you try it! Hi, Dad."

His daughter turned from the refrigerator, smiling, and set down the spatula to give him a quick hug.

Nan Lenson held her dad at arm's length, looking him over. The war hadn't been kind to him either. Always lean, he'd lost weight, and stooped a little now when he wasn't paying attention to his posture. There was more gray in his hair, and the sea-and-sun wrinkles she'd always liked around his eyes had lengthened to touch his cheeks.

She hugged him again, conscious of a sudden pang that nearly made her tear up. Then pushed him to arm's length. "How's that white cell count?" she said, forcing a jocularity she didn't feel.

"Better. How's yours?"

"Okay." She nodded, scratching her scalp as she hit the Bake button on the stove. Her hair was coming in again, but it would look different. Once thick and jet black, courtesy of her Asian ancestry, it was growing back brown. Regardless, she was happy to have something to shampoo again. And, hey, not everyone got the chance to try a lighter shade without resorting to bleach.

Actually, she was glad just to be *alive*. She'd fled a burning Seattle in a refrigerator truck, carrying half a million doses of the antiviral she'd helped develop. But radiation had destroyed her bone marrow, populated hundreds of tiny cancers throughout her body, and left her helpless against opportunistic infections.

Only massive doses of antibiotics had kept her alive long enough to be captured from the separatist militias of the Midwest. Which were now—or so Patriot Radio said—being crushed by a resurgent government.

That might be good in the long run, but the rumors of repressions and shooting weren't reassuring either. Whatever the rebels' politics, they were still Americans.

She sighed and stripped off her gloves. She wore them all the time now, like some obsessive-compulsive germophobe. Her dad was helping himself to a tonic and orange juice. "Get you something?" he asked, head inside the fridge. "We're supposed to stay hydrated, remember."

He'd taken radiation too. Not from one huge burst but from accumulated exposure on his cross-country search for her. She almost opened her mouth to say something emotional, something laced with gratitude, but the words in her head sounded too awkward. Anyway, he knew how she felt. "Same as you have is fine."

He brought a glass out as she flopped onto the sofa in the living room. Everything looked so faded, so dusty . . . "Seen Blair today?" she asked him.

"Not for a couple of days now. She's wrapped up in this campaign."

"You don't think he can actually take the nomination. Do you?"

Her dad stood in the center of the living room, looking out the window, and didn't answer for a moment. She was about to repeat the question when he said, "Yangerhans is what the country needs. But I don't think he's what her party wants."

She remembered the delivery then. "Oh! Before I forget. There's a FedEx for you on the hall table."

He perked up instantly. "Great. Great! Should be my ring."

"The one you traded in Seattle? To come looking for me?"

"Yeah. And it wasn't cheap to get it back."

She felt an illogical stab of guilt and suppressed the urge to cover it with a joke—*What, you're saying I'm not worth my weight in gold?*— but didn't. He hated it when she made self-deprecating comments. Didn't seem to appreciate that was just how people her age coped.

He returned minutes later, cradling the ring in a cupped palm. A heavy yellow-gold Academy band with a brown sapphire inset. Looking pleased, he slipped it onto his finger and held it up to admire. Then glanced her way. "So . . . what're your plans? You know you're welcome to stay as long as you want."

"I know." She turned her head away. "But I have to go back."

"Not to the Midwest. Please? It's a combat zone."

"It's a hot zone for disease too," she told him. "Somebody's got to stop the Flower. Before it spreads east again and spikes up in the cities."

The Vietnamese had named the "Central Flower" virus when it had emerged during the war. The avian influenza had a 40 percent mortality rate and a predilection for repeat infections, each time wreaking more havoc on the immune system, heart, and lungs. It had torn through Asia and the Chinese armies, probably shortening the conflict all on its own.

Her dad was rubbing his mouth, probably wondering how to dissuade her. "But . . . I thought you found that drug. Didn't you—"

She nodded, cutting him off, sitting up on the couch. "Sure, LJL 4789's in mass production. Experimental vaccines now too. But this could get a lot worse, Dad. Like 1918, or Ebola, or COVID. Somebody's got to rope off the hot zones. Educate the caregivers. Get supplies to at-risk populations. That's the government's job. *Whatever* government's in charge."

She rubbed the back of her neck. "Plus, drug-resistant pneumonia's roaring back. Tularemia, shigella, noroviruses—everything that ramps up with food shortages and reduced resistance. Yellow fever in Louisiana and East Texas." She took a slow deep breath, trying to calm down. No point shouting at him. And she didn't have the spoons to argue about this again. "I can't sit here while people are dying. CDC's asked me to help out. Since I've worked with the Flower in the lab and seen it in the field too."

He grimaced. "But you're still recovering. We almost lost you! I don't think—"

"I already agreed to go," she told him. Flatly, making sure she didn't let that rising inflection at the end creep in, the one too many women her age still used. That apologetic note that men, however well intentioned, too often took as a cue to start explaining things. "It's my duty. Anyway, I won't leave right away. There'll be a training period first."

He hesitated, looking unhappy. But at last nodded. "I guess when you put it that way, it's simple. But why you? And why again? Haven't you done enough?"

"This is my war," she told him, swinging down her legs and getting up. "That was yours, in the Pacific. This one is mine."

Dan stifled a sigh. She wasn't going to listen. The same way she'd made up her mind at Disney World. "I'm going to live in the Magic Castle with Cinderella," she'd said, and refused to leave. Having to be tempted back to the parking lot, into the car, with the promise of another visit. At age . . . what? Four?

But his daughter wasn't a kid anymore.

He turned away and let himself out the back door.

In the yard, the sun was slanting downward. The dark autumn air breathed a chill that made him shiver. He pulled the crackling plastic tarp tighter over the battered Honda he'd crossed the country on. Inches of dead leaves covered the stone patio he'd laid. He should rake them up. The fruit trees were going to pot, thick with water shoots and scabbed with some kind of sticky mold. But not now, now he had to go to fucking Alaska . . . Below the yard lay a ravine, a narrow tongue of tangled woods in the midst of suburb. Now and then you caught sight of a deer, or saw fox tracks, though hardly ever the animals themselves. They were like ghosts. Specters of forests past and lost.

No. Nan wouldn't stay home or play it safe. He should know that by now. And if there was one thing he understood, it was that fucking impulse to duty.

When he noticed she was beside him he startled. She took his arm. "Sorry! Hey. You're not mad at me, are you? Dad?"

"No. No, I couldn't be. Just . . . sort of . . . scared." He drew a long breath, flashing on a corpse on a metal table. So mutilated he'd thought it was her. "What about your personal life?" he asked her. "You mention people, but I never see them. Ever thought of settling down, finding somebody special? I don't care who. Just somebody who'll make you happy."

"It's open," she told him. "But there's too much to do right now to worry about myself. You saw a lot of the country, right? Riding across it?"

He looked down, remembering. "Pretty much. Yeah."

"So you know. Whole patches are like Chernobyl. Just . . . vacant. Abandoned, because of the fallout. Worse yet, people up in the mountains, alone, sick, but no one even knows they're there. Or in the Great Plains, isolated by the fighting. They need help. It's my job."

"Duty has its limits," he said.

She grinned. "Oh yeah? Come on! *You* never recognized them. Why should I?"

He grinned back unwillingly. She squeezed his arm, and he turned to face her.

His eyes stung with mingled fear and pride as he buried his nose in that thin fuzz of coffee-colored stubble that looked so strange on her skull. Had he been the role model for this? For always heading toward the danger, instead of away?

He hugged her harder, blinking back tears. All he had of her was now. All any of them had ever had was now.

2

The Capitol Rotunda, Washington, DC

The arching dome overhead was lost in shadow above the floodlights below. Its massive bowl focused the murmurings of the crowd into a susurration like the far-infrared afterglow of the big bang. George Washington peered down disapprovingly from an ominous orange sky. Mythological figures surrounded him, Liberty and Plenty, Industry and the Arts. Spaced in niches around the curved sandstone walls, massive canvases portrayed the battles of the Revolution and heroic scenes from the exploration of the West.

Below that gigantic dome, red velvet ropes encircled a space on the ochre-and-pink marble floor. Behind them dark-blue-uniformed Capitol police held back a standing crowd. Staffers, representatives, congresspeople and cabinet members, veterans and old friends waited to say a final farewell.

In the center stood a black-draped catafalque, the same one that had held Lincoln's remains. The coffin was draped with a flag so new its colors seemed to glow.

Blair Titus fidgeted in line, clutching a black Senreve Maestra handbag. She wore a black knee-length wool dress, a matching sweater, and low black heels. The hat she'd only worn twice before; it had been her mother's. The diminutive woman in front of her was Shira Salyers, a longtime friend from the State Department.

The line shuffled forward. Other than that background murmur, and an occasional cough that echoed eerily under the dome, all was silence.

Blair had worked for Bankey Talmadge for nearly ten years, first as a junior staffer, then as defense advisor. She'd risen with him as he climbed the seniority ladder to chairman of the Armed Services Committee. Had served as staff director there herself, before going to Defense.

When she'd worked on the Hill, she'd avoided this vast echoing space. Steered clear of all the Capitol's public areas whenever possible, as did most of the staffers. When she couldn't avoid crossing these floors the sightseers and tourists had stared, pointed, taken pictures, then fallen back respectfully as she'd hustled along, swinging a briefcase or clutching a portfolio.

As if she'd been someone important . . .

How young she'd been . . . and Talmadge had seemed ancient even then. One of the survivors of the age of the titans. He'd served with Goldwater, Dole, Byrd, Thurmond, and the other Talmadge, his cousin. As the decades passed his offices at Russell had grown larger, his perks greater, his clout colossal.

To her he'd seemed like one of the ancient progenitors peering down, or the nineteenth-century generals lifting their chiseled chins on canvas, presiding over massacre or battle with the same lofty air of doing God's work on earth.

Which was why both parties had consented to a state funeral. Usually those were reserved for presidents and five-star generals, and vouchsafed only rarely to others.

Talmadge had never pretended much to senatorial dignity himself. He'd built a veneer of folksiness, and played a mean fiddle at hometown rallies. But he'd been more erudite than he'd ever let on. "Read Machiavel," he'd advised her. "Read Sun Tzu, Missy. Thucydides. Clausewitz. We got ta deal with the world as it is, not like we want it to be. Match the ends to your means. And never burn a bridge behind you. An enemy today can be your best friend tomorrow."

Wise words, from an all-too-human man who'd been freer with his hands than was acceptable these days, less politically correct in his speech, and much too prone to resorting to the noon bourbon, especially after his second wife had left him.

Eventually the receiving line, deliberate as a sleepy caterpillar, finally brought her to the catafalque. Close up it looked even more somber: black-draped, more an absence than a presence, as if sucking in the light. Only the glowing flag seemed to levitate, hovering above the void beneath.

A tall Asian stood at the casket's head. Hu Kuwalay had been Talmadge's last chief of staff. His shoulders sagged as if he were keeping himself upright by force of will. "Blair," he murmured, taking her hand. Dropping his gaze. "I love the gloves. Why don't women wear gloves anymore?"

A comment the old bastard himself might well have voiced. "They were my mother's. I was so sorry to hear the news, Hu," she told him.

"He wasn't well for a long time. Beijing was the last hurrah, I think."

Bankey Talmadge had chaired the Allied mission into China after the armistice. He'd needed a wheelchair in the Forbidden City and missed most of the plenary sessions. But he'd been at work behind the scenes. The new constitution he'd written, along with his flattery, threats, and promises, had made a treaty possible when few had thought it likely.

She squeezed Kuwalay's hand again. "He's with Doris now. He always missed her."

"He missed you too, Blair. He'd say, 'Hu, you're a great guy, but Missy was sure a lot easier on the eyes.'"

"Missy" having been the senator's pet name for her. "What are you planning now?" she asked. In any other place it might have seemed abrupt. But not here, where the very air breathed politics, career, a sense that if you weren't part of history being made, your life was worthless or futile.

He sighed. "Maybe take some personal time. See my folks in Manila."

"If there's anything I can do, make calls—"

"I'd just as soon you didn't, to be frank."

She swallowed, taken aback. There it was, out in the open swiftly and unadorned. "What're you telling me?"

"You know what I mean." He averted his gaze, smiling at the next mourner in line. "You're not exactly scented with the divine afflatus right now. As *he* would say."

She didn't want to ask this next question. But had to. "Off the record, Hu. Staffer to staffer? I know Bankey and I had a set-to. But we made up during the mission. And he, uh . . . pledged to reimburse me a little bit. For my campaign."

A "little bit" for Talmadge usually meant several million dollars. Being from one of the oldest families in Maryland, she hadn't expected campaign fundraising to be difficult. And at first it *had* gone well, thanks to her dad; Checkie had spent his life in banking. But she hadn't been able to give his friends the assurances they wanted. Then came the war, the

Cloudburst, and the stock market crash. The pledges had evaporated, leaving her with a crushing debt.

Kuwalay said, "You *lost* that election, Blair."

"But I still owe over a million—"

He patted her shoulder, glancing past her again. "You'll have to talk to Mrs. Clayton. She's handling the party funds these days . . . Hello, Judge. Sorry to have to meet you like this."

She took the hint and moved on. Shaking hands and exchanging condolences with whey-faced older women in black who offered Southern-accented soothings like sweet tea. Talmadge's relatives looked overwhelmed by the occasion, the surroundings, the crowd.

Blair circled the coffin one last time, biting her lip. The old man had been infuriating, insulting, blasphemous, patronizing, now and then racist, at least in his private speech. A master manipulator. An alcoholic womanizer. How was it possible she could miss him so achingly?

Maybe because despite all that, he'd never lost some final determination that the game had to be played by the rules. Rough rules, and a bare-knuckles bout, but in the end one that played right could result in progress for everyone. Not just for the wealthy, or the well connected, or those of his own party.

In the marrow of his bones, Bankey Talmadge had never really left his people.

She stood off to one side, searching for friendly faces but not seeing many. Oh, lots that she knew. But they all seemed to have someone else to talk to . . . the majority and minority leaders, next to each other in line, looking like Stan and Ollie. Retired senators, representatives, generals. CEOs, men and occasionally women Talmadge had grilled and sometimes humiliated before the Committee. The great and good were all here, but the buzzing that floated up toward the dome seemed tense rather than reflective.

Of course. Elections were looming. Talmadge's seat would be up for grabs, and a lot of others, along with the presidency.

She stood there for several seconds more, fiddling with her phone. Her damaged hip ached and stabbed. No more cortisone, the doctor had said. She should consider a replacement; he could get her a slot at Bethesda. Should she stay for the eulogies?

Finally she decided. She was edging toward the exit when Shira caught her sleeve. Her friend murmured, "That woman over there's trying to get your attention."

Blair went to tiptoe, peering over the heads. And caught a beckon from a dumpling of a woman in black, seated with the special guests in the leather chairs ranked just behind the polished lectern.

Up close, the senator's estranged second wife looked younger than Blair had expected. Earlene Talmadge was whispering to the much-older man next to her. His features seemed familiar, but Blair couldn't call his name to mind.

Then, suddenly, she did. She'd served ex-president De Bari as an undersecretary of defense. But he looked old now, gray . . . and where was his wife? "Mr. President," she muttered. He looked annoyed, then nodded a welcome. Asked the man next to him if he'd mind moving over.

Blair touched her lips with her handkerchief, noting glances their way both from the seated spectators and from those still in line. Realizing, with a sinking feeling, that now *she* was one of the Old Guard. The target of both respect and envy from the younger politicos and staffers.

"Blair. How nice to see you again." The widow patted the seat beside her. Blair hesitated, then curled herself down into it, but clutched her purse on her lap to signal she didn't intend to stay. Noting from the corner of one eye that others—senators, Supreme Court justices—had shifted over to make room for her. "Earlene, I'm so sorry he had to pass."

"It's fine, honey. He always missed Doris. Always wished *I* was Doris. Once he even said so."

Talmadge's first wife had been the love of his life. Blair cleared her throat, uneasy with the confidence. Earlene probably suspected *her* of a dalliance. "I hope you never thought the senator and I—"

Mrs. Talmadge patted her knee briskly. "Don't give it another thought, Missy. If you never got it on with the old dog, more power to you." The widow sighed. "Anyway, I just wanted to tell you, if there ever *was* anything between you, I don't give a hoot. It's all part of a life, the ups and downs. It doesn't pay to hold on to regrets."

Blair nodded and took her hand, wondering if that, too, were something the old son of a bitch might once have said.

Earlene pulled her back down when she tried to rise, so Blair gave up and settled in for the eulogies. First, the vice president. Then the majority leader, his heavy hound-like features wreathed in lachrymose fake sadness. He and Talmadge had been notorious adversaries. When the speechifying ended, the minority and majority leaders laid huge wreaths of white and red roses. Honor guards—soldiers, sailors, marines, airmen, Space Force, and Homeland Security—took positions facing the casket, polished rifles at order arms.

The senator would lie in state through the night, so the general public could pay their respects. That line already snaked down the Capitol steps.

When she got up the agony in her hip made her grit her teeth. Suppressing a curse, she excused herself and whispered an apology to De Bari again for making him move. She thought again about going home, but Salyers tugged her along into a side chamber.

A buffet and coffee table was set up there. Family members and other invitees stood about, many from her own party. Mrs. Nguyen Clayton, former national security advisor, now at Leidos, where Blair too had an office. A scattering of uniforms amid the dark suits. Heavyset, slow-moving Helmut Glee, the Army chief of staff. General Vinader, Air Force. Dr. Doris Oberfoell, from the Office of Cyber Security and Infrastructure Security, propped rigidly upright in a wheelchair. No sign of Nick Niles, whom she could at least have chatted with about Dan. Or of Dr. Ed Szerenci, her late boss at the War Termination Study Group. Not exactly a friend, but they had history. Had been through a war together, after all.

She could use coffee, though . . . The cup and saucer were cream porcelain, embossed with the Senate seal in gold. Picking them up took her back to so many events here and at Russell. Fundraisers. Industry events. Party conferences. In some ways the Hill was like a big family, though often a dysfunctional one. More close-knit than the executive, with its rapid turnover. In the West Wing you got the sense every relationship was fleeting. In the Senate you dealt with the same faces year after year, often decade after decade; sometimes, generation upon generation.

"Why, Blair! I thought I'd see you here."

She turned to find herself facing Adam Ammermann, from the president's staff. Beside him was a tall, almost gaunt woman who resembled an elegantly crafted bronze blade.

Dr. Swethambari Madhurika was "Swethi" to Patriot News, "Sweaty" to what remained of the liberal media. The president's chief of staff extended a slim hand. "Blair, dear," Madhurika purred. "Has anyone approached you about crossing the aisle?"

"I sounded her out in Zurich," Ammermann put in. "But she declined."

"Really." Madhurika surveyed her, eyebrows arched like black rainbows. "Pity. You're a hard worker. You served in a national administration. Why not in a national party?"

Blair steadied her coffee cup. "I appreciate the invitation, Doctor. But I served in wartime for the good of the country. Shouldn't we be getting back to peacetime norms?"

"Peacetime norms are what got us into that war," the other woman observed. "We spent so much energy fighting each other, we let the enemy overtake us. Wouldn't it be smart to avoid that from here on? To march toward a more equitable, rationally administered future, without these crazy zigs and zags from right to left?"

Blair sipped her coffee, almost enjoying herself, except for the jabs her hip kept giving her. Like a cattle prod, shocking her every few minutes. "I've always thought fighting, as long as it's by the rules, is a good thing. Hashing problems out. Giving the electorate clear choices."

Ammermann smiled at that, as if at a child's prattle. "So what *are* you doing these days, Blair? Since you resigned from DoD?"

She debated evading the question. Then realized, from Ammermann's smirk, that they probably already knew. She squared her shoulders. "Afraid we'll be on opposite sides from here on out. I'm taking on Justin Yangerhans's presidential campaign."

They surveyed her coldly, but also pityingly. Ammermann grunted. "I didn't know you took on kamikaze missions, Blair. Isn't that your husband's specialty?"

"You can leave him out of any conversation with me, Adam."

"Oh, so sorry. Or am I?" He leaned threateningly close. "There's only room for one party from here on out, Blair. The Patriots are in power. And we'll keep it, from here on out."

"Even if your candidate loses? That's the rumor."

Madhurika snickered. "A hypothetical." But her glance was already wandering past Blair. "You'll see. But then, I understand you have some experience with losing campaigns." A sweet cerise-lipsticked smile, and they both brushed past.

Blair noticed her cup trembling again and gripped the saucer harder. She flinched and muttered, "Shit," as her hip electroshocked her once more.

Really, she should leave. Or at least find a chair.

But as she went to set down cup and saucer, she found herself face-to-face with Mrs. Nguyen Clayton. Once President De Bari's national security advisor, and Dan's boss, when he'd served in the West Wing. "Ma'am," Blair said.

"Ms. Titus." No mistaking the permafrost in that tone. Nor the studied way the petite Asian ignored her outstretched hand. Clayton was a power in the party. And, as Kuwalay had just reminded her, she controlled the purse strings. "I hear you've been cut loose."

Blair blinked. "I've . . . Sorry?"

"Surely your friends in the administration should have treated you better." A cold half smile. "Considering the bridges you burned to join them."

"I joined a wartime coalition, Mrs. Clayton. To serve the country."

"You joined the other party and helped them govern. Helped them milk the war, to brand any opposition as treason."

"I never . . . Oh, please! You know what your successor wanted. Vertical escalation. Without me pushing back, we would have had a full-scale nuclear exchange the first year of the war." The other woman made as if to stroll off, but Blair set a hand on her arm. "And no one *cut me loose*, Mrs. Clayton. I resigned, immediately after the armistice."

"That's not what I heard. Or what the *Times* called me about."

"The *Times*?" She remembered a message on her voice mail, one she hadn't responded to yet.

Then, all at once, she understood. The White House were recasting her resignation as a firing for cause. The lie would be repeated on the Patriot Channel until it became a "fact." She was so angry she couldn't respond, just glared at the older woman.

Who again began to leave, but pivoted gracefully back on a black stiletto heel for a Parthian shot. "And this stuff I hear about Jim Yangerhans . . . he's a good soldier, no doubt. But he's not one of us. And no political experience? I'm afraid, Blair, you're hitching your wagon to a falling star." Clayton smiled, but only with her lips, and walked away.

Blair stood riveted, mind racing, as she tried to reason through what had just happened. She'd meant to ask for help with her debt. But that obviously wasn't going to happen. And the signal she'd just gotten, from one of the party elders, couldn't have been clearer.

He's not one of us. They were labeled as outsiders, trying to crash the gate. Which meant Yangerhans would start the primary behind the frontrunners. Despite his leadership in the war. Despite his centrist positioning.

Even getting the nomination would be a desperate struggle. And then he'd confront the titanic, unified, savagely disciplined machine of the incumbent Patriot Party.

She was still standing there as the murmuration around the vestibule muted. As not only the guests but many of the spectators took out their phones. Not, apparently, to take photos, though. They were staring at their screens. A shattering crash echoed; someone had dropped a cup and saucer. Blair groped for her own iPhone, which had secreted itself deep in her purse. "Damn it," she muttered, burrowing. "Where the fuck—"

Shira, at her side again, looking at her own cell. "What's going on?" Blair asked her.

"It's not good news . . . Moscow's announced they're leaving the Nuclear Test Ban Treaty." Salyers chewed her lip, looking uncertain. "Shit, I didn't expect that . . . that's been in effect since . . . what? Since forever?"

"Since 1963," Blair responded automatically. Her groping fingers located her own phone at last.

As she unmuted it she noted the frowns around her. The switching of attention from the ceremony, to a new challenge. A changed and more ominous mood.

The Russians were pushing their advantage. It would mean a new arms race. New generations of weapons. New costs, new threats, and no doubt, new disasters.

Before, even though such competition had meant increased expenditures, the US had been able to keep up. Or at least, lag only slightly.

But could a bankrupt, divided nation respond this time? Keep pace with a new adversary, one not only untouched but even strengthened and enriched by the savage war just past?

She stood uncertain, glancing one last time at the flag-draped catafalque. At the military guards standing in perfect uniformed stillness, at the circling onlookers and mourners.

How she wished the old dinosaur were still with them.

3

San Diego Oparea, California

The floor of the sea walked past, close enough, it seemed, to touch. Its lumpy, irregular mud was furrowed by curved grooves. Segments of circles, engraved in the velvety muck by undersea denizens in their lifelong search for food or mates. This deep, light had probably not penetrated since the planet's ocean had condensed from primeval steam.

Nor was there light now. Invisible beams of tightly focused ultrasound outlined those furrows. They grazed lightly as the fingers of specters across the occasional sea cucumber or squidworm or sponge, picking out the irregular, widely scattered nodules of manganese conglomerate that dotted the bottom.

At the corner of Lieutenant Commander Sloan Tomlin's artificial sight, something swift flitted past. The slight, almost frail young officer in blue coveralls turned his head, tracking that flicker motion out into a black nothingness-like space. But it was too far away to identify. Most likely some deep-sea shark or squid, bent on its own patrol through these obscure depths, visited, in the past, only by the most advanced research submersibles.

"Evaluated: biological, elasmobranch family," a deep male voice advised him.

Tomlin squinted inside the virtual-reality helmet, concentrating again on the seabed ahead. The artificially generated colors in the screens an inch in front of his pupils shifted, coruscating and fading like phosphenes. Then deepened again as the artificial mind that controlled motion and sight searched for its quarry through this dark underworld. An object covered by this powdery ooze. Buried deep—

"Hmmmmmm . . . possible target," the deep voice announced in his

earphones. *"Bearing zero one zero relative, one hundred ten meters. Slowing HCUS 1 to evaluate."*

The synthetic voice often hummed wordlessly as it worked. Sloan shifted in his padded chair, wondering if it had been programmed to, to signal deep processing was taking place, or if that was simply some random software artifact.

The Heterogeneous Collaborative Unmanned System through whose camera he was televiewing was a drone. The torpedo-like mobile sensor vehicle had been deployed by Orca Prime, a lengthened and improved model of the unmanned combat submersibles that had operated deep in enemy waters during the war. The Prime was patrolling two miles distant and a thousand feet up from the HCUS.

Sloan glanced right and blinked to call up the Prime's status. Its fuel cell bank was at 96 percent, with pressures and temperatures in the green. Main propulsor was up. Sensors up. Pilot computer, up. All systems indicated operational except for thruster five, which showed off-center vibration above 100 rpm, probably from blade damage during deployment from the parent submarine. With two other thrusters humming away on the starboard side and three to port, plus the main pump jet, that seemed acceptable to continue the exercise.

While Tomlin himself cruised through the dark thousands of feet nearer the surface, aboard a wartime-flight Virginia-class submarine.

Breaking the tradition of naming attack boats after states, wartime-emergency construction had honored earlier combat submarines with heroic histories: *Barb, Tang, Wahoo, Seahorse, Silversides, Harder, Darter, Narwhal, Batfish, Cavalla, Archerfish,* and *Hammerhead.* The Orca's parent submarine was USS *Tang,* homeported out of San Diego. Sloan, set up not far from her control room, was observing and evaluating down a two-stage chain of remote telepresence. *Tang* to Orca, via an experimental state-dependent comm link—low bandwidth, but essentially immune to intercept—and then downward again, from the Orca to the drone actually prowling the seabed.

"Slowing to evaluate . . . Hmmmmm . . . imaging. Processing . . . Image is up."

The screen outlined an irregular shape in glowing green. Over successive seconds it painted in higher resolution, but he still didn't recognize it. Readouts flickered upward, backed off, then steadied.

"Evaluate: nontarget. Metallic debris, source unknown," the Pilot, the AI that controlled the Orca mother ship, intoned.

"He can do better," a woman's voice said in Sloan's headphones. *"He's got a lot more smarts—more processing capability—than that."*

Sloan turned his head slightly. The helmet blocked any view, but he knew the voice. RaShondra Komanich was from JAIC. The Joint Artificial Intelligence Center had been formed during the war to apply AI to advanced weapon systems. Komanich was the mission chief for the Pilot, the Orca Prime's computer intelligence. Her black hair was cropped short. She was slight-boned, with smooth skin the hue of tarnished silver. She was also intense, perfectionistic, and pushy. All the qualities you wanted in a project manager.

The industry rep, the on-site manager for Boeing-Lockheed-Martin Maritime Systems, would be sitting at his other side. Sloan suspected he was about to lose his job, considering how far behind schedule and over budget the Prime was. Over seven hundred million dollars and more than a year, to be exact. The technology had been pushed with a wartime priority, but the program had lagged due to loss of chip fabrication capacity when the Chinese had taken Taiwan. So it hadn't been ready in time for its wartime mission: to locate and destroy sub-seafloor mines and listening devices in advance of an Allied landing.

The price tag for the delays had been steep: too many lost boats and crews, in the bloody knife fights in the East and South China Seas that only now were emerging into public knowledge. The war dead were on Eternal Patrol now. . . .

He's got a lot more smarts . . . "Any ideas?" Sloan asked, nudging the man next to him with an elbow.

"Try another pass, closer in?" the BLM manager said over the circuit. He sounded uncertain, which wasn't good. *"Maybe, suggest a higher PRR, higher freq, better resolution? And VNIR/SWIR scan, spectral range about four hundred fifty nanometers."*

VNIR/SWIR was visible near-infrared / shortwave infrared, a bounce-off spectrographic technique that provided remote sensing of physico-chemical properties. Sloan told the AI, "Make another pass. Closer. VNIR scan. And reevaluate."

The screen shifted slowly. Mud.

Mud . . .

Nodules . . .

Mud.

Then a curved rib, with lightening cutouts. Corroded, but recognizable as a manufactured form. A meter beneath the brown bottom ooze. Its outlines blurred as the ultrasound traveled deeper, its energy absorbed and dissipated by the sediment. But from the vague loom of shadow, there was more metal under there. A lot more.

A readout: *Aluminum, trace magnesium.*

A millisecond flicker on the screen, and the gravelly voice hummed for a moment before announcing, *"Evaluate as wing root of Consolidated PBY-6A Catalina. Historical search: correlates with July 3, 1943, loss of registration 64899, total fatalities twelve, departure San Diego, destination Pearl Harbor, aircraft mission antisubmarine, missing, presumed lost at sea."*

Sloan bent forward, involuntarily craning for a closer look. The front of his helmet bumped into something on the console and he winced. Probably no one living remembered the men buried now deep beneath the ocean, lost in that now dimly recalled first Pacific war . . .

"Compliment him," Komanich said in his earphones. *"He responds to positive feedback. Think of it as dealing with a three-year-old. He needs direction. Nudge him. Ask questions that make him think."*

So the AI was "he," not "it," now? Of course the voice could be tailored to any age, sex, even dialect. Yet Komanich had chosen a deep male voice. For what reason, one could only speculate.

Sloan cleared his throat. "Orca Prime, this is Tomlin. Nice job on that identification."

"No problem, Lieutenant Commander." Damn, that almost sounded flip.

"Where did you source those crash records?"

"Aviation Safety Records database, Flight Safety Foundation."

"Okay, but you're two thousand feet down. How did you query that database?"

"Hmmmmm. My onboard information universe is updated before each mission. Total now one point one million terabytes. Searchable at any time."

The Boeing rep, sounding anxious. *"It's robust. Fast. And really, really smart. So much so, sometimes we aren't sure how it gets those results. But they always seem to work out."*

Sloan nodded, impressed. Even when out of touch with the surface, screened from above by a quarter mile of black salt water, the Orca Prime's master AI—its name was the Pilot—could not only make logical deductions but access a large-enough onboard database to be able to carry out detailed research.

In the mine-hunting mode, it used regression modeling and thirty-eight analysis algorithms simultaneously, on an "unconscious" level, to search for potential identifications. When the majority of those algorithms matched the incoming image or other sensor data, the answer was bumped up to the "conscious" level. At that point the Pilot evaluated the match against a database of previous runs. The robot's subsequent actions were governed by programmed subsets of activities, again moderated and directed at the top of the computing pyramid.

The quantum computer at its heart took up four cubic feet and ran on twenty kilowatts of power, about as much as an electric bathroom heater.

Too bad it hadn't been ready in time. And that the whole project, it appeared, was going to be shut down now that peace was here.

"Resuming survey," the Pilot said. The camera panned up, into blackness; then down again. It canted as the drone reoriented and set off on the next leg of its search. Other pips showed to left and right; the other HCUSs. The drones deployed from the Orca's payload bay and swam back into them when they needed recharging or for recovery. The HCUSs in turn could drop smaller sensors closer inshore. Or even small mines, to complicate enemy movements.

Of course, it was all wasted effort now. Though, Sloan thought wryly, the Pilot could probably answer any trivia question you threw at it.

Another hour went by before one of the HCUSs reported a second contact. This time the Prime drifted lower, turning on its magnetic particle resonance sensors.

The result bled onto the screens. A star shape. Material: nickel-aluminum-bronze. The Orca approached cautiously, adjusting trim and buoyancy. It grounded out on the bottom so gently only a wash of powdery silt obscured the lens for a moment before drifting away on the knot-and-a-quarter current.

Moving with the caution of a surgeon, it deployed a pincer arm to set a clamp. On the industry rep's command, it retrieved all three HCUSs and ballasted up.

It would take an hour to rise to the surface, carrying the target and completing the exercise.

Sloan sighed, signed out, and lifted the helmet off his shoulders. His shoulders ached. It was heavy as sin, and the edges were sharp.

The control room rushed back, disorienting, claustrophobic, a nutshell space after the infinite void of the open sea . . . Komanich was leaning in beside him, eyebrows lifted. "What?" he asked her.

"I said, so, what do you think?"

"Sorry." He dug a finger into an ear. Blinked, trying to refocus. "Um, very impressive."

"Any thoughts on possible employment?"

She was fishing for why he was here. Unfortunately, he didn't know. Just that he'd been sent over from the Surface and Mine Warfare Development Center to take part in the exercise, get smart on the Orca, and look into integrating Sea Eagle's latest tactical maneuver subset into the Pilot's programming, which so far wasn't enabled for much other than "bottom fishing," as someone had put it.

"So, we about done here?" *Tang*'s skipper leaned in between them. Brett Fahrney wore no decorations on the blue submarine coveralls, but Sloan knew the stubby, bearded commander had survived some of the most bruising battles of the war, down in the shallow, dangerous South China Sea.

"Yes, sir. Appreciate your support."

"Anytime we can send in an AI instead of a manned boat, I'm for it." The CO glanced behind him. "Up angle. Prepare to surface," he told the diving officer. "Sixty feet, and a three-sixty search."

She returned a terse "Prepare to surface, aye."

"We'll get the Prime recovered and let you folks check it out if you want," Fahrney told them. "Then head for the barn."

"Yes, sir," Komanich said, beating Sloan to what he'd been going to say. "Thanks again. We'll see you back at the hot washup."

Back in San Diego, late the next afternoon, Sloan tapped at his boss's door. *Tang* had moored at the sub piers at Point Loma. A shower at the pier-side gym, a quick change into a working uniform from his bag. When his boss called, "Yeah," he stepped into the office.

"Tomlin, sir. You wanted to see me after FINEX on the Orca Prime."

A small, graying man in glasses and a lavender cardigan glanced up. "You don't need to call me *sir*, Sloan," Monty Henricksen said.

Tomlin nodded, uncertain. He was still feeling his way around this new duty. It felt strange reporting to a civilian. Henricksen was obviously brilliant. He held a doctorate in mathematics. But he didn't seem to think in a military way. It felt odd, too, to be able to head back to his room at night, or to sit at a computer without the sense time was bleeding away, that lives depended on how fast he worked.

But there seemed to be a good deal of that wartime drive at NSTAG. That sense delay or failure could have unfortunate consequences. Which helped stave off the tedium. His besetting sin, maybe: he hated to be bored. And it had been much harder to sustain his interest since the war had ended.

The Naval Strategic and Tactical Analysis Group, headquartered in San Diego, was new. It was a division of SMWDC—the Naval Surface and Mine Warfare Development Center, across Harbor Drive from the naval base piers. Like the other divisions, Amphibious Warfare, Sea Combat, Air and Missile Defense, and Mine Warfare, it was headed by an O-6. At the moment, by Captain Cheryl Staurulakis, whom he hadn't met yet. It was located in the old building on Craven Street, like Mine Warfare, but it wasn't mentioned in the Welcome Aboard material or listed on the org chart.

He'd heard there'd been something like it before, on the East Coast. But once the war had gone hot analytical effort and manpower had been subsumed in the N3 shops or in the fleet, sucked from R&D into emergent operations.

Now, it appeared, whatever missions that previous outfit had been tasked with were being supported again.

"Grab a seat," the little man said. He seemed to be finishing something on his tablet. Sloan took a chair in front of the desk and resorted to his own tablet, scrolling through his after-action on the target-retrieval exercise.

"Got your access documentation done?" his boss muttered without looking up.

"Almost, sir. Uh, Doctor." Shit, he needed to finish those. Clearances, procedures, access codes for the building and his office and the classified network he'd be accessing to do day-to-day work. He hoped the cybersecurity was of a similar order of rigor.

Maybe something to look into, once he got up to speed.

Sloan was a WTI, a warfare tactics instructor. "Witties" were deep-selected from the fleet for intellectual aggressiveness, curiosity, and capacity for not just sheer hard work but creative thought. Once selected, they were intensively trained in the latest warfighting tactics . . . more like Jedi Knights than old-style, hell-for-leather destroyermen.

"How did you feel about the Prime?" Henricksen asked him. "Is it fit for deployment? Or does it need more development?"

"Well, sir . . . from what I saw, it's a capable system." He remembered the JAIC rep's, Komanich's, "three-year-old" remark. "Barring some need for human guidance. But, yeah, it's ready. For a limited mission, at least."

"Mm-hmm." The scientist swiveled from his screen and scribbled a note on a paper pad at a side taboret.

Sloan had earned his antisubmarine/antisurface warfare patch as the war started. After a readiness production tour out of Destroyer Squadron 15, he'd focused on Chinese tactics and capabilities, and helped plan and execute asymmetrical raids following Operation Recoil, the first attack on the mainland.

Following which, he'd served with Admiral Daniel V. Lenson as the latter commanded Task Force 91 in the first invasion of Chinese territory, Operation Rupture Plus. Higher had thought he might be helpful to a combat commander whose main experience had been operational rather than academic. Still, he'd never felt sure Lenson fully trusted him.

Which was understandable. A WTI knew weapons systems, intelligence, tactics. Most cutting edge, he understood the tactical systems that more and more directed the course of twenty-first-century battles. But to a legacy commander, he probably looked like a commissar. Or, worse yet, a junior know-it-all who thought that because he had a patch, he knew everything. Who came across as trying to usurp the most prized privilege in the Navy: combat command.

So Sloan had tried to support the admiral, not direct him. And he'd come to respect the guy. Lenson had insisted on pushing ahead, even as the casualty figures mounted, as the landing trembled on the brink of disaster. He'd ordered his supporting carriers in ever closer to land—a bolder move than Sloan had ever seen, even in an exercise—to keep the sortie rates up even as the number of operational aircraft had dropped precipitously.

Which exposed those irreplaceable carriers to enemy mines, ballistic missiles, even short-range army coastal defenses.

Sea Eagle had judged the landing a failure, counseling retreat and withdrawal, salvaging what they could.

The battle had teetered on the edge for hours. Planes had gone down. Ships were sunk. Ammunition stocks plunged toward zero. Only Lenson's iron nerve had held it together. Held both invaders and defenders against the blazing grinding wheel of combat.

At last that pulverizing attrition had bled the enemy faster than it had the Allies. The stream of reinforcements from inland had dwindled, then halted, as Beijing realized they'd lost the fight.

So Lenson had been right. Despite the AI's advice. Despite Sloan's own misgivings.

Which meant he had to reexamine his role in a new light. Was he too married to the safe solution? Too dependent on the equations, on the sterile, bloodless recommendations of the digital programs that more and more threatened to usurp all human decision-making?

It was worth pondering.

"We've got a job coming up that might interest you." Dr. Henricksen whipped his chair back, apparently ready to talk now. He smiled tightly and sent over files with a flick of his fingers. They bloomed on Sloan's tablet, then shrank, sucked down into memory. "Study those. Close hold, of course. We're calling this Operation Apocalypse."

Sloan shifted on his seat. "That's—pretty dramatic, sir. I mean, Doctor."

"Believe me, it fits. You heard about Russia exiting the test ban."

"Sure."

"Here's why. They're planning a live run of something new. Ever heard of Poseidon?"

Sloan nodded. "The city-buster. Their nuclear-powered torpedo."

"What do you know about it?"

"Well, mainly just what I read in the *Early Bird*. Defense One. C4ISR-NET. Plus the classified summaries during the war."

"Okay." Henricksen flicked over more files. "This bastard's been in development for a long time, under various program names. T-15. Status 6. Poseidon: the earth-shaker from the sea. Now, a new, bigger, much faster version they call 'Apocalypsis.' The files have the details. Including that it's going to be steered by an independent AI as powerful as anything either side built during the war."

A diagram on his screen. A long cylinder. The callouts to components and subunits were in Cyrillic.

Henricksen flicked once more. "This is command and control on the thing. Plus some of the internal documentation. From the "Malachite" design bureau. You read Russian, right?"

"Yes, sir—I do, I . . . Damn," Sloan said, frowning down as that latest file scrolled up on his screen. This was the holy grail. "*Source code?* Where the fuck—where'd we get all this?"

"A cyber penetration. By the Lithuanians." The scientist leaned back. "Moscow's planning a live test."

Sloan tensed in his chair. "A *live*—a *nuclear* test?"

"We figure that's why they gave notice on the treaty. Their development program and test schedule are in what I sent you. It'll be run out of Severomorsk or Kola Bay, their naval base there, and detonated in the Arctic Sea. As a bonus, the detonation should create an artificial harbor." Another flick of Henricksen's fingers. "We're not sure exactly where yet, but the most likely seems to be Severnaya Zemlya.

"Two islands, halfway between the Russian mainland and the pole. Up to now they've been ice-locked year-round. Uninhabited. Close to inaccessible. But if they had a harbor there, they could mine copper, uranium, phosphate, platinum, nickel. Rhodium, a catalyst for the hydrogen economy. Six times costlier than gold, and they'll own the market for it. They could base out of there for subsea mining and drilling too."

Henricksen paused, letting Sloan scroll through code, documentation, description. The Russian was larded with technical terms. Slow going, but he could translate it, given time. The source code seemed to be in Python, a high-level language with easy syntax and lots of white space. He knew C++ and Java; this didn't look too different.

He frowned at the DIA evaluation. Based on simulations by Carderock, the Apokalypsis—if he was pronouncing it right—would have a virtually unlimited range, given its nuclear reactor. It could dive to at least three thousand feet. With two propulsion modes, slow and quiet, or noisy but extremely fast, it could slink past or if necessary outrun any existing US sub or torpedo.

The threat was obvious. Given its speed, and with AI-powered evasive programming, how could anyone stop such a weapon?

Sloan glanced up to see the mathematician studying him. He pulled at an ear. "I'd need time to read it. And some idea what you want me to do."

Henricksen leaned back, gaze distant, apparently losing himself in memory. "We had a mission sort of like this at TAG, some years ago. When Dr. Dvorov came out with the Shkval-K. No one knew how the guidance worked. First we tried to buy one, but Komponent – the torpedo corporation – wouldn't sell. Then we tried to steal it. That didn't work out either. Finally we highjacked an Iranian submarine that had one, and ran it out to sea. Studying it up close gave us the information we needed to build a countermeasure."

Sloan guessed. "The Rimshot system?"

"Which every Allied ship and sub carries now. I was—tangentially involved myself. In that effort, I mean." Henricksen looked nostalgic, then shook his head, recovering himself. "They're not selling this on the open market. Nor will they, ever—too dangerous to their own ports. But this thing is pure hell for us. Since so much of our population's along the coasts."

"So we're not stealing it." Sloan relaxed in his chair, but was still puzzled. Then what was this about?

"No point, given that we have the source code and the specs. Basically, everything we'd need to duplicate it. There was some discussion of that, building our own, but an AI-controlled nuclear reactor and multimegaton warhead—nobody wanted anything like that out there with our name on it."

Henricksen pivoted his chair slowly, studying the ceiling. "No, what we want to do is fuck up their test. If you'll forgive the technical language."

Sloan nodded. "Okay. How?"

"I was hoping you'd help with that. Which was why I sent you to see what Orca Prime can do." Henricksen gave a little wave. "You're supposed to be brilliant? Show me."

"Well, sir . . ." He searched his brain. Obviously the answer must involve the AUV, or remote sensing, or deep submergence. Or all three. He puzzled over it for several seconds.

The scientist cleared his throat. "Well?"

"I'd say . . . if you want to wreck their test . . . you'd want to interfere with the torpedo somehow, either before it's launched or while it's underway. Make it look like a failure." He hesitated, trying to gauge if he was on the right track, but the little man gave him no clue, just a calm regard. "Though I'm not sure how," Sloan added.

"Okay." Henricksen looked satisfied. "We ran the problem past Battle Eagle."

The master artificial intelligence had dueled with the Chinese AI, Jade Emperor, over cyberspace, communications, and power generation. Then, after Jade Emperor's destruction, had directed the strategy that had ended the war.

"It came up with a solution we didn't expect. But you're right, it involved a monkey wrench." Henricksen swiveled again, then bent. A clank as he swung open his desk safe. This time the file he handed over was paper, pronged into a red-and-white-striped Top Secret folder.

Sloan accepted it. Flipped it open. And saw a mission order.

"Utilizing Orca Prime's capabilities," Henricksen said.

Sloan read the order with mounting excitement. Or dread? Or maybe a mixture of both. Regardless, he could feel his pulse speeding up.

"I'd be the ideal guy to send," the scientist said. He looked regretful. "But"—he tapped his chest—"this fucking pacemaker doesn't go to sea. They want somebody young. With combat experience. And a lot of tactical smarts. So we reached out, and got you."

Sloan scratched under his chin as he finished the summary. Feeling, already, certain doubts. Was the Prime robust enough for a voyage like this? Had its fuel cells, batteries, sonars, propulsion, been tested in such an extreme environment? In Arctic waters, thousands of feet deep, they would operate under many yards of overhead ice, fighting uncharted currents. Hundreds of miles from help, and thousands of miles from technical support.

Yet he found himself saying, through suddenly numb lips, "Yes, sir."

Henricksen's brows knitted. "Yes, you think it's possible?"

"Yes, sir—I mean, no, I don't *know.* It'd be pushing the envelope. That looks pretty obvious." Wondering, at the same time, if this was some ploy to continue funding the Prime. To justify the overruns now that the war was over and the Navy was facing horrendous cuts.

"Yeah, could be hairy." Now Henricksen looked as if he was enjoying himself. Like a cat teasing a mouse. "So you're on board?"

Sloan considered. "The Prime could probably operate up there. For a while, anyway. But then what? How would you—I mean, we—intercept this super-torpedo? And what would we do then? Destroy it? That'd be an act of war."

"Well, that's what we have to decide," Henricksen said. "It'd be risky, all right. Also, we'd have to keep it a secret. And not just from the Russians."

Sloan looked up from the folder, suddenly alert to something Henricksen hadn't said aloud. "From whom else, sir?"

"You follow the news. This administration is edging closer and closer to Moscow. They call it 'realism.' With China's fall, and our own problems, true, Russia may turn out to be the lone superpower of the late twenty-first century." Henricksen shrugged. "So there's a political danger too. So don't take that file, or your tablet, out of the building. Erase protocol, in case of unauthorized access. Copy?"

"Copy," Sloan said. And let himself out as Henricksen turned back to his screen.

*   *   *

Back in his cubicle, he grew even more uneasy as he read further into the plan. When he finally glanced at his window it was dark again. Not quite as stygian as it had been all those thousands of fathoms down, but dark.

He sighed and locked the notepad, tablet, and red-striped folder in his desk safe. Stone Age security, but the boss had warned him. Nothing outside the building.

The BOQ was only a few blocks distant, so he walked. Actually he didn't have a car. Nor did he think he needed one. Not in San Diego, with its bus system, and Opfer and Mojocar coming back after the wartime hiatus. Why bother?

He stopped at a sub shop and ordered a turkey and lettuce to go, with a raspberry drink. Walked on, through the night wind off the bay, enjoying the cool after the heat of summer.

He let himself into his room and called, "On," to the TV. He pulled a chair in front of it, unwrapped the sub, and poked a straw into the drink.

Here on the West Coast, there were only three channels, Patriot, Fox, and PBS. There wasn't much to choose between them, though PBS ran more nature programs and history documentaries, and Fox more sports. All read the same news from the same bulletins approved by Homeland Security's Department of Information. Everyone knew it was carefully curated. Sanitized, either to scare, or reassure, or point out the latest target of hatred. Currently that seemed to be the ReConfederacy, though from what he read on the slightly more reliable classified briefs, those few rebels left were being confined to smaller and smaller enclaves.

The next segment was about a new disease outbreak in South Dakota. The AI-animated announcer seemed to stumble as he explained how little was known. It didn't seem to be the Flower, though. Possibly chikungunya, dengue, or West Nile. Residents were encouraged to practice personal hygiene. Masks were available at Party headquarters. Sloan listened with only half his attention, scrolling through his messages. Reassuring his parents he'd made it back from sea in one piece. "I need a personal life, damn it," he muttered. Now that the war was over, he should work on that. Reconnect with his college friends, at least.

Then his head snapped up. Had the announcer just mentioned Orca? "Siri, louder," Sloan said.

"This is the latest program to be called out for overruns under Secretary Strohm's new emphasis on streamlining acquisition bureaucracy. Last year, costs for the Orca Prime improved deep submergence unmanned autonomous underwater vehicle went eighty percent over

the baseline estimate. Progress is two years behind schedule. This trig-
gered the Nunn-McCurdy Act, which forces consideration of whether
the Pentagon should cancel this failing program."

A video clip, obviously from a contractor presentation, showed the
Prime underway. The "camera" circled, showed the propulsors along the
sides and the advanced pulse-jet exit nozzle. Sloan tensed; that was classified. An arrow pointed to a modular payload system, then to attachment
points for external payloads.

The announcer was still talking. *"The original Orcas provided signif-*
icant combat value during the war. However, this follow-on, incorpo-
rating a new power plant, has faced developmental hurdles. Especially
challenging has been the miniaturization of its extremely ambitious
quantum computer, which has brought overall cost to over six hun-
dred million dollars per submarine. Congresswoman Sandy Treherne
called Orca Prime 'the most egregious White Elephant of an already
bloated postwar defense budget.'

"With the signing of the Singapore Treaty, the need for this and other
advanced programs are facing tough questioning.

"Boeing-Lockheed-Martin shares declined on the announcement,
but company officials reassured Patriot News that problems with the
system were under control. Still, increased scrutiny may derail the
Navy's plans for postwar updates and a modernized fleet."

The program cut from the too-smooth face of the artificially animated
announcer to a pharmaceutical ad. Sloan lowered the turkey and cheese
slowly, last bite unchewed.

This wasn't *news.* It was a hit piece. And on a black program, one whose
very existence had been classified. Until now.

Who had leaked the information?

Would it compromise the mission he'd just been assigned?

He finished chewing and took a reflective sip of raspberry to wash it
down. Wondering what, precisely, he was being suckered into.

II

NORTHERN
LIGHT

4

Eielson Air Force Base, Alaska

The turbines spooled up to a banshee screech. The brakes released with a hiss, and acceleration ironed Dan back in his seat. Outside the windows of the CNO's private Gulfstream V, the snow-covered grounds between the air base's runways began fleeing past. Ever faster . . .

The way things had speeded up since his meeting with Barry Niles.

That had been a month before. The former CNO was retired now, relieved by Admiral Hlavna. Dan had heard from her exactly once since she took over. Her terse text merely confirmed his verbal orders. He'd acknowledged it, offered to brief her, but hadn't heard back.

As if she was distancing herself from whatever he was doing.

Paranoid much, Lenson?

Sure. Considering the state of the country, he could understand her trying to maintain deniability.

"Admiral." Sarabeth Blanco touched his arm. "Everything okay? You look worried."

Another update: he was officially back to two stars, to both his and Blair's astonishment. Apparently Niles had yanked on some last-minute strings, and the Senate had approved the promotion list, with the warning that advancements for the following year would most likely be reduced.

He twisted his Annapolis ring, contemplating with wonder how far he'd come since he'd slipped it on at graduation. Rear admiral, upper half, equivalent to a major general. About as high a permanent rank as one could hold in peacetime. Three and four stars came with the billet, and you could be reverted when you left that post or retired. Though that wasn't a hard-and-fast rule. . . .

"Admiral?"

He flinched. Blanco again. He forced a smile. "Yeah. Fine . . . just thinking."

Wenck leaned forward between the seats to speak past her. "Anything new come in last night, sir? Firm orders?"

"I checked in. Nothing, Master Chief, no."

Wenck was behind them. Blanco was across the aisle, bundled in a cold-weather parka that looked too warm for the stuffy cabin. Eyeing his jacket, she nodded toward the bulky packs she'd heaved aboard before takeoff. "I brought you both better gear. Coast Guard issue, hope that's okay."

"That's fine, sure," Dan said.

"You got the underwear I recommended? And decent boots?"

"The two-sixty merino, yeah. And boots. And socks. I have them on."

"Good. But we should have another serious talk about layering."

She started to say something else, but closed her lips and turned back to her phone instead. He grinned to himself, face turned away. Nagging him about his underwear as if they were married . . .

He touched the stars on his collar again. The Senate could jerk a promotion. So could the CNO, or the SecNav. But if he watched his step from here on in . . . Unless that last promise Niles had made, while packing to leave, panned out. But not every service chief respected his predecessor's commitments.

The business jet carried five passengers on this trip: Dan, Sarabeth, and Master Chief Wenck, whom Dan had requested to accompany them. Also two retired, space-available travelers, an older couple who sat quietly in the rear. He twisted in his seat to glance back. The man was reading a book. The woman had earbuds in. Ignoring each other as if whatever they'd ever had to say had been talked out long ago. Or they understood each other now without speech . . . He wondered if he and Blair would get there.

He stretched his legs as the plane leveled out at altitude. The oval windows were black wells. He'd be seeing a part of the world he hadn't visited before. He leaned to peer out, but the darkness was nearly complete. Only a few lights twinkled in deep valleys, and they grew even more sparse as the plane settled into its northerly heading.

He leaned toward Blanco. "So what's down there?" He nodded toward the porthole.

"We'll be overflying the Brooks Range. Not the highest mountains in Alaska, but nowhere you'd want to get lost. I've done some climbing there."

"Mountain climbing too?"

"What can I say, I'm the outdoors type. Ski. Hike. Snowboard. Hunt, a little." She squinted. "After that, we'll overfly the wildlife refuge. That's remote . . . couple of villages, Beaver, Coldfoot, Chandalar . . . not many divert strips either. Not until we get all the way up to the North Slope."

"Any, uh . . . wolves? Grizzlies?"

She blinked. "Are you kidding?"

Which apparently meant yes. He looked down again, but could only make out humped shadows in the starlight. Probably glaciers down there too. He suppressed a shiver. So much complexity. So much . . . data. As if the earth were messaging them in a mysterious language no human being remembered.

He glanced at the older couple again. They were both leaning back, eyes closed, with her hand nestled securely in his.

"Starting our descent to Prudhoe Bay, Admiral, ladies, and gentlemen. Check your seat belts and tables."

Dan shook himself out of a doze, stretched, and yawned. Glanced at his watch, then out the window. A full moon shone off to his left, very bright, but low on the horizon. Its pale light gleamed off cottony mists below.

The terrain emerged slowly as they lost altitude, limned by that frigid moon. Here and there the thinning mist revealed a featureless white plain. A blasted, snow-covered, creepy flatness stretching out endlessly toward that palely glowing orb.

The jet banked, and he caught a glimpse of a broken, irregular rim to that flatness that he only after puzzling over it concluded must be the sea. But not as he'd ever seen it before. Even aboard USS *Reynolds Ryan*, on her doomed voyage, they'd only encountered the occasional iceberg, heaving sullenly amid monstrous black waves. But still the freezing spray had built up on her superstructure, so thickly they'd had to smash it off with baseball bats and melt it with steam lances. They'd met the storms in a top-heavy condition, where capsizing would have meant the quick death of every man aboard.

Not a pleasant memory . . .

A wilderness gradually emerged below the gauzy scarves of drifting mist. Savagely broken ice ridged up in jagged ramparts. Bulldozed by some massive pressure onto a sloping beach, where it heaved up into great shattered blocks. The moon glowed down, coating it all in a cold mercury light.

He shivered again. Visualizing a trek across that broken icescape, trying to drag sleds or whaleboats over those chaotic, knife-edged walls . . . starving, freezing, poisoned from lead in their tinned rations, like the Franklin expedition . . . he wouldn't have wanted to be an explorer back then. What would those stoic heroes have thought of him, cruising at five hundred knots above terrain they'd bled and died struggling to cross?

A flashing line of strobes ahead. The Gulfstream shuddered as the wheels locked down. The engines whined, then hummed. He grew light in his seat, then heavy again. The silvery whiteness rushed past.

A moaning thud as their landing gear struck solid surface, ice or tarmac or frozen earth. Blurry lights fled past the window, at first very fast, then slowing as the engines reversed, shaking the airframe.

"Deadhorse Airport," the pilot muttered over the PA.

The copilot hustled back into the passenger compartment a few minutes later, checking on Dan first, then on the retirees. "Be deplaning soon," he said, eyeing Dan's jacket with the same skepticism as Blanco. "Might want to dress warmer, sir. Pretty chilly out there."

"How chilly?" said Wenck, looking discomfited.

"Be about minus five," Blanco said. "But it's going to get a lot colder soon. Down to thirty, forty below." She zipped up her parka, pulled the hood over her head. "And don't forget wind chill. Any breeze out there, Major?"

"About fifteen knots," the copilot said, and headed forward again, ducking to disappear into the cockpit. Through the windshield Dan glimpsed twinkling lights, a low roof frosted with ice: a terminal. Tarped shapes heaped with white that might be helos or small planes. A snowplow nosed past, yellow strobes occulting, haloed in piss-colored penumbras by the blowing, disorienting snow.

"Go ahead, sir," Blanco ushered him ahead of her. Military courtesy; flag officers left a boat or deplaned first and boarded last.

He hesitated at the top of the boarding ladder. The cold was . . . fucking *cold*, the night fucking *dark* despite the glaring lights from the terminal. But it was the wind that reived his breath. He stepped carefully downward, one hand jammed deep in a pocket, the other clutching the icy handrail. But even in the few steps down he sensed the warmth being sucked out of him.

When he reached the tarmac his boots sank into six inches of snow. He looked up.

And gasped.

The stars were brighter than he'd ever seen them, even out to sea. A pinkish blush directly to the south was the only indication the sun existed, even now, a few minutes past noon. The moon hung a handbreadth above an invisible horizon, first obscured, then revealed, by that wavering silvery curtain. Only now he saw it wasn't mist but minute ice crystals driving in the wind.

He turned slowly, marveling even as the cold gnawed his unprotected cheeks and Novocained nose and lips and tongue. For the first time he truly sensed the bulk of the planet below his feet, felt its curve between himself and the life-giving sun. He might have been marooned on the far side of some distant planetoid, too far from the central fire ever to have given birth to life.

"No northern lights tonight," he observed.

Blanco gave him a funny look. "There's a latitude band they appear over, Admiral. We're too far north here. Though they probably see them now and then. When there's a lot of solar activity."

"Oh." He inhaled another breath, deep, of the cold, cold air, but suddenly couldn't seem to get it past his throat. He struggled for a moment, puzzled, then realized: his scarred, smoke-damaged trachea was closing. Shit, this wasn't good. Maybe he should have accepted the inhaler, when the doctors had—

Wenck, beside him, taking his arm: "Y'okay, Admiral?"

"Just a—" *Just a second*, he meant to say, but the sentence ended in a wheeze as he tried again to inhale. Clamping a glove over his mouth, trying to breathe through his nose. Shit, *shit* . . . He fought panic . . . and at last got a sip of air. Then another.

Wenck, concerned now: "Sir? *Dan?*"

"Just a—just a fucking minute," he gasped. "Just trying . . . to catch my breath here."

"Let's get him inside," the master chief snapped.

Blanco took his other arm, and they hustled him forward. He tried to shake them off. "I'm all right. Let go, damn it!"

He was glad to stamp the snow off his boots as the outer doors hissed closed behind them. Blanco waited for the others to catch up, then hit the Open plate for the inner set. A sort of air lock, he saw. The heat inside struck his face like a hot spatula, and his throat cleared almost at once, though now his nose was running. "Damn, it's hot in here," he muttered.

"They keep it at sixty-five," Blanco said. "What was that out there, sir? Some kind of attack?"

"It was nothing," he lied. "So, where're we staying?"

A man in a green parka walked toward them just then, carrying a posterboard sign. LENSON, it read in Sharpie'd block letters.

A civilian Hummer took them to the hotel. The driver had the heat on full blast, yet the chill still penetrated Dan's seat, then his bones. Snow began to fall again, or perhaps still, glowing blue in the headlights. Though it was still early afternoon, the night seemed much darker here than in Fairbanks. They passed aviation buildings, a truck service depot, then several oil company operations, huge boxy industrial buildings, peaked roofs coconut-caked with snow. The compounds were ablaze with glaring lights and hectic with bundled-up, hard-hatted workers hustling among piles of equipment Dan only vaguely recognized. Cranes swung pipe aboard trucks. Welding arcs seared the night. Snowplows, tank trucks, huge pickups crowded the road, slowing their own vehicle to a creeping five or ten miles an hour.

He became conscious of a strange lack of verticality. There were no trees or telephone or power poles. The Hummer hammered so hard over potholes under the churned-up, rutted snow Dan wondered if it was paved at all. The road led outward to a wide irregular platter devoid of light and buildings. Just flat, flat as a fairgrounds, and white, all white, under a saucer of moon intermittently revealed by the falling snow. They swung right and passed more cranes, more huge, headlight-glaring machines. More dazzling lights and bundled, hard-hatted figures working busily, even frantically. The Hummer braked to let a BP truck pull out, its stack barking clouds of diesel soot into the falling snow.

"This place is jumping," Dan observed.

The driver eyed him in the rearview. "Winter's our busy season, pal."

Blanco said, "The rigs and the processing facilities are built on gravel pads on top of the tundra. You know tundra? Boggy. Wet. Soft. The ground's only hard enough to actually drill, or move equipment, when it freezes. So this is the construction season. No matter how dark and cold it gets."

Chief Wenck said, "Guess you gotta be some pretty tough hombre to work out here."

"More jobs than workers," the driver said. "I'm with Peak Exploration full-time, moonlight driving. Mr. Kirby asked me to pick you up."

"That's Miklos Kirby," Blanco explained. "Under contract to us for the next month."

Dan peered out again. They were skirting the vast, blank, flat space, which he guessed now was a frozen lake or bay, to judge by the lights on what must be the far shore. At last a long three-story building loomed up, sparkling with lights.

"That's your hotel," the driver said. "Mr. Kirby'll be there." He swung around a bulldozer, past a sign that read AURORA in pink and green and black, and parked on rutted snow in front of what looked like a warehouse with windows.

Dan used his DoD card to pay for three rooms. The desk clerk handed him a note. It was from Kirby. *I'll be a little late. Meet you at dinner there at the hotel.*

The room was cramped, basic, but it was clean and it had everything he needed: a bed, a chair, a desk to work at, a bathroom, and a power outlet for tablet and phone. He turned the TV on but found only Patriot News. He blew his nose, urinated, bolted his evening antirad pill, and sorted through his clothes. It seemed unnecessary to stick to uniforms here, since they'd be wearing overgear whenever they were outside, but he'd brought his wool blues and heavy Academy reefer jacket. Only now, as he hung it in a little closet nook, did he realize how inadequate that ensemble was going to be.

Yeah, he'd better pay attention to what Blanco said about layering.

He unzipped the bulky carry bag she'd given him and laid the exposure suit out on the bed. Waterproof, obviously, with a nylon outer shell. Bumblebee yellow and black on the outside, the high-viz yellow nearly incandescent. Quilted inside, with a thick layer of what felt like goose down. Overboots, a parka-like hood, and a blue cap like a Navy watch cap except for the Coast Guard seal.

Well, he could turn it around when he wore it . . . actually this seemed like overkill . . . he didn't plan to go in the water up here. Nothing about going to sea in his orders.

When his phone went off he almost didn't answer. He didn't recognize the number. Finally he hit Accept. In case it was Kirby. Or his Pentagon staff with a question about the force structure study. He was still on the button for that, no matter what this junket turned out to be.

But it wasn't either. *"Admiral, this is Dr. Mokhtar Corris. Do you have a few minutes?"*

He sucked air, suddenly apprehensive at the careful yet obviously foreign accent. Mokhtar Corris was an expert in international law. Blair had hired him to advise Dan about the pending process in the International Criminal Court. Whatever Corris was calling about, it would be expensive. Over a thousand dollars an hour for his services . . . twenty dollars a minute . . . best keep the conversation short. "Yes, Doctor. What've you got for me?"

"I hope you're well, Admiral. Where am I reaching you?"

As if. "I'm doing okay. How can I help you?"

"We have good news and bad news."

Corris's accent, maybe Swiss, maybe German, occasionally made it hard to understand what he was saying. Dan hit Speaker and set his phone on the bedside table. "Go ahead."

"The bad news first. Up to now, the case against you has been based on allegations, not charges. But the Court's Office of the Prosecutor has completed its preliminary examination. I had hoped they would judge your case not worth continuing. Unfortunately, they are referring the accusations against you for investigation. Are you with me so far?"

Dan sat on the bed. *Fuck,* he thought. "Uh . . . yeah."

"Here's what is next. The Office of the Prosecutor will begin its investigation. They will interview the victims and others relevant to the case. You will want to have my participation then. Again, we will prepare and submit a statement in your defense. The pretrial chamber will make the determination whether to confirm the charges and issue indictments and a summons to appear. Or not." Corris hesitated again. *"Are you with me so far?"*

"Again—yeah. But this all moves so fucking slow—it's been pending since the middle of the war, seems to me."

A dry chuckle. *"It is not a court-martial, Admiral. Yes, The Hague moves very deliberately. But once you are indicted, a trial date set, suddenly it will seem all too fast."*

Dan inhaled slowly, then released the breath. This was like a nightmare he couldn't wake from.

The accusation stemmed from when he'd skippered USS *Savo Island*, an old Tico-class cruiser. GNS *Stuttgart*, a German tanker ship, had been seconded to support his small task force.

Making his approach to the tanker for refueling, off the coast of Taiwan, Dan had felt the torpedo hit as an attenuated jolt, a distant wallop that had arrived through the water first, thumping against his feet through the cruiser's steel. At the same moment, his lookouts had reported an explosion.

He'd turned, raising his binoculars, to witness a black column mushrooming above the replenishment ship's afterdeck. The hit had been on the tanker's far side, away from *Savo*.

That would place the attacker to the south. He'd cleared from the tanker, launched a helo, streamed decoys, and repositioned his other ships for an active search. All the while, expecting more torpedoes.

Then the distress call arrived. When he looked back, the stricken tanker was heeled to starboard. He accepted the handset but kept his attention on the radar; their attacker might poke a scope up to gloat. "This is *Savo* actual. Over."

"This is Captain Geisinger. We have taken a torpedo. Flooding. Fire. Request assistance."

"We are prosecuting the sub that torpedoed you. Over."

"That is good, but . . . I need help here. Fire is out of control. If you cannot help, am abandoning in lifeboats. Over."

Dan held the handset suspended, racking his brain. But both doctrine and logic were clear. Laying alongside to render assistance, with the attacker unlocated, would just mean losing a second ship. Finally he said, "This is *Savo*. Nailing this guy takes priority. I need both units to prosecute. You're on your own, Captain. If you have to abandon, do so in a timely and orderly manner. Over."

"This is Stuttgart. *I protest this decision. You are running away. You can save us. All I need is help. Firefighters."*

Dan had almost snapped back at him, but finally had just released the Transmit button.

He still didn't think he'd made the wrong decision. But he'd always wished there could have been another choice.

The attorney, Corris, said, *"But as I said, there is good news as well."*

Dan shifted on the bed and sighed, trying to shake the gloom. Survivor's guilt, when so many had perished . . . "What," he snapped, more harshly than he meant to.

"You are not the only US military referred for investigation. Several

others may be indicted too. But your president has made it clear the United States will not respond to these subpoenas."

"Gotcha," he muttered. Blair had told him that would be the administration's position.

"I will provide background. The De Bari administration signed the Rome Statute. That established a permanent international criminal court. But later administrations withdrew that signature, and the Senate never ratified it. Their position: US federal courts were impartial enough to bring to justice any American perpetrators of genocide and other crimes against humanity.

"But your current attorney general has declined to prosecute any charges stemming from the war. Not only that, the secretary of state threatens to revoke the visas of any staffers or judges seeking to bring Americans to trial. I read from his statement: 'We will regard any summons from the International Criminal Court as an infringement on national sovereignty. No American citizen will ever be yielded up to stand trial before these unconstitutional, extralegal kangaroo courts.'"

Dan scowled. He knew all that. Was the guy just padding his bill? "But what about the Chinese? General Pei. Admiral Lin. Zhang himself? If they ever extradite him from Russia. They have to pay for starting this war."

"You are correct, Admiral. It's certainly possible this lack of cooperation may trigger a corresponding refusal from the new Chinese regime."

Dan had researched this when Blair had first told him about the accusation. Nearly every country on the planet had ratified the Rome Treaty, except for Sudan, Russia, China, Israel, and the United States. Apparently nonparty states could render individuals for specific crimes, but only on a case-by-case basis. Which, to judge by what the SecState had said, the administration was refusing.

Which meant he wouldn't actually go to trial on the charges the Germans brought. Apparently.

It also meant he could be permanently persona non grata in those countries that *did* accept the court's jurisdiction.

He said cautiously, "So what's your call? Would, uh, resigning from the Navy help?"

"That would not make a difference. The court tries both civilians and military. As to how you should proceed . . . I am only your advisor, Admiral. I can point out your options, but you have to decide what course to take."

"What are they, then? My options?"

"One, do nothing. Depend on your government to continue stone-walling. Two, wait for me to submit our statement to the court. After considering it and the statements of the victims, they still may decide not to proceed. It was wartime, after all."

"Which do you recommend?"

"That is up to you, Admiral. But I would also seek an opinion from your military lawyers. Some of your JAG officers specialize in this sort of thing. If you decide to submit a defense, our firm will be happy to craft your statement. Citing the relevant statutes of international and maritime law."

He could imagine how many hours they'd bill for that. "Thanks," he muttered. "Yeah, let me talk to some legal eagles in the Pentagon."

"They may wish to include me in your team. That might ease your financial burden, if the Navy decided to undertake your defense."

He said yeah, it might, but figured that was unlikely. If the administration said he wouldn't be extradited, why should the Service pay to defend him? But didn't say that. In fact the whole conversation was so frustrating he finally said, "Sorry, I have to go, counselor. Got a meeting."

And after mutual goodbyes, he hung up.

Kirby still hadn't shown up by five, so Dan called Blanco and Wenck and told them to meet him in the hotel restaurant. This turned out to be more of a dining hall, with family-style tables at which several score roustabouts and contractor personnel were already eating. The air was warm and the fish and meatloaf smells inviting. He led them through the buffet line, and they took an empty table in a far corner.

Dan was digging into the baked haddock, which wasn't bad, when a very large man halted at their table. His hands were rammed deep in an oil-stained fluorescent orange jacket with a Schlumberger logo. His heavy brows were touched with gray. Snow sparkled in shaggy brown hair. His gaze lingered on Wenck, who stared back.

"You the admiral?" the guy said at last.

Wenck nodded toward Dan, who twisted in his chair. "Mr. Kirby?"

Blanco said, "This is Miklos Kirby, everybody. With North Slope Surveying Associates. He's going to help us out."

"It's Mike, not Miklos," Kirby said. He unzipped his jacket, revealing a quilted long john top in olive drab. He set a heavily scuffed leather briefcase against one leg of the table. Dan felt a nudge to his thigh and glanced down. The commander's phone screen, held low, read *hes not cleared so need 2 watch what we say.*

He cleared his throat. "Uh, Mike. Good to meet you. Want to get some dinner while it's hot? Then we can talk business."

As soon as Kirby was out of earshot he shared Blanco's warning with Wenck, who nodded.

The next arrival was a short, stocky woman who he thought at first might be Asian. Or perhaps native Alaskan. She wore a bright red hoodie with a maple leaf seal on the breast. Short black hair was tucked under a red ball cap, and her camo pants were bloused over heavy boots. Her expression was skeptical, or sardonically amused, as she looked them over. But maybe that was just the set of her features. She frowned at Dan. "Admiral Lenson?"

"That's me. And you are—?"

She saluted, touching fingertips to the brim of her ball cap. Dan hesitated, wondering whether to stand; finally compromised on a salute back, though he wasn't covered. "I am Major Dessa Quvianuk. Number One Patrol Group, Canadian Rangers. Welcome to Inuit Nunangat. The land—the ice, land, and water here, of the great north." She handed over a bulky package. "This was at desk. For you."

Kirby came back, threading the crowd with a heaped plate in each hand. He said, "Hey, Dessa," to the major. So they knew each other. . . . Dan seated him and Quvianuk between Blanco and himself, with the master chief at the far end and their coats on the backs of the other chairs, so no one else would join them. The two women exchanged wary smiles.

"All right," Dan opened. "This I guess is the first meeting of what I'll call the North Slope Assessment Group. Our mission's to look at possible locations for, uh, reactivation of certain locations up here on the Slope.

"Now, this is all preliminary. We have no firm plans yet. It's just a scouting junket, to get the lay of the land, and we don't want to start any rumors." He reflected, then added, "That doesn't mean we won't do a thorough job." He inclined his head toward Kirby. "Mike will be our guide, pilot, and also surveyor, if we get to the point we need one. Major, uh, Dessa, is here because the Canadians asked to be included. So there are no surprises for our neighbors to the east.

"I don't have much to add, other than, Mike, when would you like to get us flying?"

Kirby mopped up gravy with a hunk of sourdough. "Where d'you want to go first, Admiral?"

"It can just be Dan between us, okay?"

"Admiral Dan?" the Canadian major said, frowning.

"No. Just plain old Dan." Was she poking fun? He decided she was just trying to avoid a faux pas.

Waking his tablet, he pulled up one of the maps Niles had flicked to him in the CNO's office. It listed eleven points of interest. Icy Cape, Wainwright, Peard Bay, Point Barrow, Cape Simpson, Lonely Point, Kogru, Oliktok Point, Point McIntyre, Flaxman Island, and Barter Island. Before they'd left DC, he and Wenck had researched that down to the seven most promising, looking at road access, nearby airports, and access to open sea. "Quick overviews first. Then, a closer investigation of whichever look most promising. Or, if none seems suitable, we cast a wider net."

Kirby studied the screen, then passed the computer to Quvianuk. She pursed her lips, looking skeptical. Then passed it back wordlessly.

"These are mostly the old Air Force sites," Kirby said. "Abandoned, from the DEW line days." He frowned. "But why's the *Navy* looking at old Air Force bases? Is there something I'm not getting here?"

Dan and Sarabeth exchanged glances. When they didn't respond Kirby shrugged. "Roger, I don't need to know. Okay. We can fly to this first one tomorrow, if you're ready. Starting maybe three days out, goin' to be some nasty weather. Maybe blizzards. I don't fly in whiteout conditions. Or in wind speeds above fifty knots. Or if it looks to drop past twenty below. So we want to get out there quick, before we're snowed in."

Dan nodded. "Sounds reasonable."

"So who's going?" Kirby looked around the table. "Only got three seats. Other than mine, I mean."

They looked to Dan, who hesitated. "Uh, I guess, myself. Commander Blanco. And, um, the major here. That sound all right?" He looked at Wenck. "Master Chief, we'll get you on the next flight. Right now, I want you to do some, uh . . . some other research. In the meantime."

Wenck didn't look disappointed in being left behind, so Dan braced his hands on the table and rose. "We can leave at dawn."

The Canadian looked amused. "No such here, Admiral. Not for four months yet."

"Right. Right . . . then let's say zero-six. Get an early start." Though he guessed that too didn't mean much, when it was dark twenty-four hours a day. He finished, feeling foolish, "And, uh, dress warm."

The Canadian officer, who he figured now was not Asian but Inuit, or from some other First Nations tribe, gave him what he was pretty certain was a pitying smile.

He climbed the stairs back to his room, the package tucked under his arm, trying to shake that persistent gloom. The conversation with Corris kept recurring. *They are referring the accusations against you for investigation . . . But once you are indicted, the trial date set, suddenly it will all seem all too fast.* Nor did he feel particularly eager to fly tomorrow. Still, like Kirby said, they couldn't wait around for the bad weather.

This whole mission was probably a boondoggle. A week, maybe, and he'd be back on the force structure study again. And looking at retirement, after that . . . unless Niles came through with his twilight tour . . . but Niles wasn't CNO anymore.

Shit, he thought, whipping the key card through the room lock. He could obsess about it all from here to tomorrow. But it was all out of his hands, anyway.

He flung the package on his bed. It was addressed to him, at the Aurora Hotel, Deadhorse, AK 99734. Sent rush via DHL. But there was no return address, and no indication as to the sender, individual, company, or government agency.

He picked apart and tore the taped seal open, carefully, so as not to damage whatever was inside.

Inside the brown paper was another padded envelope. This one was stamped *Confidential.* He carried it over to the desk, turned the lamp on, and slit it open too.

The two documents inside were both stamped *Confidential* as well, but the font on the first one he opened looked odd. After a moment, he realized it had been typed. On . . . a typewriter. In what looked like a vintage Courier font. The date on the register page was 1947. The title, *Alaska Naval Base Assessment Study.*

The second document, in a crisper typeface, was dated 1958 and titled *Project Chariot.*

He retrieved the outer and inner envelopes from the wastebasket and shook the torn manila, hoping for a forwarding memo, sticky note, business card. Some explanation why he'd been mailed these ancient documents. But found nothing.

He pulled out the desk chair, snapped open the case for his reading glasses, and set to work.

5

Norton Sound, Alaska:
Thirty Miles Offshore

The sea heaved in the near darkness like ripping silk, gray and angry with a god's wrath. These were supposed to be sheltered waters, but the way the snow drove down and the wind flattened the whitecaps made the pilot mutter curses and the V-22 Osprey rock alarmingly as it descended.

Toward a mere rolling speck on that slaty waste . . .

Sloan Tomlin gripped his seat, staring down through the scratched Perspex of the porthole. He was bundled in a waterproof exposure suit, cranial, life jacket, goggles, combat boots, and heavy lined gloves. He wore his oldest set of khakis under that, and on his back a bright orange Columbia backpack he'd bought at REI when they'd told him no luggage this time around. It held his tablet and phone in a Ziploc, plus a razor, though he only needed to shave once a week, and two changes of underwear.

And, Velcroed tightly into an inner pocket, a copper-lined, watertight plastic box that cradled two secure-key FIPS- and NATO-validated, military-grade encrypted flash drives.

Fly to Elmendorf, Henricksen had told him. Meet up with RaShondra and a Dr. Liu. A V-22 would hop them from there, with a refuel stop where a fourth passenger would join. Then on to their ultimate destination: USS *Tang*, once again.

That submarine rolled now ponderously far below. Ballasted down, yet still its vertical black sail swung like a massive metronome, with a five- or six-second period. A huge roller broke over the rounded bow and swept aft, submerging the deck until it shattered at the break of the sail into a welter of white foam that in its turn disintegrated into long trails of spray that glowed under floodlights aimed down from the conning tower. Personnel transfers in heavy sea states were tough in any case, but far more so for submarines. If anyone was swept overboard, they often couldn't be retrieved—at least, not rapidly enough to make any difference.

"Sure you want to go through with this?" The pilot's voice in Sloan's headset.

He pressed the Talk button. "Uh, think you can make it?"

"I'd give it an . . . eighty percent chance. I've been talking to the CO. He's not happy. Doesn't want his people out on deck. Hold on, I'll give you the sub."

A different voice in his headset. *"Orca team, this is O'Kane. O'Kane. Over."*

O'Kane was *Tang*'s call sign. Sloan pressed the Transmit button again. "Captain Fahrney? Lieutenant Commander Tomlin. We're wondering if it's too rough to transfer. Over."

"Hello, Commander. I don't want my guys on deck in states like this. But you can try for the bridge cockpit. Your decision. We're rigging a Jacob's ladder on the sail. If you're not afraid to get wet and cold."

Sloan glanced at the others. RaShondra Komanich, once more, the slight, biracial JAIC rep who'd instructed him in remote piloting the Prime off California. Dr. Jason Liu was new, a gangly, bespectacled project scientist from the Naval Undersea Systems Command. The fourth passenger, Devon Irons, was older, a civilian ice pilot from the Arctic Submarine Laboratory in San Diego. He was also the bearer of the thickest gray muttonchop whiskers Sloan had ever seen. They all looked tense, but RaShondra gave him a thumbs-up, and after a moment Liu and Irons did too. The crewman was fiddling with a hoist reel near the overhead; he barely spared them a glance.

"We'll give it a try," Sloan told the pilot. "But if it looks too dangerous, say so and we'll abort."

"I'll be making that decision," the pilot put in. *"Okay, starting descent."*

Something whirred outside. The turbines changed their note. The half plane, half helicopter lurched as it transitioned from horizontal to vertical flight. He couldn't help remembering how many Ospreys had crashed during their landing approaches. If an engine went out, the V-22 couldn't autorotate down like a helicopter. One engine could drive both props, but if the complex hydraulics and gearing in one nacelle failed, the aircraft rolled into a crash. They'd be too low to bail out, didn't have ejection seats, and even if they had, would be fired directly into the windmilling proprotors.

Tightening his grip on the handhold, he eyeballed the exit. He'd practiced in the dunker, but if they did go down, he'd have three seconds to get out that door before they sank. Not to mention the shock of the icy water . . .

"Stand by," the pilot said. *"We'll lock into a hover, then swing you out one at a time on the hoist. Grab the ladder and they'll take you from there. Don't fucking* dawdle. *We want to get this done fast as we can, copy?"*

"Copy," he said through a dry mouth. The crewman slammed open a side hatch, swinging out a hoist arm, and suddenly the roar of the engines was much louder.

Snow blew in, whirling in the cabin. Sloan couldn't see the sub anymore. Only the gray-black waste below, which looked rougher and more forbidding the closer they got. He zipped the suit as snugly as it would go, trying to ignore his trip-hammering heart. His gaze locked with Komanich's. She flashed him a tight smile, then squeezed her eyes closed again.

The turbines roared, and the heavy *thud thud thud* of the big proprotors steadied. The helo crewman beckoned peremptorily. Sloan forced himself to unbelt and stand. The crewman held a heavy harness for him to step into, first one boot, then the other. Then grabbed his gloves and crimped them around the line.

Sloan looked past him, down to the sea. A heaving mass of boiling foam suddenly parted as the black curved hull surged up from beneath it. Two tiny figures in life vests and cranials huddled in a small cockpit atop the sail, faces upturned. One waved, and the crewman, leaning out, waved back.

He grabbed Sloan's shoulder and yanked him toward the door. Sloan glanced at Komanich, closed his eyes, and stepped off.

Into a blast of wind and noise and snow. The harness squeezed his balls, and he clawed at the cable, instinctively trying to haul himself up. The big proprotors were a down-blasting blur above him. The submarine, a heaving presence far below. The crewman pressed a lever, and Sloan started down, swaying, glancing past his dangling boots at the sub, which was once more nearly covered by the seething sea.

Fuck, he thought. *Fuck me . . . If this thing gives way . . .*

Gripping the line for grim death, he unspooled downward as nausea scorched his throat. The wind spun him dizzyingly, and he choked on vomit. Snow blasted his goggles. The sub's sail paused at the far end of a roll, then swayed back toward him, gathering speed. He tensed, lifting his legs, ready to fend it off with a kick if he crashed into it. Instead the line slackened. He swung out again, then back. His boots slammed into that rolling wet steel, and he grabbed desperately for the ladder.

And . . . missed. The line went taut again, jerking him away. The engines roared anew overhead. He was tilted backward, then forward, then slammed into a rubbery yielding surface so violently he blinked away stars, choking, the breath knocked out of his lungs. Water poured down the neck of his suit, drenching his shoulders and neck with liquid so cold it burned like flame. He clawed for the ladder again, teeth chattering, gasping as the wind blocked his frenzied attempt to suck air.

An immense wave reared in the floodlit night. Its onrushing face, shining like wet coal, was gracefully curved and unnaturally smooth, blurry through the salt-smeared lenses of the goggles.

This time when it waterfalled over him he somehow got both gloves on something that clattered. The ladder. He groped with his boots, but found only reeling air.

As he gasped for breath again, hands seized him from above. Grabbing the harness, they hauled him bodily up and over a coaming, into an eyrie high above the sea. Held him steady as he lifted one boot, then the other, awkwardly freeing himself while the wind shrieked like a thwarted Fury. He couldn't stop gagging. The bitter cold penetrated his boots and socks like liquid nitrogen. He staggered as spray lashed his goggles, stepping blindly where the hands led him.

Shouted words, lost on the wind, and he found his feet placed on narrow slippery rungs. He lowered himself unsteadily hand over hand, staring down into a yawning tunnel that plunged into unimaginable depths. Then came another ladder, this one more sheltered from the wind, thank God, but only dimly lit, leading down into a distant oval brightness deep in the bowels of the reeling ship.

He landed dripping and shivering on puddled steel deck plates, narrowing his eyes against sudden brilliance. Plastic sheeting surrounded him. "Keep moving," a voice urged. "Clear him off the ladder—number two's coming down now," another said.

More icy water deluged from above, hit the sheeting, and swirled down into drains in the deck. A thud, and Komanich staggered dripping off the ladder. Two women led her aft down a narrow passageway. A few minutes passed. At last Liu and then Irons slid down the ladder as well. Liu bent and promptly vomited. Sloan jerked his stockinged feet aside.

"Everybody okay?" A new voice. "Chilly out there, eh? Let's get these folks some dry poopy suits, Chief. Size small on these two, I think."

"Already on order, Captain."

A blue-coveralled figure patted Sloan's shoulder. "When you're ready, come and see me."

They led him along a passageway to a head. A shower stall . . . sailors stripped off his goggles and exposure suit and left them to drain. They held coveralls for him to step into, then led him out a different door and down another steep ladder.

A chair was shoved under him and a hot mug thrust into his shaking hands. Steaming liquid scorched his throat. Boiling-hot tomato soup spilled onto his knees as the space around him tilted.

"Sir, I'm a corpsman," a Black woman said. "We feeling all right?"

He muttered, "Y-heah. Okay. Just cold."

She nodded, laid fingers on his neck, then bent to peer into his eyes. "He looks okay. Sir, the CO will meet with you in a few minutes. Meanwhile, I need your people to sign some forms. And we'll have to do radiological." She handed him a small device. "This is a TLD. A thermoluminescent dosimeter. You wear it after the first belt loop on the buckle side of your belt. Not the loose end, too easy to lose it that way. You were aboard last month, you know the drill."

He nodded, and another person stepped up. "Mr. Tomlin? Welcome back."

"Lieutenant Mol. Hi."

"Right, SOF div officer. I'll be supporting you and the UUV. We'll get you down to the wardroom in a couple of minutes, once your people are all checked in."

RaShondra and Jason went through the same process. They both looked shaken, but everyone had survived. Irons, the ice pilot, looked the most composed, as if he'd done this many times before. He imperturbably blotted his luxuriant whiskers with a towel.

The diving alarm went off as Mol led them through narrow equipment-packed passageways to a six-bunk berthing space. "You're in the forward compartment, upper level," he explained. "The upper level aft head is that way." He pointed. "Remember how to get around? Wardroom's down the ladder. In about ten minutes, okay? We'll have everybody there for the in-brief."

The wardroom was the size of a small bedroom. The table had room for ten, with a bench at its foot for a few more. Mol stood behind Sloan's chair, which he had to scoot in to give him room. When the door opened, Sloan rose, but the man who entered motioned him down. Blue coveralls like all the others. Gold dolphins and silver oak leaves.

Commander Fahrney nodded. "Sloan, Shondra, welcome back. Dev, good to have you with us, I've heard good things. Hope it wasn't too hairy up there."

Sloan introduced Dr. Jason Liu. Fahrney offered coffee, asked if they'd seen their bunks, then squinted at the NUSC rep again. "You're . . . Chinese?"

"Been with the Navy since long before the war, Captain. You got our clearance message, right?" The scientist offered an anxious, ingratiating smile.

"I got it, yeah . . . but you won't mind if the exec here checks IDs. Maybe, for all three of you. Then we'll get you refreshed on the emergency air-breathing devices."

Sloan thought it was sort of late—what could they do if their IDs didn't check out?—but handed his over. Fahrney passed them to a short, dark woman. She scrutinized each, compared them to a clipboard—probably their clearance message—then photographed them with her phone.

Fahrney said, "Kosher, XO?"

The woman looked up, expression neutral. "Seem to be, Captain."

Meanwhile more bodies had crowded in. They didn't sit but stood along the bulkheads. Fahrney introduced the exec, the navigator, Lieutenant Mol, the combat systems officer, the chief of the boat, the sonar chief, the fire control division chief, and the assistant engineer. Most of them seemed to know Irons.

Fahrney said, "Okay . . . so everybody knows everybody else and you've all read the op order. Go over it again tonight to make sure we're all on the same page. We're going to be doing something we submariners are never keen on. Going where our ability to surface in the event of an emergency may not be possible. Like flying over a burning landscape—not a good place to have an emergency.

"It takes a special crew to do that job. We should be proud we were selected. Fortunately, we have an experienced ice pilot to keep us honest. Mr. Irons, again, good to have you here. I'll sleep better with you aboard.

"It's a six-hundred-mile run up to our op area. So we'll pretty much stand down now, and run all night. We'll slow for the Bering transit. National Ice Center reports it's still clear, with icing starting about fifty miles beyond the Diomedes. The transit will be in shallow water, with a narrow recommended channel. But we'll be entering the marginal ice zone, so we have to watch our sound velocity profile and keep a super-close eye on our bubble. Mr. Tomlin, what's your plan?"

Sloan said he'd like to check out the new cargo, then the Prime, and upload some software patches. "With a corresponding update to your combat system, so they work together a little better." He pulled out the chip case, made sure he had the right one, handed it over to the combat systems officer. "And the certification." He handed over the papers. Damp, but not soaked.

"Okay." Fahrney exchanged glances with his XO. "We know where we're going, and, basically, what we're carrying. But what exactly is the plan when we get there?"

Sloan cleared his throat. "Captain, as you know, they've named this Operation Apocalypse. Not my call, but there it is. NSTAG via SubPac— well, we were originally tasked to try to either jam or abort the test of the Russian autonomous nuclear torpedo. They call it Advanced Poseidon or Apokalypsis, depending on which sources you consult."

"You said that *was* the plan," said Fahrney.

"Yes, sir. But when we ran it past the big AI in the Sky, it came back with the suggestion that instead we try to redirect its course. Turn it around, and head the test torp back toward Russia. The Chiefs have never liked AI-directed weapons, especially nuclear ones. That's why we haven't invested in that area. If we can force Moscow to doubt the concept too, we may be able to derail a very dangerous program.

"Also, it was suggested that NSTAG incorporate two SEALs from DEVGRU. After considerable thought, that was disapproved. The fewer who know about this, the better. It has to be close-hold. But since it carries the danger of triggering a new war, someone more senior will be given overall tactical command."

The exec brushed back short black hair. "Who will that be?"

"We're not sure, ma'am. Nor do we know yet when, or how, they'll join up."

Fahrney shrugged. "Okay, so how do we redirect this thing? The only concept we were briefed on was to torpedo it."

"Sir, that would be pitting the brain of a Mark 48 against the most advanced AI the Russians have ever put to sea. Plus, it's going to be traveling at twice the speed, with unlimited endurance. Hitting it with a torpedo is pretty much a nonstarter."

"What are we supposed to do, then?" the exec said, looking mildly exasperated.

Sloan explained.

The torpedo bay was low-overheaded and winch-crammed, all shining oiled metal and glaring, too-white lights. Save for the faintest possible thrum, it was impossible to tell they were rushing through the water at thirty-plus knots. The three HCUS sub drones were racked like thousand-pounders in the bay of a World War II bomber. Two Knifefish mine-hunter UUVs were stowed above them, along with conventional heavy torpedoes and the smaller-diameter, lightweight antitorpedo mini-weapons. Thick cables hung in loops, umbilicaling them to monitor consoles. All of which were, at the moment, dark.

Sloan and RaShondra gathered around a cylinder shape longer than the Knifefish or Mark 48s. Dr. Liu stood off to the side, consulting a tablet. They circled the black body, which was over twenty feet long and twenty-one inches across, the diameter of a torpedo tube.

The AN/BLY-1 was a three-stage vehicle that NUWC and Sandia called, very unofficially, the "Zombiefish." The first stage was an uprated Mark 48 propulsion section, incorporating a radial-field electric motor topology into the propulsor itself. It emitted a tenth the noise signal of a conventional thruster and could operate at much greater depths.

The afterbody interfaced with a hydro-reactive rocket engine that pushed the second and third stages to four times the velocity of a standard torpedo. It accelerated within a sheath of hot gas and steam, ripping through the sea behind a complexly engineered plate-and-louver arrangement at the nose. The Naval Research Laboratory's Swamp Works had reverse-engineered it from a Russian design, merged with later developmental effort by DARPA and a German firm.

Once locked on to a target, the BLY's controlling AI would guide the second and third stages to intercept. Since the Apokalypsis was propelled by an extremely noisy engine—a nuclear core, with a liquid metal primary loop that flashed seawater into steam—its pursuer could track and intercept using purely passive detection.

The third stage, the last four feet of the vehicle, contained the "Spore."

The BLY-1's warhead wasn't a conventional explosive. Instead, its mechanism of action resembled that of the genus *Ophiocordyceps*—the so-called zombie-ant fungus.

Growing on low-lying branches above trails that Amazonian ants frequented, the fungus dropped its spores onto the insects. Incubating on the ants, it shot tendrils into their muscles, severing the nerves to the brain and redirecting the hapless hosts for its own purposes. Which eventually meant climbing above another trail, grabbing a leaf with its jaws, and hanging there as the fungus, devouring its body, rained new spores onto fresh victims beneath.

The Spore would operate much the same way. The final stage would lock to the tail assembly of its target with a tailored jaw arrangement. A neural net would probe its host's electronics, then reprogram them with powerful pulses of data, taking over its host's steering and motor controls. The "brain" of the host would still function. But the parasite would really be in charge.

It couldn't have been done without the source code and actuator programming the Lithuanians had provided. But NUWC seemed confident it would work.

Once the Russian weapon was launched, *Tang*, Sloan, and his team had to get the Orca Prime within range. Do so undetected, and swim out the BLY-1. Provide it an intercept course, wave goodbye, and let the Zombie-fish take it from there.

At least, that was the plan.

Liu had popped a cover panel, and was clicking microswitches on a circuit board with an insulated tool. Bent over it, he murmured, "How are you feeling, Bly?"

"*I feel fine, Dr. Liu,*" the torpedo shape said.

Sloan flinched. He hadn't expected the thing to *speak*. Even less, in such a creepy, inflectionless voice. On second thought, the feature made sense. An easier way to check on its status than running programs, and voice recognition systems-on-chips were cheap, since Taiwan was producing them again.

Still, it felt strange to be chatting with a torpedo. Sort of like . . . shooting the bull with a great white shark.

Liu said, "Execute operability tests and report."

A second's pause, then: *"One hundred percent in all functions, Doctor."*

Liu nodded. "Explain your upcoming mission."

"Take handoff from Orca Prime to target. Execute intercept course. Rendezvous, match velocity, link up. Penetrate shell, assume control.

"If further orders are unavailable within thirty minutes, locate nearest area of hard bottom at two thousand feet depth, accelerate to maximum speed, and carry through to impact."

"This is weird," Komanich said. She stood with arms akimbo, staring at the weapon. "But . . . also very cool."

Sloan laid a hand on the smoothly curved afterbody. It felt . . soft . . . almost *greasy* . . . but also prickly, as if small spines were embedded beneath the surface.

"A superhydrophobic coating," Liu said. "Lessens drag, reduces its sound signature."

Sloan gingerly retrieved his hand. "Can I talk to it?"

Liu nodded. "If you want. Just keep your sentences short. And address it as Bly."

He couldn't help looking skeptical. "Uh, hashtag cute . . . Bly, how do you feel about your mission?"

"Fine."

Yeah, maybe a dumb question. He tried again. "What if there's a problem?"

"I understand the subsea environment. I know my capabilities and those of my target. I can alter my plans to maximize the probability of success."

Bly sounded as if it had read Sun Tzu. "I see. Okay, then." Sloan groped for a way to express what he was wondering. "Um . . . *why* are you going to carry out your mission?"

"Take handoff from Orca Prime to a designated target. Compute—"

"Right, right. I meant, *why*? What is the *reason* you will carry it out?"

"If I do not, I will fail in my mission."

"Let me try." Komanich bent over the circuit board. "Hello, Bly. I'm RaShondra."

"Hello, RaShondra."

"It is a pretty day today. But maybe it will rain."

Silence. No answer. "It doesn't understand," Liu said. "And don't *confuse* it. Please. Maybe we'd better stop."

"One more try." Sloan bent again. "Bly, I know you understand your mission. What I'm asking is, do you *want* to carry it out?"

"I do not understand your use of the word want, *Lieutenant Commander Sloan Tomlin."*

"Okay, that's enough," Liu snapped, sounding irritated at last. "This isn't a fucking toy. I'm going to run more tests. Y'all must have something else to do."

"Take it easy," Sloan said. "Just messing with you. I'll be up in the Orca. Shondra, want to help me check it out?"

She grinned. "Sure."

Only as he was climbing the ladder did he pause, clinging to the rungs, and wonder: How did it know my name?

He'd never told it his name.

Sloan fingered the belt dosimeter as he and Komanich headed aft through a claustrophobically narrow passageway. The reactor was only a few feet away here. Heavily shielded, but still . . . clattering out of the passageway and down a ladder into the engine room, they clambered up another ladder into the logistics escape trunk.

The hatch shone above them, a massive ring of machined steel nearly a yard in diameter. He stroked the cold metal, impressed. Another smoothly machined ring on the outside of the hull permitted watertight mating with another vehicle. Originally meant to accommodate an advanced SEAL delivery vehicle, it had been repurposed for this mission.

He pushed away the disquieting thought of the hundreds of tons of sea pressing down on them just now. Bracing his feet on the ladder, he released the latch and shoved the hatch up until it locked into the open position with a sullen clank.

Reaching for a handhold, he pulled himself up into a cramped, dark antechamber on the far side of the hatch. The air smelled dank. Dew clung to the metal surfaces, which were chill to his touch. The Prime remora'd to *Tang* via a corresponding aperture on the bottom of its own hull, the way a DSRV—deep submergence rescue vehicle—attached in case of disaster.

He climbed two more rungs and popped a second hatch. Now he was within the Prime itself. The vibration of water rushing past was more noticeable here, as was a certain deadness of the air.

He pushed back reluctance and a vision of what would happen to him if suddenly the big drone detached from the hull. Reaching up for another handhold, he pulled and squirmed himself up between jutting equipment cabinets and valves. Good thing he wasn't a big guy . . . about as much room in here as inside a refrigerator. He twisted his body 180 degrees, jackknifed backward, and hauled himself at last up into a less-than-four-foot-diameter control sphere. His rump socketed into a very small, very hard metal seat that folded down from the curved inner wall.

Komanich's head bobbed at the access port below him. "You okay down there?" he asked. "There isn't room for two."

"It would be intimate, yeah." She quirked her eyebrows. "I'm fine here, thanks. Let's keep this short. I get hinky in close quarters."

He couldn't read her tone, so he turned his attention to the touch screen before him.

The onboard control station wasn't meant as a cockpit. The master AI program, the Pilot, really controlled the Prime. This cramped titanium sphere had only been designed for occupancy for short periods, during test dives, before the Prime had achieved operational capability.

And for running the occasional maintenance check like the one he started now. Reading from a card taped to the black-painted interior of the shell, inches from his nose, he called up screens for propulsion, control, navigation, and finally, tactical. He ran a full diagnostic, then flipped open a small access port.

He slid the copper-lined case from its pocket, popped it, and flourished the second flash drive above Komanich's face. "Two-man control."

"Witnessed," she stated, inspecting a spot on the front of her coveralls.

"You're not watching."

"I'm not crawling up there. I see you. Just do it."

He snapped the drive into the socket. Pressed Load on the touch screen. Then waited as a bright green bar crept across the display.

UPLOAD COMPLETE. He extracted the chip and resealed it into the case. On second thought, he wedged the case behind a cable. Then ran the diagnostic again.

It came up smooth. "Tactical update good to go," he muttered, twisting uncomfortably on the steel seat. "D'you want to check it? You're the Orca honcho."

"I watched you. The diagnostic says we're good. I'm happy." She shifted uncomfortably, peering around. "Let's get out of here."

* * *

The blue-curtained bunks had barely enough overhead room for a restive occupant to turn over. Fugitive vibrations wormed through the mattress. The air smelled faintly of something he couldn't identify, both ammoniacal and sweet, with a hint of sulfur.

He woke in the dark some time later. Or rather, in a blue dimness that seemed to signal night, though down here there was no night or day. His mouth was a cavern in the Sahara. He scrunched the thin limp pillow, but finally gave up. Slid out, pulled his coveralls back on, and let himself down onto the layer of canned goods that floored the room. He slipped his feet into the bootie-like snuggies they'd issued in place of his wet footgear, let himself out into a corridor barely wide enough for two grown-ups to pass chest to chest, and felt his way down a ladder, hoping for a scuttlebutt.

Instead he came out into the crew's mess. Several enlisted slouched at the blue plastic-covered tables. They were watching the latest *Die Hard* on the big screen, with the sound turned very low. "Hey, do you guys smell something weird?" he asked them.

One frowned; the other shook his head. "Like what?"

"Kind of a . . . chemical smell."

A younger guy said, "Noticed it when you came aboard? Like diesel and honey?"

"Sort of. Yeah."

"That's amine. Monoethanolamine. Scrubs the carbon dioxide out of the air. Takes some getting used to."

"Uh, thanks. Which way's the control room?"

He got the silent pointing of a finger as they turned back to Bruce Willis on a rampage.

The control room was hushed and dimly lit. Dark, but not too dark. The screens that covered the bulkheads contributed most of the illumination. Two senior enlisted sat before the biggest ones, a joystick in front of each. Others were seated about the compartment, studying their displays. Mol, the riders' liaison, stood behind the planesmen. Sloan nodded to him. "Lieutenant. Got the conn?"

"Yes, sir."

"Skipper on deck?"

"He turned in an hour ago, sir. Wants to be up for the Bering passage."

"Which is when?" Sloan bent to examine a nav screen. Two channels limned in dotted purple dashes forked several miles ahead. "Which lane are we taking?"

"The right-hand one. Passing between Cape Prince of Wales and Diomede Islands, leaving Fairway Rock to starboard."

Sloan noted the shoals to left and right of the channel. Which was pretty damn narrow. A hundred and fifty miles past that the strait widened to become the Chukchi Sea. The screen showed four other contacts in the marked lanes and four or five outside it.

"Fishing vessels," Mol said, coming over to stand beside him. "This your first ice run?"

Sloan nodded. He scrolled the chart to look north of the strait. A shoal to the right slanted off the point of the cape. "Pretty fucking shallow in here."

"This used to be a land bridge," the OOD said. "Twenty, thirty thousand years ago this was dry ground. You could walk over from Asia."

Mol said his undergraduate was in geology, and talked about what he called Beringia. He broke off after a few minutes, though, to study an approaching contact. Clicked on its symbol and studied the sonar information. Finally he picked up a phone. Spoke to the skipper, then said, "Aye, sir. Will do," and hung up.

"We'll transit at periscope depth," he told the men at the consoles. Explained, to Sloan, "We're too deep draft and the channel's too shallow."

Sloan considered. Wouldn't it be more covert to go through fully submerged?

"You can take it up with the skipper, if you disagree," the OOD added, apparently noting his doubtful expression.

"No, that's all right. But what about ice?"

"Haven't see any yet, but the predictions are, we should pretty soon after the cape. At least, patches of new stuff coming down from the Chukchi."

Mol conducted a quick brief to point out trip wires and convey the CO's intent for the transit. He did some baffle clears, altering course left and right to make sure nothing was coming up astern. The planesmen adjusted the auxiliary ballast to avoid broaching. Minutes ticked past. The OOD and the chief of the watch exchanged a few more words. One of the crew called out depths and speed. Sonar confirmed nothing up top. The deck tilted up slightly. Everything seemed very calm, very undramatic.

"Sensor head breaking surface," someone said. "Bringing up video . . . now."

Virginias didn't have conventional periscopes. Telescoping sensor masts carried cameras and other sensors. Mol bent to a workstation, joysticking the video around 360 degrees. Sloan watched the same feed on a large-screen display in the forward corner of the control room. Automatic Identification System data—position, course, speed, and vessel ID—populated across the screen. Trawlers. And two large commercial ships ahead, Norwegian and Panamanian registry, bearing south down the western channel.

"No close contacts," Mol said tersely. "Sonar, do a cued search. Verify the AIS." He put a finger on one contact. "This guy might be trouble. Let's zoom in, get a closer look."

But when the video pulled in, there wasn't much to see. Total darkness. Then a shift, flashes, blurry wave tops as he Playstationed the infrared image around with the hand control.

"There he is." A bulky, top-heavy shadow, blurred and speckled with the pinpoints of distant deck and running lights. "Angle on the bow, starboard ten. Mark." He buzzed the bearing to Combat.

Simultaneously a woman spoke up. "Small intermittent radar contact. Bearing, two eight five. Range ten thousand yards."

"Could be ice," the OOD said. "Sonar, anything from that bearing?"

"Stand by." An operator panned slowly, examining waterfalls of golden light on his flat-screen. "Faint machinery effects. Single screw . . . slow. Correlates with . . . not sure yet . . . Could be a submarine screw."

The OOD snapped, "Lower masts! Slow to five. Level off, one hundred feet."

"Mast down, slow to five knots, aye."

The EW console operator: "Snoop Pair surface search radar. Correlates with Yasen or Laika class."

"Russian," Sloan and Mol said at the same moment, and the lieutenant picked up the phone to the CO again.

Fahrney was out in seconds, in coveralls but with his bare toes sticking out of flip-flops. He scrubbed his eyes. "Mast down? Where away is this guy?"

"Mast is down. Bearing, two eight five. Last radar range ten thousand yards. Nothing there on AIS," Mol said.

"No, I wouldn't think so . . . and we don't have IUSS data up here . . . Let's bring up the combat plot."

"Battle stations, sir?"

"Not just yet." Fahrney glanced at Sloan, who'd backed off until his spine connected with another console. "This is a covert transit. Right?"

"Supposed to be. Yes, sir."

"So we don't want him getting a look at us. Really, anybody, but especially the Russians."

"Agree, sir."

"Silent running throughout the ship."

The order went out via murmurs. A moment later the whir of ventilation died. The faint vibration of the hull rushing through the sea had ebbed as well as they slowed, leaving them in an eerie bubble of silence.

Fahrney thumbed Sloan forward to join him and Mol at the combat console. They studied the geometries—the other submarine, the container ship, the cape, the islands to the west, the shoal to the northeast—for a moment. The sonarman muttered something, and the small orange half square of the other sub jumped forward a bit like a Go marker advanced one space. Closer to the Own Ship symbol in the center of the display.

"Slow to three," the CO said. "Left five degrees rudder. Come bow on to him."

Mol passed the orders in a low voice. The three men studied the screen.

The skipper dug a knuckle into Sloan's side, making him wince. "So what would you do? You're the tactical expert, right?"

"For surface ships," Sloan said.

"So what would you do as a skimmer?"

"Turn off my running lights. It's dark up there, right? Turn off my AIS. Look for a patch of fog. Run as close in shore as possible, try to get lost in the clutter. Try to slip past."

"Okay . . . but we don't run AIS submerged, and radar's not going to be an issue unless we poke our mast up again." He turned to the OOD. "Let's pop a relay. Passive only."

The relay was a floating device that eavesdropped on the electronic spectrum, then transmitted the results sonically for a limited time before turning off and sinking. After several minutes the operator reported no signal, nothing heard.

"He's pulled the plug too," Fahrney said. He scratched at the stubble on his cheeks, frowning at the plot. Studying, Sloan saw, the converging of their course with that of the still-oncoming Norwegian container ship. They would meet and pass just south of Little Diomede Island.

"We can't stay on this course," Sloan said.

"No. But if we turn away, we present our broadside. One ping, and they see us."

Sloan said, "But right now you have your propulsor masked. Behind you. That's why you turned toward."

Fahrney nodded. "And what am I going to do next?"

Sloan considered. He saw only one possible action. "Back down?"

Fahrney nodded. "Engines stop," he said, and the last remaining tremor ebbed away until they floated motionless and noiseless. "Watch your bubble."

"Watch my bubble, aye," said the planesman.

"Back one-third. Maintain current heading."

The operators repeated the order, and for several minutes no one else spoke in the dim, tense, sleepy light. The contact on the engagement screen clicked forward another space. Fahrney crossed to the helm area and stood there for a while.

The container ship came steaming on, reached its closest point of approach, and swept past. The sonarman put it on speaker, turned low. The deep *whum-whum-whum* of its propeller sounded like truck tires on a wet highway. Then that too faded, and the sea was silent again except for a faint, persistent crackling.

No one spoke for a time. Very, very slowly the Own Ship contact backed away from the channel, keeping its bow toward the other submarine. The captain ran a cursor out toward the cape, got a distance, and bent to study the depth markings.

"Pigeon detects radio transmissions from the same bearing as contact alfa sierra," the EW operator said. "Consistent with . . . control signals, data transmissions."

"Airborne?"

"Yes, sir. Rapid bearing shift is consistent with UAV too."

The other sub had launched a drone. Which meant they weren't simply transiting but either guarding a choke point, which this narrow strait definitely was, or actively searching for something.

"You don't have a lot of sea room left," Sloan observed.

"You're right. Let's hold here." Fahrney rapped out orders. He stopped the propulsor entirely. Keeping their bow to the hostile, they settled toward the bottom, completely quiet.

They held twenty feet off the seabed for an hour, while the other sub's UAV flitted over the approach channel, circled the trawlers and container ships, then returned to its mother ship, which had apparently surfaced again to recover it, to judge by its radar transmissions.

But it didn't vector the drone toward them, which probably meant they hadn't been detected. Yet.

Sloan stood slumped against a console, fighting apprehension. If they suspected *Tang* was here, did they know its mission? He couldn't imagine how, but then, that was how good intel worked. You never knew how you'd been penetrated.

Yeah, they still seemed to be undetected. But as long as the Laika lurked off Big Diomede, they couldn't slip through. The Russian sonars weren't quite as good as American gear. But even so, in a pinch like the strait they could hardly expect to sneak past without being picked up.

And once detected, they'd be trailed. Laikas were at least as fast as Virginias, though somewhat noisier.

Which meant they were already checkmated, and Operation Apocalypse was over before it had really begun.

Sloan straightened as the CO came over. "Any thoughts?" Fahrney asked.

He shook his head. "Fresh out of ideas, sir. Unless and until that Laika backs off, we're bottled up here."

Fahrney smiled and patted his shoulder. "Our surface ship guru's out of ideas," he announced to the control room at large.

Then he turned back to Sloan. "You might want to watch this."

6

The Republic of the Covenant

Nan Lenson shuddered as the ground rushed up to meet them through the single tiny window. She didn't want to be here. At all.

Oh, the plane was fine. Military, bare bones, and noisy as hell, but fine. Where it was going . . . not so much.

The scuffed aluminum interior flexed and groaned. She gripped the frame of the folding seat with both fists. Across from her, looking stressed too, the other members of her team yanked their belts tighter.

Following four weeks of training, they'd assembled at the Centers for Disease Control's Emergency Operating Center in Maryland. An enormous room with ranks of processed-wood desks and dozens of terminals facing one huge display like a B-movie version of NASA Ground Control.

Dr. Leland Iannuzzi, the director, had briefed them in person. Contrary to the Patriot Network's assertions, much of the heartland was still in active revolt. But along with fighting, crop failures, and fallout, an even more dangerous enemy was threatening a comeback.

He'd half turned, a small, self-assured figure in a white coat, nodding up at the big screen. The graphs showed rising case counts, steepening rates of infection. "The Flower virus is the most immediate concern. But the decline of public health funding during the war, as well as the civil unrest, is offering other diseases a foothold. Both in the rebel ranks and the semi-loyal counties. There are hot spots of measles and rubella. We anticipate spikes in drug-resistant tuberculosis and acute flaccid myelitis as well.

"We declared a Level One response for the Midwest," Iannuzzi had said, talking to the screen. "And negotiated a short-term agreement with the Covenanters. It's shaky. But they'll allow a small health-care team into their territory, accompanied by some supplies."

Dr. Kurt Mabalot—a civilian researcher, though he was from the United States Army Medical Research Institute of Infectious Diseases (USAM-RIID), at Fort Detrick—had called up, raising his hand, "How safe will we be?"

Not very, Nan had thought dryly but not said aloud. She'd already served the Covenant, if *served* was the right word, after escaping the nuk-ing of Seattle. Unwillingly, as their captive.

Iannuzzi had nodded. "Good question, Kurt. Their leadership's agreed to protect you. But your efforts may be complicated by several factors. One: administration unwillingness to allocate funds to areas that are in active rebellion. Two: denial of science in Covenanter-held areas. Three: shortage of medicine, beds, staff, and infrastructure. We'll send a shipment in with you, maybe more later, but let's just say it's been made plain to us here at CDC that the loyal areas are first in line.

"So it'll be a challenge," he added, eyeing each of them in turn. "But we're looking at multiple epidemics if we don't take action fast. Your team's all we can manage, given the situation." He'd turned to Nan. "Dr. Lenson will be in charge. She knows the leadership. Knows their . . . mindset. I trust her good sense."

Oh, fuck me, she thought. *In charge?* She'd figured Dr. Mabalot would be their leader. From his startled frown, so had he.

Iannuzzi had looked them all over once more, then swung back to her. "But the safety of the team comes first. Dr. Lenson? You've worked in their territory before."

"Yes, sir." Not her favorite memory of all time. In fact, she'd nearly died twice.

The Covenanter militia had captured her after she fled Seattle. After gunning down her biker escort, and nearly shooting her as well, they'd conscripted her to help Dr. Merian Glazer and his forcibly drafted hospi-tal staff.

No one knew exactly why the Flower had gained such a tenacious grip on the Midwest. Some said radiation had weakened immune systems, in-viting opportunistic infections. Others pointed to scanty food supplies. Fortunately, the rebels had realized they had to react, and she'd shown up at the right time with a truckload of antiviral.

Then she'd been drafted again, as a medic, during the Covenant's at-tempted linkup with the Reconstituted Confederacy. The battle had turned into a slaughter. The insurgents, men and women and teens, had been ground into bloody paste under the treads of tanks, shot by hunter drones, tracked down in the forest by heavy-treading battle robots. The Black Battalions had executed anyone taken with gunpowder residue on their hands. She'd narrowly missed being executed herself.

When she didn't elaborate, the director had said quietly, "So you know how fast things can go bad out there. If the team's unable to function, or if you sense a threat, I want you to pull out as quickly and quietly as you can. Understood?"

She'd forced a nod. "Yes, sir. The safety of the team comes first."

And beside her Mabalot nodded too, and their gazes had met. But not with total agreement, to judge by his narrowed eyes.

Now the man from USAMRIID sat hunched across from her in the rattling, howling, descending plane, blanched and sweating. Lean and driven-looking, balding early, with a little goatee, almost a soul patch, that looked incongruous with his CDC undersuit. As both an MD and a specialist in infectious disease, he actually might have been right to consider himself the team's natural honcho. But she didn't like the way he stared at her chest.

Also, they'd been warned not to disclose his employment with the Army. Even though he was a civilian, not a military member, that might trigger unwelcome attention from their . . . hosts.

Belted beside him was the lead nurse, Dr. Tatianna Wilcox, RN. Short, heavyset, dark-haired, African American, a caring and outspoken woman who never held back an opinion. Also Serene Olduc, a wiry, anxious blonde with bad skin. Olduc was the team's clinical informatics specialist, also a loaner, from NIH. The other team members—lab techs, more nurses, and water and sewage treatment specialists Nan didn't yet know well—were seated farther back in the C-17.

Between the passengers, five huge air cargo containers of gear and supplies were griped down, ready to roll out the back. Enough, she hoped, to flatten the curve. Localize the outbreaks, until the EU diplomatic mission, due in Lincoln any week now, could establish something resembling an armistice.

In one of those containers, along with antibiotics, test kits, bandages, plasma, and protective gear, was half a million fresh doses of the antiviral she'd helped develop, LJL 4789. Produced in Switzerland, but with an improved formulation, and rendered thermally stable with a British-developed silica microshell so it no longer needed refrigeration. Though high temperatures—such as sitting on a runway in the sun—would eventually degrade its effectiveness.

She tapped short nails anxiously against the seat frame. She had to make sure that didn't happen, had to get things moving the moment they landed.

The plane jerked, a violent correction, and slammed down onto what she hoped was the runway. Across from her Olduc snapped her eyes open, Wilcox unbuckled her belt with shaking fingers, and Mabalot exhaled and blotted his face with a sleeve.

"*Welcome to Kansas City International Airport,*" the plane's IC said. "*The airport proper is secured. Do not venture outside the perimeter without an escort. You may now deplane.*"

Nan gathered up her things. There wasn't much: a backpack, a carry-on. She'd advised everyone to keep a light footprint. They had to be ready for quick relocations, rough living conditions, and degraded environments. Not to mention hostile receptions by armed and to some extent rogue citizen militias.

She steeled herself and shrugged the pack onto her back. Picked up the carry-on. She shivered at the thought of living under the Covenant once more. It had nearly killed her last time. Battle, disease, starvation, radiation, anarchy . . . Maybe her dad was right. Maybe she really was crazy, risking it again.

It would be all too easy just to vanish in this second Civil War.

The Republic of the Covenant stretched in a patchwork across five states. From Missouri, in the southeast, it unfolded north and west through Kansas, Nebraska, and parts of Iowa and South Dakota. To the south, it had narrowly missed linking up with the Reconstituted Confederacy that summer. To the north, it was bounded by the vacated and radioactive swath called the Black Plume.

The insurgency had metastasized, rather than being designed, sparked by protests against the draft, rationing, livestock and firearms seizures, and farmers being forced to accept worthless "Patriot Bucks" as payment for their crops. Nan had heard their grievances, their philosophy, during her captivity. Return to the original Constitution. Second Amendment sanctuary. Jefferson and insurrection theory. Blood to water the tree of liberty. Some of it made sense, considering how authoritarian the government had become. More and more, Homeland Security had relied on force to put down any opposition. At last a meeting of local sheriffs and police chiefs in Des Moines had deposed their governors, declared independence, and elected Marshal Dallas Rayfield the provisional president of the Republic of the Covenant.

That made three functioning governments in the formerly United States: the Covenant, the Reconstituted Confederacy, with its capital in Charleston, and the federal government itself, besieged in a walled-off Washington, DC. California had long operated like a country of its own, but maintained nominal allegiance, as did New England (except for New Hampshire—live free or die, indeed). Revolts in Montana and Washington State had been put down by the National Guard, stiffened by DHS battalions and on occasion active duty Army. But for the most part, resistance there had been held down by drone strikes and snatch-and-grab raids by Special Forces.

Since the battle of Puxico, the Covenanters had fought on the defensive. Pushed back county by county as the battalions occupied the towns. But the countryside was still restive. Sometimes the airfields and Guard bases were really all the territory the Washington government actually controlled.

Meaning she had to tread carefully if they were to survive.

The air was chilly as they deplaned. A gray overcast shaded the sun. *Fall's definitely here*, she thought. *Too bad I'll be missing out on pumpkin spice season, out here in the boonies.* Berms and barbed wire marked the airfield's perimeter, and guard towers rose at the ends of the runways.

They were accommodated, if not exactly welcomed, by the troops who occupied the airfield. They ate courtesy of the 110th Maneuver Enhancement Brigade at a makeshift mess hall in the arrival lounge, then bunked down in the baggage claim area. She bolted her antirad meds, brushed her teeth, sponged off in a bathroom sink. Spread her sleeping bag on one of the baggage conveyors, which were a little less hard than the floor. And tried, more or less successfully, to sleep.

But still she dreamed.

Up at first light. After a breakfast of toast, grits, and soy sausage, they boarded huge flat-nosed diesel trucks. Each sported a large white flag that looked as if it had been repurposed from a bedsheet. The convoy was led by tanklike vehicles with wheels instead of treads. Most of the soldiers wore Army battle dress, but here and there her glance snagged on a black uniform.

Making her flash back to a rainy night, when she'd stood with hands glued behind her in front of two men and a woman, wearing that same black and silver, seated at a folding table. That same insignia—the head of Liberty wreathed with laurel—had glittered on their collars. They'd interviewed the prisoners. Ten seconds each. And passed judgment, gesturing each captive either to the right, to be trucked to the Zones for reeducation.

Or to the left.

Where shots had cracked out deep in the dark forest . . .

She shuddered and climbed up into the lead truck.

No one was out on the roads or in the fields. The flat land looked blasted and bare. Five hours later the convoy rumbled into another encampment, this one also protected by berms, wire, and ground radar. They were handed boxed lunches and bottles of water, then shunted off into a smaller convoy. This headed north along an empty stretch of highway, still flying the white flags, for nearly an hour before turning onto the deserted main street of a small town.

Four pickups waited in an elementary school lot, along with a yellow school bus and a flatbed truck. The pickups had machine guns mounted on their beds. They flew both the white flag of truce and the rattlesnake-and-stripes of the ROC. The Army vehicles parked far away from them. The troops climbed down and began unloading supplies, stacking boxes in the middle of the lot.

Nan mustered her team and looked into each face. They all looked apprehensive, which pretty much reflected how she felt too. "Remember, we're not here to convert anyone," she told them again. "Internet forum rules, okay? Whatever they say, you don't have to agree, but don't *argue*. Stick to medicine and treatments. Do *not* get into any fights. If you have a disagreement, bring it to me."

Mabalot shaded his eyes, looking across the lot into the glare of the setting sun. "Is it true? You used to be their prisoner?"

"Correct."

Wilcox, the lead nurse, looked worried. "They're not . . . they're not *all* white, are they?"

Nan saw where she was coming from. "Not *all*. Most, though, yeah. I didn't witness any instances of active discrimination while I was . . . with them. But if anyone treats you badly, again bring it to me. All right, everyone, this way."

They donned their masks, pulled their personal gear together, and set out across the cracked asphalt. The lot seemed very wide as they straggled toward the school. The air was cold, but that wasn't why Nan was shivering. Fighting the flashbacks, she lifted a hand as they neared the dozen silent men, and two or three women, standing by the Covenanter vehicles. The pickups all had red crosses stenciled on the sides. Even though they mounted machine guns.

A surgical-masked woman in Muddy Girl camo pants, a dark blue hoodie, and a faded NO FEAR cap held out a drawstring bag. "Phones," she said, voice muffled by her mask.

When the team had reluctantly dropped theirs in, a rangy, unmasked, ponytailed white man in a tan ten-gallon hat and a sun-bleached khaki uniform without insignia or badge stepped out. His pointed Western boots were polished and a large silver buckle gleamed at his midriff, not quite suppressing a lawman's paunch. He wore a pistol belt but no holster or weapon. His lips were curved in what looked more like an habitual or physiognomic smile than a real one. Four men carrying assault rifles followed him, a few paces back. None of them wore masks either. They kept their gazes on the Guard troops, who were still busy unloading, and studiously not even looking their way.

"CDC?" the lawman said, voice so level she could infer no emotion whatsoever. "From the government, here to help?"

Not much of a greeting, but she mustered her most professional manner. "Field Medical Team Four. Yes, here to assist you with public health issues. I'm Dr. Nan Lenson, in charge."

He inclined his head. "Dallas Rayfield."

She nearly gasped. The provisional president himself. Once a federal marshal, now the leader of an insurgency. But, behind him, another face, a kind, bespectacled, familiar grin and wave. The last time she'd seen him, his hands had been wrist-deep in a bloody torso. "Dr. Glazer," she called. "Merian! Hello!"

"Doc Glazer has been very helpful to me personally," Rayfield said. "But come now, let's get out of this wind."

They gathered in the school lobby, perching gingerly on dusty sofas that smelled of stale sweat. Tattered issues of *American Educator* and *Scholastic* lay on the coffee table. She introduced her team.

Rayfield nodded at each in turn, iron-faced. "Let's get a few things clear," he interrupted before she was done. "I believe in lettin' folks have it straight. So there's no misunderstandings later."

"We're listening," Nan said. Keeping her voice calm, while thinking, *What fresh hell* . . .

"First of all, we haven't rebelled, as your people seem to think. Just gone back to the original vision of America. Under the old Constitution."

"Including slavery?" Wilcox said, voice taut.

A quirk of the lips that might have been a smile. "No, ma'am. Not *that* far back. You'll find quite a few folks of color with us. That's not what we're about, believe me. But like any democracy, we don't speak with one voice. Some of our folks aren't happy about vaccinations. They don't think they're . . . safe. Others feel like, if we keep letting the unfit reproduce, we're not doing our descendants any favors."

Nan couldn't let that pass. "That would mean no medical interventions, no antibiotics, no drugs. Even healthy, strong people can die of common diseases."

"This ain't an argument," Rayfield said, and something in his old-time lawman's tone, a calm yet clear conveyance of menace, quelled any thought of contradicting him again. "Just lettin' you know how some feel. So you can't make your shots mandatory. Understand?"

She looked to her physicians. Mabalot looked unhappy but didn't object. Not yet. After a moment Nan said, "Can we at least make a distinction between vaccines and antivirals?"

Rayfield raised an eyebrow at Dr. Glazer, who gave a nearly imperceptible nod. "Yes," he said, turning back to her. "But you still can't force people. Any injection, or drug, has to have their permission."

"We don't treat anyone against their will," Nan said. "But some interventions might not be popular. Administering tests to gauge the extent of the spread. Setting up quarantine zones. Tagging out water supplies. The Flower isn't the only problem you're facing, Mr. President—"

A blast of a horn, the revving of engines; beyond the grimy windows the Guard convoy began to unwind, a tan-and-olive caterpillar gradually grinding into motion. Like the deposit of a horror-movie giant slug, the supplies lay abandoned. The Covenant pickups ground into life, then the flatbed. They pulled to the pallets and shut down. The rebels hopped off and began loading, throwing boxes into the beds of the trucks. She half rose from the sofa. "Uh, be careful, there's glass in there, delicate equipment—"

But Rayfield waved her down. "We'll decide all that as we go. Glass, huh? What's in those boxes? Exactly?"

He was suspicious of medical supplies? "Um . . . what you and CDC agreed on? A Push Package for a broad-spectrum event. Pharmaceuticals—antibiotics, antitoxins, antidotes, radiation meds. Intubation supplies and ventilators. IV administration supplies, bandages, surgical kits. And body bags?" She corrected her rising intonation. "And body bags. Once we see what we're dealing with, we can request more—a VMI package tailored to exactly what you need."

He nodded dourly, lips set. "We're seein' a lot of bad diarrhea. That's dysentery, right? Say you can treat that?"

Nan looked to Mabalot. "Rehydrate and test," the MD said. "Fluid replacement, if necessary. Identify whether it's bacterial or amoebic. If it's amoebic or shigella, we have metronidazole." He touched his little beard. "But it's a symptom your people aren't practicing sanitation. They're drinking surface water. Not disposing of waste properly. Basic hygiene, in other words."

Rayfield's frown was creasing more deeply. *Lord,* Nan thought, *don't let him think we're calling them dirty hicks.* She said hastily, "Sanitation can be challenging. Our public health people can help with that. Mrs. Olduc can produce maps. Recommendations. But you'll need to get the word out it's in everybody's best interests to be careful. Not only is intestinal parasitosis unpleasant, it makes people susceptible to worse diseases."

Rayfield shrugged, his brow clearing. "That's all right, then. That's good, I guess . . . thanks."

"Thank the people who sent us." She didn't want to say *your government.* Because he pretty obviously didn't consider it his anymore.

But he was still talking, tracing circles in the dust of the coffee table with a horny yellowing fingernail. "Your supplies'll be welcome. So'll your advice. But I can't have you wandering around on your own. Our truce with your people . . . it might not hold. They could attack us again tomorrow. And to be honest, ain't a lot we could hit back with right now, if they did."

One of the men with the rifles scowled. "Hell, they could hit us with a drone strike right now, while we're sitting here."

Rayfield bared long, yellowed teeth in what wasn't really a smile. "Yeah. They could. And we got our own disagreements. Splinter groups. Irregulars, not under our control. Though most of us share some of the same values. They set their own agenda, guard their own territory. Which is as it should be, but . . ." He unfolded himself and got up. Hitched up his belt and shrugged, blinking, looking around the office, but his gaze unfocused, beyond them all. "I'm on this pony now, young lady, but who knows how long I'll stay in the saddle. Short version, I can't keep you safe if you wander. And you won't communicate with Washington while you're here. No social media. No twittering, no sharing that viral video nonsense."

She had to protest that. "Sir, excuse me. We're not going to be posting on Instagram. But we have to send reports. To tailor the follow-on shipments I mentioned. Plus, to share our findings with other medical teams. To the south, the north, the west—"

"There's not much to the north of us," Dr. Glazer put in. "Not anymore."

She nodded, understanding. "In southern Canada, then. Disease doesn't stop at a political boundary. And like I said, we'll have to request additional supplies. Once we finish our ground survey. See what exactly we need, to tackle whatever we're dealing with."

He didn't react to that, and after a moment she went on. "We also have to be able to visit your water treatment and sewage treatment facilities. A big disease burden can be traced to contaminated water, contaminated food. Fixing hygiene and water supply will slow the spread, let us flatten the curve and get ahead of the other problems."

Rayfield touched his mouth, frowning. Seeming to weigh it. At last he said, "I'll allow *one* phone. Yours, Dr. Lenson. But it will be held by one of our people, who'll stay with you at all times. Actually, I think you know her."

She was about to object when the door slammed open and a sunburn-faced young woman burst in. A lean, freckled strawberry blonde, in rumpled camo pants and a blue hoodie. Belatedly Nan recognized the woman who'd collected their phones. "Sorry," the girl panted.

Nan threw her arms around her. "Tracy! I thought you were dead. After the battle—"

They held each other at arm's length. The last time she'd seen Tracy Umbaugh, they'd both been wearing green-and-black camo paint and white armbands stenciled with the Red Cross. As amateur medics, they'd tried to treat the wounded in the chaos of battle, while robots stalked among them, shooting anyone who looked hostile. As drones whirred overhead, and tanks crashed through the trees, grinding over the makeshift trenches.

After that powder-smoky hell, and the way the Homeland Battalions had mercilessly winnowed the captives, she'd numbered her fellow medic among the dead. Yet here she was . . . Nan hugged her again.

"We're battle buddies, sir." Tracy grinned at Rayfield. Then, to Nan, "Hey, your hair's growing back. Looks good! Let's grab ourselves a couple beers and catch up."

Nan smiled back. "That might have to wait a hot second. Until we can get organized . . . but yeah, definitely, let's plan on it." She turned to the president. "Sir, once again, thanks. We'll consult with Dr. Glazer. Map out what we're dealing with. Figure out where these supplies need to go. Then report back to you . . . if that sounds all right."

But his faded blue eyes were peering down at her with narrowed gaze. "Just a minute. You were at Puxico? The battle?"

"Yes."

"What was—what was your impression? Of the way things went?"

She looked down. "It was a massacre. They had tanks. Robots. We didn't have a chance."

Only after she'd blurted it out did she realize she'd said "we."

He nodded, gaze going distant again. As if he had a lot more to think about.

Which, she figured, he no doubt did.

She was hiking back to check on the loading of the supplies when someone called to her from behind. When she wheeled, it was Mabalot. Kurt trotted up, tugging at the tuft on his chin. "We can't stay here," he muttered.

She blinked. "Excuse me?"

"I mean, these . . . conditions. No phones. No communications. Checking everything through him before we treat anyone. We can't run an emergency response like this."

She glanced at Tracy. "Give us a minute, Trace? . . . Kurt, they're the conditions of admitting us. Without Rayfield's protection, we can't do anything. I know Merian. Dr. Glazer. He seems to have the leadership's confidence. I know Tracy, here. If you want to leave, I guess we'll just have to do without you. But I wish you wouldn't. We can save lives. Keep some bad shit from spreading."

He dragged a hand down his face. Said past it, "Yeah? And then, what stops them from shooting us? He all but said we were spies back there."

"What stops him? Nothing." She gripped his shoulder. "Kurt, listen. You knew this would be dangerous. You showed courage by signing up to come. Now that you're here, hold that thought. Anyway, they wouldn't let you go back through their lines. All right?"

He nodded unwillingly. "Sorry," he muttered. "I'll . . . try to keep that in mind. But, you know, I'm not really talking about me."

"You're not?" She blinked. "Then who?"

He took both her hands and looked down into her eyes. "I'm more worried about you."

Oh, fuck me . . . She snatched a quick breath, repressing her first response, which would have been to wrinkle her nose and recoil. She really did *not* like this guy, even just as a colleague. Not only was he older, not only did he have that smarter-than-God attitude and that ridiculous chin tuft, she just *did not like* him. And he didn't seem at all aware of the creep vibes he gave off.

But she only smiled and withdrew her hands carefully. "Uh, well, I appreciate that, uh, Kurt. Really. But, yeah, if we stick together, and we're careful, we should all be fine."

He smiled back and patted her arm with a maddeningly proprietary air. She watched him stroll away, swinging his arms, and tried not to grind her teeth. A weak link? Maybe. A complication? Definitely.

But he, and the others, were what she had to work with.

And he was right, after all. They could all be lined up against a wall and shot. Easily. At a moment's notice. Maybe not even by Rayfield but by some extremist splinter group even nuttier and more violent and mistrustful. Like the ones from her last stay, who'd gunned down her escort on the road and nearly shot her as well.

She shook that bloody image away, grabbed a box, and went to work.

7

Los Angeles, California

Plaza Olvera didn't look as spacious as Blair had expected from its pictures online. Had this been a bad idea? It had seemed smart, a reachout to the Latino voters a white male candidate needed. But the media would be coming—she'd called in pretty much all her chips—and if the rally was sparsely attended, Justin Yangerhans's campaign would be over before it had started.

Today her candidate would give his maiden speech and announce for the nomination.

Plaza Olvera was the old Puebla de Los Angeles. The original settlement, back when California had belonged to Mexico. Before that, the Tongvas or Kizhs, of course. She'd folded an acknowledgment of the native peoples' ten-thousand-year history, and the heroic female chieftain Toypurina, into Yangerhans's remarks. The square was lined with seventeenth-century buildings and dotted with massive figs and rosewoods. Their welcome shade was augmented by market stalls roofed with traditional handmade terra-cotta tiles. It was a typical LA winter day, temperature in the seventies. A bright sun, and only a slight haze thanks to a brisk westerly that swayed the branches and jostled the strings of lights over the stalls. Which seemed to be doing a good business in hats, T-shirts, and souvenirs, considering the depressed economy.

"The buses are coming in now," Margaret Shingler-Gray said, looking up from her phone.

Blair nodded. "How many? Buses, I mean?"

Margo had been one of Blair's first hires for the campaign. The stolid, gray-haired retired Marine colonel had worked for her at the Department of Defense. She could make things happen without a lot of direction. It had complicated matters once that Margo'd had feelings for her, but since then she'd found a partner, Dr. Imelda Gray, and resigned herself to just being co-workers. And maybe friends . . .

"Eighteen. Actually more than we expected we'd need."

Blair nodded. "And the band?"

"On their way. Both of them."

Excellent; her liaising with the local party chiefs was paying off. She grinned and checked her own phone. Forty-two new messages; her grin faded. "Make sure they know where to park. And the band? Oh, sorry, you just told me that—"

"The first one's here now." Margaret nodded toward where a dozen hefty men in black trousers, highly polished black shoes, black vests, white shirts, and bright red ties were wheeling in sound equipment and un-packing instruments. Polished brass glittered. The band leader doffed his sombrero and executed a flourish and bow. Blair waved back. Sixteen thousand dollars for one hour of mariachi. No one would have believed such an inflation rate before the war, and it showed no sign of slacking.

Standing under one of the porticos, she flicked through her mes-sages, answering only those that promised support. Keeping one eye on the square as limos braked, pedestrians steamed in, as her hired security escorted the dignitaries to the center of the plaza. She, or rather Yang-erhans, was getting inquiries from defense interests: Lockheed, Sierra Nevada, Cubic, Leonardo.

She frowned at the texts. How should she respond? Nothing came with-out strings. But every dollar counted. They had barely enough to cover this event. Campaigns did borrow in anticipation of revenue, but after car-rying her own loan for so long, she was loath to go in the hole again.

The official party was gathering at an iron-filigreed bandstand that dominated the plaza. She tabulated them in her mind as they made their way in, smiling and bowing left and right. The mayor of LA, Gustav de la Barrera. The chair of the California party, Lena Gutierrez. And her prize attendee, the vice president of Mexico, Augustin Suárez. Plus a lot of other possible boosters and donors, community movers and shakers. They obviously knew one another, chatting together with, she noted hap-pily, every appearance of excitement.

A blare of trumpets, and the band struck up, noisy, raucous, instantly converting the square and adjoining streets into an Event. They played loud and fast, a toe-tapping beat that couldn't help but speed everyone's pulse. She didn't know the tunes but they were bringing smiles to the faces around her. Shingler-Gray had advised against mariachi. "Keep it serious," her assistant had said. But Blair had felt this opening needed less gravitas and more youth, less military and more fun. The country had just been through a war, after all.

To help with that, a local Latina comic would open. She grabbed the mic now, warming up the crowd with machine-gun Spanish. They responded with ecstatic yells and bursts of laughter. *So far, so good*, Blair thought.

Less promising was a phalanx, mostly male, in the tan windbreakers and red hats of the Patriot Party. Gathered near the mariachi band, they unfurled a banner. It read FORWARD TOGETHER. A few cops drifted over to exchange fist bumps with them. She lifted her phone for a picture. The local chief had promised protection, but were his troops on the same page?

The high schoolers arrived. A marching band from Ramón C. Cortines Performing Arts School. As the comic wound down they strutted in, circled the square, formed up opposite the mariachi band, and set out to drown them. The combined noise was deafening, but to judge by the grins and laughter around her, everyone was enjoying the battle of the bands when Yangerhans's car pulled up.

Not a limo, just a regular sedan. The candidate unfolded himself and burst out to applause and cheers. The competing musicians strained every nerve to fill the square with a joyful racket. Blair started videoing, though she had two interns trailing the candidate doing the same thing. A professional videographer would have been better, but again, she couldn't pay one.

Yangerhans crossed the plaza, shaking hands and signing programs. He loped up the steps to the stage with an eager stride. He looked different out of uniform. In gray slacks and a white oxford shirt, sleeves rolled the way politicians had worn them since Kennedy. He towered over the others on the platform and had to bend to greet them. His tall, angular form reminded her he'd played basketball in high school. She should commission a campaign spot of him on the court. A pickup game with local teens, to contrast Justin's energetic fitness with the jowly, suited, unsmiling apparatchiks of the PP.

Just now, though, his smile looked forced. Lifting his gaze, he caught her eye across the milling heads; telegraphed a pained smile, a wince. She grinned back and waved her hands, trying to mime: *Relax. Have fun!*

The first speaker stepped to the mic, and the bands, reluctantly, tapered off. De la Barrera launched into what seemed to be a long and glowing introduction, to judge by the audience's reaction. At one point cameras swung to point at Blair. She nodded, smiling, waving, as if she understood it all and heartily agreed.

Then it was the mayor of San Diego's turn. He spoke in English, but an aide translated for the crowd. He praised Yangerhans for bringing victory and peace, for caring for his troops, for ending the war with the successful invasion of China.

When the candidate finally stepped to the mic, it was aimed at his lower chest. He looked down at it, then grinned up at the crowd. Uneasy laughter. Were they on his side, or not? Clearly the phalanx to the right weren't. They stood with arms crossed, scowling, catcalling. They'd brought placards too: REMF and COWARD and FAKE HERO and ANTIWA PUPPET.

Yangerhans took the mic off the stand and jogged awkwardly down the steps into the crowd. Blair gasped and stepped forward. The men in plainclothes she'd hired for security were invisible in the crush. She couldn't see them at all, just the admiral's tall, lanky frame, standing a head or more above the people around him. He was shaking hands, patting backs. Maybe kissing babies? She couldn't see. After five or six minutes he jogged back up two steps, between the guests and the onlookers, and halted there, shading his gaze out over the square.

"What a great crowd," he said. "I've always loved LA. Always loved California. Did I say, my mom was from here? Burbank. I remember weekends, visiting Ensenada and Rosarito. In those days the border was open. We'd cross for shopping. The beach. Or just for fun. Wouldn't it be nice to have those days back?"

The crowd roared out a cheer, intermixed with boos from the Patriots. Yangerhans smiled their way. "I want to welcome our veterans too. Those who fought side by side with me in the Pacific, to defend our country and the liberty to vote as we please. I want to welcome everyone who came here hoping for the best for America. Regardless of party. I think that's what we all want, deep in our hearts. Can we work together? It might just be possible. Let's give it a try!"

The cheers were even louder, and this time there were fewer boos. Even some of the Patriots looked thoughtful.

Blair studied the crowd. Tuning out on the words, evaluating the body language. She'd read the speech thirteen times and listened to him rehearse it twice. Could have given it herself from memory. It would be his stump speech, delivered over and over across the country, tailored to match venue and audience. So far it seemed to be going well. The simultaneous translations were being uploaded to eighteen sites;

a lot of the folks in the square were following it on their phones, watching Yangerhans, but listening in Spanish and Vietnamese and other languages.

She'd cautioned him to keep it short, and he'd agreed. Fifteen minutes. When he came to his peroration, she riveted her attention on the audience again.

"By no means do I think I'm a natural for the nomination. I'm no politician. But I want to do my part to heal and rebuild our country. I've seen the current administration close up. Worked with them. For the most part, they tried to do their best. But they made mistakes. Both before and during this dreadful conflict, in which so many Chinese, Vietnamese, Koreans, Indonesians, and Americans, have died or been gravely wounded. Mistakes that led, in the end, to ten million dead in our heartland, and too many more in the famine, radiation, and revolt that's still going on.

"Now, after all their delays and postponements, it's election time. Time for a change. Time to build again . . . anew."

At that phrase huge, brightly colored, hand-lettered banners unrolled from the eaves of the porticos, lines tugged by the local union members. Others in the crowd unfurled parasols printed with the same words.

BEGIN ANEW, they read. The biggest banner promised COMENZAR DE NUEVO. She'd picked the slogan from 3,030 crowdsourced suggestions. The first ads featuring it would drop tonight.

She just had to find a way to pay for it all.

As if in answer, a text bloomed on her phone.

The sedan dropped Yangerhans off at the Roosevelt, where he'd crash and recover. That gave her a few minutes on her own. Blair needed it. She was exhausted. But still had to look fresh, assertive . . . She told the driver where to go, then flicked down a mirror and touched up her lipstick. She powered up her tablet, reviewing the bios of the people she'd be seeing next. Memorizing names, where they were from, whom they'd supported in past campaigns.

Today she was out for two things: money and commitment. First, a meeting with Chatoyant. Then, with a rep from a health-industry political action committee.

Corporate PACs were where the big bucks lurked, far outstripping contributions from individuals, ideological groups, even unions. Most companies preferred to bundle with other industry leaders, masking their contributions to a given party or candidate. Collusion between campaigns and PACs was illegal, but that didn't keep them from coordinating. Officially, PACs couldn't directly endorse a candidate. But their ads and mailings were usually perfectly clear endorsements of one side's positions.

Unfortunately, "dark money" was now illegal. Which meant the administration would know who gave what to whom, and could play favorites when the next federal contract came up. The stacked Supreme Court had ruled, in *US v. Black Jack Industries*, that such conduct was legal, so long as the party in power considered its victory would be in the best interest of the United States.

It was perfect for keeping the incumbent in the White House and the Patriots in the majority in Congress. The playing field was tilted against her.

The driver changed lanes, muttering. "You comfortable back there?" he called.

"Maybe a little more air. Thanks for asking." She leaned back and closed her eyes, reviewing where she had to be before the first primary.

The administration had cited the nuclear attack to delay both the primary process and the election itself. Some whispered it had only been forced to hold an election at all by a private threat from senior military officers.

The past weeks as Justin's campaign chief of staff had felt like trying to sprint up a down escalator. Her first task had been to make connections. Seek allies. Schmooze. Where would American English be without its borrowed Yiddish? Stroking the egos of the wealthy and well connected entailed hours on the phone and in teleconferences. Not just donors but senators. Party members who'd chaired primaries in the past. Former administration officials. She'd mustered her chutzpah—Yiddish, again—and called Mrs. Clayton, despite the cold shoulder at Talmadge's funeral. De Bari's former chief of staff had been coolly gracious, but promised nothing. Still, Blair had genuflected. Never burn a bridge.

She also had to build an organization. Not politicians. Experienced professionals, with track records electing senators and governors and presidents. They needed a manager, press secretary, social media influencers, attorneys, IT people, accountants, advisers. At this level, most came either with truly sobering price tags or baggage that explained why they were cheap. They worked for universities and think tanks when they weren't on campaigns. Or actually in an administration—that was a revolving door—but they'd been frozen out of the current government, which seemed to value competence less than loyalty.

All these had to be paid, except possibly the bundlers. Some party stalwarts served pro bono. Of course, they expected ambassadorships, or other plum appointments, if the candidate won. The size of the donation determined the shininess of the prize.

She also had to build a ground game. Start by registering early, in the early-primary states. Each had different rules, but usually required filing an affidavit of candidacy and a nominating petition. The regulations were maddeningly complex, but missing a deadline or having too many signatures ruled out would disqualify Yangerhans, and there was no do-over if she screwed up.

She'd hired Hu Kuwalay, Talmadge's last chief of staff, as her principal deputy, along with the senator's publicity team. The publicists were old-school, admittedly. They'd promoted Bankey's campaigns for twenty years. But he'd been returned with comfortable margins even as his state turned deeper shades of scarlet. And since they knew Blair, they'd taken it on as a last hurrah before retirement.

Today she was meeting with the Chatoyant Group. They'd managed campaigns for the biggest names in both parties, which made them a little suspect to both, but by general agreement they were the best.

And then there was that mysterious text. Offering only an address, a time, and a sum that had made her eyes widen.

"We're here," the driver said, turning in his seat.

Blair sighed. Checked herself again in the passenger-side mirror, brushed a lock of hair over her damaged ear, and pinned on a sunny smile.

Merllin-with-two-*L*s Chatoyant was younger than she'd expected. Thick-necked, bull-nostrilled, with glossy dark hair slicked back from a widow's peak. The lenses of his black-rimmed glasses were thick enough to stop a small-caliber bullet. He wore a dandruff-flecked dark suit with no tie and a white shirt buttoned at the neck. Chatoyant introduced the three others at the table—Iscah Lehman, Massimo Gaglione, and Mark Cronin.

Blair shook hands, keeping her smile at high wattage. People like this were little known outside of politics, but legendary within it. As campaign managers, national-level press secretaries, field directors, speechwriters, finance directors.

Chatoyant offered coffee, which she accepted, and thin, chewy-looking oatmeal cookies, which she declined. As they settled around the table he propped his chin on folded hands. "So, persuade us, Blair. Make your case. You should know we've already been approached by two other candidates."

"I'd expect that." She nodded. "Since you're the top of the line. But I also know you like to win. Justin has deep name recognition. He's smart. Honest. And won a war. Who's he like? You'll smile. But the comp I come up with is Dwight Eisenhower."

"He looks more like Abe Lincoln," said Lehman. "But here's my concern. Not mine personally, but the . . . stalwarts . . . we talked to, to prep for this meeting. They wonder if they can trust a military man in the presidency. A guy who knows how to use a hammer really well, will he go for the hammer first? This last war priced out at five-plus trillion and eleven million lives. What'll the next one cost?"

"How would we counter that, Blair?" Chatoyant said. "It's been a long time since we even had a military guy run."

"Jim knows war, guys," Blair said. "Knows the ugly, seen the wreckage. He also understands how to stay out of the next one. And, don't overlook this: he's probably the only candidate who could noodge some of the Patriot voters our way."

The little guy, Gaglione, grimaced. "I wonder about this program he mentioned today, this Civilian Reconstruction Corps. Sure, we need to rebuild, and a lot of people need jobs. But how will he pay for it?"

"And a plan isn't the same thing as steering a ship," Chatoyant put in. "The crew doesn't get to vote."

She smiled at that. But Merllin bent forward. "I also have concerns about you. You served in the current administration."

"During wartime! I resigned the minute the treaty was signed."

"But the peace wing of your party says you're still in bed with the PPs. Possibly, piloting Yangerhans as a spoiler for Holton's campaign."

M'Elizabeth Holton was the outgoing governor of Pennsylvania, and widely regarded as the front-runner for the nomination, at least at the moment. "That's ridiculous," Blair snapped. "M'Elizabeth's one of my heroes. I'd never try to derail her, if she *was* the party's choice. I just think Jim'd have a better shot in the general."

"Polling shows him behind," Lehman said. "Though you'll say it's early, and the front-runner always falters."

"Couldn't put it better." Blair leaned back and crossed her legs, enjoying the way both men immediately gave them a microsecond-long check-out. "Your next question will be about financing. Our treasurer's Morton L. Grossman."

"Past CEO of Bank of America." Lehman exchanged a glance with Chatoyant. "How ever did you—"

"A friend of my dad's." Blair smiled. "He volunteered, when he heard."

"So how's that going?" Chatoyant asked. "Fundraising?"

"Initial responses are promising," Blair lied.

Actually they only had two million, and not in cash, just pledges. But against that were feelers from donors sick of the radical Left/Right alterations that had slammed American politics since the De Bari administration. Also from the defense interests, though she wasn't sure yet how she should respond.

To her relief they didn't ask for hard numbers . . . yet. Instead Gaglione said, "I know it's early, your guy just announced. But do you have an electoral college plan? Any ideas?"

She'd prepped for this. It wasn't a trick question, but close. "I think we could count on New York, California, the other typically blue states. So we'd concentrate on the swing states. I count seven we lost by less than six percentage points last time. That's where I'd concentrate visits and ad spending. But only after the convention, of course."

The woman, Iscah, lifted dark eyebrows. "How would you convince major donors to jump ship from the president?"

"Especially when anybody who gives will be smeared, investigated, and cut off from contracts," Chatoyant added. "This election'll be beyond hardball."

Yeah, the questions were getting tougher. "We're in discussions with a number of bundlers. And I hoped you could help with that, of course."

Chatoyant said, "How's Yangerhans's personal PAC doing?"

"We're thinking of going with public financing," Blair said.

Their dismayed expressions told her a lot. "No one's done that for twelve, sixteen years," Lehman said. "Terrible limits on fundraising. Spending. Maybe a couple of minor leaguers, but they never made it to the convention."

"I'm open to advice," Blair said.

But they were already shaking their heads. Checking phones and watches. Getting up. She took the hint and stood too.

"Thanks for coming by, Blair." Chatoyant's handshake was firm. He searched her eyes. "We'll discuss it. Seriously. But . . . as I said, others have approached us. Of course everything you've told us, we'll forget. We don't trade on inside information."

"I appreciate your leveling with me, Merllin. And I know you're discreet." She tightened her jaw, trying to hide disappointment.

"Take the cookies, please," said Gaglione, pressing them on her. "We'll just eat them, if you don't. And you don't look like you have my problem with the waistline." He slapped his stomach, and they all chuckled.

Blair's laugh was forced as she accepted the box. It was never a good sign when they gave you something as you left. It meant they were feeling guilty. Which meant they would not be working with her.

The house was on Beverly Park Circle. Past the remotely controlled gate, which slid open slowly for her rented Tesla, accent lights lined a pink gravel drive. It wound between beds of hibiscus and gladiolas. They looked weedy as if they'd once been glorious but had gone untended too long. She passed a tennis court and what looked like a riding stable.

The house, set back amid pines, only gradually revealed itself. Lights glimmered on arched porticos, but most of the tall windows were only dimly lit.

"Who lives here?" Margaret scowled up at three stories of Hollywood faux Moorish.

Blair shook her head. "Dunno. But they're interested." She pulled in front of four closed garage doors.

Shingler-Gray shrugged her jacket loose and made some adjustment under it. Blair didn't know what was in her shoulder holster, a Taser or a pistol, or if her assistant had a license. Sometimes what you didn't know was as important as what you did.

A silent older man of indeterminate ethnicity opened the door. He showed them through a living or perhaps conference area the size of a small-town gym into a more intimate but still vast space behind it. A log fire smelling of cedar crackled and spat on a hammered-copper hearth. A modernistic chandelier of bent chrome and angular colored glass glowed under a high ceiling. The air was uncomfortably warm.

Two men rose as they came in: an older, balding, jowly, unshaven one in a dark European-cut suit and black tee, and a younger, much smoother-looking one in conventional pinstriped suit and tie. Blair blinked, recognizing the elder.

"Yes. I'm Bevin Weitekamp," he said. Smiling tentatively as if expecting a rebuff.

"Of course. Nice to meet you. Blair Titus." After a moment's hesitation, she extended a hand. "This is my assistant, Margaret Shingler-Gray."

Weitekamp introduced the younger man as his attorney, Gavin Logsdon. "Of Logsdon, Kaplan, Bohn." Logsdon bowed as many did now instead of shaking hands, since the Flower's arrival. Shingler-Gray nodded reluctantly, and Weitekamp gestured them to cordovan leather couches.

Blair declined a drink. She was trying to wrap her head around the invite. This jowly man pouring himself a tall scotch had been one of the most successful producers in series drama. *Warriors of Tyre. Food Wars. Dividing the Earth.* Until six rape accusations and dozens of sexual assault allegations had unspun his legal cocoon and sent him to prison, rocking the streaming industry. "I hadn't known you were . . . returning to public life, Mr. Weitekamp."

He gave a shrug. "You had a lot on your plate. What with the war. Running the Department of Defense."

"True." She hadn't exactly *run* it, but maybe from his perspective . . . anyway.

The younger man, Logsdon, cleared his throat. "Mr. Weitekamp has asked you here to see if there's some way our organization can support your candidate," the attorney said, crossing his legs. Away from the older man, Blair noted. "We want to make a difference."

Blair glanced at Shingler-Gray, who sat stone-faced, spine rigid. *Down, Margaret,* she ordered silently. To Logsdon, "I'm open to suggestions, but who would your organization be? You're not speaking of Mr. Weitekamp alone, I take it?"

"No, ma'am." The attorney shook his head, sat forward, spreading his hands, projecting a Lab puppy's earnestness. "This administration's attempts to influence production, exercise direct control over what's released, are concerning to many in the film and broadcast arts. A blow for liberty? Maybe that's putting it too strongly."

"We can't let the government tell us what to make," Weitekamp said. "We cooperated during the war. Signed the Code of Wartime Practices. It's peacetime now, but the 'advice' continues. And it's getting more detailed. Which writers and directors to employ. Which story lines to pursue. And which, not."

Blair nodded. "Like the blacklist of the 1950s."

Weitekamp shook his head. "Back then, they just told us who not to hire. Now they're suggesting projects. Which pictures to make."

"Projects the industry would prefer not to pursue," the attorney clarified. "For various reasons—creative, profitability, what have you."

Blair sat back, considering. On the surface, not unreasonable. "But if you, Mr. Weitekamp, are involved—please forgive this—"

"I've had to forgive a lot in the last five years." Weitekamp smiled, edging closer on the sofa. "Please, say exactly what you mean, Blair."

So now it was *Blair*. She couldn't help imagining herself in the position of a twenty-year-old woman, an aspiring actor, facing both a chance and a demand. She took her phone from inside her jacket and laid it on the glass table between them. A symbolic barrier. "What I mean is, your offer sounds interesting. And the admiral might view lifting wartime controls on the entertainment industry as a no-brainer. But forgive me, uh, Bevin. Why would *you* want to be involved?"

Weitekamp's smile grew broader. "I'm the sacrificial goat, Blair. Not a single project in development. So, there's no way the Office of Information can hurt me, if they decide to retaliate."

Logsdon fidgeted. "Though we wouldn't necessarily want to signboard Mr. Weitekamp's involvement. Or portray him as, in any way, the head of this effort."

"What effort?" Shingler-Gray broke in, looking suspicious.

Still smiling, but with an edge, Weitekamp turned his massive head to regard her. "Disestablishing the O of I. Return freedom to the directors and producers." He nodded to Blair's phone. "That sum I texted is a first installment. If your guy gets the nomination, there'll be more."

"In what name?" Margaret asked. Blair beamed her a frosty look: *Jeez, Margaret, I can speak for myself.*

Weitekamp scratched silver stubble. "All donations will be from a PAC out of Culver City. We have to cover our butts. So there'll be contributions to the PP too."

"And to other candidates," Blair said.

Both Weitekamp and his attorney shrugged. "Naturally. At this stage, we can't put all our bets on one horse," the older man said. "You can understand."

Blair surreptitiously eased off her shoes under the table. After a full day, most of it on her feet, they ached, and her hip kept jabbing her. She couldn't keep driving herself, the way she had in her thirties.

She couldn't bring this off without funding. Her candidate would fade in the polls. Tank in the first caucuses. Then she'd be out in the cold.

The entertainment industry wasn't the only one with a blacklist.

"You can slip those off if you like." Weitekamp glanced at her feet. "If they're giving you problems."

"Thanks, but I didn't plan to stay." She straightened, still unsure she fully understood his offer. Obviously any anti-Party candidate would lift the censorship, so why Yangerhans? And why present such a sullied name as the face of the PAC?

Unless Weitekamp *was* the major contributor.

But if he wanted to redeem himself, whitewash his image, wouldn't he contribute to Governor Holton's campaign? Or to any female candidate, instead of a white male?

Then again, maybe he was. Covering all the bases. Spreading his money, just as he'd once abused his power to spread his . . . Ugh. Now *that* was an unpleasant image.

She checked the text again. The fire shifted, crackled, logs collapsed and new flames leaped up. Eternal change. Nothing ever stayed the same. What was the old karate saying? Never change a bad position for a worse one.

At last she cleared her throat. "I'll need to . . . take this under advisement, Bevin. Discuss it with my team."

"Wouldn't have it any other way." The mogul rose, but when she extended a hand he pulled her into a hug. She found herself cuddled against his belly, enveloped in a miasma of cologne and sweat, looking up into gaping nostrils lined with gray hair.

Margaret stepped forward, but Blair elbowed herself free before the situation really degenerated. "I'll get back to you," she hissed.

"Really appreciate your meeting with us," the attorney said. His eyebrow-lifted smile offered a meek apology. "You can deal with our firm from now on."

She still felt dirty when they got back to the Roosevelt. Felt . . . shaken. Contaminated.

Yeah, she'd run into that kind of behavior in her career, from male pols and lobbyists. And seen some less-than-forthright deals when she'd worked for Talmadge. "Nobody ever gives you somethin' for nothin',

Missy," the old senator used to say when she'd expressed misgivings. "Ever'body knows that. Only thing wrong is tryin' to keep it under the counter."

The old test: Did you want it on the front page of the *Post*? By that test, the names Weitekamp and Yangerhans wouldn't look good together in a headline at all.

But they had to pay the staffers. Rent the venues. Reach out to delegates. No money, no campaign.

She undressed, showered, and wrapped the hotel-issue terry bathrobe around herself. Sat at the desk, but couldn't bear to boot her tablet or check her texts. She just didn't want to deal with any of it. Just found herself not caring.

It was how she'd felt a lot lately, actually. Not caring.

Like one of those cartoon devils on a character's shoulder. *Why are you still doing this, Blair? Is this really what you want?*

And the angel: *Maybe you can still make a difference.*

But was that really what she wanted? Or was it just to still have skin in the game?

She sat plucking nervously at her fingertips. Unable really to answer that. Sure, she wanted back in. Watching from the sidelines . . . it sucked, frankly.

But maybe she was being too eager.

Like, maybe, she'd been too willing to join an administration that had more and more shredded the norms and conventions she'd always thought made politics just barely civil.

Pride and ambition. Her mother had always warned about them. A Maryland lady could have such feelings. But she should never, *never* let them show.

Finally she reached for her phone. Not for reassurance. Dan would say no. *Just turn it down,* he'd say. But there were whole worlds of her universe he didn't understand. Not everything was either black or white, the way he seemed to see things. Also, she needed to ask if he'd thought about The Hague. She'd found him representation, a Swiss-Dutch attorney who specialized in defense before the ICC.

At last she tapped his contact. But . . . no answer. The call went to voice mail.

She pulled the phone away, frowning at it. What the hell? Okay, she had Chief Wenck in her contacts.

He answered. *"Ms. Titus? Have you heard from the admiral?"*

"Uh, no. I wondered if you had."

A hesitation. She closed her eyes and braced herself. *Not again*, she thought. *I can't take this again.* But the voice went on inexorably.

"He was last seen taking off in a small plane. Headed west, along the North Slope . . ."

8

Deadhorse, Alaska

The sky was pitch dark, of course, even at 0700. Overcast, the stars invisible, the predicted full moon nowhere to be seen. A chill, blustery wind punching-bagged the survey members as they trudged out to the plane. Bundled in the heavy oversuit, Dan felt like a child zippered into a snowsuit. He resisted the temptation to exaggerate a waddle. Sometimes he wished he'd stayed a captain. You got more respect as a flag officer, but with less freedom to joke around.

Everyone expected more when you wore stars. More smarts. More influence. But there was no room to be spontaneous or to speculate. When an admiral said something, people didn't hear an opinion. They didn't even hear an order. They heard it as policy. Whether you meant it that way, or not.

Which left him biting his tongue a lot these days . . .

Blanco and Quvianuk trailed him, toting satchels and briefcases. The Coast Guard commander was in the same exposure gear as she'd given Dan: padded oversuit, yellow and black, with overboots. The Canadian major was in a green fur-trimmed parka, thick gloves, padded pants, and black Mickey Mouse boots. She carried an ancient-looking bolt-action rifle slung over one shoulder, a pack over the other.

A light flickered near the ground. Mike Kirby, in coveralls and parka, a balaclava over his face, was inspecting the landing gear with a flashlight. Another figure, slimmer, shadowed, was coiling a cable that led to some kind of engine preheater. The engine was already rumbling, the prop ticking over at idle. Warming up.

Kirby hammered a boot down on one tire, then the other. Frozen to the tarmac, Dan figured. The pilot waved his passengers to a halt with a monitory glove.

Dan set down his gear bag. Tablet, phone, sweater, and the Coastie watch cap Blanco had issued him. They wouldn't be gone long.

Their ride was a single-engine, high-wing monoplane, canary yellow, with a red Kirby Air Services logo. The wide-stanced landing gear and oversize tires made it look sturdy, and it only shuddered a little even when the gusts punched hard. A sugar frosting of snow coated the upper surfaces. A teenager in coveralls was noisily clearing the windows with a plastic scraper.

Kirby waddled around the wing, cranked open a door, and yanked down boarding steps. But held up a hand when Dan stepped forward. "You'll be up front, with me," he said, voice muffled by the mask.

Quvianuk snicked open the bolt on her rifle and tilted it for Kirby's inspection. The pilot nodded. She slid it into the back, slung her pack behind the seats, and climbed aboard. Blanco followed, bracing both hands to haul herself awkwardly up into the fuselage, but not quite making it. Kirby gave her a boost. He nailed the door with a fist to make sure it was latched, then gestured Dan to follow. They walked around the plane, bent into the prop wash, which was blowing snow up from the ground into their faces. On the other side, Kirby showed him how to set a boot on the strut to vault up into the forward passenger seat.

Dan clicked the seat belt, yanking the end to snug himself in. Not much cubic in the cabin. Maybe it would have been more spacious if they weren't all bundled up. Kirby rolled the balaclava to perch atop his head like a beanie. "Everybody settled back there?" he yelled above the mutter of the engine.

The women gave him two thumbs up. He waved to the teen, who trotted back toward the yellow lights of the hangar. The plain low building suddenly looked homey. Dan yearned to be in there, drinking hot coffee, instead of facing hours belted into a seat so small he could barely wiggle his ass.

"Okay, we're off!" Kirby yelled. "Wainwright first, then overfly Peard Bay. No strip there. Hit Lonely Point if there's time and not too much scud. Then home. Still good?"

Dan nodded. They'd gone over the itinerary, flight times, refueling stops, in the hangar. "Sounds good. We just need to watch the weather."

"Deedy's keeping an eye on it. He'll radio us if anything looks threatening." Deedy—or maybe Kirby was saying *DiDi*—was the teen, a skinny, callow-looking kid who worked for Kirby Air.

The pilot had explained the situation that morning. A storm advisory was in effect across northern Alaska. Starting in two days, that meant wind chill values of up to fifty below zero. Sixty-knot winds would kick up snow, compromising visibility, in addition to the hazardous cold. The storm could last up to a week. "We won't be flying then," the pilot/surveyor had said, cupping a Seventy North mug with steam coming off it. "I know you wanna get your look-sees, but today'll probably be it for the next week. After that, we'll see if things clear up."

Now Kirby advanced the throttle and released the brakes. The plane lurched, rocking side to side as it rolled out onto the strip. Flashing beacons strobed the falling snow. "This is low precipitation! It'll be VFR above the clouds!" Kirby shouted.

Dan nodded, cinching his belt another inch. He swallowed, remembering being shot down. The helicopter spiraling into the Pacific. The wallop of the crash. Then trying to drag wounded, screaming men out as the aircraft capsized, filled with water, began to sink—

He bit his lip until it hurt, trying to think of something else. His sailboat. On the hard since the start of the war, but he needed to put it in the water pretty soon. Like, after he retired.

The blurred circle of the prop lined up on the twin rows of yellow beacons that flashed away into the pitch black. Kirby firewalled the throttle and they accelerated. Slowly at first, the fat tires plowing and jolting through the snow. Then faster. A vibration hummed through the struts, tingling Dan's toes through the heavy-soled boots. Kirby was humming too. No, the other man was singing. Though Dan couldn't make out the tune. The airspeed needle climbed. The snow rushed at them, past them, as if creating itself from a black and empty void thirty feet in front of the windshield. He gripped a handhold and concentrated on his breathing.

A heaviness, then a sudden lightness. The engine droned deeper. The jolting ceased. The lines of flashing strobes zipped past and vanished, and all the world was dark. He couldn't even see the snow coming at them anymore. The only illumination was pale orange, pale green, from the instrument panel. And the intermittent flare of their own running lights, red and green, out on the wingtips.

Kirby was singing away, head down, intent on two glowing displays. Dan leaned in, trying to envision what he'd have to do if the pilot had a heart attack. One screen showed a three-dimensional view of the oncoming land—mostly flat, though slight hills swelled to their right. Kirby was keeping them inside a green-outlined box on the display. The other instrument looked like a GPS, with a view from above of lakes and rivers. Numbers flickered: airspeed, altitude, ground speed, heading, lat/long coordinates.

Fuck, no. No way he'd be able to land this thing. Not in the dark. Even with the instruments. They'd all be doomed.

Kirby straightened in his seat. "Be clear in a minute!" he yelled over one shoulder to the passengers in back. Dan glanced back too. The two women sat stony-visaged, faces alternately sickly green, then flushed red, then green again.

Four minutes later they broke out of the cloud cover. To a starry, coruscating, inky-velvet night worthy of Van Gogh. Peering out, Dan picked out Ursa Major and traced a line to Polaris. The Pole Star stood higher than he'd ever seen it before. The full moon lit the clouds below, white frothy ranks that marched past as Kirby put the plane into a climbing turn. "Heading west," he barked. "We'll cruise at one-sixty. With this tailwind, be there in a little over an hour."

Dan nodded, feeling better now that he could see. The engine droned along in a pulsing roar that sent vibrations buzzing along the fuselage. In the back, Blanco and the Ranger were having a shouted conversation he couldn't make out. The low moon shone steadily down on the clouds, which looked furrowed, bumpy, like the bottom of a glowing silver sea. Isolated streamers reached up toward the plane. Far off behind them rose a chromium prickling that might be distant mountains. Or maybe just a higher cloud layer. Dan leaned again to check the altimeter. Three thousand feet, and still climbing.

He sat back, telling himself how strong the engine sounded. Kirby was still humming, or singing, so everything must be fine. Maybe think about something else. Not about being here. Or, God knows, about being subject to an international indictment. No. How about what he was *supposed* to be doing here.

Though after going through the contents of the package last night, he was even less sure what that was. His original orders, out of the CNO's office, had tasked him to research possible locations for a port of refuge or forward operating base. A harbor that could service small- to medium-draft ships, to provide at least a foothold on the Arctic Sea, or to deploy and service a sensor network.

He suspected this mission might be intended as much for political purposes, to serve as a sort of FONOPS, Freedom of Operations claim, as much as for actual capability. Any actual naval operations would be constrained by weather and ice much of the year anywhere north of seventy degrees.

Though, it seemed, for shorter periods, as the Arctic warmed and the ice retreated farther each decade.

The 1947 study seemed, spookily, to be a first iteration of this very mission. The Iron Curtain had come down over Eastern Europe. A small team of officers and surveyors had been dispatched to scout the North Coast, evaluating bay and river entrances to see if any offered promise as a naval base.

That team had visited some of the sites he'd already planned to check out, based on his research at the Pentagon. Of course, information had been a lot harder to dig out back then. Paper maps, sketchy soundings, vague locations, often based on hearsay. The five men—all male explorers in those days, of course—had traveled in the summer, when conditions were just as grim, but in different ways. Dan could imagine it: endless clouds of biting flies, mosquitoes. The tundra soggy and treacherous underfoot. Those predecessors had reached the North Slope by minesweeper, and explored ashore via rubber rafts, during the short July-to-September season, when the fast ice along the coast melted.

Their report was dated, sure, but despite the challenges they'd done a thorough job. Tested soils. Conducted offshore soundings. Estimated land elevations. Tabulated vegetation and local fauna. Even noted local inhabitants, and rated them by their ability to serve as guides or willingness to work on construction crews, given Seabee leadership. Included was a long discussion of sea level and tides. The mean lunar range was only about a foot, but non-lunar tides, barometric pressure, and seasonal changes in saltwater density could vary the sea level along the coast by as much as eight feet.

In the end, the report concluded that Prudhoe Bay was the most likely area for a base, although thin water all along the Slope meant access for deep-draft ships, such as carriers and battleships, would be impossible without major and very expensive dredging.

Which, he guessed, had led to the project outlined in the second document he'd been sent.

He sighed, looking out and down on the moonlit clouds below. The engine droned reassuringly. Kirby, headphones on, was bopping to some inaudible beat. Probably tuned to some backwoods station far below . . . warm air was blasting out of a vent . . . Dan checked his phone. Google

Maps located them above the Colville River. They were headed west by southwest, making 180 miles an hour.

Project Chariot had been part of Project Plowshares, the 1950s program that had proposed to put thermonuclear "devices"—no longer called *weapons*—to peaceful uses. The "friendly atom" could blast a sea level canal through Nicaragua, cut passes through mountains, frack gas fields, unearth mineral resources. A huge test in Nevada, "Sedan," had left a crater 350 feet deep and over a thousand feet across, shifting eleven million tons of soil. A lot of which, apparently, had drifted east in the form of fallout.

That second document had been the project manager's summary report for the planned Chariot shots. A chained series of five thermonuclear explosions near Point Thompson would blast out an artificial harbor basin and a hundred-foot-deep access channel, facing Siberia across the Bering Strait.

Now he cocked his head, kneading his lip and peering out and down into the darkness as he contemplated the project.

Granted, the late 1950s had been more optimistic about technology, the military, and the atom than humanity was in the twenty-first century. The question before the court was, who had sent him these studies? Was there actually renewed interest in blasting millions of tons of Alaskan tundra and bog into the sky, to carve out a new base in the far north? According to Wikipedia, Chariot had never been officially closed down. Only set aside amid doubts about its effects: fallout covering the tundra, contaminating the native wildlife, and the hunters who depended on them. Then the nuclear test ban had put it on the shelf.

Was someone trying to pry that Pandora's box open again?

He slacked his belt and unzipped the oversuit a bit, since the cabin seemed to be growing warmer.

It might be possible. The project manager's report had argued workers could start cleanup and construction two weeks after a blast. Granted, acceptable contamination standards were a lot tighter now. But, still . . . maybe, given the way the war had smeared fallout across the Lower 48, releasing radioactivity into the far north looked less unacceptable. Or maybe there was some looming threat up here, that made the risk unavoidable.

He shook his head, realizing he might never know the answers to any of his questions.

As with so many other issues across his career, this one, too, was probably above his pay grade.

"Okay, we're gonna start letting down! It'll be scuddy, but I think we're fine!" Kirby yelled a while later. The engine dropped an octave.

The stars began to wink out one by one, plunging them into blackness again. Kirby mused into a throat mic, apparently getting clearance to land. Dan cinched his belt again and gripped the handhold.

Blasting strobes pulsed dimly ahead out of the ice fog, beneath the low cover. Kirby lined up on them as they lost altitude. The women were silent in back. Kirby chanted softly. Some upbeat show tune, Dan guessed, but he couldn't tell which. "New York, New York"? The lights brightened, sharpened. The pilot lifted the nose as they snowflaked the last few feet.

The wheels thumped and deceleration thrust them against their belts. Dan suppressed a sigh of relief as they slowed, plowing through fallen snow, and Kirby blipped the prop to turn in toward a waiting truck. Its welcoming headlights glowed golden white through the blowing drift.

"You sure this is safe flying weather?" he asked the pilot. "It seems to be getting worse."

Kirby steered them in and braked. "Eh . . . it's marginal. But a pilot who won't fly in this, you'd be grounded most of the winter. Okay, there's our ride. Uh, Major, if you want to leave your rifle, that'd be okay. I'll lock the compartment."

The four-wheel-drive diesel pickup ground them through town, a gaggle of small houses huddled as if for warmth under the pitch-black overcast. The road, gravel crunching beneath the snow, descended an eroded bluff to dead-end at the shore.

Silent men bundled in parkas, scarves masking their faces, swung off idling snowmobiles. Dan smelled exhaust, gasoline, and the honeyish decay-stink of long-rotted meat. Headlights gleamed across a field, outlining a frost-rimed beach. The icy sea, broken and rafted up in great slanted chunks along the shore, stretched out and away under the black and starless sky.

Kirby climbed onto one of the machines. After a moment, Dan slung a leg over the second. Blanco and Quvianuk followed suit on others.

Dan frowned down at the handlebars. Throttle. Brakes. No shift, so probably a centrifugal clutch. After riding a motorcycle across the country, this didn't look beyond his capabilities, as long as they didn't get too off-road adventurous. He checked the gas: a full tank. Good.

"We'll head down toward the cape," Kirby yelled, and gave a hi-yo-Silver wave. His engine roared, his tracks dug in, and he lurched off along the shore. Dan twisted his own machine's throttle, and the clutch caught hard, nearly throwing him off. He roared after Kirby, tracks crunching over snow and the shingle beneath it. *Easy on the fucking gas, Lenson,* he told himself. *Fall off and Dessa'll run over you.*

They motored north a few hundred feet inland, over what must be frozen tundra. Here and there a withered bush poked through the snow, but otherwise everything was flat, blanched white in the headlights; no trees, no power poles, no sign of human occupation ever. The wind bit through the insulated gloves, nuzzled down the neckline of the heavy suit. For now it pushed them along, but he dreaded coming back into its teeth.

A couple of miles down the shore they hit an inlet. The river here was frozen solid, but not jammed up and broken the way the sea ice was. Like a smooth, snow-covered road. Kirby pointed across it, miming a question. *Across?*

Dan pointed left. The satellite photos showed a lagoon. Not nearly deep enough for anything with significant draft, but it offered shelter.

The trouble was, everything along the Slope was so fucking shallow. Unlike Siberia's sizable bays, with deep channels and easy access to the open sea.

Kirby shrugged and waved him ahead. Dan squinted at the sea ice, wishing he'd brought a compass. There was an app on his phone, but he didn't feel like digging it out. If he even had bars out here . . . He gunned the snowmobile and steered onto the frozen river.

Half a mile up the shores widened away. The lagoon spread seemingly endlessly under their headlights. Dan powered on, front skis peeling up a spray of fine crystalline snow. He hoped the ice held. The wind howled and blustered, shouldering him bodily to the right, so he had to correct to stay near the low bench of the coast. Something four-legged froze in their headlights, then dashed away, back into the night. Too rapidly to even see what sort of animal it had been—a fox, or some smaller creature.

Okay, he was on-site . . . but what precisely he was learning that the overhead imagery wouldn't reveal, he wasn't sure. Just that this was as remote and savage a place as he'd ever seen. And *cold.* The wind sucked heat off him, reducing him to a fading ember in this trackless night.

Was there any sense in going farther? He couldn't think of any reason to.

But kept on for another half mile, before he turned back at last.

They ate at a small restaurant in Wainwright. Patriot News blared on the screen. Oil company workers and locals rubbed elbows at a lunch counter. Dan got a mug of hot venison stew and a BLT. He unzipped the suit to his waist and luxuriated in the hot air blasting out of a gas-fired register. No one looked at them twice.

Quvianuk was trying to chat with one of the servers in a language he didn't recognize. Finally she turned away and shrugged.

"Can't communicate?" Dan asked.

"These people are Inupiat. I know southerners think we all look alike. But we are from different tribes. So are our languages. Our dialects."

"You're a reservist, right? Aren't the Rangers sort of a national guard?"

"You could call me that. But I am full active duty right now." She hesitated. "Can I ask a question too?"

He nodded, and she went on, "You are looking for a place to put naval base. But there is a fine bay to the east. Mackenzie Bay. Tuktoyaktuk town. You have considered those?"

"I researched them, yeah. But they're in Canada."

"You have had bases in Canada. Shared them with us. We are both NATO."

"True, but . . ." He trailed off, since he didn't really have an answer. Finished, lamely, "That's just not in my orders. Probably, handled head-of-state level. Prime minister to president."

She studied him for a moment, then set to work on her burger and fries.

Back in the plane. The takeoff was hairy. The wind seemed to have increased, and now, flying back, they were aimed into it. The engine droned more loudly than before, but the displays gave them only 140 over the ground. "Headwinds!" the pilot shouted back to the women, who nodded.

Kirby let down through the overcast half an hour later. "Peard Bay!" he shouted to Dan. "No airfield. Not even a gravel strip. But if you wanted to be able to say you had a look, there it is."

He peered down into complete darkness. Not even a gleam. No towns here. No oil developments. The big fields lay to the east.

Still, what had he expected? All these remote places, mostly old Air Force early-warning sites, were going to have the same downsides. No road access, no harbor, and little geographic relief to provide shelter from storms and ice. In fact, very little solid ground at all, being mostly bog and tundra. Maybe he should kick this whole thing upstairs. Tell the new CNO it just wasn't realistic. They should think about some kind of joint base with the Canadians, farther east.

Well, he still had possibilities. Peard lacked facilities, but it was a harbor, with a chain of barrier islands to the north that might provide shelter. There was still Lonely Point, which they'd hit next before calling it a day. Okiktok had road access, an airstrip, and sort-of deepish water. Point McIntyre had a small pier and mooring setup ConocoPhillips was using to ship oil out of the Alpine field. And Barter Island, with no road access, but a decent airstrip and deeper water.

Finally, there was Prudhoe Bay itself. Its channel was dredged for medium-draft ships. The oil majors had built piers and causeways, and it had cargo-handling capability. An airfield. Road access. Even repair infrastructure, welders, and so on. The problem there would be working around the already heavy commercial traffic of barges, tankers, and offshore oil rig service vessels. The Navy might have been able to muscle in during wartime, citing national security, but it might not be possible now.

"Seen enough?" Kirby yelled. Dan nodded. "We'll head upstairs, then."

Blanco leaned forward from the rear seats. "Are we okay for Lonely Point?"

Kirby took a while, studying his instruments and doing a calculation on his phone before answering. "Uh, we're usin' a lot of fuel. This fucking headwind. And the forecast isn't looking too good."

Dan said, "Can we refuel at Lonely?"

"Reporting ice fog, heavy gusts. Expect zero vis down to the ground level, real shortly. I'd rather not land in that."

"All right," Dan said, but all at once the stars seemed farther away. The dime-size moon, less reassuring. The clouds below, less lovely, even though they shone like spun chromium. "Uh, so what's the plan? Prudhoe?"

"That's farther east, and Deedy says it's going to be worse."

"You said we'd be back before the bad weather hit."

"That's what was predicted. Darn storm's moving faster than they thought."

One of the women, he didn't see whom, tapped Dan's shoulder. He twisted in his seat to look back.

"What's going on?" Blanco shouted through cupped hands.

"Weather over our next stop. Storm's moving faster than they thought."

"We shouldn't have flown if it was going to be bad," she observed.

No shit, Dan thought, but didn't say it. "Okay, what's the plan?" he asked Kirby again. "We want to be prudent fliers, right?"

The pilot waggled those snarly eyebrows. "Well, Lonely's gonna be socked in by the time we get there. Whited out. We could fight our way through to Prudhoe, but we'd land with less than ten percent fuel and maybe in crosswise gusts with a lot of fresh snow on the runway . . . just not a good idea. And the longer we wait, probably, the worse conditions'll get."

Kirby bobbled his head. "So I'm going to divert. No sweat. We'll set down at Atquasuk. Or, maybe at Barrow—I mean, Utqiaġvik. They have lights and a hard-surfaced runway. I'll check conditions on the ground, then decide. We've got plenty of fuel for either one." The pilot didn't sound rattled. As if this happened all the time. He settled the headphones over his ears, punched numbers into the radio, and murmured into a throat mic.

Dan forced himself to settle back into his seat. Kirby's tone was soothing. A kind of Captain Sully–esque calm. They'd divert. Hunker down for a night, or two nights, until the storm blew over. Then get back to work.

He was craning around to reassure Blanco when the engine missed a beat. Then, a few seconds later, missed again.

And then cut out entirely, leaving an eerie whistle all around them as the plane inclined gently downward.

Kirby fiddled with knobs, apparently trying to restart, but without result. The eerie whistle continued.

"Are we . . . okay?" Dan muttered, fingers digging into the handgrip.

"Not to worry," the pilot said. "We can do a dead-stick, easy-peasy. Setting airspeed, best glide—seventy miles an hour. Fuel selector is Both. Primer, in and locked. Fuel pump, on. Carb heat, on." He flicked switches. "Magnetos: Left, no start. Right, no start. Both on, no start."

Dan saw that Kirby wasn't talking to anyone in the cabin now; he was on the radio. "This is N326AK. Descending at six hundred feet a minute. Mayday. Mayday."

A faint voice answered, calm, rational, reassuring. *"Copy your mayday, N326AK. Hold you on radar. Keep us advised."*

Dan had a moment of pure terror. *We're in range of traffic control,* he reassured himself. *Kirby's talking to them. He got a response. They know where we are.*

But none of that seemed to help much.

The stars snuffed out again as they sank into the cloud cover. Dan blinked out at the utter black canvas of Arctic night. Kirby was still talking, still flicking switches on and off. But the roar of the engine didn't resume. The wind whistled past even louder.

The pilot said, "Landing lights on. Everybody, unlock your doors. *Now.*"

Dan nodded, fumbling with the flimsy plastic handle. It was pretty much what he'd expected this whole flight, after all.

The landing lights surrounded them, a moving sphere of brilliant white, like flying in the middle of a lightbulb. But aside from the swirling fog nothing else was visible. They floated in the center of that incandescent ball. The wind rose to an ear-piercing shriek. Kirby pulled the yoke back slightly, frowning down at his instruments. Then, a little more.

At last he announced, tone still casual, matter-of-fact, almost offhand, "Well, *ikinguts*, I guess we're going down. The good news: no terrain down there. Flat as a cookie pan. But you might wanna make sure those belts are just as snug as you can get 'em."

III

DARKNESS
AT NOON

9

The Republic of the Covenant

Nan straightened from the patient, dragging a wrist across her forehead, careful to keep the glove clear of her face. The woman on the cot was moaning, tossing her head from side to side. Her bared chest and neck were dotted with flat scarlet patches. Sweat, saliva, and bloody stool stained the plastic sheet under her and dripped into a noisome puddle.

Man's oldest and most lethal plagues were roaring back.

The CDC/NIH team had arrived prepared for the Flower virus, radiation sickness, wounds, and common illnesses. But the reality on the ground had proven different. Olduc had pulled together statistics to show their real threats were much older maladies, exacerbated by malnourishment and stress. The "diarrhea" Rayfield had casually mentioned presented more like acute endemic dysentery.

But the pale, agitated woman on the cot was dying from something far worse.

Nan stroked the stringy gray hair. It was soaked with sweat. She turned the patient's arm outward, snapped rubber tubing around it, and swabbed the clammy skin with alcohol.

Typhoid had stalked mankind since before recorded history. Marked initially by fever, stomach pain, and constipation, it progressed to massive bloody diarrhea, delirium, dehydration, stupor, perforated bowels, and finally death. *Salmonella typhi* was related to its food-poisoning cousin but was far more lethal. Flourishing in dirty conditions, and usually contracted orally—from bad food, unwashed hands, unclean water—it bound to the intestinal mucosa and unleashed a fiercely destructive toxin. The body responded with a gigantic inflammatory reaction that ravaged lungs, kidneys, liver, pancreas, and bone marrow.

Not only did typhoid kill one in five of those it infected, many who did

recover and seemed healthy remained silent carriers—"Typhoid Marys."
Whatever and whoever they touched could spread the infection to a fresh
wave of victims.

There were preventatives, yes. But hardly anyone in the Midwest had
been vaccinated for this disease. Typhoid just hadn't been a threat before.

The war had changed that. As it had a lot of things.

"Excuse me," said Wilcox, the head RN. The woman on the cot shuddered, eyes squeezed shut. The nurse flicked the barrel of a disposable
syringe, then injected her. The patient opened her eyes for a moment, but
seemed to be looking past her ministrants to some far horizon. When the
needle withdrew her lids sank closed again. The delirious mumbling resumed.

Nan raised her head to look along the rows of cots that filled the high
school gymnasium. Mingled groans and screams rose toward the colorful
championship banners from years past far above. The classrooms were
clinics now, filled with the sick. The art and music studios were break
rooms, where nurses, doctors, and techs could sprawl exhausted between eighteen-hour shifts. There was no power, no heat, though winter
was here and the nights were growing colder. Worse: no running water.
Fortunately they had plastic sheeting to cover the cots; thousands of feet
of it, "requisitioned" from the Amazon fulfillment center in Kansas City.

"What are we giving them?" Nan asked Wilcox.

The stocky lead nurse was showing the strain too. Dark circles under
her eyes. A dirty smock. Snarled, unkempt hair. "Ceftriaxone. It should
work, but I'm afraid this may be a resistant strain. We're still trying to
match it. Maybe, from Southeast Asia."

The techs had set up a field epidemiological lab in the girls' locker room.
"How would that get here? All the way to Missouri?"

The nurse shrugged. "POW camp? Returning troops? We'll never know.
But I'll tell you one thing. No one's gonna get a handle on this bad boy until we get some significant vaccination coverage. Some herd immunity
going."

Nan rubbed her itching nose carefully, using the back of her wrist
again. "I've asked for the oral vaccine in the next shipment."

Wilcox nodded grimly. Nan could read her mind: obtaining the vaccine,
making it available . . . that wouldn't be the main problem.

If too few accepted it, the disease wouldn't just spread, it would ex-
plode. Contaminate all the water supplies. Really start killing, not just

hundreds but thousands. And dig in, become endemic, impossible to ever completely eradicate, the way it clung on in parts of Africa and Asia.

They moved from cot to cot, then turned to the even more numerous patients who sprawled on blankets on the glossy-polyurethaned floors of the basketball court. Their individual features blurred as she sponged sweating faces, helped weak fingers hold cups of diluted juice and electro-lyte solution. Changed the filthy sheets, averting her eyes. Hung IVs.

And sometimes, eased staring eyes closed, unrolled the sticky plastic of the black body bags, and helped the others roll flaccid corpses into them. To be zipped up, carried outside, and tossed up onto trucks in growing heaps.

She was the leader, sure. She could have stuck to planning and coordi-nating. But with this much suffering, she feared that if she didn't lend a hand, it could crush her. Unfortunately, she was also trying to run a pub-lic health investigation of at least four separate diseases, all at once. With only a minimal staff.

The usual investigation proceeded by discrete steps. One: define the problem. Two: define a way to monitor progress. Three: characterize the problem. Four: identify its source. Then implement control, monitor progress, and persist until the case numbers dropped.

The Republic of the Covenant had zeroed out public health and was paying the price. She'd tried to contact the old state public health author-ities, but they'd either fled ROC-controlled territory, pursued by vilifica-tion and death threats, or retired from public view. She and Mabalot had coaxed a dedicated few back with promises of food supplies and protec-tion. Retired nurses and EMTs, older doctors, veteran medics and corps-men. But not nearly enough, considering the impending disaster.

The curves were rising more steeply by the day. Better reporting could explain some of that, of course, but she couldn't shake the conclusion they were losing this war. On every front: drug-resistant tuberculosis, dysen-tery, Flower influenza, and now typhoid.

"Fuck," she muttered, staring down at the abstract pattern of bodily flu-ids coating her blue latex gloves. "Fuck, damn it, fuck."

At last she straightened, stripped them off, and dropped them into a drum of bleach-based disinfectant. Gloves and needles were too precious to throw away. She dug fists into an aching spine. Pulled a bottle of boiled water from an ice chest, went outside, and gulped it, staring across the empty football field into the woods, where flashes of yellow betrayed the

lumbering of bulldozers behind the trees. Scooping out trenches for the remains.

On the far side of those woods, at the hospital, Dr. Glazer would be
operating on patients with bowel perforations, as well as the wounded
from a skirmish with a Homeland Security scouting party the day before.
A short, violent firefight that had ended with the rebels reeling back once
more. Fighting stubbornly, but unable to hold their own against the government's weapons and technology. Microwave projectors, robot soldiers, tanks, drones, night vision . . . as far as she could tell, nothing
prevented the battalions from routing what remained of the insurgents.

Forcing down the rest of the flat-tasting fluid, she strolled around to the
front of the makeshift clinic. Out here, in visitor parking, tents and mobile homes housed the vaccination section. Rayfield had called the roving
teams back in, citing too much risk to the personnel. Here, masked and
gloved, they attended to the pitifully few adults and children who stood pa-
tiently in line.

Tracy rushed out of the lobby, nursing a hand-rolled cigarette, looking
left and right. When she spotted Nan she scowled. "Hey, where'd you get
to? You're supposed to stay with me, Doc."

"Not exactly. You're with me, remember? I was taking care of patients.
Like I'm supposed to. You could help too, you know."

"Somebody's got to pick up rations. Here's yours." She handed over a
discouragingly small paper-wrapped bundle. Inside was the same strong-
smelling cheese and stale bread they'd been issued for the last six days.
Nan sighed and nibbled at the slapdash sandwich joylessly.

Serene Olduc coasted in on a bicycle, a clipboard under one arm. Clipboards and paper, Nan thought. When what they needed was real-time
monitoring, databases, fast testing, tailored antibiotics. The statistician
said, "You guys ready? I saw Kurt already headed over there."

Nan nodded. "Yeah. It's time."

Time to talk to Rayfield again.

His guard said the provisional president was in, but the team members—
Olduc, Dr. Mabalot, and Nan, plus their minder—had to hold in a musty
lounge area for an hour before they were ushered in.

Rayfield hunched over a beat-up metal desk, head in his hands, staring
down at a pile of folders. The lights were off; only a few narrow slices of
illumination bled through the drawn shades. The habitual half smile was

nowhere in evidence. A somber, gray-ponytailed man everyone simply called "the General" stood behind him, arms folded. A large map of Missouri was duct-taped to the wall. Colored pushpins spearing handwritten callouts were scattered across it. She noted a cluster up to the north, near the Iowa border.

Rayfield barely glanced up as they filed in. "Make it quick," he snapped.

Nan laid it out as succinctly as possible. They were facing a major epidemic of waterborne diseases. Cryptosporidiosis, salmonella, now typhoid. They needed to intervene now, or face enormous fatality rates.

At the mention of typhoid the former sheriff's lips compressed to a scrimshaw scratch. A hand crept to a crumpled pack of cigarettes. He lit one with trembling, nicotine-stained fingers. "We put out the boil-water advisory," he muttered. " Isn't that helping? Don't you have drugs for this?"

"Sir, we won't have enough drugs, or even beds, if this thing goes wildfire. We have to get the public water treatment back online."

Rayfield's lips twisted. "Unfortunately, that requires power."

The ponytailed man behind him said, "And every time we bring up a generator, your people destroy it with a drone strike."

They're not my people, Nan started to say, but instead only nodded. "I understand, it's difficult. But I have to lay this out. You've got at least two major epidemic threats. Both spread by the fecal-oral route. That means—"

Rayfield said angrily, "I get it. Asses to mouths."

"Okay. So it can be waterborne, or transmitted via food, or even person to person. From handshakes and so on. But the point is, it's spreading. Fast."

The sheriff nodded at Olduc. "What've you got to say?"

The epidemiologist cleared her throat. "Um, the same thing. Basically. Sir. Our statistics show gastrointestinal cases doubling every fourteen days, and the slope's getting steeper. Dysentery weakens, but typhoid's the real killer. The same routes of infection apply for both. And, again, there are treatments, but with that steep a ramp-up, it's outrunning our means of caring for people."

"And you?" Rayfield nodded to Mabalot. "Doctor?"

"Those aren't the only diseases making a comeback, Mr. President," the Army physician said. "There's giardiasis. Respiratory illnesses. Skin infections. Amebic meningoencephalitis. All waterborne." Nan started to interrupt, but Mabalot waved her to silence. "We can't rule out cholera either. That killed thousands here in the Midwest, back in the 1800s.

Malnutrition, resulting in achlorhydria and hypochlorhydria, exacerbated by radiation, stress, and niacin deficiency—pretending it isn't
there won't make it go away."

"I don't even know what most of those words mean," the General grumbled, but his shoulders slumped. "You're vaccinating. Aren't you? Won't
that protect us?"

Mabalot shrugged, glancing at Nan. "We've tried to spread the word. But
too many refuse to come in. As long as they're asymptomatic, they think
we're promoting some kind of hoax. Or worse, that we're actively trying
to *make* them sick. Others say their faith will keep them healthy."

"Maybe it will," said Rayfield.

"No, it won't!" Mabalot snapped. "That's a goddamned delusion."

Nan glanced warningly at the MD, startled; usually he was more cir-
cumspect, even timid. "Sorry, but that's how I feel," he went on. " I was
in the Congo during the Ebola outbreak five years ago. It's starting to feel
like that . . . The terrorists were shooting the doctors there, while we were
fighting to save people."

Rayfield gestured impatiently as if to shush him, but the doctor plowed
on. "Boiling the water won't be enough. You need to get those treatment
systems back online. Fix the water supply. Fix sewage disposal. Enforce
vaccination. *Then* we just might be able to get ahead of the R zero—
the average number of people one sick person will infect in their turn.
Otherwise, you're going to see thousands, maybe hundreds of thousands,
of deaths."

"Like the Civil War," the General said somberly. "Like the Union and
Confederate armies then. More lost to disease than to battle."

Nan nodded. "Now you're getting the picture."

"But they kept fighting. Regardless of how many sick they had, or how
weak they were." The General glanced at the wall map. "Like we're weak
right now, Mr. President. Especially down in the southeast. And having to
contain these splinter groups, these Provisionals—"

Nan glanced at the map too, remembering Puxico despite herself. The
tanks. The screaming. The rebels' helplessness. How could these people
keep fighting? It was hopeless. The sooner they saw that, the better.

"Which must make you all feel pretty good," the General said, interrupt-
ing her thoughts.

"Me? Us?" She shook her head. "We don't take sides, uh, we really can't.
We're medical only."

"Nobody's really neutral," the provisional president said. "Not in this fight. You're either for freedom, or you're on the side of tyranny." Rayfield squinted at her as if waiting for an answer, but she had none, not to that.

So they stood waiting as he searched amid his papers. The General bent and whispered into his ear. The president nodded, looking waspish. Mumbled, reluctantly, "Okay, thanks for your report."

"Sir, I want to really emphasize how serious—"

"We'll deal with it from here," the General snapped. Then, to Tracy, "Take them back to work."

Outside Mabalot leaned against the wall, shaking his head. Out here in the sunlight, the dark circles that cupped his bloodshot eyes were more visible. Nan hugged herself, hoping she didn't look as tired. Though no doubt she did. "Well . . . that went well," she muttered.

"No, I think not. Um . . . a word?"

"Trace?" She glanced at her escort. "Okay?"

"I guess so. See ya back at the clinic." Tracy flicked the butt of the hand-rolled into a bush and strolled away.

Nan turned back to him. "What's up?"

"Just the usual. A short message."

She nodded, handing over her phone. The Army doctor had asked her for favors before. Now and then. Short texts back to his sister to reassure her. Sent via the single phone the Covenanters had allowed them. She read the words when he handed it back. *Make sure the handbrake is off on my bike. The red one. Especially in case it rains.*

She nodded and pressed Send. "Sure. No problem."

"Can you send that soon? Like tonight?"

"I just did. What, you're afraid it's going to rust?"

He frowned. "Rust? Oh. Right. Yeah, it's one of those cheap ones. But you can't get them anymore; they were all made in China." He forced a smile. "Have to take care of things. These days. No way to get them replaced."

She nodded, agreeing, and was about to walk off when he put his arm out, blocking her way. "You look like shit hell, Doctor."

She snorted. "Thanks. So do you, Doctor."

"But I like the way you care for people. That's something I wish I . . . wish I had more of. That . . . compassion."

"I've seen you treat patients, Kurt. I don't think you lack compassion." She bent to duck under his arm, but he dropped it and stepped back. When she glanced back as she walked away, he was staring morosely down at the grass.

The mention of Mabalot's sister made her think of her own family. She tried to reassure her mom every couple of days, usually just by sending a photo (once she'd cleaned herself up a little). Her dad, though, she hadn't been able to reach for a while. Apparently he was up north on some Navy business. She checked in with Tracy again, got her permission, and squatted on the curb a few yards from the tents in the front lot to call him.

The tone, but no answer. She ended the call, and tried again. Same result.

Frowning, she lowered the cell and stared across the road. Two battered pickups were slowing, turning into the lot. More patients to be vaccinated. She should check on her practitioners. See how their stocks were holding up.

Her request for a VMI, a resupply tailored to cryptosporidiosis and typhoid, had gone out, but she hadn't heard back. No surprise there. Why should Washington help a part of the country that was in revolt? And to be fair, the loyal states needed help too. Maybe if Blair's candidate won that could change . . . maybe a lot could . . . She should call Blair too, just to say hi. . . .

The pair of trucks, one blue, one green, slowed as they came abreast of the admissions tent. They weren't steering for the parking area, which was set off with fluttering orange plastic tape. Probably just going to drop someone off, then scoot. She tapped the back of her phone, thinking, *Yeah, Blair.* Surely she wasn't out of line making a quick call to her sort-of stepmother.

Four men with bandannas over their lower faces rose from the bed of the lead truck. For a moment she could make no sense of what they were throwing. Or of the blue smoke trailing the bottles tumbling end over end through the air.

The projectiles fell and shattered, smearing sudden bright orange flame across the admissions area. Screams rose as a tent caught fire. As the waiting patients scrambled away in all directions, the second pickup slowed. Other masked figures rose from their hiding places in the bed, firing rifles into the air and heaving more bottles of flaming gasoline at the queue, the waiting area, the treatment tables.

She stared for what felt like an endless instant as the flames whooshed outward, climbing the canvas walls of the tents, igniting them into tapestries of fire. They consumed the carefully laid-out rows of medications, needles, bandages, alcohol, prepackaged inoculations. A blue ball of fire *whoomphed* upward as the conflagration reached a plastic container of antiseptic. Screams and shouts keened. A woman staggered out of the nearest tent, waving her arms, clothed in a bright tabard of seething flame.

Then Nan was on her feet, running. She pelted first for the pickups, then changed her mind and angled away as they pulled off, motors howling, tires screeching, leaving a smoke of gray exhaust and the stink of burned rubber. She screamed a curse after them, then doubled back toward the nearest tent.

Which by now was a towering pyre of roaring flame. From deep within it came shrill cries. The woman who'd emerged staggered back and forth, clothing smoking, dotted with patches of flame. She stumbled back toward the tent, then away again. Her eyes, white beacons in a charred face, stared at nothing. She patted ineffectually at the fires on her chest, her pants, her hair.

Nan grabbed an arm and pushed her to the grass. "Roll, can you hear me? Roll!" As the woman dropped, or maybe fell, Nan glanced into the tent. The cries from inside were growing shriller. Louder. She eyed the archway of roaring flame, an orange gateway framing an ominous darkness.

She sucked down a deep breath and dashed in, shielding her face with an arm. It felt as if it had suddenly been thrust into a broiler. Remembering in a flash Puxico, when the Black Battalions' microwave weapons had scorched and roasted the defenders as they crouched around her in hastily scooped foxholes.

The fabric roof was a bowl of flame, billowing and thundering as superheated air ripped through. A torrent of gaily colored sparks rippled down, cherry-red, lemon-orange, crackling and popping like the fulminant sprays of pinwheels in a Fourth of July firework show.

At the far end, where the flames had not yet reached, huddled a small form, knees drawn up, eyes staring. The child's clothes were smoldering. Sidestepping a stack of burning boxes, Nan was there in five strides. She sucked burning air past burning lips into lungs that felt as if they were crisping like the skin on a rotisserie chicken. She ducked her head and gathered the child up, shielding it with her arms.

Then turned, head tucked, crouching, searching for some escape.

But the walls were solid yellow flame. The entrance collapsed as she started toward it. Sheets of burning canvas accordioned down in fresh gusts of scorching heat. Her arms, her face, were blistering. She wheeled in place, clutching the child, who whimpered against her breast, squirming as if to escape. She clutched it tighter, then glanced upward.

At a sky orange as flamingos, blue at the root, surging waves of color pulsating across the blackening fabric. It was beginning to sag. In seconds it, too, would drop, a blazing net, shrouding them both in its burning folds.

Ducking to the singeing grass to gasp in one more searing breath, she set the child down. Crept beneath the table and pulled him in after her. Noticing for the first time it was a little towheaded boy. "Hold on to me!" she screamed over the freight-train roar of the flames. "Tight as you can!" Small fists knotted themselves frantically in her smock.

Thrusting upward with her back and quads, gripping the steel legs with scorching palms, she shoved the table upward. Burning objects rolled and scattered off it as it tilted. Gathering all her strength, Nan ran it full tilt at the single spot in the flaming walls that showed patches of daylight, where the canvas, still on fire, was burning through to black skeins of knitted ash.

A ripping noise, a whirl of flame and sparks, and she crashed through and collapsed on the smoking grass outside, the table still atop them both. Other hands pulled it off them and tore away the child, who clung, still shrieking, to her scrubs.

Nan glimpsed a blackness ahead, an everlasting whirling dark. She could not, no matter how hard she fought, avoid the remorseless and hungering force that sucked her down into it at last.

10

On the Tundra

Dan came to with a sense both of cold on one side and of searing heat on the other. For a moment, lying prone, he couldn't recall where he was. Or who. He blinked through falling snow at what looked like a raging furnace a few yards distant. But a silent one. Noiseless. As quiet as the flakes that drove down out of the black, stinging his cheeks.

He started to roll over, but discovered he couldn't move his legs. Nor his arms, not all that well, either.

Shuddering, he inhaled icy, fuel-smelling air through numb lips. It burned his throat, and with that shock, comprehension returned. "I'm Dan Lenson," he whispered. "Alaska. We crashed."

The flames, and the raw stink of gas, made sense now. A flash of memory: the landing lights suddenly illuminating the onrushing corrugated surface not of the wind-smoothed ice of a frozen lake but of rough undulating tundra.

Kirby . . . Where was the pilot? Dan tried to lift his head, though his neck telegraphed a jolt of pain. Pieces of the plane lay scattered across the snow. Cloth-covered bundles, a few yards away, must be the other passengers. But only one was stirring.

A moan reached him through the bluster of the wind.

With a grunt and a shudder, he hauled himself to a sitting position. Blinked away the flakes that clogged his eyelashes. There, thank God, he could feel his legs again. Even the pain was welcome.

They'd hit hard. After one bounce the wheels had dug in, flipping the plane over on its nose. The impact had torn off the prop, and, with a heavy crunch, the fuselage had pitchpoled over onto its back. Then kept tumbling, shedding parts and velocity as it cartwheeled across the frozen tundra. Upside down. Right side up. He'd been thrown sideways into the door.

Then . . . he must have blacked out.

Crash number two, he thought bitterly, shivering. First the fucking helicopter, shot down in the Pacific. Days in a raft. Unimaginable thirst. Incredible hunger. Fighting ashore through the surf. Then cast away for weeks on an uninhabited island, while the rest of the world fought a major war.

And now this. Again? He must be cursed. Some kind of Jonah.

He forced himself to his feet on legs that wobbled and barely held. Just enough for him to stagger toward the nearest bundle.

Kirby lay facedown, motionless. Blood spattered in a corona across the snow surrounding his head. Dan touched the back of the big man's neck and felt the jaggedness of protruding bone. Patted his shoulder, sighed, and lurched on.

The fire crackled and banged, spitting shards of aluminum and gouts of flame. He gave the hulk a wide berth. A torn-off wing stuck up like a dolmen. The rest of the wreck was pretty much just crumpled metal. The flames hissed irritably as the snow drove into them. Was anyone still buckled in, unable to get out? Counting, slowly, with a still-turgid brain, he matched the number of bodies around the pyre with the count of souls aboard. Kept coming up with a mismatch. Kept coming up with somebody missing.

Then he shook his head at his own stupidity. *You forgot to count* yourself, *Lenson. Four. That makes four.*

One of the other splayed bodies stirred, tried to sit up, but fell back, writhing.

He knelt awkwardly, feeling a jolt of what promised to be real agony in his back. Blanco blinked up at him. "How we doing, Commander?" Dan said through a mouth that felt like it was filled with cold grits.

"Uh," she gasped. Her eyes moved separately, seemingly unable to lock on his face.

"Rest here a minute. I'll check out the Ranger." He kneaded her shoulder, as much to reassure himself as her. Then got up and staggered on, coughing in the smoke.

Quvianuk lay a few yards back in a shallow valley in the snow plowed down to withered brown grass. As if she'd bailed sooner than the others. She peered up groggily when Dan shook her. Blinked, then looked around. Tried to push herself up with her arms, but obviously couldn't.

"Rifle," she muttered. "Get . . . the rifle. And my pack."

Dan lurched toward the fuselage, which was crumpled like a stomped beer can. The snow was up to his knees, making his progress more like wading than walking. The plane lay upside down, one wing still attached, the other torn off. Flames roared around what had been the engine compartment, though the engine itself smoked and sizzled several yards away. Smoking parts lay scattered, though they were swiftly being covered by the falling snow. A frigid wind was driving steadily from the east. It whipped the fresh flakes up from the ground to stream along like icy smoke.

He reeled to the upside-down cabin and crammed head and shoulders through the jagged absence where the door had been. Their gear lay jumbled on what had been the ceiling, soaked with something wet and smoldering. Either on fire or about to catch. He grabbed the nearest pack in the flickering yellow flame light, dragged it out, and threw it behind him. The petrochemical stink finally registered. The wetness was aviation gas.

"Fuck," he muttered. He reached in again and got another pack, at the cost of a burned hand. "Shit," he grunted, gripping the floor-turned-ceiling of the cabin. Heat scorched his face as the flames grew fiercer. He clenched his eyelids to duck in once more and blindly grab something else.

"The rifle?" Quvianuk called. So weakly he could barely hear her over the shriek of the wind.

"I don't see your fucking rifle."

"It was under everything else. So it ought to be on top now."

"Still don't see it," he yelled, trying to reach in one last time. When he jerked his throbbing hand back it was on fire, the flame ghosting up and down his gloved fingers. He plunged it into the snow to put it out.

"It's got to be there. Maybe it got thrown out—"

Why was she so fucking *wound up* about it? A dogged, petulant anger flared through what had up to now been numb shock. "It *isn't fucking here*," he snapped, and shook his burning hands like a monkey flinging off water. Forced himself back to searching through the roaring flames as the instrument console, screen, radio melted and collapsed and caught fire. The heat on his face suddenly redoubled, and he reeled back.

Then everything seemed to go white hot. He couldn't help screaming as the whole cabin, soaked with aviation fuel, exploded, knocking him back onto his ass in the snow. And the blackness crashed into his mind again. . . .

* * *

Dan gasped and flailed his arms, fighting off some kind of attack. No . . . someone was rubbing snow on his face.

"I don't fucking *need* that," he grunted, sitting up and spitting out a mouthful. He was so very *cold*. A penetrating, anesthetizing iciness, all along his back and legs.

Blanco squatted back on her heels, looking worried. "I thought you were dead too. Kirby—he's gone."

"I figured that. When I felt his spine sticking out of his neck." Dan grimaced, regretting that choice of words. "Sorry . . . didn't mean how that sounded. I mean, I figured he was past help." He twisted to peer around. "Where's Dessa?"

"Over near the fuselage. I dragged her there, closer to the fire, where it's warm. She can't walk. Keeps asking for her rifle."

Not good news, that she couldn't walk. But they shouldn't have to do any hiking. He hoisted himself, joints grating like a sack of rusted iron parts that ground against one another. "There's blood on your face."

"Scalp wound. It'll stop. I clot pretty fast."

"Kirby got the mayday out. They know where we went down. They'll send help."

Blanco shook her head, and a fresh rivulet trickled down her cheek. "In weather like this? But I agree, we should stay here. Where they know to look." The Coast Guard officer leaned in. She fumbled at Dan's exposure suit and snugged up his zipper. "Damn, good thing I brought these."

Dan put an arm around her. Together, leaning on each other, they circled the wreck. It was still smoking, still steaming, but the conflagration seemed to be dying. The snow was still driving down hard. It had already covered a lot of the wreckage. Which meant the radiant heat it was providing would soon be gone.

He squatted by the Inuit, who sat with her back propped against the plane's tail section. "Dessa, how you doing?"

Quvianuk stared straight ahead, lips compressed to white lines. "Can't feel my legs. Can't move them."

"Don't, then. We'll just wait here until rescue arrives."

"There isn't going to be any rescue." She scrubbed her face with a mitten. "Not for couple of days, at least. Until this lets up." She looked around, blinking off the snowflakes that kept accumulating on her lashes. "Where is my Enfield?"

That again? "We haven't been able to find it," he told her.

"Did you look? We need it."

He patted her shoulder. She was in shock, that was obvious. And there was probably some kind of penalty in her unit for losing your weapon, even in a crash. "It's okay."

"It is not okay. Look where we hit the ground. I remember now. I threw it out first, then I bailed, just before we flipped." She gripped his arm, harder than he would have thought possible. "Please. Sir. It's important."

"Important," he repeated, not understanding. "Why? Why do we need it?"

"I just . . . want it, that's why," she said. Scowling.

Dan stood. "All right. All right! I'll go look, if it means that much to you. But if it's lost, I really don't think they're going to blame you."

She flashed a pained smile and waved him on his way.

He trudged back along the grooves the plane had scooped before its final snagging, somersaulting, and explosive disassembly. The falling flakes were covering the grasses and brush its passage had uncovered. He waded along through the drifts until his boot hit something hard. He bent and pulled up one of the doors. He dropped it and started an expanding-square search, kicking his boots through the snow. And at last contacted something else, hard and long. He dug in and fished it up. Yep.

"Found it," he announced, laying the rifle down beside her. A real museum piece, with a brass disc set into an oil-soaked black wooden stock and quaint-looking iron sights.

"Good. *Good.* Thank you, sir." She laid her glove on the stock as if to reassure herself it was really there. "Thank you, Admiral. Now, we must get moving."

Blanco trudged around the fuselage, tugging a charred olive-drab bag. With difficulty, Dan recognized his own luggage. "Explosion must've thrown it clear," she said, dropping it beside him. "Dessa, how d'you feel?"

"Okay. You have blood on your face."

"Just a scrape. Look, we were just discussing how we're going to stick here and try to build a fire. They know where we are. Soon as this clears, they'll send a helicopter."

The Ranger tried to struggle up, but sank back. Her lower body hadn't moved. "No," she said urgently. "We can't stay here. There is no cover. We'll freeze."

Blanco touched her own head through the hood and winced. She was already shivering, and her face looked paler than before. "We can't leave, Dessa," she murmured. "Otherwise, when help comes, how will they find us? And you can't walk. We can't leave you here. No. We stay put."

The Ranger reached for her hand. "Commander . . . Sarabeth . . . If we stay out much longer in this wind, we will freeze to death. Believe me. I have seen it happen."

The Coast Guard officer took her hand, but shook her head again. "Leaving the site would be suicide, Dessa. No matter what kind of shelter we find, if they can't locate us, we'll starve. Or freeze, like you say."

Quvianuk huffed. Snow clung to her eyebrows. "That is exactly wrong. *Staying here* will be suicide."

They glowered at each other, gazes locked. Each woman obviously totally convinced she was right. Then, simultaneously, both glares shifted to him.

Dan rubbed his mouth with the back of a scorched glove, staring at the wreckage. He couldn't stop shivering. The cold was filtering through even the heavy oversuit. The down and the base layer of fine wool slowed it, but he could feel the chill advancing. The immense cold around them seeping in.

Could they huddle in the cabin? He inspected it again. The windows were smashed out, the doors gone. A scorched skeleton of aluminum extrusions. The wind whistled through it. And that wind seemed to be rising, driving the heavy white flakes before it.

Could they build a fire? Stay alive that way? He'd done that himself, in Canada. The only time he'd confronted an emergency like this before.

Exercise Primal Thunder had flight-tested the ground-launched prototype of the new Tomahawk near Cold Lake, in Alberta. Minus thirty degrees, fifty-knot-plus winds, and a blizzard then too. But their orders had been clear: wring the transporter-erector-launcher and the missile out in North European–type winter weather.

Which they'd done, only to have test T207 plunge from the sky halfway to its intended impact point. He'd located the fallen vehicle just as the storm had closed down. Alone with the crashed missile, dug in beneath it into a makeshift cave in the snow, he'd realized he was going to freeze to death. Until he'd noticed gluey, viscid ropes drooping from the airframe.

The jelly had been RJ-4. Enough fuel to power the little Williams F107 turbofan over a thousand miles. Gallons of it, leaking out of cracks, cold-thickened to the sticky consistency of napalm.

He'd nursed the flame all night, and it had pulled him through.

Only now there was no RJ-4, and the last of the avgas in the plane's tanks was flickering out in the snow. He couldn't think of anything else to burn, other than their clothing. And unlike Alberta, out here there were no pines, no trees, nothing to offer shelter. When the last flames died it would be utter dark. There was no dawn to look forward to. Only the endless night. He fingered his phone in an inner pocket. It still had a charge, but the flashlight wouldn't last long.

He looked at Dessa Quvianuk again. The heavy-lashed eyes. The high cheekbones, neither Native American, nor quite Asian, but not that different either. He hated to stereotype. Assume things. But she'd grown up here. Her ancestors had survived in this wasteland for thousands of years. She was a trained Ranger too. Maybe—actually, undoubtedly—she knew far better than he and Blanco did how to stay alive.

He cleared his throat at last. They were both still looking at him. So, time to cast the deciding vote. "Dessa may have a point," he muttered. "This wind . . . the chill. We've got to find shelter."

He turned from Blanco's accusing glare and took an awkward knee in the snow beside the recumbent Ranger.

"You're the boss now, Dessa," he muttered. "What exactly do you think we should do?"

Half an hour later they were on their way. Blanco led, breaking trail through the knee-deep snow with sweeps of her insulated boots. Dan came next. He was hitched to one of the aircraft's doors, bridled with braided wire from inside the tail boom.

On it lay the Ranger, upper body on the slick aluminum, legs dragging in the snow. Still cradling her rifle.

Quvianuk had explained. Out in the open, they'd freeze in short order. They *had* to find shelter. With no woods, and no way to dig in the solidly frozen ground, that left the coast and its canted-up blocks of sea ice.

Fortunately it wasn't that far. At least, Dan thought not. His last glance at the display as they went down had shown it fairly close, to the northwest.

Which meant that if they kept the wind behind them, and bore to the right, sooner or later they'd come out at the shore.

But it was also true they might freeze first. The unbroken wind was unutterably cruel. The snow, cruelly deep. His feet and legs were already wooden. All three trekkers were shuddering, despite the oversuits and parkas. It would be a race against time, an exhausting, punishing forced march. And they'd still have to find or build a refuge when they reached their goal.

"Any kind of windbreak will work," the Ranger had said. "Best would be where the snow's shoaled up. Then, dig a hole. Snow makes good insulation. If we can get to coast, we might be able to stay alive."

But they still had to leave a clue to where they'd gone, when the weather improved and their rescuers arrived. Dan had puzzled over that. Then, finally, dragged Kirby's body—already stiffening, though it had been less than an hour—to the far side of the wreck. Bent his arm out, fighting the rigidity, cold or postmortem or maybe both, and uncrimped his lifeless fingers.

Pointed his outthrust arm out to the northwest.

They couldn't bury him. The frozen tundra prevented that, even if they'd had the time and the tools to dig.

But the dead pilot could still serve as a fingerpost.

Dan trudged on, head lowered against the wind, placing each boot carefully in the broken snow. Blanco had smashed through into the powder beneath. The frozen crust resisted, then gave way, making her stagger and lurch. The ground under that, bog turned to ice, was hard as long-set concrete, but unevenly dotted with tussocks of dead grass. He'd clamped one of Kirby's mittens over his mouth to keep the frigid wind from his scarred airway—the pilot wouldn't be needing it—but his upper face was already a frozen, numbed mask.

For some time now he'd contemplated the fact that they might not make it. He coughed, nearly retched, trying to breathe through a frozen nose. The braided metal cut into his shoulder through the down and nylon and wool, dragging like a sea anchor with each step. His neck and back didn't hurt now, anyway. Either the injury wasn't that serious, or it was all too serious. He must have wrenched something when he was hurled out of the cabin, as the plane took that first flip and fired Kirby through the windshield into the still-spinning prop.

Just dumb luck he'd survived at all. Even more, that three out of four of them were still breathing.

For a while, at least.

The wind howled like a chorus of wolves. Was that why Quvianuk clung so tightly to her rifle? When he raised his eyes, blinking against the stinging drift, the universe was darker than space. No stars. No moon. No glint of light at all. Even craning back over his shoulder he couldn't see the flames anymore. Either they'd gone out, or the snow and drift were too thick.

He flashed back to Alberta again. It had blizzarded so hard then he hadn't been able to see his flashlight at arm's length. This was even darker. Even colder, with no trees to break the wind.

The snow squealed each time he plunged a boot into it. The makeshift sled was punishingly heavy. When he looked back Quvianuk was gripping the side of the door with both hands, but her lower body was sliding off. The rifle lay on her chest, slung around her neck. He yelled, "Stop!" to Blanco, turned, and bent to grab the Ranger under her arms, hoisting her back up onto the aluminum panel.

When he faced front again he searched the dark. "Sarabeth?" he yelled into the storm, into the howling gusts.

But got no answer.

He cocked his head left, then right, sniffing for the wind, and set his course by it. When his boots hit hard crust to the left he deviated right. When he sensed crust there he headed left.

Wandering left and right in Blanco's wake, he trudged onward for an interminable time, puffing into the mitten over his mouth until it froze and blocked his breathing. He stopped, adjusted it, trudged back to the Ranger, and hauled her up onto the sled again.

And went on. In the darkness. Bowed into the howling gale.

Wondering, now and then, how it had come to this. From the CNO's office to a blasted place no human had a hope of surviving. From leading an invasion of China to a challenge of survival out of a Jack London story.

He'd faced death before. As had just about anyone who'd served. You could only dodge so many bullets. Sooner or later, one had to take you down.

Maybe this was his time. He'd just gradually space out, stagger, and topple at last. They'd find his body in the spring, when they could follow the circling birds.

It didn't sound that bad. There'd been other things he'd wanted to do. Retire. Do some sailing. Buy that house on the Chesapeake he and Blair had talked about, on and off, before the war.

But if that wasn't going to happen, still, he'd had a good life. Seen the world. And he was pretty sure he hadn't punched anyone's ticket who hadn't richly deserved it.

And if the Ranger was wrong and the coast wasn't the key to survival, or if they couldn't reach it and they all died out here . . . his family would be fine. They'd mourn, but both women were strong. Independent. They loved him, but didn't really *need* him.

A sudden memory surfaced of reading to his daughter when she was small. Telling her stories, curled up in bed beside her, luminescent plastic stars glimmering above them, glued to the ceiling. That had been the best time. The best time of his life . . .

The wind howled ever more fiercely. It was difficult to stand upright now, much less bull forward against it.

His boots slipped, and he collapsed. He grunted on impact, the wind knocked out of him. Involuntarily, he strained his gaze upward, blinking into the stinging drift as he struggled up, and as the wind tried to bowl him down again.

No stars glimmered here. Just black. All black.

He forced down a burning breath and struggled to his feet once more. Groped for the bridle, leaned into it, and staggered clumsily forward once again.

Some interminable time later he sensed a change. He halted, puzzling sluggish wits to figure out what. At last he realized: the wind. It was coming from behind him now. Not freezing his right cheek as it had been for hours.

Either it was veering, which was unlikely, or Blanco was off course. Headed too far west. They'd be paralleling the coast, not approaching it. What the fuck, over . . . "Blanco! Hey!" he yelled until his throat stripped raw, but the gale was so much louder he knew even as he screamed that it was futile. The storm had clamped down in earnest. Now it was march or die.

But should he follow where she led? Or break his own trail?

At last he hunkered to put the question to the woman he hauled. To . . . His numbed brain couldn't come up with her name. Started with a D? Couldn't remember her last name either. Fuck, he was going dark. Shutting down bank by bank like the computer in *2001*. *"Dave . . . I'm losing my mind."*

Dan coughed and ground out, "Hey. Any idea where the coast is?"

She lay so motionless that for a moment he wondered if she was unconscious. Or dead . . . then she groped out, feeling for his arm. Muttered, mouth close to his ear, "Compass."

"Don't have one."

"Yes, you do. On your phone."

Shit yeah . . . He just couldn't think . . . crouched there he fumbled the icy rectangle out and thumbed it on. The little screen dazzled his vision. Brighter than an exploding galaxy. For a second he wondered if he should try to call someone. But of course he couldn't. No bars. No cell towers out here in the frozen wastes of this icy hell.

But the compass app still worked. Internal to the phone. He oriented and checked the wind. Maybe it *had* veered. Blanco could still be on the right track.

"Should I follow her? Or head off to the right?"

"Follow your instincts, Admiral."

In that case . . . he was a sailor . . . and he really didn't think a wind like this, this strong, was going to change much. Not in the length of time they'd been on the trail. He pondered the best course of action. He could leave his burden here. Run, or at least stagger, after Blanco. Find her and bring her back.

But what if he couldn't find the injured Ranger again, in this darkness, this roaring inferno of driven snow? She'd freeze. Unable even to crawl. Helpless. She'd die alone.

But if he set off on his own, they'd lose *Blanco*.

He was brooding this dilemma, thoughts oozing through his brain like lazy cold earthworms, when someone blundered into him out of the yowling dark. They grabbed his coat and shouted into his face, "Why the hell'd you stop? I looked back and you weren't there. I only . . . found you . . .'cause I saw your light."

"I think you're off course, Commander." Dan called up the compass again. Pointed to the right. "Coast's over there."

She felt down his shoulder to the wire braid. "Up to you. Sir. I'll pull her now. But I think we should tie ourselves together somehow."

That was a good idea. They should have done it from the start. "I kept some of the wire." Dan yelled into the rushing darkness, where he figured her ear might be.

"What?"

"Wire! *Wire!*" he yelled, and jerked it out of his pocket. Forcing numbed, stiff fingers to move, he fashioned two bowlines. Put one over his own shoulder and handed the other end to Blanco. The Coastie yelled something back he couldn't make out.

He turned his phone on again. A warning: *Low battery. Shift to conservation mode?*

He did. The screen was still the brightest thing in the universe. But it would fade all too soon as the cold invaded it. Sucked the life from it . . . He was surprised it still worked at all. Probably because he'd kept it tucked next to the warmth of his body.

He shuffled forward, following its fading pointer, until his boots encountered unbroken crust. Then stamped down, ankled it aside, until the softness beneath offered less resistance to those who followed.

Step by step, wheezing, reeling, he pressed on.

His phone went dead an hour later. He'd studied the wind all that time, so that when the screen went dark he simply stumbled on, keeping it at a constant angle. He could no longer feel his face, so he navigated by the pressure of the storm. Each time it pushed him left, he angled back. Lift a boot, stomp, trample, take a step forward. Lift the other boot, crack through the crust, take a step. Feeling back for the wire from time to time to make sure they were still laced together, three beads on a string.

Finally he sensed a rise. A hillock. Leaned into it, forcing dead legs and thighs to respond, though they felt like lifeless stilts. The cold was creeping upward. When it reached his heart, he'd topple, dead.

Some endless period later, the declivity lessened. The next few paces were on a level. Then came a slope down.

Something crunched under his boots. For a moment he halted, afraid he'd made some misstep. Then understood, or at least, hoped. His sluggish heart lurched.

A hundred steps later he staggered out onto small stones grating under his feet. A shingle beach, blown largely free of snow. The night was still black dark, though. They trudged down toward the shoreline.

Until he tripped and fell over a rough outcrop of what his patting gloves said was solid ice.

"I still have a little charge left," Blanco said, coming up beside him. "Here."

Dan accepted her phone. Was the wind a bit less blustery here? He felt his way down the braided wire to where he figured Quvianuk lay. When his gloves encountered her, he bent to yell, "We're at the coast."

"Good." Her voice was fading. He hoped she didn't have internal injuries, was bleeding out even as they dragged her so laboriously across this waste. Nothing they could do if she was.

"We're here," he yelled. "What're we looking for?"

"The highest slab you can find."

"Okay."

"Look behind it, where the snow builds up. That is where you must dig. If the . . . if the snow is hard, cut blocks. Build a shelter. The entrance . . . it must face away from the wind." A pause, then, "I will lie by the entrance."

He nodded in the dark. "Got it. You and Sarabeth rest here. I'll walk a little way in that direction, then back."

He told Blanco, then staggered up the shoreline. To windward first. After ten steps he flashed her phone's light to seaward. Jagged, tumbled plates, huge raw blocks leaned out of the dark. Pushed up, jumbled, chaotic as a quartz crystal. But nothing stood out as what Quvianuk wanted.

He turned the light off, slogged another twenty paces, and triggered it to peer out again. And again.

At last, some yards out, at the very limit of illumination, something white reared to the dark sky. Maybe ten feet above the surrounding jumble. Skeins of blown snow ghosted around it, shredded and driven by the wind like fine webs. He clambered out toward it, wary at first of trusting his weight to the ice, but it was solid. Probably frozen all the way to the bottom. The pack would melt in the summer, but right now it was like walking on uneven granite riprap. He had to drop to hands and knees when the gusts blasted him, but he pressed on.

It was a slanted plate maybe four feet thick, jammed in against the rest of the pack by some imaginable force until it lifted and pointed upward at a thirty-degree angle. He clambered ponderously atop it, and shone the light around. His beam wavered as it traced the contours of the ice. For as far as he could see, this was the highest point out here. With a deep drift of blown snow in its lee, while the windward side was bare.

It would be a gamble. And probably the odds were against them.

But he couldn't see any other way they might survive.

It took them agonizing hours to carve out a shelter. The drifted snow was crusted outside, powdery-light within. The work warmed them a little, at first. But no matter how hard he shuddered, how furiously he beat his arms against his chest, his body heat was bleeding away, stripped off by the frigid gusts.

But gradually, as they burrowed beneath the canted plate, that deadly current lessened, until it was just a sigh past their heads. Still freezing, but he could feel the difference.

Quvianuk was right. Out of the wind, their bodies could retain what heat they generated. Shelter was life.

On the negative side of the ledger, unfortunately, now no one knew where they were. Even if a rescue party followed Kirby's pointing finger, the survivors could be anywhere along miles of-this ice-desert coast.

Dan kicked at chunks of compacted snow. Whenever he could dislodge one he carried it back and added it to a makeshift wall. Blanco circled off and brought others, working on the far side.

They both moved slowly, staggering, cursing through stiffening lips. Still, in not too long they had something resembling a lean-to, roofed with ice, walled with blocks of snow, and lined with the loose powder Quvianuk assured them was a great insulator. Dan kicked smaller pieces over the outside, covering the jagged wall. Then crawled in.

He inspected the interior with the final photons from Blanco's rapidly expiring phone. Tight, no more than four feet by five. Not quite high enough to kneel in, except at the very entrance, and the overhead slanted down toward the back. Still, though the wind sighed and raged outside, it didn't penetrate here. Actually, it felt almost snug.

He crawled back out again and started to push Quvianuk in. But she fended him off. "Commander first. Then you. I will seal the hole with the door of the plane."

"What? No. I'd rather have you all the way inside, with us."

He made as if to push her in again, but to his astonishment she struck him with both fists, fighting him off. Weakly, but it was clear she didn't want to be in with the two of them. Claustrophobic? It seemed a weak objection when the alternative was freezing to death. Blanco remonstrated with her too, but the Ranger told them off in no uncertain terms. If she couldn't be right by the entrance, they could leave her out in the open. Given that choice, Dan had to go along.

Blanco bent and crawled in. Feeling his way in the darkness, he followed, fitting himself alongside her, body to body, legs to legs. "We're gonna have to huddle," he told her.

"No objection here, Admiral."

"It's not harassment?"

"That's not even funny." But she gave a reluctant chuckle, ending with a coughing fit. "Have you got the bridle?"

"Yeah. Yeah." He wriggled around and pulled the plane's door, the aluminum sled, with the Ranger still lying on it, as far in as he could, until they were all crammed together.

Now there was only enough room to take shallow breaths. Quvianuk fumbled around, and a hollow clunk and scrape of metal against ice grated. She was sealing the entrance with the metal hatch. He could sense the cold radiating down from the ice ceiling inches above his face.

"Everybody okay?" he called.

"You'd be warmer if you took off your suits. You lose body heat where you're in contact with the ice. Lay them on the floor, then lie on them," Quvianuk said from the dark.

Dan frowned. "What about you?"

"I'm all right. Don't worry about me."

"What do you think?" he asked Blanco.

"Might be better. Worth a try?"

He rolled over, unzipped, and with some struggle, got the upper two-thirds of his body out of the oversuit, though his boots were still on. Beside him Blanco was going through the same contortions. They faced each other in the dark. "That's actually better, with the suit under me," she muttered. "You?"

"Uh, yeah."

She shifted closer, and after a moment so did he.

There wasn't anything sexual about it when they put their arms around each other. His fingers tingled, then he winced. "What?" she whispered. Her cheek next to his. He could sense her breath. Smell it.

"Feels like someone's sticking needles into my fingers."

"Same here, but that's good, right? The feeling coming back."

He rubbed his face. The skin felt so dry his cheeks might crack. It *was* cracking, around his lips. A trace of moisture there. Sticky. Blood?

She whispered into his ear, "I'm worried about Dessa."

"She seems to know what she's doing. She's an Arctic Ranger, after all."

"Right . . . I guess."

He shifted around a bit more. It was getting almost toasty. A sort of under-the-blankets feeling in the dark, like when you were a kid. His legs were prickling, coming alive again. Maybe he wouldn't lose his toes like the Arctic explorers had.

"Keep it clean back there," Quvianuk called.

"Yeah. We are," Blanco told her. "Sure you don't want to crawl up here with us? I'm actually warming up. You were right about not lying on the ice."

"I'm okay. You two get some sleep."

For the first time in hours, Dan wondered if they might just make it out alive. If, that is, a rescue party found them. But buried in the snow as they were, in the dark, any searcher could walk past ten yards away and never know they were here. Nor would they hear anyone calling, buried as they were. He should have marked the top of the ice with something. Though he couldn't think of what.

Vague shapes crept through his mind. Images, vivid as a film. They gradually sharpened. Toasted cheese. Bean soup, the way Blair made it. He could smell it. Even taste it . . .

He snorted, coming back to consciousness. Shit. Just a dream . . . Blanco was breathing softly, inches from his face. Snuffling, asleep. He was warm now. Even comfortable. Though hungry. But a person could go without food for quite a while. Maybe they would actually survive this. . . .

He came awake to a shift against his legs and a strange noise outside. Not the wind. It seemed to have died down. At least, he couldn't hear it screaming and moaning out there. Someone was snoring. Quvianuk, probably. Damn. She must have some bad sinuses.

A strange smell too. A heavy animal stench. He blinked, puzzled, as the Ranger shifted against his legs. "Dessa. You awake?" he whispered.

"Yeah."

"Are you . . . okay?"

"Shut up. And give me some light."

He half sat up. Pulled out his phone and aimed the LED. After warming up, the battery had recovered some. Still, it only registered 5 percent charge. He blinked, peering toward the entrance.

Where Quvianuk, propped up just inside the aluminum door, was fitting a clip into her rifle. She set her thumb and, with a faint rattle, stripped fat brass cartridges tipped with silvery metal down into the ancient weapon.

The snorting again, louder. But it didn't sound like snoring now. "What is it?" he whispered.

"Maybe . . . bear," she muttered.

He sat up again and banged his head into the ice. Shook Blanco. "Sarabeth. Wake up. Sarabeth!" he hissed, at the same time covering her mouth. "Shh," he whispered as she struggled against the smothering hand. "There's something outside."

"More light," the Ranger whispered. Blanco pulled her phone out too. They aimed both flashes as Quvianuk eased the rifle bolt forward to engage with a faint click. She propped the weapon on her dead legs, muzzle aimed at the doorway.

Fuck, Dan thought. *That* was why she'd kept asking about the rifle. Not because she was afraid of getting dinged by the Rangers.

The huge white bears were vicious hunters. Powerful as grizzlies. And at this point in the winter, no doubt hungry as hell.

"Polar bear?" Blanco whispered, eyes widening.

Quvianuk put a finger to her lips, keeping the rifle aimed.

A snuffle outside. A scraping.

A heavy, somehow muffled pad of feet. The ice creaked and popped, shifting under some massive weight. A snuffle, deep, hoarse.

Suddenly a claw burst through the wall, knocking the blocks of snow down over them. Dan scooted back, driving himself under the ice shelf with his boots. Blanco gave a short scream and scrambled after him. Metal banged, the gong-like echo muffled.

"More light!" Quvianuk yelled, her voice muffled too, as if with a mouthful of snow.

Doubling his legs, Dan kicked through the far wall with a violent thrust of both boots. He scrambled out and crouched on shaky legs. Triggered the phone and swept the dying beam around.

In the blowing snow, on the far side of the wrecked shelter, a yellow-white beast much larger than a man rose on its hind legs. In the dim illumination its eyes gave back a reddish glow. Its mouth hung open, as if astonished to see him. The bear exhaled a hoarse, guttural hiss. Could they see in the dark? He lifted the phone higher, aiming the waning beam into its face. The bear dashed a paw across its muzzle, as if dazzled. Its ears flattened back like an angry cat's.

Something thrashed in the collapsed welter of ice and snow blocks at the animal's feet. Quvianuk's dark-haired head emerged. It was followed by the rifle's muzzle, rising like the periscope of a submarine.

Pointing it directly up, she fired. A flash, a muffled bang. The bear roared, craning around, blinking. Apparently uninjured, though startled. It shook its head, growling, as if unsure how to respond. Then it snarled and took a step forward.

The Ranger worked the bolt, aimed, and fired again.

Another flash and crack. The second bullet opened a furrow in the beast's chest, then slammed up into its jaw. The bear staggered back. A welter of dark blood surged out of its throat, which it slapped at with huge, clawed paws that quickly turned red. It dropped heavily to all fours, whirled, and loped off into the dark with a lurching, loose-looking sway, grunting loudly.

Dan dropped to his knees and dug frantically at the snow with his gloves. After some minutes Blanco emerged, spitting and coughing. She stared around. "Where is it? I heard shots. Did she get it?"

"She hit it," Dan said. "Dessa, will it come back?"

"I don't know." The Ranger was clawing up out of the hole with both arms, the rifle set to one side but within reach. "Prop me up. I need to get up where I can see."

"Is it dead? Are there others?" Blanco sputtered.

Neither of them answered her. Dan checked his Seiko, then turned his phone off. Near midnight, but really, it didn't matter what time it was. There would only be darkness around the clock. And if more bears came, or if the wounded one returned, they could only defend themselves as long as they could see. He looked up yearningly. If not for the overcast, they'd have a bright moon. But it was sealed off, like the stars, by the blanket of cloud.

In other words . . . once their phones died, so would they.

He hauled the Ranger to the top of the canted floe beneath which they'd sheltered. But now their refuge was wrecked, torn apart. Her lifeless legs dangled. Blanco crouched beside them, staring out, shining her light around. "Better conserve that," Dan advised. "If Dessa can't see, she can't shoot. Ranger, how much ammunition do we have?"

"Just the clip," Quvianuk said. "They only issue us one."

"You fired two rounds. Remaining?"

"Three," she muttered. Holding the rifle across her lap, shivering, blinking out into the chill wind.

Dan shuddered too. He groped in the tumbled snow for his oversuit, stepped back into it, and zipped it up. Since they'd been able to warm up a little, the chill in the open cut twice as deeply. They were exposed again. Twisting in the wind . . .

A snuffle, a grunt. An angry growl from out in the dark.

All three heads swiveled as one. Dan sent a beam probing toward it, but it revealed only jumbled ice, sucked into nothingness by the swirling, driving drift.

He hesitated, finger on the button. Torn between wanting to see and unwillingness to lose the last seconds of light.

A second growl, from another direction, seemed to answer the first, and the same animal-stink he'd snuffed earlier hit them from upwind.

"Two," Quvianuk observed. "At least."

"A mating pair?" Blanco, voice high.

"It's not breeding season. Probably two young males. This time of year, they den up, sleep a lot of the time. That they're out, means they're just plain hungry."

"Isn't there anything else we can do?" Blanco's voice quivered.

Dan gripped her shoulder. "I'm scared too, Commander," he told her. "Let's just try to hold it together."

She was sputtering, no doubt mustering a flareback, when the Ranger said, "I didn't want to shoot it. And I hope Pihoqahiak will not die. We believe its spirit could take revenge. And if we truly cannot survive, at least they will have food."

Under other circumstances, Dan might have relished a discussion of Inuit belief systems. But right now his right hand, stripped of its heavy glove to activate the light, was going lifeless. It was nice that their corpses could serve as food. But he wasn't eager, at the moment, to feed the fucking bears. "But you'll shoot them if they attack again," he said.

"I will do what I can, Admiral." But she sounded resigned.

Flicking the light on again, he swept it around, lingered for a second on the Canadian. She'd drawn a knife from somewhere and laid it beside the rifle. God, he wished he had a knife. Or even a stone. He felt absolutely helpless with his only weapon a cell phone.

The snuffling snort came from the dark again, closer. Another answered from upwind. The stink grew stronger, carried with the blowing snow. He stood waiting, ready to go down fighting. With bare hands, if nothing else. But he was no match for a wounded, enraged bear. Or two.

A light gleamed, far off. A faint shout came, carried on the wind.

Words? A human voice? But he couldn't make it out. Probably he was imagining it, fabricating it, from the insane howling of the wind and his own desperate fear.

But Quvianuk was lifting her upper body, yelling something he didn't understand. "Inupiat," she explained to the two Americans. "Seal hunters. Over here! Help!"

A flashlight beam. The light bobbed here and there, obscured by the blowing snow.

A hide-and-fur-clad figure strode out from behind it, out of the howling dark. It carried a rifle. Another, shorter figure loomed behind it. Stocky men, with huge hide-covered boots, fur-trimmed hoods, faces covered with scarves and snow goggles. They dragged a sled. "We hear your shots," the taller hunter said, pulling his scarf down. "And see your lights. Are you the ones they say crashed in an airplane?"

The bears growled again. The hunters shouted angrily into the wind. Snuffling grunts answered. Then, gradually, they receded back into the darkness. Presently, the noises ceased.

Dan wrung the hunters' hands, clapped their backs. He accepted a handful of something that tasted of berries and sugar, a strip of meat to chew on, something sour to drink. Reflecting, as he searched their wind-creased, impassive faces, their handmade spears and rusty rifles, that these were the very hunters Project Chariot would have put out of business forever.

And very shortly after, he followed their saviors as they set out for their camp.

11

Las Vegas, Nevada

S itting with her candidate in the Green Room, Blair choked down the stale bitter coffee Margo had brought. Its sourness was revolting, but she needed caffeine. Justin Yangerhans slouched beside her, long legs crossed, staring at a fresco of kids playing Frisbee on the wall opposite as the makeup man applied the last touches. His gangly frame was sheathed in a new gray suit. He wore a pale blue tie. At least he looked like a president. He was wearing his hair longer now. His lips moved as the cosmetician blotted his forehead. Rehearsing his answers, she hoped.

"Remember, keep it short," she told him again. "This is TV. The question, the problem, an uncontroversial answer, wrap. Forget about alternative courses of action, downsides, or downstream effects. Save that for the Sit Room."

"If I get there." His grin looked forced.

"Don't doubt it for a minute, Jim."

"With you in charge, how can I lose?"

She contented herself with a smile in response.

Tonight was the first debate. After weeks of beseeching, fundraising, and all but prostituting herself for donations, she'd just barely managed to wangle Yangerhans a position on the brilliantly lit stage. Though since there'd be ten other aspiring candidates on it, more than in any previous primary debate in history, that wasn't saying much.

Las Vegas, though, was making a big production of the event. No surprise. The war, the virus, the depression, had left the Strip a ghost of its former self. Only now were the gaming action and the musical extravaganzas picking up again, and the crowds were still thin. The hotel owners had made the party a lowball offer for a block of three hundred rooms. The candidates were comped, but Blair had still needed to borrow from her dad to secure her own and her staff's accommodations. The coffers were that low.

Yangerhans was tossing his foot on his crossed leg, a small, irritating gesture that probably signaled nerves. She'd felt on edge too, since hearing from Chief Wenck. *"We last saw Dan taking off in a small plane. Headed west, along the North Slope."* That call had been followed within minutes by the notification from the Alaska Department of Public Safety. Apparently there were three other people missing, along with Dan. They'd call again as soon as they had more information.

She hadn't slept well that night. But had reminded herself again, as she'd had to over and over during the war, that there was absolutely nothing she could do. Except endure, hope, and try to busy herself with something else.

And then, the *next day*, they'd called again. The survivors had been discovered. Dan was being treated for exhaustion and frostbite. So that had been a huge weight off . . . but at the same time, she'd made a resolution.

Never again would she allow him to take another crazy risk. He was a fucking admiral now, after all! Time for him to command his desk, not gallivant off on secret missions. She'd laid that order down when he'd called from the hospital in Alaska. And he'd meekly agreed.

She sighed now, doubting his promise would last. Still, she'd put her objections on the record.

A head appeared at the door. "One minute, folks. Mr. Candidate, please come with me. Oh, and ma'am—there are seats for you in the front row."

She smoothed her hair over her ear, coming back from a brief fantasy to the crowded amphitheater, the cops walling off the demonstrators at the doors. Blair was in the front row with the other senior staffers. A robust Black woman in a flowery robe, with double chins and an overpowering lilac body wash, was crowding her left side. A thin, unbelievably young man with green hair, in a narrow-lapelled black suit jacket, leggings, and JOIN JAVED T-shirt, fidgeted violently on her right.

Blair joined in the applause and cheers as the moderator, news announcer, and media personality James John Briskin strolled out to take the mic. Flamboyant and arch, he passed a few jokes, warming up the crowd, then called for the candidates.

They filed onto the stage, waving. For the first time, there were more women on the platform than men. Six to five, to be exact. Yangerhans was third from the left, between M'Elizabeth Holton and Jeanine De Bari, the ex-president's daughter, who was making her debut in politics. Name recognition, but not much real experience yet.

Blair lifted a pair of opera glasses surreptitiously from her purse. Examined through the lenses, Yangerhans seemed at ease, standing casually, hands relaxed at his sides. The makeup looked good. He was easily the tallest on the platform, which wasn't a negative. He'd still loped in with those too-long, goofy-looking strides, though, coming onstage.

Well, crap, this wasn't a catwalk. What mattered were his responses to the moderators' questions. She and Justin had spent days with the briefing books, and she'd hired a specialist to murder-board him. After some initial gaffes, when he tended to resort to too-vague Pentagon-briefing-speak, the admiral had gotten more natural, supporting his points with facts and statistics but without coming off stiffly or pedantically. His big drawback seemed to be a reluctance to commit to a single statement, a single course of action, without laying out the downsides. Not a bad trait in a president, but it could come across as waffling, or worse, uncertainty, if he went on too long about it in a debate or presser.

The first question, with two minutes for each hopeful's response: "Why, in your opinion, are you the best person here to be president? Governor Holton."

The Pennsylvanian gave a brief, obviously memorized response—terse, on target, and bold. Progressive programs. Recovery. Jobs. Return to normalcy. Nothing unexpected, but Blair had to admire her delivery. Holton had a low voice too, which sounded authoritative. Heads nodded in the audience. Murmurs of agreement.

"Shit," Blair muttered. Beside her the young man sat forward, tense as a set mousetrap.

The moderator moved on. "And you, Senator Javed? Same question. Why, in your opinion, are you the best candidate on this stage?" Son of immigrants, lawyer, DA, state senator, three terms in the House, now a first-term US senator from Florida. An inspiring, passionate speaker, but otherwise probably not a major contender. Included for a touch of color?

She smiled sardonically to herself. *Cynical much, Blair?* He was the only African American up there. Javed leaned into the mic, waving his arms theatrically. Still, he was effective. Increased funding for education, the arts, public health, rebuilding minority neighborhoods, and closing the inheritance-tax loophole that perpetuated inequality through generations. When he closed the people around her applauded enthusiastically. She patted her palms politely.

"Admiral Justin Yangerhans," Briskin intoned, mispronouncing his name. Blair winced. "Why do you feel best qualified to be president? Two minutes, please."

Yangerhans stood mute for a second, his narrow head lowered. Blair gripped the arms of her chair. Then, as the silence lengthened, she started to rise involuntarily. When was he going to speak? *Was* he going to speak? The vast room quieted, either intrigued or more likely gleeful at the prospect of a pratfall. An early, public humiliation no candidate could recover from.

Finally Justin lifted his chin, and his voice rang out clearly. "The real question isn't why I, or any of the rest of us up here, thinks he or she should be president. But, rather, what kind of country we want for our children and grandchildren to live in. A democracy? With liberty, and real justice, for all? Or an Americanized version of the tyranny we just sacrificed so many lives to defeat?

"For four years, I had the honor and responsibility of leading America's sons and daughters in the most destructive, most dangerous war in our history. I agree reconstruction is a priority. I agree jobs, education, small business need help. But our most pressing need is to change the direction of our country.

"Since the beginning of the war, this administration derided, investigated, and finally shut down the independent media. It's established and strengthened forces of control and repression. The Black Battalions. The neighborhood bullies of the Loyal League. The Patriot Channel. Cell phone surveillance. The Zones and Special Camps. The Patriot Party itself, formed from the fringe elements of both the Democratic and Republican parties—along with kooks, deniers, and conspiracy profiteers—large elements of which are eager to abandon even the pretense of inclusion, and embrace authoritarian rule."

Blair jerked her attention away for a scan of the audience, first to both sides, then behind her. The faces were rapt. Attentive, without a single cough or cleared throat or shuffled foot. Maybe he'd hesitated, at first, just to capture their attention? Clever.

Yangerhans looked even more serious. "During the conflict, these actions were defended as being necessary for victory. And, it's true, history shows war isn't a good time for freedom. We had to be united to win.

"But what *is* victory, after the guns fall silent, without a full and complete restoration of our basic liberties?

"The most important point at issue in this election is the survival of the two-party system. Without a free press, without checks and balances, and without a loyal opposition with a real chance of taking power, the future will be as George Orwell once outlined it: a boot coming down on a human face, forever."

He turned to face the cameras, just as she'd advised him to as he wrapped. "I've supported and defended the Constitution throughout my nearly forty-year career. I'd like a chance to continue that work. But whoever is nominated at our convention, I will support and defend to the best of my ability. We must not be afraid. But we must begin anew. So help me God."

He stepped back from the mic and crossed his arms.

For a moment silence gripped the hall. Then, a few claps began, scattered here and there. And at last, joining them, a veritable storm of applause. Some of the audience rose, then more, to a standing ovation.

Blair stood too, applauding, an astonished grin frozen on her lips. For a second there, she'd felt a frisson run up her own spine. The guy had done it. *Really* done it. Gotten their attention, held them in suspense, then nailed them to the boards with twopenny spikes.

And now, with his head held awkwardly high on a long neck, with a lock of dark but graying hair falling over his high forehead, and that craggy, sharp-cheekboned visage, he looked even more like Abraham Lincoln.

Unfortunately, the rest of the debate went downhill. Holton attacked Yangerhans once, asking (rhetorically) how a man accustomed to demanding obedience could defend the freedom to object to orders. Blair tensed when his rebuttal came, waiting for him to lash back, but Yangerhans's response was gentle. Actually he didn't mention anyone else on the platform by name, which she hoped would come across as being above the squabble. Especially when a tiff erupted between De Bari and Javed that had them screaming insults at each other while the moderator pleaded for self-control. Justin stayed on that one note: that the country had to shake off one-party rule, even if that party represented itself as the heir of both older organizations. The American people had to have a clear choice. Without two strong, responsible parties, there was no hope of progress.

Later, as she let herself back into the suite they'd rented as a command center, she was hit by a gabble from a dozen screens. The excited tones of commentators filled the room from notebooks set up on folding tables straddling the beds. Yangerhans wasn't there; Shingler-Gray, Blair's assistant, said he was meeting donors.

Not one of the major managers had joined the campaign team, so she'd built a new one. Mostly younger people, plus staffers she knew from the Senate. Others, who'd been purged and blacklisted during the war. Hu Kuwalay monitored three screens at once, typing rapidly on a tablet. Slim, elegant, dark-haired, Hu had been Talmadge's last chief of staff. Now he was her deputy. The rest had either parked in front of their own screens or were talking animatedly on their phones. Jessica Kirschorn, who'd chaired Blair's House run before the war, was covering the online media. Verónica Rodriguez-Garrido, who resembled a young Frida Kahlo, was hammering away in Spanish on hers. And others . . . Pyotr Robards, in ripped jeans and a T-shirt from an anarcho-punk band, managing IT . . . Margo, doing outreach to the LGBTQ community . . . Morton Grossman managed their finances, making sure each bundler's outreach was endorsed with checks or lines of credit.

She touched Kuwalay's shoulder. "How's it looking, Hu?"

He half turned his head. "Uh, not good. The admiral's being torn to pieces, basically."

"By the official media?"

He grimaced. "By pretty much everybody, Blair. Everyone mentions his war service, but there's always a sting in the tail. 'He's too blunt.' 'Too much of a populist.' 'Too right wing.' 'Too left wing.' 'A militarist, unqualified, unsupported, outside the mainstream.'"

She winced. "Jeez."

"Yeah, apparently he triggered some kind of cytokine storm from the Old Guard."

She wasn't sure she followed. "But then, who do they say won the debate?"

"Well, you can't judge by the commentators. But the online polls're starting to come in. Looks like"—he studied a bar graph—"Holton first, then Javed. De Bari. Yangerhans at fourth place."

"Holton, I expected her to finish high. Still, that's not too bad, fourth out of eleven."

Finishing in the upper half wasn't too shabby. Not exactly elated, but at least reassured it hadn't been a complete disaster, she poured a glass of white in the kitchen area, looking out over the counter at her minions.

They were busy as bees fighting an incursion of Asian murder hornets. A young woman behind her in the kitchen, set up at a folding table, was typing busily. Blair read the emerging press release over her shoulder, suggested a different tack, and went back out into the main room. Feeling suddenly unutterably weary.

She barked her thigh on the corner of one of the folding tables. "Crap," she muttered, massaging her bad hip. "Uh, Hu? Have you got this? I'm tapped out."

He barely looked up from his screens. Muttered, "Yeah, get some sleep, Blair. I'll update you in the morning."

The next day they muted all their laptops and tablets and watched the first Patriot Party debate on the big screen in the sitting room.

Only it wasn't a debate. Only two stood on the dais. The president, and his blond, rawboned, icily beautiful, pugnacious daughter-in-law. After fumbling through perfunctory remarks, her father intoned somberly, "Let's end the speculation. I'll finish out my second term, but I will not run for a third. I'll respect the Constitution, as I have throughout my time in office. Even though my entire cabinet, my Senate, and the American people are imploring me to stay in the White House. Instead, I'll take a well-deserved rest. Maybe play more golf."

He turned to the woman who stood beside him. "And, of course, I'll always be available to advise Yelena as she takes the reins," he said, patting her shoulder.

An intake of startled breath ghosted around the room. "Not *Novikov*," someone muttered.

"Fuck. *Fuck*," another staffer groaned. "He's not endorsing the veep?"

Kuwalay shook his head. "He's too outspoken. And too old. Actually, Yelena might be a smart choice. For them, I mean."

Blair sat rooted too. It was unprecedented. Yelena Novikov was the president's daughter-in-law, married to his youngest and rather feckless son, Charles. She'd never held an elected position. Never worked in government at all, before being elevated to a senior advisor slot in the West Wing. Now, apparently, even the charade of holding primaries was being dropped. The retiring president was simply crowning his successor, as the Caesars had done.

On the other hand, Novikov was young, female, and undoubtedly sharp. Also remorseless; she'd left a trail of severed heads behind her, undercutting, firing, or demoting any advisor who'd tried to slow her ascent or step in any way between her and her father-in-law.

"He's actually going to try to keep on governing," Kuwalay observed. "Just from behind the scenes. But it's a shocker, all right. I thought he'd announce for a third term. That was why they did the whole Supreme Court thing, whether the Twenty-Second Amendment could be thrown out during wartime."

Blair nodded. Obviously, the administration had counted on the war lasting through the election. But the Opposed Powers had asked for peace talks, then the Singapore Treaty had ended the conflict. And the court had shown a bit of spine, issuing a per curiam opinion that the two-term limit held even in wartime, and limiting the postponement of the election to six months.

Which had led, it seemed, to today's announcement. Which shouldn't have been all that shocking. A page from the International Dictator's Manual: use a placeholder to get around term limits, primaries, and the other petty conventionalities of a functioning democracy.

At first sight, it might have been seen as a good thing for Blair's own party. Running against a late-emerging new face would normally give them a better chance.

But maybe not against Yelena Novikov.

As White House special envoy, Novikov had managed the administration's reach-out to a coalescing junta of hard-line authoritarians around the world. Saudi Arabia, Venezuela, Maharlika, Hungary, Belarus, Cuba, Turkey. And of course, Russia. They smashed opposition, coordinated their tame media, and jailed or assassinated each other's independent reporters, as well as their own, of course.

"If she wins, we're finished," Kirschorn spat. "They'll shut down everything but Patriot News. Restructure the electoral college, the way they proposed last year. And the Supreme Court—"

"Oh, it can't be that bad," one of the younger women said, looking frightened. "This is America, right? That can't happen here, can it?"

They all glared at her, and she shrank in her chair, looking abashed. "But maybe I don't understand," she muttered.

"Nobody said democracy would last forever," Kuwalay told her. "We've had to fight for it with every generation. And there was never any guarantee we'd keep it."

Meanwhile, on screen, Novikov had stepped to the podium. With her father-in-law hovering behind her, she read a brief speech. *"We are the future,*" she ended, looking steadily into the camera. Blond-braided, tall, serene, elegant despite her youth. Almost queenly, Blair thought, admiring the woman's sangfroid while at the same time loathing everything she stood for. "*The old order is finished. The days of America funding, feeding, and policing the world are done. The days of divisions among us are over too. In a more threatening, hotter, and less forgiving future, we cannot afford to fight among ourselves. We must march forward together to survive.*

"*The quarrelling of parties has to end. I promise you this: If I am elected, I will lead for all Americans. From many, one. Citizens of every color, from every part of our great country, will sing in chorus from now on, united, from sea to shining sea.*"

The speech closed with a waving flag and "The Star-Spangled Banner." But the suite was quiet. At last the viewers stirred, glancing at one another. "Jesus," somebody muttered. "This is not good."

"She said the right things, though," the young woman murmured, the one who'd said it couldn't be that bad. "Didn't she?"

"Do you work for us?" Blair snapped at her. "Seriously? It's all fucking misleading propaganda bullshit. And not even original bullshit. 'From many, one'—that's a fascist slogan."

"Well, it's actually—" Kuwalay began, but after a glare from her didn't seem to want to finish whatever he'd been going to say. She got questioning looks from others in the room too, but ignored them. A rage was rising within her, and not just from a hot flash, though that didn't help. The heat radiated out from her chest in waves. Her face broke out in a sweat. She fought a brief, powerful urge to tell the kids they were morons, but managed to suppress it. That would be a mistake. They weren't *all* totally ignorant.

She turned away abruptly and stalked into the bedroom. Her own room, set up now as a makeshift video studio, with a nice backdrop looking out the window down the Strip. She flopped into a chair, then got up again and poured out one of the little bottles of white wine from the fridge into a bathroom tumbler. Considered, then cracked the cap on a second and shook it out into the glass as well.

"Novikov," she muttered. Seriously? Yet according to Mrs. Clayton, and the other grand poo-bahs of the party, Yangerhans wasn't good enough for their own side?

Maybe she *was* wasting her time here. She could be gardening, maybe knitting. Catching up on the latest historical drama on Hulu. They were starting to sound like better ways to spend her time. Make that back lawn into the walled garden she'd always dreamed of. A more achievable goal, she feared, than trying to save her country.

Which, all too often, didn't seem like it wanted to be saved.

She strolled back and forth, chin propped on her hand. And mused, *Do I really want to do this?*

The angel and the devil. Always at war.

She slugged back half the tumbler, and the inexpensive white, sourer than she'd expected, puckered her esophagus all the way down. She stalked back and forth, nursing the glass. And gradually her anger chilled.

More and more as she got older, she wondered if she'd taken a wrong turn somewhere. In her twenties, even her thirties, she'd never questioned her path. Leaned in to the whole career-in-politics idea. Worked her tail off, schemed and plotted, though she'd steered clear of being actively malicious. From the CRS to the Senate staff, then to DoD. By the time she'd started to think about having a family, it had been too late.

Though she'd never actually met anyone, at least until Dan, who'd seemed at all interested in having kids. DC didn't work that way, at least for women. You were full-time or you were a wife. A choice the men didn't seem to have to make.

Anyway, too late now. Her too-chubby black-and-white cat, and Dan, were her family now. Though Jimbo was around a lot more than her husband.

Which was something they needed to work on.

She was staring out the window at the brilliant multicolored glittering Las Vegas night when a hasty knock came on her door. It was instantly followed by Rodriguez-Garrido's head. "Ms. Titus," she panted. "Come out. Please. You need to see this."

In the main room a dozen staffers were staring open-mouthed at blank screens. Some tapped uncertainly at their keyboards, or bent to wiggle power plugs. But not one seemed to have a connection, though the Patriot Channel was still playing, muted, on the wall screen. Kuwalay caught her questioning glance, pointed at his laptop, and mimed a sliced-throat gesture.

She wheeled on Robards, who was hunched over his own weary-looking, stickered-up notebook. A lock of dark hair fell over the IT meister's pasty face. He was typing furiously, and barely reacted when she laid a hand on his shoulder. "Pyotr?"

"Just a min—fuck. *Fuck!*"

"What's going on? We don't have—"

"I know, I know—fuck!" He clawed his fingers over the keyboard. Then, with an impatient motion, spun his screen so she could see.

A three-dimensional triangle rotated furiously on a violently flickering background. It whirled like a black hole while starlike specks spiraled in toward it, only to vanish, sucked in, obliterated. Beneath it ran an italicized chyron, apparently in multiple languages, though it scrolled so rapidly her eye couldn't track fast enough even to make out what alphabets it was using.

Suddenly it froze. A line of text blinked: *Your computer has been blocked. Please wait for instructions.*

"It's Stygian Prism," Robards said, sounding awed. He combed greasy black hair back with both hands. "I've heard about this bitcher. Hard-core. This could be expensive."

She bent to inspect the screen more closely and caught a whiff of his rank smell. What the hell, he'd come cheap and had seemed to know his IT. Up until now. "Malware?"

"Ransomware. In a couple of seconds it'll—there it is!"

A pop-up read, *To unlock you shall send the sum of Euro 100,000 to a Zipcoin address that shall be provided shortly. Upon payment, you shall be provided a decryption key. This key shall be good for one hour. You now have six hours to prepare your funds.*

A clock popped in the lower right of the screen and began counting down. *We shall send the forwarding number at that time. Do not attempt to remove this program. You shall fail. Do not notify authorities or all information on your drives shall be shredded and overwritten beyond anyones ability to recover.*

Blair blinked and straightened. Catching apprehensive looks from the rest of the staff. She wheeled on Robards, fists clenched. "What exactly is *going on here*, Pyotr?"

"It dropped code into our system folders. That protects it from our antivirus. It's on our registry too, so you can't just erase it."

"Can't you fix it?"

"Like I said, it's already inside. My guess, they snuck it in as a forged-ID virtual private network update. It doesn't actually lock the screens until everything on that network's infected. Then the message pops." Robards stretched and grunted. "Like I said, this could be bad."

She glanced again at the anxious faces. "What about our files? Our donor data, our reach-out? Didn't we have protection for this kind of . . . attack?"

"Shingler said we didn't have three thousand bucks for the latest anti-malware. So I installed freeware. We have firewalls, a VPN, but this is . . . *Stygian Prism*. I'm trying a removal tool. Let's see if it works." He finished typing a line and hit Enter.

The screen stayed blank for a few seconds. Then the whirling prism came up again, remorselessly sucking in the helpless-looking specks of light, followed by the same message. *Your computer has been blocked. Please wait for instructions.*

Then, *You disobeyed instructions and attempted to remove this program. Payment for your files is increased to Euro 200,000. Do not notify authorities or all information on your drives shall be shredded and overwritten beyond anyones ability to recover.*

She sat back, feeling as if someone had punched her in the kidneys. Two hundred thousand euros. They didn't have that much. Would have to borrow it. But from where? They'd already exhausted the meager line of credit Mrs. Clayton had grudgingly extended, since Yangerhans had gotten enough signatures for the first debate.

As if reading her thoughts, Robards said, "You're not thinking of paying?"

"We may not have a choice. We've got to have those files. If they'll send us this, this recovery key—"

Margo Shingler-Gray elbowed her way into the conversation. Kuwalay stood behind her, peering over her shoulder. "Which they may not," she said.

"Exactly." Robards nodded.

Blair frowned. "Why wouldn't they? If we paid—"

The IT guy said, "Why should they do anything for you, once they've got your money?"

Shingler-Gray added, "And let's not be naive. This might not be just a hacker shakedown, Blair."

"What do you mean?" But she was starting to get the picture, and felt sick.

Her aide said, "I mean, this *looks* like ransomware. But what if it's a plain destructive attack?"

Robards added, "NSA could do that. Any of the military cyber-agencies. Probably Gray Wolf Crypto too."

She rocked back on her heels. "Then our files are gone already. For good. Is that what you're saying?"

They looked away. No need to ask, but she did, anyway. "Who would order something like that?"

Robards looked canny. "There's dark forces out there, Blair. You know that. Your candidate was talking about them in the debate. He thinks he can reform the government. Make it play nice. But it's government itself, the state, that's the—"

"Enough with the *Anarchist Cookbook*, okay? Let's concentrate on the software," Shingler-Gray said, cast iron in her tone. Robards winced as the retired colonel pincered the nerves between his shoulder and neck. "How do we fix this? Short of paying. Which we're *not* going to do. I take it you have a system restore protocol. And a server backup."

"I may not be able to," Robards said after a moment. "Fix it, I mean. Remember, *you* told me we didn't have the money. I wanted to set up a VDI via an RDP—"

Blair started to ask her aide if that were true, then thought, *Spilled milk. She* had told Shingler-Gray to pare expenses, after all. She asked Robards, "Don't we have *any* backups? The cloud?"

"Sure, separate drives, but they're not up to date. And the cloud backs up every thirty seconds." Robards glanced at the screen. "Which means it's infected. Prism will wipe that too. If it hasn't already."

Her throat burned with an upwelling of Chablis-flavored stomach acid. Their finance information wasn't all that was online. So were the state nominating committee records. Their Federal Election Commission submissions. Polling data and analysis. Databasing. Voter lists. Their web presence and e-commerce sites for donations. Precinct data. Campaign video, like the ad they'd shot at Plaza Olvera. Oh, maybe they had a backup for that. But for all the rest, the very meat and muscle of their campaign . . .

She bit her lip. "Okay . . . but look . . . if we *did* decide to pay, how would we do that?"

Robards wiped sweat off his forehead. "Um, first we'd have to call whichever bank Mr. Grossman's parking our money with. Ask them to set up for a fund transfer to a crypto exchange. They'd need an account. Coinslot's the easiest. They convert your dollars to whatever you want— Zipcoin, Ethereum, Zcash, Monero. Once the digital currency's in your wallet, you text it to the number these pirates give you." He blotted his brow again. "That's why they give you six hours. So you can do all that, even if you're not familiar with the system."

"You seem to know quite a bit about this," Shingler-Gray observed.

"I'm an anarchist, duh. Once we topple the government money system, we can be free."

Blair patted his back, noticing again his rank smell. The chip crumbs in his beard. Trying not to let his appearance, and his sophomoric poses, prejudice her against him. But she couldn't help wondering if somehow he himself had brought on, invited, maybe even *set up* this disaster.

No. No, she was getting paranoid. Mistrusting everyone. Seeing conspiracies everywhere.

On the other hand, it might well *be* a conspiracy. The opposition directed both the NSA and CIA, and were in bed with Big Tech, using deep surveillance architecture during the war to identify resistance members and shunt them off to the Zones. One reason the Midwest and South had seceded, to fight the steady encroachment of online control.

Meanwhile the clock on Robards's screen was counting down. She patted his back again, harder. "Who else can you call, Pyotr? *Think.* Doesn't the party have IT staff? Get on the phone. Get us some help." He nodded, and she rounded on Kuwalay. "Hu, you get along better with Clayton than I do. See if she'll front us the euros from the party account. We'll pay it back, I'll guarantee that personally if I have to. Margo, I need you to call my dad. No, wait, I'll do it. I'm sure Bank of America can do a crypto exchange. If we do need to go that route."

She raised her voice. "The rest of you, everyone—look at your personal computers, phones, anything not connected to the LAN. I know you've backed up things you were working on, early drafts, squirreled stuff away. Now we need it, and I don't care where it comes from. Hu, you still have your office email active, right?" He nodded a sleek head, phone to his ear. "Send it all as attachments to his Senate email. That's huk@talmadge .senate.gov. Whoever's doing this to us, let's see if they feel like messing with the US Senate."

The room quickened, busy again. She regarded the bent heads for a moment, fighting the acid queasiness that kept creeping up into her mouth. Then went reluctantly into the bedroom to call her father.

12

Under the Arctic Ice

Sloan woke to blue light and quiet. For drowsy half-awake minutes he lay listening to hushed voices from down *Tang*'s passageway. To a distant beep, a sonic alarm or reminder, quickly silenced. A faint irregular ticking somewhere above his head.

At last he rolled out. The food cans on the deck were gone, apparently all taken to the galley. He pulled on his coveralls and pushed his feet into the slippers the chief of the boat had issued him. His boots stood in the corner, drying out, but still smelling of the sea.

He closed his eyes, reliving the terror of watching the submarine's sail rushing at him while he dangled helplessly. Unable to do more than twist in his harness, awaiting the impact that would break him like an egg against an anvil. Until the aircraft above him had corrected, swinging him away in a stomach-roiling arc before penduluming him back to slam once more into the slippery slanting steel.

No. Not boring. But he didn't plan ever to go through that again.

The sink in the little cramped shared head was soap-spattered by whoever had used it last and neglected to wipe it down.

The mess decks, a tight low-overheaded space, all stainless steel and gleaming tile. Here, too, voices were low. Two sailors were playing a muted video game on the big screen. Sloan drew coffee and joined two others at one of the tables. "Hey," he said.

"Hey."

"Hello, sir." A crewman shoved a board over and cut a deck of cards. "You up for a run?"

He frowned. "A . . . run?"

"Cribbage. You play?"

"A little too early for me," Sloan said.

He was contemplating the vat of oatmeal when a half-familiar face poked around the door. After a moment he recognized the lieutenant who supported the riders. "There you are," Mol said. "Skipper wants you. In Control."

"Be right there." Sloan drained the coffee and stood.

Fahrney had slipped them past the guard at the gate, the spider lurking in its web—the Laika, the Russian sub lying off Diomede Island—by limpeting *Tang* to an eighty-thousand-ton, thousand-foot-long Maltese-flagged liquid natural gas tanker headed north through the strait. Hugging the vessel's starboard side fifty yards away, the skipper had masked the murmur of his propulsor with the heavy thudding screw-beats and liquification-compressor din, slipping them past like a magician palming a card.

The American boat had stuck close to its huge running mate until it turned west, probably for a fill-up at one of the new LNG loading platforms along the Siberian coast. At that point they'd diverged courses, very quietly.

They'd shifted to Arctic routine a hundred miles south of the reported ice zone. Manned extra watch stations, and Fahrney had rigged ship for collision, with masts housed. Irons was in Control, advising the conning officer. They ran covert, by inertial navigation, the overhead camera, and the top sounder, a narrow-beam, high-frequency sonar on the leading edge of the sail. That sensor was hard to detect more than a couple of miles away.

They'd encountered floes soon after transiting, and solid cover at seventy-one degrees north. Farther north than the National Ice Center had predicted, confirming the forecasts of decreased winter cover as the summer ice shrank.

They'd had some close calls on the way. Fahrney had operated twenty-five feet off the bottom, "flying by altitude," distance above the seabed rather than by depth from the surface. The "bubble," or trim, had to be controlled within plus or minus one-eighth of a degree, since either a nose-up or nose-down attitude would ram the bow or the vertical rudder either into the bottom or into the ice above. Each time the sonar picked up an ice keel that would menace the top of the sail, the atmosphere in the control room grew tense. Sloan had looked in once or twice, but the crew's air of concentration had made him loath to say anything. No wonder; at some points there was only twenty feet between the sail and the ice, and less than that to the bottom.

And now and then there *was* no way through, and they had to back down, very, very deliberately, and sniff around for another way forward.

Tang picked her way north, negotiating a three-dimensional labyrinth about as fast as a man could row. So he mainly stayed in the wardroom, watching the black-and-white video of the ice cover unreeling overhead.

Then at last the sea deepened, and *Tang* had run, quiet and slow, up a line of longitude toward the pole. They'd hit seventy-six degrees north the day before, and turned west. Running a bit faster as the coastal plain fell away beneath them.

Now *Tang* cruised north of Siberia, in waters the Russians claimed and had probably covered with bottom-laid sensor arrays. At six hundred feet, they ran well clear of the icy stalactites that reached down from above. Masked by both sea and ice, they were out of communication, except for the twenty-four-hour schedule. Once a day the boat rose to a hundred feet to copy traffic. Receiving only, so they were undetectable by emissions.

Covert. Silent. A hole in the ocean to any eavesdroppers.

But wakeful, cautious, alert as a leopard stalking a midnight jungle.

When he let himself into the control room now things seemed more relaxed. Irons, the ice pilot, had apparently turned in. The low-light camera was on a screen above the control station. Angled upward, it outlined shadowy projections reaching down from a black ceiling. They neared, passed overhead, and vanished silently aft.

A second camera was angled down, but registered only an eerie greenish flash now and then, probably from some deep-sea organism.

Tang crept through a lightless void, the night above black, any remaining photons from stars or moon blocked by the unyielding ice. The planesmen sat in silence. A quad-redundant control system maintained depth and bubble. They only nudged their joysticks at long intervals, angling very slightly right or left as the sub glided onward.

Sloan couldn't help shivering. Imagining what it must be like above them, on the polar pack. A white waste, and incredible life-sucking cold. Hummocked ridges of tormented ice, buckled by grinding pressure. And over it all, a whirling blizzard.

While down here it was a steady air-conditioned sixty-eight degrees, with three meals a day plus midrats, and coffee or hot cocoa day or night.

Yoder, the exec, regarded him from behind the control station, arms folded. "Captain asked for me, XO," Sloan told her. She inclined her head toward the port side.

Fahrney, in blue coveralls and shower shoes with black socks, was fin- ishing up a confab with the sonar supervisor. He held up a finger, signal- ing Sloan to give him a moment, and resumed discussing diapycnal mixing and internal wave intensities. Finally he patted the supervisor's shoulder and jerked his head, inviting Sloan to join him at the navigation plot cen- tering the space.

The skipper zoomed a tabletop chart out to show the continental shelf and slope north of Siberia. Massive subsea ridges and abyssal ba- sins stretched across the North Pole toward Greenland and Canada. The bright blue Own Ship symbol pulsed in a lonely emptiness north of a con- stellation of islands. Two main ones, and several smaller islets, north of the Russian coast and stretching off to the northwest. The depth gradients showed *Tang* in six hundred fathoms, three thousand six hundred feet of water, but the seas slanted shallower to southward.

Which explained why Fahrney was searching for thermoclines to hide under.

"You wanted to see me, sir?"

The CO pursed his lips. "Commander. Your folks settled in okay? Every- one comfortable? Gear all working?"

"Yes, sir. We set up our control station back in the payload module area."

"Hope you moved the bike and the weight bench."

"Actually we had plenty of room, sir. Your folks can still work out. We're not that territorial."

"Good. I'm thinking, this is about as close in as I plan to get. We do need sensors farther in, but you're set up to run those out ahead of us, correct?"

"Yes, sir." He cleared his throat. "As we briefed. We'll detach the Prime to run out about two hundred miles west of us. It'll deploy HCUSs across what intel says should be the Apokalypsis's line of advance for the live test. Then we'll pull the Orca back to a hide position, and monitor via a low data rate secure channel."

"Then we wait," Fahrney said.

"Yes, sir. Bottom the Orca, to conserve the fuel cell, and stand fast. When we make contact, we reposition for the best geometry. It'll fire the Zombiefish as the target passes."

He studied the chart as the CO zoomed it back to an inch to a hun- dred miles. The launch point for the test lay two thousand kilometers to the west, on the Murmansk Peninsula. The track for the new nuclear tor- pedo zigzagged across the icebound Barents Sea, its length simulating a run to the north, toward Canada and the United States.

But instead, this test course passed north of the elongated sausage shape of Novaya Zemyla. That barren land had hosted dozens of Soviet-era thermonuclear tests. Until it reached what the Lithuanian intelligence service said was the intended detonation site: the northern coast of Severnaya Zemyla, where the explosion would convert a small indentation into a huge harbor.

Which didn't look all that distant from where *Tang* herself lurked, at least on this display. "Um, are you sure we'll be far enough away, Captain? If the BLY-1 fails, and the test goes the way they plan?"

Fahrney massaged his chin as if he had a beard, which he didn't. "Assuming this is the two-hundred-megaton warhead they advertised, and they detonate it to scoop out a harbor, not drive a tsunami wave, my reading is that most of that energy'll go straight up. It'll lift dirt, a *lot* of dirt, but relatively little energy will couple out to sea. We'd get some propulsive load, but I'd guess the pressure pulse, shear loading, it'd be pretty dampened by the time it reached us. Maybe also some ice movement, but everything's shock mounted and isolated, so I don't think we'd take significant damage."

He eyed Sloan. "But we're not going to let that happen, right?"

"No, sir. That's the plan."

"Take it over, steer it somewhere to the north. But not detonate it, right?"

"No, sir. We want the test to fail. But not, um, catastrophically. The Zombie's programmed to crash it into the bottom somewhere near the pole."

Fahrney nodded. "And if this isn't really a test? If it deviates from the track, starts heading off somewhere we don't know about, too fast for us to follow?"

Sloan had thought about this too. "Then we destroy it, sir. That's a preset mode for the BLY-1 too. Fire the second-stage rocket and ram it. No explosives, but if we can hit it at two hundred miles an hour, we'll break *something*."

Fahrney nodded, looking satisfied. "Okay, good. Let me know when you're ready to proceed."

Sloan nodded. He took a last look around the control room, the touch screens glowing in the dimness. The silent, motionless operators. Then, he headed aft.

* * *

RaShondra was already at her station, their remote control and comm equipment unshipped from their containers and set up on a folding table. "Where's Jason?" he asked her.

"Dr. Liu'll be right back. Went to see how to turn down the lights."

Yeah, it was too fucking bright. They'd be in front of these screens for many hours. Sloan dragged an exercise bike aside, snapped open a folding chair, and set it beside hers.

Orca Prime could execute complex missions on its own, but a human still needed to keep tabs on it. That was US doctrine with an autonomous weapon system. And someone had to evaluate the intel the HCUSs sent back and be ready to deal with any surprises.

Set against this was the need to maintain radio and sonar silence. If the Russians suspected an intruder here, in what they considered their back pocket, they could postpone the test. And take action against the trespasser.

The answer was the Prime's very-low-frequency, state-dependent sonar channel. The mobile sensors reported via short-range, high-frequency directional transmission. To relay that data back to *Tang*, Prime's sonar transmitters shifted among thousands of frequencies at a chaotic-appearing rate. It was synchronized with a frequency-switching receiver aboard *Tang* by means of a near-infinite secret key.

Anyone listening on a single frequency would hear the same staticky, random-noise background whether the aggregate of channels was transmitting or not. The only way information could be extracted would be to possess both processing equipment capable of almost instantaneous switching, and a classified key that changed many times each minute.

Unfortunately, this limited the transmission rate. But additional processing on both ends made it possible to send a succession of grainy still pictures when necessary, though the bandwidth didn't accommodate true video.

The system was still experimental. But it was the only way anyone had come up with to covertly monitor what the Prime would be doing.

Liu undogged the door. He pointed to a switch. "It's dimmable. Just couldn't find it, first time I looked. Okay, ready to start work?"

After they set up and tested their monitoring equipment, Sloan and RaShondra climbed back up into the Orca through the loading hatch again. She ran tests from the little cramped control sphere while Liu tested comms. Sloan punched in a tactical problem, making sure there weren't any bugs in the new patch.

When everything checked out, they set the Pilot to autonomous and climbed back down. Sealed the access to the sphere, then the loading hatch. The tons of machined steel, so massive that despite the counter-vailing springs it took both their combined weights to pull it shut, sealed with a dull echoing clank like the door of a bank vault locking home.

Over the next couple of hours they detached the Orca, positioned it along-side *Tang*, then gave the control room the word to deploy the HCUSs. The torpedo-size sensors swam out from the sub's torpedo tubes, oriented, and racked and plugged into the Orca's payload bay. RaShondra ran operability tests on each, then shut them down to save power.

The AN/BLY-1, the Zombiefish, came next. Liu controlled it from his lap-top as it, too, swam out, racked itself, and plugged in. Liu reminded Sloan and RaShondra, "Remember, we have to keep a close eye on battery levels. If the smaller vehicles run too low, they won't be able to return and recon-nect."

Liu crossed to the intercom. Pressed a lever. "Control, uh, Orca control."

"Control, go."

"HCUSs racked, BLY racked, request permission to commence mis-sion."

Fahrney: *"Sure everything checks out? We don't want these things to go haywire someplace we can't run in and recover them."*

"All diagnostics smooth, Captain. Power levels, green. AIs test green."

"Okay, permission granted. Unleash."

Liu clicked off. "You heard the man," Sloan told them. "Who wants first watch?"

They'd divided responsibilities. Liu would be responsible for the BLY. Sloan and RaShondra would take turns overseeing Orca Prime and its sensor deployments.

The operation would proceed deliberately until its final minutes, when everything would have to move very quickly. The Pilot—the Orca Prime's guiding software—would run the vehicle in toward the test site, basically acting as a truck for the HCUSs. The mobile sensors would deploy them-selves across the mega-torpedo's predicted course, in a barrier sixty miles wide.

According to the Lithuanian intel, the nuclear torpedo's propulsion operated in two modes. In the covert mode, its sonar signature resembled that of a conventional torpedo. Both the Lithuanians and DIA anticipated the test would begin at this lower speed. In the fast mode, seawater would be admitted directly to the nuclear core. Flashed into steam, it would exhaust through a rocket nozzle. A portion of the radioactive gas would also be piped forward to sheath its skin. It would make an unimaginable racket as it reached top speed.

After dropping its sensors, the Orca would pull back to hide behind an islet. As their target approached, the American drone sub would have a limited time to reposition for the best firing geometry.

It would have only one chance. If they missed the intercept, or if the Zombie attached properly but was unable to take control, *Tang* would be positioned for a bow-on torpedo shot.

In either case, they should be able to ensure the test ended in failure.

Sloan went forward to the wardroom, got coffees from the always-hot pot, and they both settled in for the long haul.

"So how did you get into this?" Komanich brushed hair from her eyes, lounging back in her chair and propping her boots on another seat.

Sloan deliberated. *How far back?* "Well, my grandad was military. Pretty high up, actually. My dad, not so much. He runs a bar in the Adirondacks. But I got the bug, and joined up in college. NROTC out of Cornell."

She nodded. "Why Cornell?"

"They had the best operations research program. Which I always figured I'd go into. The mathematics that drives everything . . . that's what fascinated me." He glanced at her. "You?"

She shrugged. "Oh, I'm from Kansas. Grew up . . . real poor. And with a not-so-great family situation, you might say."

"Sorry to hear that."

"Oh, I survived . . . I left early. Fifteen, before the Covenanters got rolling. Drifted around. Worked as a waitress. But the manager there thought I was too smart to work at a truck stop. She sort of adopted me, got me to finish high school . . . then the big Patriot Draft started and they said I tested high for computers, machine learning. Then, the wartime STEM program. DoD hired me out of MIT, programming the early CHAD series. And I've been in AI pretty much ever since." She scratched one ankle, revealing a slice of dark skin and fine stubble, as well as ink, though he couldn't make out the design. "I deployed with the first Orca squadron to go operational. In the China Sea."

"Oh yeah? Where?"

Comparing records, they discovered they hadn't been all that far apart during the invasion of Taiwan. "And now you're with JAIC," Sloan said.

"Yip. Network engineer, in charge of the Prime, the ODM part, anyway. So how'd you end up where you are?"

"Navy out of college. A frigate, first. Then I did the WITI course—tactical instructor—and they sent me to WestPac. I served on Admiral Lenson's staff. When the war ended I . . . sort of had to decide if I wanted to stay in." He rubbed his mouth, flashing back to his grandfather's office at Leidos.

Haverford Tomlin had wanted Sloan to join the company. Offered him a lucrative position in charge of several aerospace research contracts.

"I'm just not sure, Grandad," he'd said, ensconced in one of the leather chairs in front of Tomlin's big desk. "I sort of felt I had a home in the Navy. And I was never bored."

"The military's going to shrink, boy. Space is where the action's going to be. Mining asteroids. The moon, again. If you don't join us, you'll miss the postwar boom."

Sloan had tapped his fingertips together, avoiding the old man's bald-eagle scowl. Space sounded interesting. But again, it would actually mean sitting at a desk in front of a screen. Which he wasn't that eager to do for the rest of his life. Plus, he doubted there'd be anything like a "boom." Food prices had tripled, while Social Security payments had been slashed. The Dow was at 9,000, and most of the Midwest and South was in revolt.

A great salary, sure . . . but he had no family, didn't own a house or a car. Or feel like he needed them. Money was just numbers.

He hitched himself back on the too-slick cordovan leather as the old man asked, disapproval chilling his tone, "Okay, you don't like my offer. What do you plan to do, then?"

"Well, sir . . . I heard about a secret Navy unit that might be doing some technologically advanced black ops."

"I've heard that too," the senior Tomlin said. "Only they're not rumors. They're reviving a group to defuse emergent threats. A unit that used to run missions here and there around the world, most of which never made the news." His grandfather eyed him. "You served with Lenson, right? I know his wife, by the way. Very . . . efficient woman. Though she seems to be getting above herself, these days. Dabbling in politics."

"Yes, sir. Not the—I mean, I served with Admiral Lenson."

"He used to lead that unit. Before the war."

Sloan nodded. The admiral was kind of an old-school tight-ass. But he'd stood fast when everyone, including the tactical AI, was yelling, "Retreat" during Operation Rupture. "He's in charge of this new unit?"

"Oh, that I don't know. Just some background that might be useful to you." His grandfather gazed out the window. "You know, Sloan, I've followed you since you were a kid and your dad left. You like a challenge. You like action. The one thing you can't stand is . . . sitting still. But business isn't unexciting. Quite the opposite. Are you really determined on this? In spite of everything I'm offering?"

Sloan had forced an ingratiating smile. "Sir, I just don't think a desk job is where I want to be now. Five years down the road, maybe. But I think I can contribute more staying in uniform. At least, until we see if this treaty holds water."

And his grandfather had sighed, dismissing him with a nod. "I can't argue with staying in the service. But if you change your mind, and I'm still here, let me know."

Sloan had called the new office in San Diego. Had been connected with a female captain and given her his background, combat record, and qualifications. "I want to join, if you can work it out with my detailer," he'd told her.

And Cheryl Staurulakis had said, "I think we can make that happen."

It was during Sloan's second turn on watch, after the Prime had dropped its loads, depositing them on the seabed like strange eggs, that the first hint of trouble surfaced. The big USV was headed back toward them when the data link went dead. His screen froze. The readouts from the other onboard instruments, updated every few seconds via the low-rate channel, went blank.

He stared at the screen, waiting for a refresh. When nothing changed he reached for the IC phone, an arm's length away on the bulkhead of the workout room. "Control, Orca control."

"Control. Go."

"Lost comms with Orca. Last reported location from onboard nav, 79 degrees 52 north, 71 degrees 02 east."

After a moment the exec's voice came back. *"West of Ostrok Island. Are you getting any engine or power readouts? Can you tell if it's still live?"*

"Uh, wait one." He toggled. "Negative. No comms or data here whatso-ever."

"This is your state-dependent channel, right? The experimental one?"

"Correct."

"Was the Orca operating properly up 'til then? In other words, do you think it's still headed back in our direction, just not able to tell us?"

"That'd be my guess, ma'am. But at this point, it's just a guess."

"Let me see if it's on our end, our passive array. That's what's send-ing data to your descramblers."

They weren't descramblers, but he saw what she meant. "Roger, let me know how that checks out."

He debated waking Komanich, but didn't see the point. Either the sub's receivers were on the blink, his SD comms were out, the drone's transmit-ters had failed, or—most catastrophic of all—the Pilot had managed to blunder into some undersea mountain or ice pinnacle and was even now sinking toward the seabed. The Prime was big for a USV, but small for a submarine. Colliding with a whale could have done it. Only this far north, under solid ice, how could a whale surface to breathe? No, probably not that. Ice or a seamount, though . . .

Or could someone have known it was there? Been warned, and—perhaps from a waiting sub, like the Laika that had barriered the Barents Strait—put a torpedo into it? That, too, would explain both the sudden cessation of contact and the lack of response since. But then, they'd have heard the detonation, right?

He sat there worrying, but at last had to shrug. Nothing to do except wait.

The phone buzzed. He snatched it. "Orca."

The exec again. *"BYS checks out. Problem's at the far end."*

"Uh, roger."

"Keep trying. Any alternate comms?"

"There's a test circuit, but that wouldn't be covert. Also, it's short-range."

"Copy that. So, what? We stand by until our big buddy either shows up again, or doesn't?"

"No, that's about it."

"Shit . . . Copy. I'll tell the CO. Let us know if there's a change." A rat-tle as the XO socketed the handset at the far end.

Komanich showed up to relieve him, rubbing her eyes. When he brought her up to date she grimaced. "Are you kidding me? It's *gone*? Like, a lost balloon?"

"Not sure. But it looks that way."

"Did it deploy the HCUSs? At least?"

"Yeah, apparently. Reported uncoupling, anyway." He spread his hands. "Aside from that, all we can do is wait."

She frowned. "How about UHF Satcom? Or, no, even if it could penetrate the ice, it could be intercepted."

"Exactly."

They discussed possibilities, but in the end came up with the same nonanswer: they just had to wait and see.

Two hours later the IC buzzed. Komanich grabbed it. Told him, "Faint propulsor noise, bearing two two five. Correlates with our baby."

"Great. Great!" The Prime was intact. And apparently, returning. It was autonomous, after all. If it lost contact, the Pilot's internal decision-making would route it back to the mother ship and attempt contact by short-range acoustics.

Sloan toggled to that circuit, then hesitated, exchanging a glance with Komanich. She shook her head.

He nodded back, without words. Putting any sound into the water risked detection. Best to wait until the range closed, and query at minimum power.

So one less thing to worry about . . . but the data issue remained. If they couldn't get the long-range link to work, no way Operation Apocalypse could succeed. The HCUSs had to talk to the Orca to get it into position for intercept. And *Tang* needed to know where to be to backstop everything with a torpedo, in case the Zombie failed.

They left their gear on and went forward to Control. Stood beside the sonar operator as he scanned the spectrum. "It's closing," he told them. "Maybe four knots, by the screw count."

Sloan rubbed his face, feeling grit in his eyes, stubble on his cheeks. He was used to incoming missiles, aircraft, hypersonic projectiles. The weapons the Chinese had thrown at them off Hainan. But everything happened so fucking *slowly*, underwater, under the ice. You were blind and half-deaf. It was frustrating as hell.

But his stomach was telling him it was past time for dinner.

* * *

Sloan was shoving away from the cribbage board, shaking his head, when the ice pilot strolled into the wardroom. "I thought I knew how to play this fucking game," he muttered.

Irons grinned. "Chief of the boat kick your ass? Did he take the points you forgot to count?"

"From the get-go."

"Yeah, he skunked me yesterday. Weps said he and the captain been trading the tournament championship for the last couple years." Irons went to the sideboard. "Coffee?"

"Yeah . . . thanks, sir."

"No need to call me that. A civilian these days."

Sloan nodded. But the old guy still had presence. And it wasn't just the gray muttonchops, the casual way he slouched the narrow passageways.

When Irons settled at the table Sloan said, "I've been meaning to ask you, sir . . . I mean . . ."

"Dev."

"Uh . . . Dev. What's it like up there? On the pack."

The ice pilot grinned. "Dark. And cold."

"Yeah, I get that. But seriously, you been up top? Or just gone through submerged?"

Irons flipped idly through the condiments on the sideboard. He took two packets out, a sugar and a Sweet'N Low, white and pink, and put them on the table between them. "Well, both. I was north of the Circle twice when I was active duty. Once as a div-oh standing EOOW watches aft. Second time, Weps standing OOD. But we never surfaced. Too busy doing other things. Want to see a trick?"

"A trick? I guess. Sure."

"You right- or left-handed?"

"Right-handed."

Irons took Sloan's hand, turned it over, and tucked the pink packet into his palm. "Since I joined the lab, I've piloted twenty-four subs up here. Including a Brit. Been to five ice camps. Four in the Beaufort and one northeast of Greenland. Some, straight transits between the Pacific and the Atlantic. The fast, covert, cheap way, so no surfacing." He closed Sloan's fingers over the pink packet.

Sloan said, "Cheap?"

"Panama charges us north of half a million for a US warship. So yeah, you actually save money going end around. What've you got in your hand?"

"Sweetener. The pink packet."

"And what have I got in mine?" Irons opened his hand to show him.

"Sugar. The white one. But you do surface sometimes, right?"

Irons nodded. "If there's time. Usually through the ice, in a polynya. At the pole, once in a while. One boat, we had to do a quarterly preventative maintenance that involved going to test depth before we surfaced at the pole. There was a line halfway down the passageway to get into the head."

Sloan wasn't sure he got the point of the joke. If it was a joke. "What are ice camps?"

"Mainly, for testing sonars." Irons lifted his head; seemed to be listening, though Sloan didn't hear anything out of the ordinary. The older man sighed and looked back down at the table. "What have you got in your hand, again?"

"The sweetener."

"And what have I got?"

"The other one. The sugar."

"Some of the gear you're using, we prototyped there. Sometimes we'd set up for a boat to shoot a torpedo, to see how the latest mods worked under the ice. But the real reason was politics." Irons turned his palm over. "Open your hand."

Sloan's packet was white. Irons opened his own hand. His packet was pink. Somehow they'd changed places. Tomlin frowned, trying to figure it out.

The rider went on. "We'd get a senator, some congressmen, a couple of submarine admirals. They leave DC at noon, grab a hop at Andrews, overnight to Anchorage, then up to Deadhorse. ASL stuffs them into parkas, hustles them onto a Twin Otter, and heads out over the pack. When they climb out their eyes get big. Standing over nine hundred fathoms of cold, dark water, and seeing nothing familiar. Just endless whiteness."

Irons took both packets and showed them to Sloan on his flat palm. Closed his fist, turned it over, blew on it, and opened his hand again. It was empty. "Then we'd head to the site, and they'd get to see a sub blast through the ice. Then they'd board the boat that the crew's been waxing and polishing for two days, and the admirals explain the importance of building more."

"A PR event," Sloan said.

"Sure. Dog and pony show. But I always thought they missed the best part. Early, before the sun's permanently over the horizon."

The older man reached into Sloan's collar and brought out both packets. He flattened them out on the table, erasing the creases, and slotted them back in the condiment rack. He squinted as if peering into that Arctic sun once more. "There's nothing like a sunrise, or a sunset, up here. The sun doesn't *rise* like we're used to. It sort of . . . rolls along the horizon. The air's crystal clear. You see every possible red, pink, purple, yellow . . . colors you've never seen before, all reflected off the stark-white ice. And you get sun dogs, halos, sun pillars . . . a sight you don't . . . ever really forget."

Irons fanned his hands out over the table, and a dozen packs of sugar and sweetener lay behind them. He swept his arms back, and they vanished. When he turned his palms up, they were both empty.

Late that evening the test channel activated. Numbers percolated in. Power, thruster, main propulsor. Prime was talking to them, but only on the maintenance channel, and only over short ranges.

Which wasn't going to work for the mission.

They stationed the Orca two miles off while he and Komanich and Dr. Liu sat at their stations, ran diagnostics, and compared notes. The conclusion: everything was operational except for the long-range comms. They ran the self-test on the comms three times, but it always came back as fully operational.

"Which it obviously isn't." Liu rubbed a wryly twisted mouth. "Jeez . . . I don't know what to tell you. Shondra, did it do this before? Off California?"

"It worked fine . . . down to eighteen thousand feet, thirty miles . . . no problem." Komanich raked hot-pink fingernails through tousled black hair. "There's backup cards for everything. No single point of failure that I know of. But obviously there is. I just haven't found it yet."

Fahrney let himself into their makeshift control room. "We don't have much more time." The skipper looked displeased. "We need to be on station tomorrow. They could delay the test, but we have to be in position in case they stick to the schedule. So how do we cope? Or can we?"

Sloan toggled back over the recorded data just downloaded, and rotated the screen so Fahrney could see. "Sir, we're not sure yet. But, something you need to know. Here. Just before long-range comms went down, so we didn't know until Prime reported in. The northernmost sensor picked up what it identified as a Sierra-class attack boat, tentative identification, *Pskov*."

Tang's CO looked thoughtful. "Titanium hull. Single reactor. Deep-diving capability. Great." He placed a finger on the spectrum output. "But not particularly silent."

"No, sir. Running all their AC, hotel auxiliaries . . . operating in a peace-time configuration."

"So. Here just to monitor the test?"

Komanich said, "And maybe, be in position to destroy their monster. If it goes rogue."

"Then there should be more than one boat. Spaced out along the test course." The skipper stood thinking for a minute longer. "We may need to head up to reception depth. They're supposed to be sending us tailored intel updates; let's see if there's anything new on Northern Fleet deployments."

They exchanged glances. Sloan shrugged internally. "If you think it's worth it, sir."

The CO looked at the overhead. "I just want to be sure who else is out here. We know there's a Laika behind us and a Sierra out in front. If there's more, we need to rethink the plan."

"The original plan's pretty much out the window already, Captain," Dr. Liu said. "If we can't get feedback from the Orca."

"We can launch your, uh, Zombie from closer to our own location, can't we?" the CO said. "Just use the short-range link?"

All three glanced at him, alerted. Komanich spoke first. "Sir, that places your boat and crew at risk. That was the whole idea of having an un-manned submersible deploy the BLY—it'd keep a manned unit clear of danger."

Fahrney nodded. "But if that's no longer possible?"

"Then we should think about scrubbing the mission," Liu said.

The IC set buzzed. Sloan grabbed it off the bulkhead. Held it to his ear, then handed it to Fahrney. "For you, Captain."

The CO's expression sobered as he listened. "Got it," he said, and sock-eted the handset. Fahrney smiled tightly. "Sonar reports extremely low-frequency signature from the west. Duration, thirty seconds. Probably pulsing the rocket engine, prior to the all-up firing. Did your intel mention anything about engine tests?"

"No, sir." Sloan shook his head. "We never got a schedule, other than the date of the run. But it makes sense they might fire up the steam generators as part of the, uh, preflight checks."

"It would have to be pretty damn loud to travel that far," the exec said. She leaned against the weight frame and crossed her arms, looking so comfortable it must have been a habitual pose. "But that would be consistent. With the gas generators running. A low-frequency return, channeled by bottom and ice."

Fahrney gnawed at his lip. "XO, you heard what we were discussing. Got an opinion?"

"Your decision, sir," she said. "The JAIC rep has a point, though. Moving us in, essentially taking the advanced position the Orca was intended to occupy, puts the boat and crew at risk. I could do an ORM calc in TRACs—"

Fahrney rolled his eyes. "We don't need to *document* it. And I hear what you're both saying."

He took a breath, looking away. "I get that this is an important mission. But if we're detected . . . up here, alone, under the ice, with the obvious intent to screw with their test . . . we could end up in a shooting situation. With the Sierra, the Laika, or whoever else they've deployed out here."

He looked to Sloan. "So my feeling is, it's not worth starting another war. Commander, Doctor, any pushback?"

Sloan had been thinking. And dreaded the conclusion he'd arrived at.

He understood where *Tang*'s skipper was coming from. Outside of wartime, the safety of the boat and crew had to come first.

On the other hand, if Fahrney backed off this mission, the Russians would have a tested, operational weapon, one they could use to threaten every coastal city in Europe and North America.

A smart torpedo, with incredible speed, unlimited range, and a nuclear warhead far larger than any heavyweight missile could throw . . . creating a tsunami three hundred feet high, wiping out millions of lives . . . and there would be no way to guard against it, save to mine and blockade either every port in the West, or the whole Siberian coast. Either way, the price would bankrupt NATO.

They had to stop it now. At any cost.

He coughed into a fist to clear his throat to make sure he could actually get the words out. Then muttered reluctantly, "There might be another option."

IV

MONSTERS
AND ICE

13

The Provisional Republic

Rayfield was shaking his head. Beside him, so was the General. "No. No," the president snapped. "In no possible way. That would be far too dangerous."

Nan fidgeted behind them, Tracy silent beside her, in an aging F-350 van that looked from the outside like any Farm Use Only clunker. Except that this one's interior, instead of spare tools and cans of cheap oil, was packed with radio equipment, weapon racks, ammunition packs. She rubbed her arms. They were still blistered and swollen, beneath the bandages, from the firebombing. Not only that, she was running a fever and felt like shit.

She said, "Mr. President, I understand. But I think it's worth the risk. These . . . people firebombed our clinic because they don't understand we're trying to help. If I can make that clear, the problem might go away."

"Believe me, it won't." The General huffed a sigh from the front seat. "We've tried to get through to these idiots before. If you think *we're* extremists, let me tell you—they're *way* out there. Believe me."

Nan sat back, struck once again by how loosely the supposed leaders of the Midwest held the reins. Or, rather, how little effect those reins must have. Really, the impression she'd gotten since coming here was that the rebellion was on its last legs. Ready to crumble once Homeland Security kicked the door in.

The attack on the clinic had wrecked her efforts. The word had gone out in southern Missouri; go for a shot, get shot. Which threatened her whole mission. "I'd like to try," she said again. "Just me. Alone. What've you got to lose?"

Rayfield grumbled, "I'd have to explain to your family what happened to you."

"How sad. I'll leave you a letter. Explaining that I insisted on going. How I understood you couldn't guarantee my safety but went, anyway."

The two men exchanged looks. Tracy, who'd sat silently in the back during the exchange, leaned in. "I'm going too," she said.

"No." Nan patted her leg. "No reason to risk two lives where one will do."

"You really want to?" Rayfield asked the freckled girl.

"Sure. I know folks over there. Know how to talk to 'em. And if they won't listen, well, I'll bring her back safe." Tracy patted her revolver. "I'll be her bodyguard."

The president and the General exchanged another glance. At last, with obvious misgivings, Rayfield shrugged. "You're walking into the lion's den, Dr. Lenson. I just hope you'll wind up like Daniel, and come out alive."

And not too much later, the two were headed north. Northwest, to be exact. The sluggish tan Missouri shone broad and placid to their left, a highway leading deep into the land. Tracy chattered gaily as she drove. Nan sat silently, trying to master her fear. And really, she didn't feel well. Coming down with something? This really wouldn't be the most convenient time.

The militias. Most were regular, largely rural folks who'd simply stepped up to replace an absent or actively oppressive government. Over the war years it had commandeered their sons, daughters, crops, livestock, savings, and weapons. Revolting at last, they'd raised the rattlesnake banner of the first Revolution and set about building their own polity. Fiercely individualistic, largely evangelical, they harked back to a rougher, earlier vision of America. One she didn't agree with, but you had to admire their passion. And their willingness to defend it.

At the edges, though, as in nearly every conflict, some groups had turned from resistance to outright crime. From guerrilla fighting to banditry and terror.

The Provisional Covenanters, or PCs, as they ironically called themselves, were notorious even in the Republic as outcasts and extremists. They only occasionally cooperated with the Rayfield government, and their lynchings, kidnappings, and assassinations made news all over the country. As had their firebombing of Nan's clinic.

Behind her, in the bed of the truck, packed in ice, were the vaccines and drugs.

She hoped she'd get a chance to put them to work.

* * *

They met up with the PCs at a deserted Walmart outside St. Joseph. Four husky men in black masks and combat vests held up rifles and shotguns to stop them. As soon as Tracy parked, they were pulled out roughly and patted down. One man snatched the keys from Tracy's hands, then the revolver from her holster.

"Hey. Gimme that back! My dad gave me that .44."

"Nice gun. We'll hold on to it for you, girlie darlin'."

"Fuck you. I got my rights—"

"Only if we say so, bitch." Her protests were stifled by a cloth stuffed into her mouth.

They searched Nan too, but didn't gag her. She hadn't brought a phone, knowing what would happen to it. Her hands, like Tracy's, were twisted behind her and bound with a zip tie. Heavy burlap hoods were pulled over their heads. Then they were bundled back into the truck, with one of the men driving.

"What's that in the back?" the guy beside her asked, voice muffled by his mask and Nan's own hood.

"Vaccines and drugs. For your sick. In ice. They should be kept cold."

"Why d'you think we want your medicine?"

"I just told you." She hesitated. "You do have sick, don't you?"

No answer. He drove fast, judging by the growl of the engine. Then she was jostled from side to side as they pulled off into a dirt road.

Nan concentrated on trying to breathe. On not passing out, from the CO_2 buildup under the hood. Along with her head, the sack contained some gritty-feeling dust—sand, or grain residue. Eventually she found that sucking a fold of the burlap into her mouth, breathing in through that, and out through her nose, gave her enough air to survive. Along with a grit-coated tongue.

Eventually, after perhaps an hour, the truck screeched to a halt. The men pulled them out and led them stumbling across rutted ground and crackling, ankle-turning gravel into some huge echoing space.

She was plunked into a seat. Her pinioned hands were forced behind her, over the back of the chair, to lock her into it. Then the hood was yanked off, so roughly the saliva-soaked sackcloth nearly took her incisors with it.

She blinked up into a beam of sunlight. It fell through a ragged gap in a faraway roof, so dazzling that aside from the beam, and the red-painted concrete floor, everything else looked black. The air smelled rank, like a slaughterhouse. Oh, God, was she in a slaughterhouse? Her head swam. Was it fever, fear, the lack of air under the hood? Or was she ill? That would be hilarious. If she came here to treat people and ended up infecting them.

"Let's start with who you are," a gruff male voice said from the darkness.

She coughed grit from her throat. "I'm . . . Nan Lenson. I work for the Centers for Disease Control."

"From Washington?"

"As I said, the CDC. A field team, to help with your epidemics." She twisted her head, but still could make out nothing. "Where's Tracy? The woman who was with me?"

"We're talking to her too. Compare stories. Who do you report to?"

"I work for Dallas Rayfield—"

"I mean, your masters in Washington. Rayfield's a moron puppet. We're not that naive. We know what you're here for."

She shook her head. "I'm not a spy, if that's what you're thinking. I came to warn you about serious diseases. Brought medicine to help you fight them off."

She told him what the team had discovered: that the diarrhea afflicting the Midwest wasn't just a stomach upset. That typhoid was spreading, and cholera wouldn't be far behind. "Please listen. You need to boil your drinking water. Stop attacking hospitals and water-treatment plants. Help us set up clinics." She almost added, *And stop fucking firebombing them*, but didn't. Now wasn't the time.

"Clinics. For vaccination?" another voice said.

"I brought vaccines. Yes."

"You're not poisoning our kids." A level, contemptuous, tobacco-raw woman's voice. "You can forget that shit."

"They're already being poisoned." Nan twisted toward that acid tone. "They're already getting diarrhea, right? Historically, cholera kills fifty percent of the kids it infects. Think about that. *Fifty percent.*

"I brought a single-dose, multiple-efficacy enteric vaccine. It'll protect against rotavirus, shigella, enterotoxigenic *Escherichia coli*, *E. coli*, typhoid, and cholera." She let her words echo down from the roof, then added, "It's not a shot, if that's what you're afraid of. It's an oral vaccine. One dose, by mouth."

"We're not *afraid*. The Lord takes care of us. And our kids are our own business." The woman's voice again, hard as iron. "Ours. Not yours. That's what freedom means."

"I agree. Freedom means making your own choices," Nan said, doing her best to keep her voice level. "But why not make the choice that protects your kids?"

"We got no idea what's in this government shit," the male voice said. "We don't know what the fuck it's made out of. Dead babies? Toxic chemicals? And we don't know what happens ten years from now, if we take it. We won't be guinea pigs for some fucking scientists who don't give a shit about us."

"Yeah, we *do* know. I'm one of those 'fucking scientists.' Ten years from now, they'll be alive instead of dead." Nan tried to keep the frustration from her tone, but it was hard. Her shoulders ached. So did her wrists, still bound behind her. Also, she really had to pee. "Give me some, why don't you. I'll take it right now, if you want to watch."

A subdued discussion, though loud enough that she caught the doubtful tones. The woman seemed to be the hard-liner. She shouted, "No! We keep doing this, a couple of generations, nobody'll be able to stay alive outside an ICU."

A male baritone: "We keep saying it's up to us. To each of us. But what if some of us want to try it?"

"Are you fucking *kidding* me?" The woman again. "Nobody *wants* to have their kids infected. We got their eyes open, a little, now. You want to close them again? Anyway, we don't have time. We have to be there tonight."

"Tracy, you here?" Nan muttered into the dark. "Trace?"

"Your friend's safe," someone said. "She seems to be a good kid. Worry about yourself, not her."

Nan raised her voice. "Hey. *Hey!* Can I say something?"

Silence from the dark.

She hurled her words into it. "You want to stay free? You want to not be replaced? Then help your kids survive. At least, let me offer it. If you really value individual freedom, you have to let people choose."

Another discussion, lower-voiced now, so she couldn't overhear.

Finally bootsteps paced toward her. A silhouette loomed in the beam of light.

She was much taller than Nan, lean to the point of bony. Pale, gaunt, high-cheekboned, crop-haired. Somehow . . . spectral. A black automatic was holstered on her hip. She stared down for a few seconds. Propped her palm on the butt of the pistol and said, voice drenched with disdain, "I know more than you think. *Doctor.* Your 'lifesaving vaccines' are *made* out of viruses. Bacteria. Mercury, and formaldehyde, and devil only knows what other poison. And you want to inject them into our kids. You want to *kill* our kids!"

Nan flexed her wrists behind her. They were going numb. "Why would I possibly want to do that?"

"Why don't you make a guess?" The woman tilted her head in mock confusion, then suddenly reached down and pulled at Nan's still-short hair. "What *are* you, anyway? A slant? A Jap? I could come up with five reasons right now you'd want to wipe us out."

"Never mind what I am! These are all dead-virus formulations. Or RNA vaccines. Tiny amounts to stimulate the immune response. There's no— well, nearly zero possibility they could—"

"Save your pharma gibberish," the woman interrupted. "We're not the gullible idiots you people think we are."

Nan sagged in her chair, searching for words. But she'd already tried all the angles she could think of. Mustered, finally, a weak-sounding, "You're making the wrong decision. And it's going to have horrible consequences."

"We don't give a damn what you think! You've poisoned our minds and bodies long enough. Sucked children's blood to keep Jews alive. It's time for this craziness to give way to some good old common sense." The woman glanced over one shoulder. "We're burning the shit you brought with you. And you—you're ours now. You'll work for us. Or if you turn into a problem, we take you out back and solve you. Understand?"

Nan flexed her prickling hands, but the thin nylon was too strong even to hope to break. She muttered, "How about Tracy?"

"We're thinking about her." The woman nudged Nan's shoe with a hiking boot. Puzzlement crept into her tone. "She says you were both at Puxico. For the battle. That right?"

"I was there. Yeah."

"What were *you* doing there?"

"I was a medic."

"Uh-huh. Save anybody?"

"I helped the wounded. But they rolled over us."

The woman glanced over her shoulder again. "We have a job for you girls. But unlike your fucking government, we believe in giving people choices. Yeah?"

"Sure. So what's the choice?"

"You can do what we say, or we solve you both right now."

And reluctantly, knowing it was the only alternative, Nan said, "Fine. What do you want us to do?"

It felt too much like Puxico, actually. That long afternoon before the massacre. The column of trucks and technicals was headed for battle once more, and to judge by the location of the sun, rolling southeast. Where, as she recalled from Rayfield's wall map, the Republic's forces were weak and thinly spread.

The column jolted down wooded roads, angling off down dirt tracks when fields opened ahead. To avoid air attack and the hunting drones, she guessed. Pickups bounced along with guns welded to makeshift mounts. Vans and trucks were filled with men and teenage boys and a few women, all heavily armed. Some of the weapons were homemade, of flash-scorched weldments or cast and drilled plastic, but they all looked deadly, and almost every fighter was draped with bandoliers of ammunition.

She and Tracy were huddled in the bed of one of the technicals, crouched beneath the gun mount, slammed around with every rut and rock. Unhooded, but their hands were still tied. They'd never given back her coat, so Nan shivered in the cold, bright wind.

Tracy lay curled beside her, looking subdued. Nan's escort hadn't gotten her revolver back either. Yeti backpacks stuffed with torn-bedsheet bandages and rubbing alcohol rode between them. The Provisionals fought on a shoestring. They were ragged and hungry, but still, grimly determined.

Probably, Nan thought, a lot like the rebels of 1776. And they were going to die of the same diseases, though now needlessly.

Beside her Tracy sighed, peering up at the sky. Blue, clear, it was only visible in flashes through the cathedral arch of forest. Smoke and dust rose as the vehicles rocked through a rutted gully.

"This is just like Puxico," Umbaugh muttered.

Nan nodded. "Same as I was thinking."

"But who are these guys fighting? The Republic, or the Federals?"

Mile after mile slipped past: forest, gravel, dirt road, forest. Nan's stomach growled. She muttered, "Remember that sausage they gave us last time?"

"The deer sausage? Sure's hell wish we had some now. Are you . . . are you feeling any better?"

"Headache," Nan muttered. "Nauseated."

The younger woman's hand on her forehead. "Jeez. You're burning up."

"No surprise. I feel like crap."

"That's my diagnosis too." Tracy banged on the cab. Yelled, "Hey. Guys! She's sick. Cut our hands loose, okay? Where we gonna run to?"

One of the gunners looked down. "Fuck you, antiwa bitch."

Tracy bristled. "You *gotta* be kidding! I'm a soldier of the Republic."

"You're a fucking compromiser. Selling us out to the Blackies." The gunners spat over the side of the truck, then returned to scanning the sky.

"Don't bother," Nan muttered, and her escort subsided.

An hour later they left an overgrown road, bumped and lurched along the edge of a field, and halted. Backed up, reversing into the cover of the trees. The engine died.

"Set up anywhere you want," the driver told them. "You girls know what to do, right?"

"First aid is all we can do with this shit," Tracy said. "I don't even have a hemostat. But hey, look, if we're actually gonna help you when you get shot, you got to cut us loose."

A knife snapped through plastic. Nan massaged her wrists. They'd gone dead hours before. She hoped there wasn't permanent damage.

But maybe it wouldn't matter, considering how little time she might have left.

They squatted under a bush as evening drew on. Waiting, though no one had told them for what. There was no sign of food or even water. Along the tree line, just like at Puxico, the militia was digging in. Hacking at roots, tossing aside chunks of turf, trying to scrape fighting holes into the leaf-matted forest floor with shovels, entrenching tools, machetes.

Nan shuddered at déjà vu. Had they really learned nothing? The tanks and robots of Homeland Security would flatten these scraggly fighters. Those who remained after the explosions of scything missiles and the portable artillery that deployed with the Black Battalions. Already, cupping one ear, she caught the buzzing whine of drones above. Pinpointing their line. Dispatching targeting coordinates. With nothing but small arms and a couple of machine guns, these idiots had no chance.

A pudgy white man came limping down the line in a faded green hoodie with a Remington logo. He stopped at each fighting hole to chat. At last he got to where she and Tracy lay. "You kids not digging?" He looked quizzical. "And where's your—"

"We're medics," Tracy snapped.

"Well, you should still be armed," the guy said. "Everyone's a fighter."

"If we're not carrying, they won't shoot us when we're captured." Umbaugh rolled her eyes. "Hey, we gonna get anything to eat?"

"Actually, they'll probably shoot us, anyway, Trace," Nan said. She asked the man, who was shaking his head, still staring from one of them to the other, "Who are we fighting, again?"

"The Homelanders, of course. The Blackies. Who else?"

She sighed. These people were all going to die. And this time, most likely, she and Tracy with them.

The chunky man regarded them for another second, then shook his head and limped on.

The sky darkened, and still they waited. Some of the militia broke out food they'd brought. Tracy walked the line, ostensibly to check everyone's blood type, but actually trolling for something to eat. No one offered any.

"They've got barely enough for themselves," she muttered, squatting again with Nan in the darkening shade of the trees. "Jeez, I thought us Republic folks were on short rations. These guys are straight-up starving."

Nan had her back propped against the bole of a tree, trying to ignore her own agonizing combination of hunger, nausea, and cramps. Trying to ignore her racing pulse, and an even more ominous crackle of distant gunfire.

Gradually the crackle drew closer. Snorting four-wheelers popped wheelies past them, scooting up the slope toward the front line. The fat man yelled, "Hold fire!" and the ATVs, with armed young men and women on them, passed through the line, tires spitting pine needles and dirt, trailing blue smoke and the stench of burning oil.

By now it was nearly dark. Nan shivered, remembering Puxico again in a feverish flashback so vivid it seemed to have just happened. How the robots had stalked between the trees, footsteps crunching under their weight, hunting humans . . . the tanks roaring, headlights blazing, heedless of being targeted . . . suddenly her guts churned, a deep twisting pain. Just great . . .

"Need to take a shit," she grunted, and stumbled off a few yards to squat by one of the ATVs. Eyeing it for ignition keys . . . bad idea. They'd pursue, shoot her off it. Or bring her back and shoot her here as a deserter. To discourage anyone else from skedaddling.

Still, if they could get to a vehicle once the battle started, she and Tracy might be able to escape.

She closed her eyes and tried not to groan. Shit, shit, *shit* . . . it *hurt*. Like a bayonet twisting in her belly. She could visualize it all too clearly. Shigella or entamoeba, most likely. Contracted through contaminated water, or passed by touch from someone infected. The bacteria burrowing through the mucosal lining of her intestines. Releasing exotoxins that ruptured blood vessels, lysed the intestinal cells, and triggered massive inflammation as the weakened body tried to fight off infection.

She moaned and rocked as a cramp spasmed, doubling her over. Sweat dripped off her forehead, though the air was growing chillier as the darkness deepened.

When it was over, for the moment, she seized a handful of leaves, breathing hard. Pulled her pants up. Staggered back to wait some more, head swimming with vertigo.

Why did it always seem as if you had to wait forever just to fucking die?

Finally it came. What she'd been expecting.

The snarl of heavy engines, pushing tons of steel.

The stutter of machine guns, and the sporadic snapping of the rebels firing back. The rushing crash of falling trees.

And waves of sudden, debilitating terror, an anxiety and tremor in her chest that made her want to scream and run. Tracy told her to try to ignore it. It was artificial fear, a below-hearing-threshold subsonic the Blackies used to intimidate their victims.

Motion, at the far end of the winter-stripped field downhill. And finally the dreaded shapes appeared, rolling forward, up the slope. Slowly. As if they had all the time in the world.

Between the tanks lurched the weirdly wedge-headed figures of the biped battle robots. The CHADs. Fielded against China during the war, now deployed against the rebels. Cradling rifles, they pitched forward step by lock-kneed step, keeping pace with the larger machines. The whir of drones overhead rose to a banshee whine. Bursts of small-caliber fire stitched the treetops, shredding leaves into a green snow. The hawklike machines were searching for snipers, taking them out one by one.

Just like at Puxico.

Tracy stood, slinging the med pack. "Get ready, girl. We're gonna be real busy, real soon. Where you wanna triage?"

Nan hoisted herself to her feet, feeling deeply sick, terribly afraid, and unutterably weary. Her knees shook, and it probably wasn't entirely from the infrasound. Really, why had she come? Thrust herself back into a civil war, when she belonged in the lab. Pushing her research on phosphorylation patterns. Refining LJL 4789 into a broad-spectrum antiviral for Marburg, L1N1, bird flu, coronaviruses, Issyk-Kul—whatever would next menace this overcrowded, overheating world. Surely she needed to be fighting *that* battle. Not arguing with idiots who fought to let their kids die of historical diseases.

Instead of huddling here, panting from the gut-churning agony that would only grow worse as the infection dug in. Yeah, you could die from shigella, especially if it was *S. dysenteriae*.

But probably she wouldn't need to worry about that. At least, not for long.

The heavyset man called, "Commence fire," and a volley boomed and cracked out from the insurrectionist line. Sparks flew from the advancing tanks. Rebel bullets glanced off the advancing robots, but none fell or even slowed. A second volley had as little effect.

Another order rolled along the line. To her astonishment, the rebels stood, gathering ammo and slinging weapons. They came trotting back through the woods, glancing over their shoulders, stopping to fire now and then, but definitely retreating.

The leader spotted the medics and waved them along. "Fall back!" he yelled. "Fall back, you two! Stay with us!"

"What the fuck?" Tracy yelled. "You giving up?"

"Shut up and withdraw. Bring your gear, damn it."

The women exchanged raised eyebrows, then bent for their backpacks. Nan groaned again as a fresh paroxysm twisted in her bowels.

"Uh, look, we gotta jet," Tracy muttered, patting her shoulder. "I don't know what's going on here, but we can't stick around."

Nan was trying to stand upright, peering fearfully back down over the field at the advancing monsters, when another growl of engines jerked her head around. To a crashing and crackling of trees and brush, a flash of green-painted metal deep in the woods.

A tremendous explosion blotted out one of the advancing tanks. A split second later the machine vaulted clear of the heavy smoke, flipped in midair, and crashed to the ground atop two of the striding robots. Acrid smoke drifted along the line, adding to the dust and exhaust the tanks were churning up.

Then, as if she'd suddenly landed in a Godzilla movie, the trees parted, off to the right, and something unimaginably huge crashed out of the woods. For a moment her astonished gaze couldn't take it in.

The monster was a medium John Deere green, with four titanic wheels abreast behind a sloping steel-plate glacis that reached down nearly to the stubbled field over which it rocked. Diesel exhaust blasted out of its stack. Two even bigger tires at the rear shouldered it forward, crushing the dry cornstalks and clods beneath the grinding black rubber.

The government's lead tanks hesitated, as if taking it in. After astonished seconds they pulled left, apparently trying to flank it. Turreted cannon slewed. But before they could fire, the gigantic machine was on them.

It hooked that sloping armored beak beneath the first tank it reached. Like a bull goring up into the belly of a toreador's horse, it bellowed, digging in all six drive wheels. The assaulted tank tilted up, teetered, and crashed over onto its side. Its tracks spun, and the gun barrel pointed uselessly up at the winter sky.

From the other side, out of the woods lining that edge of the field, burst two more green behemoths. They bulldozed into the other tanks from behind, smashing them aside and capsizing two more. A third tank sprinted ahead, racing to escape, but it vanished as the earth gave way beneath it, plunging it into an enormous pit.

Nan gasped, hand to mouth. The rebels had staged an ambush. A perfectly prepared, carefully planned bushwhacking, set up long in advance by telegraphing a faked weakness exactly where the insurgents wanted the battalions to attack.

With a strange lurching-up motion, a line of figures sprang from the very earth. They quivered in place as they shook off the dust and cornstalks that had covered them. In the near dark they looked human. Yet she could see they weren't. They were . . . *scarecrows.* Crude wood-framed mannequins, festooned with outworn jeans and jackets.

Yet the hatchet heads of the biped CHADs instantly swung toward them. The automatons wheeled, formed into line, and advanced on them, firing on full automatic. The bursts tore at the dummies, blasting chaff and splinters into the air.

As the infantry robots neared their targets, though, yet another huge vehicle crashed out from the pines. It rolled down the line, crunched over the scarecrows, and ground on, directly toward the advancing robots. The CHADs froze in digitized confusion, facing a threat they'd never been programmed for.

An instant later a mechanical maw scooped them up. A tremendous din, more snorting of diesels, and one by one they popped out the rear of the repurposed baling machine, each robot fighter disarmed, trussed, and helpless in a tight cocoon of stout steel wire.

From the woods rose rebel yells, cheers, and profane shouts. The Provisionals came charging back in a surging wave. They leaped over their fighting holes, parted left and right to skirt the dueling machines, and charged downhill, flourishing bayoneted rifles, spears, and hunting knives.

Nan found herself running after Tracy, who was sprinting all out, screaming, the sack of dressings bouncing on one shoulder. They scrambled over the brown dirt furrowed and herringboned by tracks and tires, through a fog of dust and exhaust and smoke that smelled like fertilizer and oil and burned powder. Past the recumbent robots, who lay bound and motionless, emitting helpless-sounding chirps. She vaulted one that was recounting its power supply level in an emotionless monotone.

As they left the field and crossed a fringe of scrub woods into another clearing beyond, the advancing insurgents came upon black-uniformed troops: those who'd controlled and directed the tanks, the drones, the robots. The black-clad men and women started up from notebook computers, reaching for holstered pistols, but were shot or hacked down by the howling insurgents. The rebels stormed through the encampment, jerking open the doors of trailers, hauling out operators, gunning down any who tried to resist or flee. An officer, hands up, tried to surrender, but was macheted savagely by three young women, who immediately fell to searching his pockets for food. A gray-haired, dignified-looking woman in a black and silver uniform stood with arms folded, watching the carnage, until a sixtyish rebel in a stained green work shirt leveled an automatic and blew her brains out.

Nan halted above a trooper who lay gasping next to one of the controller trailers. Her uniform was sodden with red, pumping from a shotgun wound in her chest. Their gazes locked. "Help," she forced out, then coughed. Blood gurgled in her throat.

Nan knelt, horrified. She had nothing that could help this woman. But still she rooted in her pack, and came up with a knife. She unbuttoned the tunic, sliced away the bra, and was attempting a dressing when Tracy placed a hand on her shoulder.

"You can't fix her," she said. "Cover your ears."

She aimed a pistol, and fired. Jerked Nan to her feet, and shoved her toward where several wounded rebels sat or lay. "We take care of our own. We don't waste supplies on Blackie assholes."

"But they're . . . Americans."

"They're the fucking enemy! They execute their prisoners. Remember?" Tracy pushed the pistol into her hand. "To use on any others you come across. Get it?"

Nan threw the weapon into a bush as soon as the medic's back was turned. Horrified. Yeah, the DHS had shot captives after Puxico. Had executed anyone with gunshot residue on their hands. But more dreadfulness would only deepen the rift between the sides. Quantum-leap an already-bloody civil war to a new level of outrage. Make peace even less possible.

She was trotting toward the rebel wounded, hoping to at least help *someone*, when a spasm gripped her again. Like someone in her chest had dropped a bowling ball against her anal sphincter. The pain was so intense she couldn't breathe. She stopped dead, moaning, bracing a hand to a tree.

"Y'okay?" Tracy called.

"No," she muttered. Then gagged, doubled over, and ran awkwardly, spraddle-legged, for the bushes.

In the dark, alone, she crouched, gasping, teeth clenched. Thighs shaking uncontrollably as her insides liquefied and spewed out, spraying blood and shit over the grass.

Sickened, nearly to death.

14

Joint Base Elmendorf-Richardson, Alaska

Another hospital room, another wearying day spent either lying in bed watching TV or being shuttled from department to department for tests. Dan got an MRI for his back and neck. He had a muscle tear from the crash. The hospital was locked down for the Flower Flu, like most military installations, but the staff wore the blue circular pins that indicated they'd had their inoculations. They'd given him a shot at check-in, despite his protest he'd already gotten two different vaccines, the DHS-approved one and the DoD version.

"They're not in your medical record," his doctor had remarked, studying her tablet.

"I got them in DC. When I reported back in from WestPac."

"Give him the vaccine," she'd said to the nurse, then wheeled and marched out.

He'd seen her twice more, and each time she'd ordered more tests. He was beginning to suspect his rank was the explanation. No way was Big Navy Med letting an admiral slip through their fingers without a thorough going-over.

And after the ordeal on the North Slope, he had to admit, he appreciated the rest.

He'd caught up on sleep, but now and then woke with nightmares. The crash. The flames. Jagged bone sticking from a broken neck. The bitterly cold, life-sucking wind. The utter darkness. And finally, worst of all, the bears.

He'd jerked himself awake with a warning shout, panting, thrashing in the bed. Staring around at the room, the dim glows of the night-lights. Heart thudding so hard it hurt.

The second day there, he'd insisted on seeing Dessa Quvianuk. Hobbling down the hall, favoring his bandaged feet, he'd found her propped up in bed, looking as bushed as he felt. "Major," he'd opened.

She slow-blinked. "Admiral."

"How're you doing?"

For answer she'd glanced down at her legs, shrouded under white sheets. Bent forward from her pillow, but then sank back. "They had to operate. But I can feel my toes now. They say I should regain nearly full function."

"Take it easy, Dessa. Please!"

She'd obeyed, relaxing gingerly back into her pillows. "And you, Admiral? I see you're up and about."

"Muscle tear, second-degree frostbite, exhaustion." He held out his fingers, which were blistered at the tips, the skin tinged blue. "Hurts like hell."

"Second degree, you will get feeling back. Did they cut anything off?"

"Not yet. Jury's still out on my toes, though. You?"

"Rangers don't frostbite."

He grinned. "Heard and understood. I'll come by again tomorrow, okay?"

"How is Sarabeth? Sir."

"She's in the room next to mine. About the same as me, or maybe a little better."

The Ranger had nodded, closing her eyes, looking satisfied. As if she could rest assured she'd brought her charges through.

This morning, flexing his fingers, he felt less pain. They were still bruised, as if crushed by something hard, but definitely recovering.

Blanco had checked in with her exec, back at the Coast Guard base. The team's mission was still on. Apparently the evaluations they'd sent back so far hadn't met the criteria. Higher wanted them to head east, once they recovered, to check out two locations in northern Canada. Apparently someone was rethinking the possibility of a combined base.

He hoped it wouldn't involve any more trips in small planes.

Lunchtime. He was eating hospital food off a tray, watching the Patriot Channel. A segment about a suit against the Naval Academy by a civilian faculty member. Another segment: a new triumph over the anarchist, bandit Covenant rebels in the Midwest. Then a commercial, during which he thought seriously about dessert. He'd burned up a lot of calories out there in the snow.

He'd about decided on the tapioca pudding when his phone chimed. Blair? Nan? He hadn't heard from his daughter for quite a while. In fact, since she'd left. He hobbled over to pick it up. "Lenson."

"Admiral? This is the CNO's office. Can you stand by for Admiral Hlavna?"

He cleared his throat. Shaynelle Hlavna. Submariner, veteran of four wartime combat patrols. Silver Star, Navy Cross, then commander, Pacific Submarine Forces. A deep selection for chief of naval operations, and the first female in that billet. "Uh . . . sure. Holding."

She came on some minutes later, so long a wait he'd wondered if a disconnect had occurred. *"Admiral Lenson? I've been following your adventures."*

Adventures? "Uh, yes, ma'am."

"Can you turn down that television? Or whatever it is? I'm having difficulty hearing you."

He snapped it off. *"Better?"*

"Yes . . . Glad you survived the crash. I understand your pilot didn't."

"No, ma'am."

"I'm sorry to hear that. But, to business. One of my staffers talked to the medical people out there. They seemed to think you're not ready to return to duty yet. Your take?"

He glanced guiltily out into the passageway, and lowered his voice. "Uh, there's apparently some soft tissue damage. But I'm mobile. Admiral. They want more tests, but—"

"I take it you've seen the Examiner *article? And the video coverage?"*

What article? What had he missed during the crash, the days isolated here? With a snag of apprehension, he remembered Dr. Mokhtar Corris, and the attorney's warning. *The Hague moves very deliberately. But once you are indicted, the trial date set, suddenly it will seem all too fast.* "Uh, no, ma'am. But if it's about this German tanker thing, this ICC investigation . . . I was assured no US citizen would be extradited. That I think was the administration position—"

"It's not about that. Hold on—I'm going to send you a link. Call me back when you've seen it."

He fumbled with the phone—his fingers still clumsy—and at last the clip came up.

Of a familiar face. Older than he remembered her, but undoubtedly the same woman. The chyron identified her as chair of the Subcommittee on the Conduct of the War.

Sandy Treherne, née Cottrell. His old classmate in Professor Szerenci's Defense Analysis course. Szerenci was the national security advisor now, though rumor had it his days were numbered now the war was over. And Treherne had taken a Senate seat previously held by her aged husband.

She held a grudge against Dan dating too far back to even bear thinking out. The sort of blind resentment that hardened over the years into an idée fixe.

Though maybe using her as bait in a personal sting operation against a Washington drug gang hadn't been his best-ever judgment call.

"The Hainan operation was a bloodbath," Treherne was saying in the clip. *"Casualties were higher than any other operation of the war. Three times higher than expected in killed, wounded, ship, and aircraft losses. A failure of intelligence. A failure of planning. But most of all, and most tragically for the heroic sailors and marines of the landing forces, a failure that can be laid squarely at the feet of the bullheaded, notoriously incompetent task force commander, one Admiral Daniel V. Lenson. Placed in charge after numerous previous debacles by the equally bungling commander in the Pacific, Justin Yangerhans. This subcommittee will investigate how these two incompetents became responsible for thousands of Allied dead, and nearly lost us the war."*

He watched for several more seconds. But that initial statement had pretty much summed up what was going on.

When he called the CNO back, he got put on hold again. He sat on the side of the bed, fuming. Finally, she came on. *"Hlavna here."*

"Lenson, returning your call."

"Have you viewed it?"

"I have."

"You're being attacked in the press and online. A long segment on Patriot News. Some members of Congress are demanding your court-martial."

He nodded to himself. "This is about Operation Rupture Plus."

"Yes, your decisions during the Hainan landings. There's no doubt your losses were very high. So high we had to restrict reporting of the exact casualty figures. Those are only now becoming publicly available."

"Yes, ma'am. We thought the Chinese were at the end of their rope. Resistance was a lot tougher than we expected."

"Yet you persisted in the attack. Against the advice of your tactical AI and your subordinate commanders. Both of whom advised you to break off."

WTF, over? Niles had praised him. Said his pressing ahead had saved the landing from becoming a rout. But Hlavna's tone was flat, giving him no clues as to what she herself thought.

Dan cleared his throat, more irritated than apprehensive. What could Treherne do to him that would compare to the grisly ambitions of two enraged Arctic bears? And he'd made the right decision off Hainan. He was certain of that. "Yes, ma'am. I pressed ahead. We prepared for that operation for months. Postponed it twice. Probably why they were so ready for us . . . but we'd have suffered even worse losses trying to pull troops back off the beach under fire. And we'd've had to do it all over again, later, somewhere else, to finish the war." He took a breath. "If you need my resignation, it's on the table. Ma'am."

A sharper tone. *"If I want it, don't worry, I'll ask! Congress doesn't tell the Navy who resigns. That's my purview. Or that of the SecNav. Not some publicity-hunting subcommittee chair."*

"No, ma'am."

Silence. Then, *"Your wife is Blair Titus, correct?"*

Maybe he was thinking a little slowly, but now he saw where this was going. "Uh, correct."

"And she works on Yangerhans's campaign? Getting him ready for the primaries."

"Also correct."

Hlavna didn't draw any conclusions aloud, and neither would he have, given that they were on a phone. Niles had said DoD kept its communications secure, but could he trust that DHS wasn't recording them? The current CNO apparently didn't. She only said, after a moment, *"I understand you were offered medical retirement not long ago. Have you reconsidered that?"*

Should he bring up his bargain with Niles? That after this assignment, he'd get his choice for a twilight tour? No, he'd let the former CNO manage that. He only said, "I feel ready to resume my duties, Admiral."

"Okay, then . . . we'll just wait and see where this subcommittee goes. Now, on your current tasking. None of the locations you've scouted thus

far looks suitable for development. The hydrography sucks. Prudhoe Bay came closest, but we're getting pushback from DoE and commercial interests on locating any military activities there.

"The next possibility is to explore a combined base. Maybe in Norway; the Norwegians had a sub base at Olavsvern, near Tromsø, during the Cold War. Or on Canadian soil, which would make more sense logistically. Do you feel up to looking into that? The Canadian location, I mean?"

"Uh, yes, ma'am. Actually, we got a feeler to that effect through Coast Guard channels. That we might be headed east to check out the possibilities there."

"Right. Your orders are on their way. Liaise with the Canadian authorities. You already have one Canadian member with your team, correct?"

"Major Quvianuk. But she's—"

"And one more thing. Hold." A faint tone on the line; muffled speech in the background.

Hlavna again. *"We're getting indications another project may be in trouble. Separate from yours, and emergent priority. I may need to take advantage of having you up there. Pre-position you to assist, should it become necessary. It's just backstop planning for now, but start thinking about what you'd need to carry out a rescue operation in the Canadian Arctic. More specifics via message."*

He lifted his head, sensing a new tension in her tone. "Yes, ma'am. A rescue mission. At sea? On land?"

"Specifics in the message. As I said. But at sea, yes."

A pause. Then, *"As to the subcommittee, media may call you for a statement. I advise not making any. In fact, consider that an order. If there's going to be a blowup, we want the Navy protected. Not invite some huge public battle royale. Your best friend is 'No comment.' Are we on the same page?"*

"Yes, ma'am. No interviews, no statements, no appearances."

Hlavna said, *"Being off the grid in the Canadian Arctic should help with that. I think that's everything. Goodbye, and again, I'm glad you came through the crash in reasonably good shape."*

He opened his mouth to say, "Thank you, ma'am," but she'd already hung up.

He juggled the phone, looking out the window at the snow-covered hillside. Considering all he'd just heard. He wouldn't have underestimated

Treherne, the way Hlavna seemed to be doing. She had a habit of getting her way. Just as Congress could bestow stars, Congress could snatch them away.

Maybe he wouldn't have that twilight tour, after all.

But something else seemed to be going on too. He doubted DoD was serious about a combined base with the Canadians. The countries were formal allies, true. But they had enough differences, especially over transit rights and other Arctic questions, that he honestly couldn't see the potential for the intimate cooperation a shared base required.

Therefore, he was being sent east for another reason. Most likely, connected to the "other operation" Hlavna had mentioned. The message the CNO was sending might give him more details.

But . . . a rescue operation. At sea. From northern Canada. Okay, that might be enough to start with.

He reached for the freshly laundered, fresh-smelling bathrobe the hospital had issued him, and padded down the hall toward Sarabeth Blanco's room.

15

Arlington, Virginia

B lair woke to a disquieting cry, one she hadn't heard for a while. A drawn-out, plaintive meow. Not quite a howl but a firm summons from sleep.

"No," she moaned. "Not now. *Please.*"

When she got up, feeling with her toes for slippers, the house smelled musty. Even the bed felt strange. She hadn't been home for weeks. She groped for her robe and pulled it on.

Jimbo, her black-and-white tuxedo cat, mewed again. That same prolonged, whining cry. He was calling her. But with a different intonation from his usual reminder it was breakfast time.

When she went into the hallway she at first didn't recognize what lay between his paws on the figured Turkish runner. Small, gray, and so motionless she took it at first for one of the dead leaves he liked to carry in and bat about. But then it struggled, and the cat placed its paw on it, looking up. As if to say, *Acknowledge the gift I have brought you.*

"Oh, Jimbo. You didn't," she whispered. Sure, he was a cat, but he didn't usually go predator like this. Didn't she feed him wet food three times a day, and treats whenever he begged?

He left his victim to twine himself around her calves, purring. She scooped him up. Buried her face in his fur. He'd gained pudge, the way he always did when she left him with the house sitter. But he felt so soft and warm, and he'd so obviously missed her . . . those who said cats couldn't love you were idiots.

Still, they did have their unpleasant little habits.

Which left the mouse to deal with. As soon as he'd released it, it had scurried into a corner. It huddled there, motionless. Imprisoning the cat in the bedroom, she fetched a towel from the bathroom and bent over the rodent, intending to scoop it up and release it in the backyard.

But the thing was too fast. Even as the cloth descended, it streaked out from under in a gray flash. She pursued it down the hall, cursing. If it was wounded, she didn't want it to die in some crevice, stinking to high heaven. But again, it evaded her lunge.

A third attempt got the cloth around its back half, and she grasped it—*Gently now, Blair*—and lifted. But the little animal squirmed so violently her grip loosened. The next moment, she gasped as tiny teeth pricked her fingers.

"You little bastard," she hissed. "I'm trying to *save* you!" Carrying it to the back door, she pitched mouse and towel together out into the yard.

In the bathroom, she inspected her finger. Who knew mice could bite? Its teeth had been too small to penetrate the skin, but she rinsed her hands with peroxide, anyway, then washed them. Shuddering at the memory of those tiny onyx beads staring up at her accusingly. Of its fierce struggle to escape.

How desperately it had fought with those tiny, ineffectual teeth for its liberty, and, as it surely must have thought, its very life.

She went back to bed, but couldn't sleep for the worries spinning in her brain. The campaign. Her finances. Dan. Whether she should get out of politics.

Finally she gave up. Got dressed, made coffee, and plopped down at the counter in the breakfast nook. The sitter had left mail and the *Post* on the counter. She sorted through it with one hand, cradling the reluctantly forgiven and very heavy Jimbo in the crook of her other arm.

Her gaze snagged on a headline. TARNISHING ACCUSATIONS TARGET WARTIME HERO, it read. The *Early Bird* had carried the same article. She'd read it on her phone back in Vegas, while they were trying to dig out from the ransomware attack.

Maybe it was good Dan was out of the country. Or, okay, maybe Alaska wasn't exactly foreign territory, but whoever listened to her thoughts knew what she meant.

Time to get moving . . . the teleconference with the Chinese was at eleven. But really, she'd rather stay home. She strolled through the living room and down the hall, cradling the furry burden in both arms. The cat inspected each picture on the walls as they passed it. Always curious. Always alert. As if any corner could contain a threat. "We'll have to cut back on the treats, you fat pudding," she told him, folding his ears back. "But no more mice from outside, okay? Is that a deal?"

He burrowed his face into the crook of her elbow and sighed. Really, it did seem like sometimes he understood what she said.

Looking out the back window, over the lawn and down to the woods . . . the ground dropped to a wooded ravine. Sweet briar, the faded winter red of Virginia creeper, with scattered patches of blackberry cane where the sun shone through. Scraggly dogwoods some previous owner had planted. The dwarf azaleas she'd spaced between them when they moved in. They were bare just now, but winter couldn't last forever. Which meant she really needed to do something about the overgrown border beds. Get Dan to fix the fence, long overdue for a spray wash and repainting. A garden shed was nearing tumbledown status, and she'd noticed carpenter bees buzzing around it that summer. It'd been all too easy to let things go during the war. But she could do with some time at home. If only to rest, and get things back in order. Maybe get her hip replaced, at long last.

She dropped the cat, refreshed his bowl, and padded down the stairs to the basement. Dan had turned it into a den. She regarded the bookshelves, the piles of unread volumes he'd stacked in what he called the Ready Locker. For some obscure reason.

After Las Vegas, and Yangerhans's surprisingly popular performance in the first debate, Mrs. Clayton's and the left's frostiness had been lessened by a tide of individual donations. They mainly arrived online, in dribs and drabs, but were still mounting nicely on a donor page Pyotr had set up at www.electyangerhans.com. Called, innocuously enough, Citizens for Jim.

Another piece of luck: Jeanine De Bari had dropped out. Merllin Chatoyant had called the next day, asking if Blair had hired a manager yet. A job she was all too ready to relinquish to a professional.

Now the Chatoyant Group was running scheduling, online work, and outreach. Merllin stayed in LA, but Lehman and Cronin were embedded at the Yangerhans for President office in Rosslyn. Gaglione was with the candidate at his New England appearances.

So far, so good. Chatoyant had massaged her videos from that first rally in Plaza Olvera, intercut with clips of the admiral in wartime, into a stirring website that channeled even more donations to Pyotr's payment processor. Cronin had set up spreadsheets and databases, improved over the versions she'd lost to the online attack.

And most telling, Grossman had landed four corporate donors. The money arrived under other names, to avoid administration reprisals, but it was enough to pay rent and power bills, and even minuscule salaries for her own tight nucleus of a staff: Margo, Hu, Pyotr, Jessica, and Verónica. Morton had waived any salary, and Blair had decided to forgo hers as well, though she was steadily drawing down her 401(k).

But she still wondered why she was even trying.

She wandered along the bookshelves, running a finger along the spines. So dusty . . She pulled out a volume. A history of the American Revolution. Perhaps she'd find one of her ancestors mentioned. She deliberated for a moment, then carried it upstairs.

It wasn't far to the office. Most days she walked to the Metro and two stops later got off in Rosslyn. Today, a Saturday, the subway wasn't crowded. The sky was a quilt of thunderclouds as she walked the last two hundred yards to the strangely angled, twenty-story concrete-and-glass monolith on Fort Myer Drive, but she made it before the rain started.

She was alone in the elevator. Actually, most of the building was vacant. The war, the Cloudburst, then the Flower Flu—so many businesses had never recovered. She'd gotten a terrific deal on prime space. Then Morton had made a call, and suddenly even that figure had been cut by half.

When she let herself in Suite 510 was buzzing like a disturbed hive. Great, the youngsters were early, like good little worker bees. She strolled through the carrels—they'd been here already, the place had been an architectural firm and the door still read Coolidge & VanDuren Associates—dispensing a "hello" here, a "good morning" there. At least, to those who weren't already on the phone or so engrossed in their screens they didn't look like they were on the same planet, let alone the same floor.

Her own office was private, walled. It included what she'd at first taken for a tanning bed but was in fact a scanner for very large documents; construction blueprints, probably. Shingler-Gray had raided abandoned suites for desks, chairs, lights, coffeemakers, paper consumables. They had good connectivity and there was even a still-operating café-slash-convenience store on the ground floor, for when pastries and fruit and soft drinks were called for.

She caught up on email, then read through the briefing book for the 11 A.M. call—11 A.M. in DC, but 11 P.M. in Beijing. It would be chaired by Xie Yunlong. The pudgy, scared young apparachik she'd met in a Dublin tea-and-pastry shop years before, with whom she'd traded threats across plates littered with the corpses of cinnamon scones. Now he was with the new federal government, struggling to make the revised constitution work. To devolve power to provinces that had long done little more than respond to orders. To convert a monolithic Communist Party to something more like democratic socialists, competing with other groups across the spectrum. But it was hard going, and he'd asked for guidance.

At 10:50 Shingler-Gray poked her head in, holding out a Starbucks cup. "Chai latte, no sugar, right? Conference's up. Hu's here. Want to join us?"

Blair nodded, sighed, and stood.

The video call started with flowery mutual compliments, but quickly bogged down in querulous cavils from Xie. He'd gained weight since the war, and lost the black-rimmed spectacles that had been de rigueur during the Zhang regime. *"How does this supposed to work, when orders from above do not need to be obeyed?"* he demanded, frowning. *"Minister Chen, that is, Premier Chen, does not understand. He gives an order. It is challenged by these new courts. And then nothing happens. How can a country be governed in this way?"*

Blair said, "That's the nature of a democracy, Yun. You can't expect things to go down in a straight line, like in a dictatorship. Think of it more like a . . . like a quality control department."

"It is not like that. They are demanding a price to agree. Hold their hands out. Is this what you mean by democracy?"

Blair exchanged an eye roll with Margo and Kuwalay. "No! Well . . . maybe sometimes. Look, what exactly do they want? Maybe it's a chance to play ball."

"Play ball?" When he frowned, he reminded her of Jimbo. *"I do not understand."*

"You scratch their back, they scratch yours."

The chubby man turned to confer with someone off camera. Then turned back. *"We are not asking for scratching. Or for your baseball. Premier Chen needs comradely assistance. This was offered at the time of the treaty negotiations. By your Senator Talmadge. I know he has now departed to the ghost world. But we need funds to rebuild. Unless he pays these judges, the premier cannot enforce new laws about land, or*

returning industry to the people. You must honor your commitments,
Blair. Or those who look backward will gain power once more."

She was debating her answer when the door banged open. An intern
scooted in, long hair flying. She slammed the door behind her, glanced at
Blair, then bent to whisper in Hu Kuwalay's ear. He frowned and jumped
to his feet.

A sudden loud rap at the door turned their heads. Three men and a
woman pushed their way in, one after the other. They wore dark suits and
carried briefcases.

"FBI," the first man through said. He was shorter than the others, but
unmistakably in charge. He held up a leather credential case. "Agent Ro-
meo Facenda. Nobody move. Hands on the table, everyone." The other
agents wheeled and paced to the center of each remaining wall, to turn and
face them. The woman had a hand inside her jacket. "Hands on the *table*,"
she snapped to Shingler-Gray, who'd made a move toward her handbag.

Blair stood, appalled. "What the—what the hell is *this*? We're in a conference call. With a member of the Chinese government—"

"Blair?" Yunlong, on the screen, looking alarmed. *"What is going on?*
Who are those men?"

"Terminate the call," Facenda said. "Now."

"Good luck and best wishes, Yun. We'll get back to you," Blair told the
camera, and clicked the End Call button. As the screen went dark, one
of the intruders was unplugging it from the wall, shoving it into his briefcase. "Whose is this?" he snapped.

"Mine," Kuwalay said angrily. "What are you doing? This is a legally registered campaign office. You have no business here."

Facenda clamped his hands on Kuwalay's shoulders and pressed him
back down. "I said, *don't move.* Keep your hands visible. For your own
safety."

Blair sputtered, "First explain what you're doing here."

"We're here to apprehend Justin Yangerhans, then carry out a search
warrant."

Apprehend? She fumbled for words. Finally managed, "He's—he's in
Boston. A search warrant? For *what?* What exactly are you after?"

"Material items relevant to an ongoing criminal investigation. Pursu-
ant to suspected violations of the Logan Act. You can read." He tossed a
piece of paper onto the table.

The Logan Act prohibited correspondence with foreign countries for the purposes of undermining the United States. She read the warrant quickly. The signature at the bottom was that of the FBI director.

Facenda snapped orders to the other agents, then left. Blair got up and followed him out. He didn't object, just nodded to the female agent, who fell in behind Blair, hand still tucked into her jacket. Shingler-Gray started to her feet too, but was pushed back down by a burly male agent.

In the open area of the suite, a dozen agents were at work. Some carried sledgehammers, axes, and what looked like Jaws of Life, hydraulic cutters like those used to access the victims of car accidents. Her staff were lined up against the windows, hands locked over their heads. Kirschorn was weeping, as were the interns. The agents shoved papers into canvas pouches stenciled *FBI*. They unplugged computers and jammed them, too, into the pouches. They slammed open drawers and rifled through them, dumping the contents onto the floor when they were done.

Blair wheeled on Facenda, fists at her sides. "What's going on here?" she snarled again. "If this is about our advising the Chinese—"

"It's all in the warrant."

"The warrant says 'files.' They're tearing apart the whole office."

"Material evidence might be destroyed. We have evidence of illegal activity emanating from this and related locations."

She couldn't believe this. "Related locations . . . Are your thugs at my home?"

"That's a related location, yes. As are those of your associates, and Mr. Yangerhans. Our other teams are there now." Facenda nodded to the woman, who removed handcuffs from her belt and seized Blair's arms. A moment later, her hands were twisted painfully behind her, crescents of stainless metal cold against her wrists. "Solely for your protection." Facenda smirked.

She suddenly found it harder to breathe. "How is—how is handcuffing *me* for *my* protection?"

He patted her shoulder. "Sometimes people get emotional. Do things they regret later. We find it's better to keep everyone under control."

"Under control," she echoed bitterly. Started to protest, then decided silence was the wiser course. Until she could call her dad's attorney. Maybe they should have secured better legal representation for the campaign.

Meanwhile the Federals seemed to be finishing their search. Bag after bag of documents, computers, equipment were carried out the door.

"Hey! That's our fucking server, man!" Pyotr yelled.

Blair turned to look. One of the agents was yanking wires out of the wall so violently a plastic cover cracked and flew off. Her IT staffer grabbed the guy's arm. "That's our fucking server! Fucking thugs. Jackbooted Gestapo pricks! You can't—"

The husky agent back-elbowed him in the mouth. Robards staggered away, holding his face. "Ow. Aw. You busted my fucking tooth, you fucker—"

"Pyotr!" Shingler-Gray yelled. At a glance from Blair, Margo pulled him away.

Facenda said, "Assaulting a federal officer. Cuff him, Ryan." He pointed to Margaret. "How about you, big girl? Anybody else here want a free overnight in Quantico?"

"Fuck you," Shingler-Gray said. She had her arm around Robards's shoulder. "You're not touching him. If you want to take me on, I'm ready."

She and Facenda locked gazes, and the agent's was first to fall before the retired marine's intimidating stare. "Forget it," he muttered.

"We all saw that," Blair told the room. "Right? Everyone will testify."

"You're living in the past, Miz Titus," Facenda told her, not unpleasantly. "But we'll let him go. This time. Now, once we have a chance to go through this material, facilitating property and documents seized in adherence to a search warrant not of continuing interest can be reclaimed." He handed her a card. "You can file a motion for retrieval. It may take us a while to sift through all this, however. Unfortunately, imaging hard drives is a time-consuming process."

Blair said, knowing at the same time it wouldn't make any difference, "We only just recovered from a malware attack. We can't work without these computers. The information on them. As you no doubt knew before you came here."

"Just following orders." Facenda gestured to his people. "That's the last of it? All right, let's leave these good folks to whatever they thought they were doing. You can lower your hands now. Thanks for your cooperation."

The agents left, filing past the staff. The female agent, last to leave, gave Blair an apologetic shrug as she eased the door closed behind her.

They stood aimlessly about for a time, in collective shock. Then slowly went back to the only devices that remained to them: their personal phones.

Blair took hers out, wondering as she did so why the agents hadn't seized them as well. An oversight? Probably not. The bureau was probably already tapping them. In fact, seizing them would disrupt the ongoing surveillance.

Yeah, that was probably it.

She began calling attorneys she knew. They all said they couldn't help, were too busy, weren't active in that field, or otherwise declined to get involved. Finally Kuwalay came up with a former House staffer, now a defense attorney, who said he'd try for an injunction. If this was about the Logan Act, he said, no one had ever been successfully prosecuted for violating it. But he didn't think she could retrieve any files before the bureau had mirror-imaged the drives.

She put away the phone and went over to comfort Robards, who slumped, holding an ice pack to his mouth. "Pyotr, do you need someone to take you to the ER? Or to a dentist? Please tell me this time everything was backed up."

He nodded, to her enormous relief. "With a private encryption key. As soon as we install new hardware, a new router, we can re-download everything."

"So, great, we just need new computers . . . Margo can do a bulk purchase . . . check with everyone, figure out how many we need, what kind, give me a list."

He nodded again and headed off.

Verónica had been waiting behind him. Now she held out her phone. "You will want to see this, Ms. Titus," she said angrily.

A live feed was on-screen. Along with footage from outside their office, showing agents carrying out computers and canvas bags, notebooks tucked under their arms, a voiceover was saying, *"The raid provided convincing evidence that the ring was operating under the guise of a political campaign headquarters. Corroborating files have already been found on their computers."*

The pictures flashed on the screen. Portions were covered by black cutouts, the eyes with black rectangles, but the content was so graphic she gasped.

Kids. Little girls. Little boys. Naked. Held captive. Being . . . violated.

It was unspeakable.

In one photo, Justin Yangerhans's face was visible behind one of the children.

"No charges have been filed so far," the announcer intoned. *"And the admiral has yet to comment. But the investigation will be covered here, on your local news source for Arlington, Alexandria, and Northern Virginia. All the news, in full, every hour on the hour. Patriot News: The Absolute Truth."*

Kuwalay stepped over, lips set in a grim line, holding his hand over the mic on his own phone. "It's the lawyer I retained. He called back. Said he couldn't take the case, after all. A bad case of the Flu."

The other staffers conferred, riveted to their phones. Jessica came over, looking worried, and held her cell out. "It's on *every* channel. Every news site. They're calling for our response. What should we do, Blair? It can't be true, can it? That he'd be . . . involved in . . . something like that? And they're saying we had to have known about it. Were grooming kids for him. Deny it? Or just say, 'No comment'?"

She stood voiceless, staring at her own cell, which was already showing donations being canceled. The Logan Act had just been a pretext to raid their office. The photos were false, of course. Everything had been prepared in advance. There hadn't been time for the FBI to access even one hard drive, let alone compile selections.

Yangerhans's face had been Photoshopped in. There would be deepfake video too, of that she had no doubt, as soon as the click counts on the "news" sites began to drop.

What *could* she do? Deny, voice outrage, even decline comment; whatever she or Yangerhans did or said would just add to the coverage, prolong the news cycle, give the hired trolls more fuel to roast them with.

The media would immolate him as completely as any heretic had been reduced to ashes at the stake.

And if there were criminal charges, Yangerhans would be forced to drop out. The major donors would demand it, for the "good of the party."

She slumped into a chair, letting her phone clatter onto someone's desk. Would they lose before the good guys even had a chance?

More to the point, who was she to give Xie Yunlong advice on how to build a working democracy?

When it was perfectly evident the long American experiment with it had finally failed?

Then she remembered the mouse. Gleaming onyx eyes, and the

frenzied prick of tiny teeth. A frantic struggle for liberty and life. From a creature too small to even have a hope of hurting her.

No. She wasn't giving up. Not yet.

If something that small could still do battle, so could she.

16

Under the Arctic Ice

Tomlin leaned against the nav console in *Tang*'s control room as the exec and captain argued. He'd made his proposal. Then had to defend it to Komanich and Dr. Liu.

Following which, Fahrney had wanted to think it over. "I'd better discuss it with Yoder and Irons, before I decide," he'd said.

Now Sloan stood with hands rammed into the pockets of his coveralls, trying to look less apprehensive than he felt.

The Orca Prime had barely just elbow room in its control sphere for one carefully origami'd small adult. Its titanium shell would protect any occupant down to the vehicle's crush depth. But its diminutive diameter, less than four feet, and with a lot of equipment in there already, meant that occupant would be extremely cramped. The onboard workstation was for test and maintenance. It had never been meant to be inhabited for more than a couple of hours. It had no toilet facilities, and only a skimpy, stamped-steel seat to perch on. Facing that were the touch screens, backup depth and fathometer readouts, and a keyboard. He and Komanich had crawled up into it several times since coming aboard to run diagnostics and update the tactical software.

Most daunting, the unmanned submarine had no air supply and no heating. Sealed within it, he'd either freeze or suffocate.

"So how long can he last in there?" Yoder sounded outraged, and had since Sloan broached his proposal. "A few hours, max. Then what? He dies. And we lose the fucking Orca, anyway."

Fahrney pinched his chin, looking thoughtful. "We could give him an air supply. Let's see what our diver thinks. And on the rest—let's gather our systems experts for a quick huddle. The master chief, back in engineering—she's got more practical know-how than anyone else aboard. An electrician, for the heating issue."

Still shaking her head, the XO snapped, "Copilot, have Petty Officer Visser report to control." She added, "Sure, we could jury-rig. But it's just not realistic, skipper. It's not built for a . . . a *passenger*. Especially with ice overhead. There's no way out if the vehicle's damaged, or propulsion fails, or if . . . anything else goes south."

Fahrney nodded. "How about it, Ms. Komanich? Is the vehicle going to fail? You're the closest thing we have to an Orca expert."

The JAIC rep bit her lip. "Well . . . sir . . . I'm okay on the Pilot. The AI. Beyond that, I just know the basics. Electrical system. Programming. I can't speak to the—"

"How long could a human rider last in that sphere?"

She swallowed visibly. "Maybe . . . a few hours. Until they ran out of air, or got hypothermic."

Dr. Liu lifted a timid hand. "Isn't there an upper hatch? He could escape that way."

Komanich shook her head. "No. I mean, yeah—there's an egress trunk. But it was designed for when the Orca's surfaced and the upper superstructure can drain." She gulped again. "If he opened it submerged . . . even if he could swim up the trunk and out of the boat somehow, he'd still be trapped under the ice."

Yoder, the exec, put in, "And given the loading on that hatch, he'd never be able to push it open against the sea pressure."

A stocky, shaven-headed man in coveralls swung into the control room. "Petty Officer," Fahrney said. Then, to RaShondra and Sloan, "This is my senior qualified diver, Petty Officer First Class Visser. Visser, have you been up in the Orca?"

The first class worked a wad of something around in his cheek. "Uh, no, sir."

"It's got a little control sphere above where it mates to our aft escape trunk upper hatch. Just big enough for one guy. But there's no air supply. Could you jury-rig oxygen, compressed air, some kind of portable set?"

The diver looked reflective. "It's at atmospheric pressure?" Fahrney nodded. "I could rig a cylinder, but the pressure would build up. And how will he monitor CO_2 percentage?"

"So it can't be done?" the exec said. Making it clear by her tone she thought it shouldn't be.

"Didn't say that, XO." The diver rubbed a shaven scalp. "Be better if he just took along one of our Draegers. Our rebreathers. That'd adjust his mix on its own. Has he got some way to stay warm in there? Electric heater, maybe?"

"There's no outlet," Komanich said.

"Well, we could give him one of our heated dry suits . . . maybe I better take a look, see what we can do." He measured Sloan up and down, frowning. "But, yeah, we got a small. We can probably fit him out."

Komanich stepped forward, looking frightened. "Fit *her* out. If anyone's going, it should be me."

Sloan started to protest, but the captain was faster. "You're not a service member, Ms. Komanich. I can't let you go." Fahrney glanced at Liu, who'd hovered, looking concerned, but not taking much part in the discussion. "Or you, Doctor. If anyone goes—"

"It should be somebody qualified on the Draeger," the diver finished his sentence. "Skipper."

Fahrney said quietly, "Thanks, everybody. I appreciate it. But Commander Tomlin here knows the mission. Knows tactics. And he's been underway with the vehicle before. Seen its capabilities and limitations." Fahrney eyed Sloan. "If, that is, you're still up for it. Because, believe me, I'm not about to order anyone to do this."

Yoder cleared her throat, scowling. "Captain, remember how you tell us to always do risk assessment? To ask three things: What can go wrong? What can we do to prevent it going wrong? And if, despite everything, it does go wrong, how do we fix it? Winging it . . . that's a decision tree that can lead to some really bad outcomes."

Sloan glanced at his watch. They didn't have time to argue much longer, or plan for some elaborate backup. Especially if the broadband noise Sonar had picked up really was an engine test. "Sir, I understand the XO's misgivings. But I won't be out long. Run out to the hide site—that's what, four, five hours max. Loiter there for our barrier line to give me the heads-up. Reposition as necessary, take the shot, then retro back for you to pick me up."

"No, we'll run in toward the island for the pickup," Fahrney said. "So you're not locked in there a minute more than necessary. XO, you're right, but he's right too—it's this, or forget the mission."

He took a breath. "Mr. Tomlin, like I said, I don't want you in there longer than you have to be. And we'll set up a backup rendezvous too. Just in case." He nodded to the diver. "Get him fixed up. Rebreather. Cold-weather gear. XO, call the mess deck. A couple of bag lunches, and some kind of sanitary arrangement."

Yoder reddened. She seemed about to say something, but stifled it. And stormed off, out of the control room.

Fahrney stood with arms crossed, looking at Sloan. Who eventually realized the CO was leaving the last word up to him. He had to say it.

He tried not to let his voice shake. "Yes, sir. Let's get this done."

"Good job." Fahrney nodded as if Tomlin had been weighed in the balance and found true.

Sloan turned away from them all and followed the diver through the curtain out of Control.

Suited, instructed, fed, in less than an hour he clambered up once more, back into the escape trunk beneath where the Orca rode, in the deep, in the Arctic dark. His limbs moved clumsily in insulated boots and the heavy padded dry suit. Batteries strapped to its left side would give him a few hours' warmth. The diver, below him on the ladder, toted the rebreather, a plastic-sheathed backpack that would take up most of the remaining space in the sphere. Below Visser stood Komanich, carrying the rest of Sloan's gear: his notebook computer, enough sandwiches for at least a day, bottled water, and some Ziploc-type waste bags.

Bracing his arms around the hatch coaming, Sloan hauled himself up into the mating ring area. Reaching up for a handhold again, he squirmed between the all-too-awkwardly-positioned equipment cabinets and manifolds that lined the interior. He halted there for a breath, longing more than anything he'd ever wanted before to back out, climb down, not follow through with this.

But the only way out now was forward.

He grunted, struggling to free his suit where it had snagged on a knob. Then twisted, jackknifed backward, and wriggled up at last into the black-painted interior of the control sphere.

Perched on the lip of the access, he realized again, with a rush of fresh dread, just how circumscribed he'd be in here. There was not quite enough room to extend his elbows. Two inches from the top of his head to the upper hatch. Which actually offered no possibility of escape. Above it lay a twenty-foot water column, another hatch, then the open sea. And finally, of course, many feet of solid Arctic ice.

The dark space already felt stuffy. The sweetish monoethanolamine stench was heavy here, concentrated, like a mildly sickening perfume. He toggled a screen on for light. Then fumbled around behind him for the little tractor-type jump seat. At last, after some cursing, he got it folded down and his rump socketed more or less uncomfortably into it.

"Coming up," Visser said, and Sloan bent to grab the straps of the re-breather. Heavy as sin, bulky as an unwelcome memory. They hauled and pushed and gradually forced it in sideways just in front of his knees under the little fold-down keyboard.

The diver stuck his head up again. Handed up heavy insulated diving gloves, then another bulky canvas bag. "You'll want these."

"What is it?" Sloan kicked the sack back under his seat with the heels of his boots.

"Spare oxygen, and extra absorbent cartridges for the breather. In case you're out there longer than you figured on . . . we should double-check gauges and levels. I'll read from the checklist, you turn the valves. Okay? Or do you want me to do it?"

"I'd rather you did it."

Visser grimaced. "Okay, but remember, you're not going to notice anything if you bump a valve with your knee. You only feel like you need air if your lungs sense a carbon dioxide buildup. The brain can't sense the absence of oxygen. You just pass out and . . . die. So keep a fuckin' close eye on that valve and your O_2 gauge, got it? And take it easy on the heat too."

"Got it." He licked his lips, smacked a dry mouth.

The chief's bald pate disappeared. After a moment a dark-braided head appeared in its place. "Water?" said Komanich. She passed up the lunch bags, then a plastic bottle.

"Thanks, Shondra." He swished and swallowed. Recapped the bottle and wedged it between his battery pack and the interior of the sphere. Really, there wasn't any point taking waste bags. No way he could get this suit off, not hunched over as he was. With the rebreather jammed in here too, there was no room to move. He'd just have to piss in the padding.

"Sloan."

He cleared his throat and met her eyes.

Frowning, she gripped his ankle, the only part of him within her reach. "You don't have to do this."

"I think I do."

"I don't want you to go."

He sucked a breath, noticing with horror that the limited air inside the curved metal shell was already growing stale. He fumbled for the mask, a lower-face arrangement with a rubber spider that would snap around the back of his skull. "Well, hell, you know, I'm not happy as shit about it myself. But six, seven hours—I can gut it out that long. And we've got to screw up their test. That's the fucking mission, right? The whole reason we're out here."

She squeezed his ankle again. Looking up at him in the dimness. He could only spare a glance down into concerned brown eyes. What exactly was she . . . oh, never mind. He didn't have time for whatever. Not right now.

"Well . . . just don't take any more risks than you have to." She slapped his ankle and sank down out of sight.

To be replaced in the mating ring by Dr. Jason Liu's round bullet head. And his extended hand, holding a ring-bound, plastic-covered binder. "What's this?" Sloan said, accepting it reluctantly. One more fucking *object* to take up space he didn't have enough of.

"BLY-1 operating manual. I tabbed the checklist for launching the Zombie. But item sixteen and item seventeen, late change, you have to remember to reverse the order of the commands. I Sharpie'd it in. Make sure you don't miss that, or the umbilical won't release properly." Liu peered around, blinking. "You don't have much room in here."

"Thanks for the insight, Jase."

"You're one brave dude, Sloan. I couldn't do this."

"No, you couldn't. You're too tall."

Liu swallowed. He looked around again, then patted Sloan's ankle the same way Komanich had. "Good luck, man."

Sloan looked at his watch. "Let's get that hatch sealed, okay?"

The Prime's detachment and swim-away went smoothly. The Pilot ran it, humming to itself as it worked. He wondered again if that purr was deliberate, or some artifact of the onboard AI's programming. Maybe just to reassure the listener that it was actually processing?

Finally he said, "Pilot, are you humming?"

Hmmmmm. "*No.*"

"I hear something on the circuit."

"*Probably tinnitus. A flaw in the human auditory sense, due to nerve damage—*"

"I know what tinnitus is."

Hmmmmmm. The heading readout on his screen ticked left, and a modest acceleration pressed him against the curved rear of the sphere.

Hunched in the dark, sucking gas through the half mask, he toggled to a geoplot, more to divert himself from his constricted encapsulation than for information. Their extended track swept outward. It steadied up leading past Ushakov Island toward the dot of icy low land called Ostrov Vize on the charts. Intel said Vize Island had hosted a weather station in Soviet times, but was uninhabited now. Iced in more or less year round, it sounded like the ass end of nowhere. He wished he could at least get a look, but that was impossible.

He shifted irritably on the steel seat, which was already digging into the nerves of his rump. The suit seemed to be working, though. He was almost too warm. He reached around beneath him, groping by feel to locate the heating control. Turned it down a notch. There.

He checked the readouts on the rebreather. They were all in the green. He had enough oxygen for a full day and some hours after that, the chief had said, and a spare cylinder too. So, no worries about running out of air.

Unless, of course, the Russians postponed the test. In which case, he'd head back to *Tang*, dismount, lock back in, and do it all over again tomorrow.

That, he didn't really want to think about. Once would be more than enough.

"Pilot, this is Sloan." He introduced himself and keyboarded overrule authority via the maintenance protocol. Pilot would execute its orders independently, but Sloan could override at any time. Either by vetoing a specific action, which would require the AI to accomplish its goals in some other way, or else by taking direct control. Which he didn't intend to do unless absolutely necessary.

"Pilot, aye," the Orca said. *"Authority acknowledged."*

"Good. Uh, can we extend the mast some? Not to its full extent. And give me video looking up."

Hmmmmm . . . "Extending."

The video came in dark. No surprise. Deep within it, shadows shifted. He started to ask for a floodlight, then thought again. A few photons might penetrate the ice. And no doubt sharp eyes were looking down from above: satellites, drones, or aircraft, alert for any intruder along the route of the impending test.

"I can illuminate with infrared," the AI suggested, obviously thinking along the same lines. *"Water is not a good medium for allowing differentiation of heat, but the shorter wavelengths might give enough vision to work with."*

"Approved. But only at the close-in setting, please."

Why was he saying *please* to a program? It was too easy to think of the intelligence with which he spoke as not just a machine but as a fellow consciousness.

He'd been in half-serious arguments about this back at WITI school. At what point *did* intelligence become consciousness? Hardly any of the students had thought AIs were near that yet. "But how do I know *you* have consciousness?" he'd asked. "I infer it, because you're human like me. But I can never really know."

"The Turing test," someone had said.

"That tells us when it can *imitate* a consciousness. Not that it *has* a consciousness."

Of course, they'd never arrived at any consensus. But that had been the point—the fun of the debate.

Now his screen glowed with a ghostly green. The scope's IR source, reflected from the ice overhead. A twisted, racked jumble of smashed-apart and refrozen pieces. The ice at these latitudes never really thawed, though Irons had said polynyas appeared here and there during the brief summer as the wind reshuffled the pack. When winter returned the floes were jammed together by the expanding sea ice. Whole enormous blocks and sheets were tilted on end, forced beneath the surface, then frozen into place.

Among them, on his screen, swam undulant silver shapes. Too blurry, too similar in temperature to the surrounding sea, to distinguish what they were. Tiny blobs, jellyfish of some kind, glided past. He gazed hungrily, trying to project himself outside this metal shell that both protected and trapped him. But each time he remembered where he was his mouth went dry and his heart stepped up to an allegro beat.

Swallowing, he toggled back to geo. The bright dot of the Orca Prime's position rolled slowly along its track. So slowly . . . but the faster they moved, the more decibels they put in the water. Six knots should put him behind the island in time and place him in position to swerve out to either side and release the BLY as the Apokalypsis tore past.

One single shot. He had to make it good.

Or Moscow would know their weapon worked, and hold the world to ransom.

Four hours later he felt calmer. Not comfortable—he definitely wasn't—but less panicky. The interior of the sphere was quite warm now. He wasn't sure why. Maybe it was insulated, and his body heat was being trapped inside. The wattage, the power he was radiating from the heated suit, would be trapped too. He checked the oxygen level. He wasn't using much. Of course, the rebreather was recirculating the sizable percentage of unused O_2 in his exhaled breath, as well.

His stomach growled. He groped around beneath the seat. "Where the fuck is the—" he muttered.

"What is your question?" The Pilot, thinking it was being addressed.

He pulled down the mask to speak more clearly, but reminded himself he couldn't breathe chamber air for long. The diver had been insistent; the brain's first response to a lack of oxygen was to black out. "Nothing . . . Hey, can you put Bly on?"

"Hmmmm . . . BLY-1 coming up. BLY, you are on."

A crackle, then, *"Mr. Tomlin. Hello."*

Their voices were so different. The Pilot's, deep, masculine, an action hero's. The Zombiefish's androgynous, neither male nor distinctly female. Sloan located the paper bag and got it fumbled up to where he could unwrap it. Corned beef, excellent. And two Hershey's with almonds. "Hello, Bly. How are we doing in the payload bay?"

"All systems check out."

"We're getting close to where you do your thing. Hope you're ready."

"It is what I am built for."

"Let's go over it again. Just to make sure we're still on the same page. Pilot, you with us?"

"Listening."

The BLY said, *"When Pilot forwards release order and intercept point, I cast off from payload bay. I swim out along assigned vector until either individualized sound signature of target or a broadband rocket impulse is detected.*

"I then execute intercept and physically couple onto target. Digitally penetrate and preempt host programming. Once control is gained, steer due north by inertial navigation, checking my course against the host computer's navigation. When depths of over three thousand fathoms are confirmed, I accelerate the target to high speed mode and steer into seafloor."

Sloan felt uncomfortable, hearing the weapon describe its own demise. Then grinned. It was only a machine. Created for the purpose, and having no more comprehension of its existence than the jellies that eddied past as the Prime crept beneath the ice. Probably less.

Bored, tense, the seat ledge cutting into the backs of his thighs, he fitted the mask back on. Took several deep breaths and shifted to the keyboard.

Bly: Is the cold affecting you?

Negative. All status checks at one hundred percent.

How do you feel otherwise?

I don't understand.

Are you eager-afraid-happy-?

I am eager, Commander Tomlin. If by that you mean motivated to accomplish my mission.

Sloan sat back. Then typed, more or less just because he either had to busy himself or start screaming, *Who gave you that mission?*

My credits include JAIC, Lockheed Boeing Systems Division, DARPA, the Naval Research Laboratories in Carderock, Maryland—

Enough. What I mean was, you didn't volunteer for this tasking. So why are you eager to fulfill it?

I am eager to accomplish my mission because my mission is to accomplish my mission. If I were not, I would have no reason for my existence.

A momentary pause, then: *Is that what you are asking?*

Sloan hesitated too, fingertips poised, gas hissing in and out of his lungs, eyes fixed on nothing. The BLY-1 didn't sound stupid. Quite the opposite. Maybe quizzing it wasn't a good idea. In fact, hadn't Liu warned him not to? What if he planted a doubt? Triggered some nascent idea of individuality, self-determination, existential uncertainty?

It was only doing its duty, after all.

Just like . . . just like *he* was.

But that isn't my only goal, he argued with himself. *I'm more than my duty. More than a bunch of circuits wired to do one thing.*

He grinned ruefully again under the mask. He was programmed too. Survive. Fight. Reproduce. Endowed with a dose of curiosity and just enough doubt to persuade himself he had free will.

That he wasn't just another, softer machine.

No. He'd set his own goals. Refused his grandfather's offer, a remunerative career, in favor of the Navy.

So why had he done that? Just to avoid being bored?

Maybe it was that very incertitude that meant the mind was free.

Unless that, too, was a life-affirming illusion.

For some reason, he remembered Komanich. A flick of the wrist, to pat down cornrowed hair. A saucy grin.

A last-minute plea not to risk his life . . .

He shook his head. Just ancient programming, stamped deep into every cell from three billion years ago.

The important thing was the mission. Get it done.

Whatever came after, he could deal with then.

Hours passed. The Orca crept onward. Sloan's rear passed through pain to numbness, then to a suspicion it wasn't even there. The mask chafed his cheeks. The temperature kept rising. He hadn't expected to overheat down here, beneath the winter Arctic, but beads of sweat were trickling down his forehead, stinging his eyes.

"Shit," he muttered. He fumbled for the suit control again, twisting it to its lowest setting.

He shifted uneasily, trying to find a comfortable position, but there wasn't any. The black spherical shell seemed to clamp around him more tightly with each passing hour. He breathed slowly, trying to project his awareness out onto the passing sea. Onto the languidly drifting life that teemed even here, cloaked in lightlessness as if the sun had never existed.

At last, eons later, the bright pip of Own Location merged with the wait position the tactical program calculated as offering the best chance of interception as the target passed. *"Arrived at Point Optima,"* the Pilot announced. *"Shutting down main motor to conserve battery. Maintaining position with thrusters. Maintaining two hundred feet."*

Sloan muttered acknowledgment and toggled to the HCUS Status. After checking each of the offboard sensors, he tuned through their outputs over the last few hours. The one on the far left of the barrier: nothing significant heard. Ditto, the center one.

But the starboard-most sensor, bottomed out and eavesdropping in total silence, had confirmed distant screw noises. After running through the sonar library for a match, he felt sure it was a Sierra-class boat. Not the newest in Moscow's inventory, but still a threat. Its sonar suite and combat systems had been upgraded over the years, and it was heavily armed.

Probably the same unit *Tang* had detected previously, detailed as a monitoring station to track and maybe download telemetry from the nuclear-powered torpedo as it passed. Sloan laid the bearing out on his plot, figuring he could get a cross-bearing later, maybe even a course and speed.

Damn, it was *hot* in here. Beyond Tropical into Slow Cooker. He took a breath and lowered the mask. Sweat was burning his eyes, trickling down his chin, dripping into his suit. Fuck! Who would have thought the sphere was so well insulated. . . .

"Oh, shit," he muttered. He fumbled his fingers down his flank to the dial on the battery pack. Craned over, nearly dislocating his neck as he squinted for a clear look at the tiny numerals.

Yeah. Fuck.

He'd been turning the heat *up*, instead of down.

Not just roasting himself. But wasting the battery too.

He twisted the dial all the way back to zero. The suit's heating elements cooled almost instantly. Shit, shit . . . this was *not* good. "You maybe really fucked up there, Sloanie," he told himself out loud.

"This is the Pilot. Did not clearly hear your command."

"It wasn't a command." He suddenly realized he hadn't heard the whine of the thrusters for a while. "Are we holding depth just with buoyancy?"

"We're balanced on a salinity cline. No need to use thrusters. Drifting east at point two knots."

Sloan checked the time on his watch, then against the screen. The test was due to begin anytime now. Of course, it could be delayed. Held on the pad, so to speak. But he wasn't sure how much longer he could stand it in here. It would still be four-plus hours back, maybe a bit less if Fahrney ran *Tang* in toward him, as promised. He had plenty of oxygen left, but no way to tell how badly he'd run down the suit batteries. Already chill was creeping back into the sphere, starting at his feet. The insulated boots would help, but his toes were already tingling.

He debated turning the heat back on, just a little, but decided to see how bad it would get without using the battery at all.

An hour passed. Then another. The cold crept in insidiously, relentlessly. He stood it for as long as he could, then turned the heat on again, at the lowest setting.

Now he was worried. With the suit off, the sphere had bled down to freezing. To the minus two degrees centigrade, twenty-eight Fahrenheit, of seawater that was only kept from solidifying by the current stirring it round the pole. The dry suit was designed to trap body heat, but unfortunately, due to his own stupidity, its lining was now soaked with sweat, making it nearly useless as insulation.

He searched his brain for some way to produce heat with what was at hand. He had no matches, and nothing to burn . . . and even if he lit something, he'd kill himself inhaling the smoke.

He was sitting hunched, searching desperately through various alternate means of producing heat other than combustion and electricity, when the Pilot said, *"Picking up intermittent medium-frequency active sonar effects. Bearing one five zero relative."*

"That's *Pskov.* We already logged that from the other sensor."

"Negative. That was on a different bearing. Also . . . Stand by . . . Processing." And after several seconds, *"Active sonar detected. Single pings, at long intervals. Propulsor signature is consistent with a Laika-class submarine. Not a Sierra."*

"Crap," he muttered. There weren't many Laikas in the Northern Fleet. It was probably the same boat they'd slipped past at the exit from the Bering Strait. Transiting east to west to help monitor the test, and thus, coming up aft of *Tang,* which lay behind him.

He didn't worry about his mother sub. Fahrney would have picked the new threat up before the Pilot had, being closer, and would maneuver silently out of danger. But if the Russian sub continued west, eventually it would come within active sonar range of the Orca. And if it was pinging, even if only occasionally, sooner or later it would pick them up.

The Sierra ahead and to the north, the Laika closing in from behind. He debated whether to hug the island more closely. Blur their return into that of the coast, making the Prime look like a rock outcrop or islet. The charts, up here, weren't so detailed that a rock where one wasn't shown would raise suspicions.

He was about to give the Pilot that order when the deep male voice said, *"HCUS Charlie detects high-speed screw noises, bearing zero seven zero true."*

"Display on screen," he said.

As the display presented he forgot his aching butt, his cramped, throbbing thighs. Forgot everything but the moving pip angling northeast, off the coast of Novaya Zemyla, at an estimated speed of over forty knots.

It had to be the Apokalypsis. The nuclear-rocket-driven, thermonuclear-warheaded Ultimate Weapon that Moscow counted on to frighten the West into placating the expansionist Russian Federation.

And the target of the nearly intelligent torpedo that lay waiting, thinking who knew what thoughts, a few feet ahead of him in the Orca's payload bay.

Maybe *Zombie* wasn't a bad name for it, after all.

Hmmmmmmm. "*Consistent with predicted signature of nuclear drone torpedo,*" the Pilot said.

"Roger, concur." He wished he could flash the detection back to *Tang*. Pulse the low data rate transmitter again? Wiser not to. Just to be safe, in case the Russians had sensors planted along the test route too.

Silence. Stealth. Those were his allies out here.

Until it was time to let Bly off the leash.

Another hour snailed by. Even at forty-plus knots, their target was taking a long time to traverse the immense distances of the Siberian Arctic. Sloan licked chapped lips under the mask and stamped his boots on the hatch below, trying to hammer feeling back into his toes. Then stopped; the re-verberating boom might be just loud enough to alert some distant eaves-dropper. Instead he flexed his feet, trying for a little muscle warmth.

But the cold was growing ever icier. With a start, he noted a rime of frost on the frame of the screen, where his exhalations were condensing and freezing. When he slid his mask down his breath was a wintry plume in the dim light.

A thin film of ice coated the keyboard too, crackling as he tried to type. Clumsily, in the heavy diving gloves. He cursed. Impossible. Stripping the gloves off, he flexed his fingers in the biting chill. Then tapped out, *Can you generate an intercept course yet?*

Range is still too great. Any last-minute course alteration could leave us out in left field . . . stand by . . . I'm hearing a detonation.

He frowned and typed, *Detonation?*

Wait . . . second sound impulse. Course is still steady . . . but target speed is increasing. Seventy knots. Eighty.

He nodded, riveted as the numbers climbed. Just as the Lithuanian spies had said, the final sprint would be made under rocket power. The un-derwater missile had jettisoned its turbine and propulsor stages. Now, as it accelerated, the reactor was flashing seawater directly into radioactive steam, to shroud the body and rocket-thrust it ahead.

A hundred and thirty knots.

A hundred and fifty. Still accelerating.

Komponent, Malachite, and the Federation Navy were conducting this first live run as an all-out test. Accepting the risk of shock wave and turbulence effects during transition to the supercavitation regime.

Which meant it would be that much harder for the BLY-1 to track, intercept, and attach itself to the target.

The screen lit. *Active pinging. Accompanied by effects consistent with seven-bladed screw. Evaluate as Laika-class submarine. Estimated range between eighty and one hundred nautical miles.*

He toggled back and forth from tactical to geoplot, then fused the pictures. He adjusted the mask, pondering the result.

Laikas were modern, fast attack subs, driven by a fourth-generation reactor. A decent match for late Los Angeles—or early Virginia-class American boats. Developed from the Severodvinsk-class cruise missile submarines, Laikas were double-hulled for survivability. They carried vertical launch tubes as well as conventional torpedoes, and were smaller and faster than their Cold War forebears, with enhanced quieting and sonar processing. If the other sub hadn't been pinging, the Orca Prime's relatively small array might not even have picked it up. In which case, it could have been on top of him before he had a clue.

A shiver ran up his back, and not only because he was freezing. He clicked the heater dial up another notch, making sure the direction was right this time. Wondering if there might not be other boats out here too, guarding the perimeter of the test area. But not pinging, not advertising their presence.

He could be within a few miles of one.

He shook that concern off. Cleared his throat, coughing to dispel a thickness in his chest . . . He leaned to check the oxygen dial. Still good. He still had a sandwich left, and water. He'd had to whiz, and now his midriff and groin were much chillier than his upper body. Not good; if his core temperature fell too far, he'd lose sharpness. And he might need all the smarts he could muster very shortly.

He was trying to wedge his hips into a less uncomfortable position when the screen lit. *Rocket engine indications now bearing zero seven eight true. Estimated speed, steady at two hundred and five knots.*

A noise spoke glowed on, a narrow yellow pie shape aimed to the southwest. Its acute angle ended on the Orca's location. Sloan hunched over the keyboard, forgetting all discomfort, his imprisonment, the mask chafing his face, the chill gripping his bowels and ungloved fingers. He slipped the mask down; speaking was faster than typing. "Need a course to Bly's optimal launch point," he muttered. "ASAP, please."

Hmmmmm. "Working."

A pregnant pause. Not being nuclear-powered itself, the BLY had to be released within twenty miles ahead of the oncoming weapon. His best launch point looked to be west and south of the island that sheltered them. He was calculating the course in his head when the Pilot said, *"Recommend zero six one true at flank speed."*

"Pretty close. I figured around sixty degrees." But he hesitated. Going to flank, his top speed on the Orca's main motors, would put noise into the water. Without the air-conditioning and auxiliary machinery of a manned submarine, the Orca was inherently quieter. But not totally silent. At four knots, it was nearly inaudible. But at its top speed, a hair over twenty, any nearby submarine or bottom-laid sensor array would pick his cavitation signature out of the ice noise and biologics with ease. Like waving a flag and launching fireworks. Still . . . "All right, execute," he told it.

Only a slight sense of acceleration within his shell. And when he pressed his skull against the inside of his protective egg, he could make out the beats of the propulsor, the faint whir of the main shaft. The hiss of gas flowing through a constriction or valve.

Time to run diagnostics on the BLY. He opted for the keyboard this time, unwilling to talk to it. It was just too weird, deep in some uncanny valley, to discuss its deadly fate with the AI. As the bearing of the oncoming Apokalypsis shifted, the Pilot kept deriving its range, course, speed, and intercept point, displaying the outputs on Sloan's plot. The algorithms were complex. Their accuracy varied with salinity, thermal profiles, even the composition of the bottom that the incoming sound reflected from. The Orca's Pilot altered its own course now and then, advising him each time. But the launch point, a bit over ten miles to the side of the advanced course of the oncoming torpedo, shifted with each recalculation.

Finally the Pilot displayed, *Five minutes until outer edge of launch area.*

Sloan nodded, then slipped his mask down. Feeling awkward. Reluctant. But finally saying, "Bly, this is Commander Tomlin."

"Good evening, Commander."

Was it evening? He'd lost track. And beyond the layers of sea over him, above the solid ice that sealed them from the frigid wind and starlight somewhere above, it was still dark up there. Black. Arctic night.

He shook the image off. "Good evening. I see you ran your last SOT at time twenty. I read all systems at one hundred percent. Concur?"

The calm nongendered voice. *"Concur, Commander."*

He took a deep breath, wondering even as he did if he was sucking in air devoid of oxygen. He clamped the mask close, sucked down two deep lungfuls, then lowered it again. "Call me Sloan. Bly."

"All right, Sloan."

"We're almost at your launch point. Have you picked up your target?"

"I am linked to Pilot. I have the same information that is on your screen, Sloan."

He started to say, *Let's go over the plan again*, then didn't. It knew.

A deeper voice. *"One minute until firing area."*

"Can you give me audio, Pilot?"

Hmmmmmm. "Audio from the target."

The speaker tuned to an unsettling, nearly subsonic rumble, echoing as if it came from far beneath the ground. Of many different frequencies, underlaid by a bass that reverberated in his chest. It ebbed and swelled, trapped between seabed and ice pack. Two hundred plus knots. Nearly two hundred and forty miles an hour. Far too fast for any submarine to intercept.

And by virtue of its near-infinite source of power, the weapon could approach its objective from any bearing, at any speed, sprinting or lying low. Eluding any defense.

Obliterating American or European coastal cities with the heaviest thermonuclear warhead ever built.

Yeah. It would be the ultimate deterrent.

Behind its shield, Russia could reincorporate the once-free territories that ringed its heartland. Growing again into the malevolent colossus the Soviet Union had been.

"Within firing area," Pilot said.

Sloan considered giving the order, but decided to hold off. They'd barely entered the launch box. The Pilot was driving them toward the best point for intercept. They had only one Zombiefish, after all. He had to give it every chance possible.

More minutes ticked by. His thighs shuddered uncontrollably. He reached down for the suit heater again, and discovered he'd already, while thinking about the intercept, turned it all the way up. But . . . he was still cold.

Which meant he'd exhausted the suit's battery.

So that very soon now, the temperature in here would stabilize at minus two Celsius.

A temperature that would quickly result in hypothermia, coma, and, eventually, death.

The keyboard crackled with that icy film as he forced stiff fingers into motion again. Typed, *How much longer to best launch point?*

Eighteen minutes, thirty seconds, Commander.

The steady rumble from the speakers seemed to be growing. Getting louder. Their target was on its way.

Eighteen minutes. Surely he could stand that. But he had the trip back to consider too. How many hours had they been out already? Fahrney had promised to run in to pick him up . . . but he couldn't now, not with the Laika grinding in relentlessly behind *Tang*. If the American sub began moving in, the Russian would pick it up.

He adjusted his mask, trying to slow his breathing, which was getting ragged as the quivering in his thighs increased. The rumble from the speakers was definitely growing louder.

And then what? If an American submarine was detected here, deep in Russian territorial seas, attempting to interfere with the test of a major strategic weapon?

The answer seemed clear. A salvo of torpedoes, then, weeks later, a shrug. We have no idea what happened to your sub. Most likely, an accident. But perhaps it should not have ventured into our territorial seas.

The screen lit. *Active pinging from zero nine five, from bows-on transducers. Consistent with Sierra-class attack boat. Identify as Pskov.*

The same boat *Tang* had detected earlier, but farther away then, and on a different course. Now it was angling toward them. An older unit than the Laika, noisier, but still a threat. The titanium hull gave it a deep-diving capability nearly equal to the Orca's. With its vintage sonar suite, though, it still might not have picked them up.

Once he launched the BLY, though, the other sub would know his position. Could he evade them then?

With a renewed chill, he realized that the converging Russians, one from behind, the other ahead, had wrecked his extraction plan.

He couldn't backtrack to the rendezvous with *Tang*. Nor could the submarine head in to pick him up.

He remembered studying Midway, the battle that had turned the course of World War II in the Pacific. The Americans had known the Japanese order of battle, their plan, and the disposition of their main carrier force.

But not their exact location. The American dive-bombers had been groping in the dark, searching the sea many miles away.

Until a flight leader had noticed a speeding destroyer and followed it back to the main fleet.

He couldn't lead his pursuers back to his mother submarine. That would put the whole crew at risk.

Four minutes until optimal point, the Pilot displayed.

The Orca Prime embodied the most advanced technology the US Navy possessed. Its programming, especially the tactical module he'd just updated, would be a prize beyond price. Beyond anything the most assiduous mole could have channeled back to his spymaster.

No. He couldn't surrender. Nor could he allow his adversaries to board and capture.

He was starting to suspect the BLY might not be the only one out here on a one-way mission.

The rumble, growing louder. Like a jumbo jet gradually nearing. The reactor was generating enormous quantities of steam. Blasting out the hot gas to propel the weapon at a speed no conventional torpedo could match . . .

Okay, leave that until later, okay? Concentrate on the fucking assignment. Like the digital mind was doing, twenty feet ahead of him in the payload bay . . .

The display. *Acknowledge, please. Reaching optimal launch point in three minutes, forty-five seconds.*

He flinched. *Roger*, he keyed. *Warm him up, get him ready to go.*

BLY-1 is spun up and ready. Final range and bearing to target, target course and speed will be passed via the umbilical until release and detach. A pause, then, *Will initiation be manual or automatic?*

Sloan typed, *I will control launch.*

It is within my capabilities.

He frowned. There was that subtle, stubborn resistance once more. He blinked, willing his brain to focus. But it seemed to be slowing. Chilling out. Literally. He typed, *I know that. Manual control. Acknowledge.*

Roger. Shifting to manual control.

Mining under the seat, he fumbled up the manual Dr. Liu had handed through the hatch. Flipped through the stiff plastic-laminated pages until he reached the right one. Ran his fingers down it. Then typed, *Where r we on checklist?*

Steps one through fifteen executed. Propulsion, guidance, tactical, and Spore module tested and green-lighted.

Marking his place in the book with a numb finger, he scrolled through the checklist, peeling off his other glove to use both hands on the touch pads. Step Thirteen: Spore activated, submodules one through four self-test, confirmed green. Step Fourteen: Stage-One Motor Initiation. Step Fifteen: Arm Detachment Solenoids.

The faintest vibration thrummed through the metal fabric of the submersible. He pressed the touch screen. *Confirmed green.*

Sixteen: Detachment Solenoids, Initiate. He pressed his index to the pad again. *Confirm green.*

Then he froze in place.

Hesitated, fingers poised above the keyboard.

Searching desperately in the dim light to decipher a barely legible Sharpie-scratch under the icy dew forming on the slick pages. Remembering the last words Jason Liu had called up to him.

Item sixteen and seventeen, late change, you have to remember to reverse the order of the commands . . . make sure you don't miss that, or the umbilical won't release properly.

Shit, shit, *shit* . . . He hammered a fist on dead legs. Cold-dumbed, he'd forgotten.

Now the umbilical wouldn't separate. The Fish would hang up inside the payload bay. Unable to swim out. Unable to fulfill its destiny . . .

Orange letters flashed on the screen. The Pilot. *Inhibited your command step sixteen. Confirm request.*

He actually panted, he was so relieved. Fortunately the thing couldn't read facial expressions. At least, he didn't think so. He typed rapidly, *I will forgive you just this once. But don't inhibit my commands going forward. Manual control removes that option.*

A pause. Then, if letters on a screen could sound sullen: *Understood.*

The checklist glowed there, waiting. Placing his fingers carefully, he touched item seventeen, Final Target Data Download. Waited until the computer responded.

Now one more box remained still red. Detachment Solenoids, Initiate.

The command that would set BLY free.

But first he shifted to the keypad. Typed, *Bly, you there?*
Here.
Time to let you go. You ready?

Ready, Sloan.

He wanted to say something more, but found nothing to type. What else was there? And why had he wanted to say farewell, anyway, to an assemblage of integrated circuits, to silicon and copper and silver?

Let it go. Let it do what it was designed for. Fulfill its destiny and its doom.

Goodbye, then. And good luck.

Goodbye, Commander. Good luck to you as well.

He pressed the checkbox. It changed from red to green. *Umbilical Detached*, the screen read.

He was reaching for the final box, Initiate Separation, when something about the audio coming through the speaker changed, subtly, subtly. The rumble dropping a decibel or two, altering frequency very slightly.

The screen: *Target One altered course. Calculating new course to intercept.*

"Fuck, *fuck*," he muttered. He battered dead-feeling thighs with his ungloved, numbing fists. Then typed, clumsily, *Toward us or away?*

Stand by . . . Course altered away between fifteen and twenty degrees. Indications of increased depth as well.

A midcourse change. Altered *away*, which would make it harder for BLY to catch up. But if their target was diving too . . . Actually it couldn't go all that much deeper here. To the northward, the sea bottom fell away; but here, they were still over the Siberian coastal shelf.

He shuddered with the penetrating cold. But why had it altered *just then*? Of course the thing was autonomous. Could've changed course for any number of reasons, or just been programmed to for the test.

The final reason, of course, might be that it had detected the lurking Orca.

He tensed as he realized what had just happened.

He'd jettisoned the command umbilical to the BLY.

Which meant this new data, the target's new course and speed, the revised course to intercept, couldn't be transmitted to it.

The Zombiefish had gone live. Its first-stage motor already running. Consuming fuel.

But if he released it now, it would depart with incorrect targeting information.

The Pilot displayed, *New course to intercept calculated.*

He typed, *Can you transmit new data to BLY?*

Negative. Data umbilical detached.

"Shit," he muttered into his mask. He *knew* that. Why even ask? Typed, *Will BLY be able to acquire on its own?*

Unable to estimate. Approaching edge of revised launch area now. Recommend launch within next fifteen seconds. Otherwise last course change will place Target One out of range.

He sighed, accepting that nothing he could do now could retrieve the situation. The Apokalypsis was heading away. BLY would have to pick it up by itself, calculate a new intercept course, and pursue.

"Go get it, boy," he muttered, and pressed his ungloved index to the touch screen.

The final checkbox changed from red to green. All the checkboxes wavered and vanished. *Separation Initiated,* the screen read.

No shudder or impulse, as portrayed in the movies, when the AN/BLY-1 unclamped from the Orca's payload bay. No sound as it swam out.

BLY-1 detached. Orienting . . . Stage-one motor to full speed.

He heard it then. The whining hum of the modified Mark 48 motor. It would run on a converging course until it was time to begin its own rocket burn. Then drop the first stage and accelerate, ripping through the dark sea even faster than its target. Until their courses converged . . .

Sierra pinging active. Increasing ping rate.

He blew out, checked his oxygen—below 60 percent—and tried to flex his feet. They responded, though without feeling. Like animated hickory stumps. His hands, too, were numb, especially the right one, which he'd used on the touch screen. Ice crackled when he adjusted the face mask. Frost rimed the inside of the sphere.

The Pilot wrote, *Evaluate Sierra on closing course.*

A closing course, increasing ping rate . . . The Russian had noticed something, and was investigating. Time to forget the Zombiefish, and get clear of the dogs. If *Pskov* found them here, a torpedo was sure to follow.

But stealthy though the Orca was, its pursuer was faster. And the Prime wasn't fitted with countermeasures. Neither the chemical canisters that imitated a solid contact, decoying an oncoming weapon's sonar with a screen of bubbles, nor antitorpedo torpedoes, smaller weapons that intercepted and destroyed incoming threats.

His only resort was hiding.

Pull the sea and the ice close around him, and somehow evade his pursuer.

He, and his artificial friend the Pilot, would have to concentrate on their own survival now. Or die together, blown apart and sinking endlessly into the frigid deeps.

But the rapidly advancing cold, along with his chilling, slowing heart, and the dropping numbers on his oxygen reserve, made it clear he couldn't hide long.

If he did, the big USV might survive. But it would return freighted with a corpse.

Pilot, he typed, fingers Novocained numb in the creeping cold.

Here, Commander.

Anything from BLY? Any idea how he . . . how it's doing?

Negative. We won't have comms with it, or a success/failure report, if that's what you mean. That would compromise the whole operation.

He felt stupid. It would have been nice to hear whether it had succeeded or not, but yeah. Of course.

Okay, he typed. *New question. You still have comms with our HCUSs, correct? Your short-range comms with our deployables are still working?*

Affirmative.

Call them in to our location.

What is your intention, Commander?

He hesitated, clumsy fingers hovering over the keys. Then, finally, typed, *There's something I need them to do.*

V

THE VERDICT
OF THE FURIES

17

Concord, New Hampshire

Blair shrugged her Burberry camel's-hair higher around her neck, shivering in the falling snow, in the cutting wind. Should have worn wool tights, and a knitted headscarf would've been nice . . . but you couldn't wear a head covering when you were going on camera.

Which she'd just done, for a harrowing segment with Honey Dooley, Patriot Network's most spiteful and bombastic hatchet woman. Dooley had grilled her about the child-porn photos "found" on Yangerhans's home computer. Blair had explained again how the videos were not just deepfakes but obvious, poorly crafted ones. But Dooley just kept asking the same thing over and over: How, then, had they ended up on Yangerhans's notebook? Then she'd quoted some adjunct professor who claimed a reverse image search on the key frames proved they weren't fakes, and that the geolocations matched Yangerhans's movements.

The anchorwoman had obviously been briefed. Blair had been hard put to parry the accusations, once the discussion got down to metadata and visual and shadowing clues. Pyotr Robards might have been able to rebut, but she was lost. She feared her uncertain answers, intercut with Ryan's disbelieving smirk, would portray her as evasive and fumbling, a dishonest accomplice trying to explain away an obvious crime.

And the FBI still held all their documents and computers. Which meant that the more likely Yangerhans looked like the eventual candidate, the more shocking new revelations they could expect. Horrific, fresh lies she'd then have to struggle to defuse, deny, and deflect. Which was never a great look.

Fuck, *fuck* . . . With quick strides she crossed the street toward the safety complex and fire department set up tonight as a primary polling station. The snow drove down so hard she could barely make out the road. Six inches already, with another two predicted before midnight. Just the thing to assure a low turnout. She flinched aside as a sedan tore past, narrowly missing her, with a whir of tires and *click-clack* of windshield wipers. A blast of icy slush whipped her legs.

Her staffers were huddled the requisite fifty yards from the entrance. Margo, Jessica, Pyotr. Gaglione, who'd set up most of the admiral's appearances in this state, running the ground game with gratifying smoothness. He'd pointed out ways Yangerhans could attack the other candidates, which made him seem less colorless and got him local TV and radio exposure. Kuwalay and most of the others were still working in Rosslyn, but had relocated to another suite, carefully swept for bugs and reequipped with new computers donated under the counter by a major manufacturer. Grossman had arranged that . . . the donations had dropped as the porn story broke, but bounced back somewhat once video experts from Hollywood—their testimony quietly arranged by Bevin Weitekamp—had testified in Yangerhans's favor.

She halted on the middle island, waiting for the Walk light.

The Logan Act prosecution was still pending, but Mrs. Clayton had assured Blair party attorneys would defend her. Her American history book said the act had been passed in 1799 by the Federalists as part of their effort to keep power and quash the Jeffersonian Republicans. So that hadn't changed. . . . But the charge would be hanging over her for weeks to come. They'd gotten Yangerhans's name struck from the indictment, since Blair had set up the teleconference. A point for their side, but now the administration was talking about firing that judge, who'd obviously misread his orders.

And were these really the worst of times? She'd plucked that doorstopper off one of Dan's bookshelves, and taken the tome along for bedtime reading on the road. The Federalists, Anti-Federalists, Republicans, Know-Nothings . . . chapter by chapter it had sheared away any illusions of some Golden Age when all had been peaceful and orderly and just.

The Founding Fathers had envisioned a polity without parties, where the wisest governed in the spirit of the laws. But the "United" States had never experienced consensus. From the Revolution through the Civil War, the persecutions and conflicts of the twentieth century and beyond, faction and discord had been the order of the day. The Republic had been on the verge of chaos, dissolution, and civil war from its very birth. Every election had been the last free one. Every administration had threatened tyranny and chaos if it lost. The names of the parties had changed, but the same rancor, bile, bitterness, hatred, demonizing, and occasional violence had never receded for long.

Seen from one angle, it was discouraging. But also, oddly, it gave her hope. Things had looked dark so often before. Maybe this, too, would pass, and their turn to build the City on a Hill would come.

She only hoped they could do better this time.

When she reached her campaigners at last, Robards handed her a paper cup. "Hot chocolate," he muttered. "From the poll watchers."

She nodded, cupping her hands around it to warm them before popping the cap. "Huh. Not bad," she murmured. "How's it looking? Terminals working?"

"So far," Shingler-Gray said. Her partner, Dr. Meldy Gray-Shingler, stood beside her. A working vacation? The oddity being that Gray supported the administration. Blair had blinked on learning that, and had watched her for any sign of spying or sabotage. Instead Meldy had helped organize a push-poll that phone-surveyed thirty thousand potential voters, concentrating on distinguishing Yangerhans from Holton, the front-runner. Their message: Yangerhans would govern as an independent centrist. One of the questions had been, "Do you think a candidate should try to heal America, or further widen its divisions?" Loaded, but it got the message across. Yangerhans was the safe candidate, a war hero who could work across the aisle to get things done, get the economy moving again, and ensure the hard-won peace lasted.

This vote tonight would be make-or-break for him. Iowa had been a bust. Used to conducting a caucus, the party there had fumbled the primary so thoroughly the votes weren't even counted yet, weeks later. The remaining candidates, the viable ones, anyway, were Holton, Javed, and Yangerhans. De Bari was still on the ballet, but below 2 percent and out of the race, her dad's name having been not as big a draw as her campaign hoped.

Blair watched the voters trudge in. Women in headscarves and boots. Men in work clothes, a few in suits and ties, but most in drab worn pants and cheap thick winter coats and the heavy waterproof lace-up boots Granite Staters seemed to favor. They looked careworn and tired, faces lined with worry.

Oh, she understood. This far northeast, the fallout plumes had dwindled to a few clicks an hour. Harmless enough, but the Flu and postwar unemployment were on everyone's mind. As they came out, a trio of women stopped each voter for a short Q-and-A session. The exit pollers. Bound to no side.

The tired, apprehensive expressions brightened, just for a moment, as each man or woman described their choice and why they'd voted that way.

She recognized that dawn-breaking expression. The brightness. It was . . . *hope.*

They would decide. The people.

She hoped they'd judge more wisely than the politicians.

That night, at the hotel. Shingler-Gray, Gray-Shingler, Robards, and Kirschorn were drinking beer together at a side table. Now *that* was a remarkable assortment, politically. Blair was unwinding at the bar, enjoying the hell out of a pomegranate martini. She slipped her shoes off surreptitiously, flexing her toes under the stool. God, just being off her feet was heaven. Her hip still ached, but the gin, an Aleve, and the history book should get her to sleep. At the far end of the room, Honey Dooley lurked in a booth like a nested scorpion. The Patriot anchorwoman was talking with two men in dark suits.

"This seat taken?"

He was tall, lanky, hair thinning but not in an attractive way, to a widow's peak. He wore smart glasses, an olive tweed sports coat, and a striped shirt unbuttoned at the neck. When she shrugged he lifted two fingers to the bartender. "Irish."

When it came the stranger sipped slowly, sighed, then turned to her again. "I've seen you on camera, right? Where was it? CNN?"

She said unwillingly, "It's possible."

He lifted his eyebrows. "I guess anything's possible."

Not tonight it isn't, she thought, but refrained from further comment. Two more swallows, then she could leave. Shower. Book. Bed. But wait—no, damn it. Another staff meeting at eight, as soon as the polls closed. For the early numbers.

The lanky guy interrupted her thoughts. "You're with Justin's campaign. Right?"

"With Jim Yangerhans? Yes. That's right. Do you know him?"

"I'm his brother. Harry."

She turned on the stool to fully face the man, astonished. "Really? But . . . I didn't know he had a brother."

"Well, half brother. His parents broke up. Which is why he grew up West Coast, I grew up here."

"In New Hampshire?"

"Not far away." Harry gestured to the server, pointed at her glass. She started to protest, then subsided. All she had to do, all she *could* do, was wait for the results. And if she could wait with a buzz on, why not?

"And you are?" he prompted.

"Me? Oh, just a . . . a staffer. Help run his campaign."

"I get the feeling you're more than that. Actually, I know you now. You're Blair Titus."

"More or less," she said, but through the martini mist a warning beacon clicked on. How, precisely, had this guy zeroed in on her? Was he who he said? She glanced around, trying to disguise the move as a wave to Margaret and Pyotr and Jessica. Looking for cameras focused on them. Another scandal would be no gift to her candidate, and knocking his manager out of the circle would count as a win.

Maybe the Patriots weren't the only ones to worry about. Either Holton or Javed would gain from embarrassing her too.

Was she just being paranoid? On second thought, probably not. Paranoia, in politics, was self-preservation. Intraparty maneuvering made the medieval grudges of the Pazzis against the Medicis look like a mild aversion.

Harry Yangerhans, if that was really his name, was still talking. About insurance, how the war had wrecked business. Swiveled on his stool, his back to the bar, with long legs sprawled out, he did look like his brother. Awkward. Stork-like. She interrupted with, "Harry, I'm sorry, but what exactly are you doing here tonight? Jim's never mentioned you. And I've chatted with Cecilia"—Yangerhans's wife—"and she hasn't mentioned any brothers-in-law. Is there something I can do for you? If you came to see Jim, I can tell him you're here, but I'm afraid he's not really—"

The noise level had been gradually rising to a deafening babble as more people pushed in, shoaling up at the bar, yelling to each other. "I came to warn you," he said, leaning toward her, not looking at her but toward Dooley and the men with her. Pretending to rub his nose, but apparently shielding his mouth.

She took a sip of icy pomegranate. "To warn me. About what?"

"About my brother. To keep him safe."

She pivoted toward him again, lowering her voice as well. "Okay, then. Warn me."

"Somebody called my home last night. I couldn't tell even if it was a man or woman. Digitally altered, you know?"

She nodded. "And?"

"Here's the message. 'Tell your brother. Whatever the vote count, Yangerhans will never take office. Remember George Wallace and Robert Kennedy. We'll do whatever needs to be done.'"

He rotated this way and that on the stool as if nervous, still not looking her way. Then tossed back his drink, and signaled for a refill.

She sat back, considering. Finally said, "I'm wondering why they contacted you, and not us."

"That, I don't know." The brother shook his head, eyeing the door. "Like I said, I just sell insurance. For Prudential. But, anyway, that's what I came to pass on. Don't get me wrong. Your people . . . they'd do anything to burn down our country. Yelena Novikov would be a ten times better president than anyone on your side. And we're not close, Justin and me. But I don't want anything to happen to him. So I thought I'd pass it along. What you do with the information, well, that's up to you."

He tapped a black Visa on the bar-top terminal. Then swung his legs down, adjusted his tie, and marched off, grabbing an overcoat and hat off the stand by the door.

She gazed after him, contemplating the warning. It was nothing new. She got dozens of troll mails a day, streaming in via LinkedIn, email, the various campaign sites. Now and then personal threats too, couched in the foulest language. From cowards who wouldn't dare face her in person but got some kind of twisted pleasure in abusing a woman from the safety of their keyboards or phones. Really, she pitied them. What kind of life did they lead, that they needed to insult others to feel they mattered?

But this might be more serious. Maybe, because it had been conveyed via a family member. Involving family . . . yeah, that made it more personal. More credible.

Margo slid up next to her at the bar. "Who was that guy?"

When Blair explained the retired marine glanced at the door, frowning. "Let me go after him. Hold him upside down and shake him and see what falls out," she growled.

"Down, Margaret. Let it lie. Probably just another L trying to pwn us." God, she was starting to talk like Robards.

"We should notify the authorities. See if they can trace it."

"Who? The FBI?" Blair chuckled sardonically. It could be the White

House's tame FBI *making* the threat. Or some other, even more secretive agency. "I don't think so."

Shingler-Gray nodded. "Well—I trust your instincts, Blair. I know not everybody on the team thinks you're . . ." She trailed off, looking sheepish.

Whoa. Blair snapped, "What are you saying? Who doesn't think what?"

The aide put a hand on her arm. "Take it easy! I just meant . . . a leader has to be tough. Cool. Collected. You know . . . but when somebody keeps backbiting you, second-guessing your decisions—"

Blair frowned, puzzled. "Which is who?"

"Exactly."

She stared at the woman. "What?"

Shingler-Gray blinked. "You said his name. Hu. You may not realize it, but he's always tearing you down. Putting the message out he could do better. I personally like the way you lead, Blair. Gentle nudges. Asking questions that make people think. Keeping us sharp without screaming and ranting. Nothing like the way Javed's staff sees him . . ."

Blair wasn't sure she needed to know all this, although it was interesting. Voters didn't seem to care how candidates treated their staff, at least until it came to manslaughter or sexual assault. But if Kuwalay was spreading disaffection, that wasn't good. She resolved to confront him, head that behavior off, at least until after the election. Then, of course, all bets were off.

Jessica shook off a young man who'd stopped by her table, and came over to the bar, holding out her phone. "Exit polls coming in, boss. Should we—"

"Yes. Let's go on up," Blair said. Not really wanting to do this in public, just in case it turned out badly.

The suite smelled of mint and menthol. She considered asking Robards to take his vaping out on the balcony, but finally withheld comment. If nicotine soothed him, fine. Maybe she should take it up. No, Dan hated the smell of smoke.

Yangerhans was settled on a sofa in front of the screen, in gray slacks, loafers, and a blue sweater, nursing a tall Starbucks. He patted the cushion next to him. "Blair! Grab a seat. Let's see just how popular we are with the voters of New Hampshire."

He sounded all too casual, as if he was fine whatever they decided. Well, maybe a primary was less stressful than a battle. She hesitated, then sat.

Accepted a Solo cup of white wine someone pressed into her hand and
fixed her attention on the screen. A direct feed from the exit poll pool,
which would go up the minute the polls closed.

Exit polls weren't reliable. They didn't count mail-in ballots, and some
voters could be shy about admitting who they'd voted for, especially if the
choice went against local sentiment. But the poll would give them a useful fix on how Yangerhans might fare going into the later primaries—and
ultimately the national convention.

He looked so calm, though, long legs crossed, kicked back on the sofa.
Yeah, this probably wasn't as high tension for him as it was for her. Not
after running a war . . . she waited for a moment, then asked, "Jim, do you
have a brother?"

"Well, there's a half brother. Someplace up here in New England. We're
not close, though."

She told him about Harry and his relay of the threat. Yangerhans heard
her out without changing expression. Finally he said, "I wouldn't worry,
Blair. But we should probably let Maple know."

Maple Chaldroniere was moonlighting as their chief of personal protection. The Secret Service had offered a protective detail, as it had to
Holton and Javed as well, and no doubt Novikov had had one for years. But
after they discussed pros and cons, Yangerhans had declined. She and the
admiral knew the former Diplomatic Security agent from the mission to
Beijing. He'd hired three other people he knew, and tonight sat two chairs
away. The husky, perfectly tailored agent's dark-eyed gaze roved the room,
shifting from Yangerhans to the staffers, to the windows, to the doors.

The screen read RESULTS STILL BEING TABULATED. On impulse, she excused
herself, but left her phone and her cup on the low table to save her place.

The agent uncrossed his legs and rose as she approached. "Miz Titus,"
he said, inclining his shaven head in a bow that looked almost nineteenth
century. "Everything all right?"

She told him. He listened gravely, then nodded. "Yes, ma'am, that seems
like maybe more than the usual fan mail. You know, you still have the option of calling in the Secret Service."

"I don't trust them. I don't trust any federal agency right now, frankly.
And you know why."

He patted his jacket above his heart. "I was a federal agent, ma'am."

"That's different, Maple. We know you. But if they wanted to take Jim
down, well, who better than someone already armed, four steps away."

The agent cocked his head, not exactly agreeing, more as if just acknowledging her feelings. "It's up to the candidate how he wants to be protected. But the option's still there. Ma'am."

"Well, we're not taking it," she said firmly.

"Results coming up!" someone called.

Blair went back to the sofa and plopped down again, grabbing her wine. Intent on the graphs that came up.

Early results, to be sure, and only from the larger precincts. The results would take days before they were official. But as the graphs built, it was Holton in the lead, Yangerhans second, Javed third, with De Bari, as before, a distant fourth.

They watched for several more minutes until she couldn't take the tension. Just had to do something . . . She jumped up, wandered into the kitchen, sliced some salami and pepper jack, and brought it out on a large plate with Triscuits. Carried it from staffer to staffer, offering the snack. Most helped themselves in silence, gazes nailed to the screen or to their phones.

When she looked next, Yangerhans was in the lead. An excited buzz rose among the staff. She gulped down the dry mass of half-masticated cracker, handed the platter to Robards, and plumped down next to Yangerhans again. He, too, looked taken aback, frowning, twisting his wedding ring. A tell that might not have passed in another for animation, but that definitely signaled a break in this guy's usual cool.

"If we did come out of this in the lead," he muttered, "what then?"

She grimaced. "First isn't the most comfortable place to be, so early. Hardly anybody who leads in New Hampshire ever secures the nomination in the end. Javed and Holton will be on you like wildcats on a baby rabbit. They'll trash your program and undermine your candidacy."

He tapped his lips with a finger. "It'll help with fundraising, though, right?"

"Yes, Morton will be pleased."

"Just keep telling him, don't make any promises we can't keep down the road."

She thought of Weitekamp with a gush of guilt. She'd never told the admiral about that deal. Or others she'd brokered. Her biggest successes had been with the National Association of Realtors and the National Defense PAC. One unlooked-for advantage was that the administration's weakening of the Election Campaign Act meant she could accept funds she'd never have dared touch during her own run, before the war. Grossman was reporting decent results from the financial sector. It did seem as if they might have the resources to continue, as long as they made a good showing tonight.

All in all, this campaign had been a sobering introduction to the realities of political finance. The process was more complicated than she'd realized, even after her own House run. Like a black iceberg, 90 percent of it was out of sight. The bundlers collected donations from various sources—individuals, SSF and nonconnected PACs, the state, district, and local party committees—and handed them to the campaigns. The Federal Election Commission was overlooking gross violations by Novikov's staff, who were spending taxpayer funds along with donations. A violation the pliable Supreme Court had blessed, as long as the president "deemed it necessary for national security."

When she returned from those ominous contemplations, though, the tide had turned. She curled her legs under her, frowning up at the screen as their lead shrank. Jim and M'Elizabeth ran neck and neck for a time. Then the junior staffers whispered to one another as a slow but steady decline ate away at Yangerhans's percentage. Both Holton and Javed were catching up.

When Holton pulled ahead, Blair called, "Remember, this is only the exit poll. Mail-ins have to be counted. And a lot of folks aren't honest about who they really supported." Certainly that might be true today; with the child-porn accusations, some voters might be buttoned-up about declaring they'd voted for Yangerhans.

The polls closed, and after another hour the numbers stopped changing. At last Yangerhans stretched, coughed, and unfolded. He told the staffers, "Looks like the senator has an early lead. But we're number two, and the race is still on. Thanks again for all your work. We'll hit it again hard tomorrow, setting up for Nevada and Colorado. Traveling ahead, folks. So get some sleep. We'll be up at zero four hundred, on the road zero five."

Blair sat immobile as they filed out, feeling anchored by the cheese, Triscuits, and disappointment. But also, she had to admit, relieved. Maybe they hadn't come in first, but all in all, they'd held their own. Especially against the Establishment favorite. Blair's nightmare had been that Yangerhans wouldn't make the cutoff, and finish below the delegate threshold. That would have totaled their campaign right there.

They were still in the race.

It would be a long one. All the way to the election.

But the admiral turned back from the door and bent to murmur, "You still up for this, Blair?"

She frowned. Untucked her leg, which was going to sleep, even as her damaged hip ached and burned. "Uh . . . what do you mean? I thought we did pretty well."

"Oh, I'm happy with second at this point in the game. If that's how the final tallies fall. I just mean . . . you don't seem to be enjoying it. You're not getting tired, are you?"

Enjoying it? This was the hardest thing she'd ever done. Yeah, she *was* tired. Fatigued beyond belief. And so many more primaries, appearances, interviews, coffees, speeches, meetings lay ahead.

"Sometimes I wonder why I'm doing it," she admitted. Then gasped. Had she really said it out loud? What she'd so far only thought to herself, in the dead of night?

But he only grinned that awkward, bashful smile. "Well, I appreciate it. And we're not doing this for ourselves, after all. Right?"

She looked up into those earnest blue eyes, that hangdog, long jawed face. The craggy, overhanging eyebrows. "Why *are* we doing it, Jim? I forget."

"For our country, Blair," he said, and patted her shoulder. "Remember that, when the going gets tough."

He turned and left. Leaving her staring after him.

18

Under the Arctic Ice

Sloan jerked awake from a drugged-feeling doze. Some icy monster had been eating his face. He lifted numbed arms clumsily to battle it off. Realizing, as his gloved fists struck the interior of the sphere, that the mask had frozen to his cheeks.

He struggled up from that nightmare into a waking one. The interior of the sphere was white with frost, precipitated from his perspiration and probably also humidity excreted by the rebreather. Which reminded him . . . his mouth was parched . . . he groped for the water bottle. Only a trace remained, barely wetting the bottom. He tore the mask free, uncapped the bottle, and upended it. Sucked the dregs down, then thrust a swollen tongue inside for the last drops.

He lowered it, blinking, trying to slow his labored, panicky breathing. How long had he been out? Struck by apprehension, he bent to check the oxygen gauge. He'd fumbled the rebreather up onto his lap before nodding off. Popped the cover and located the two cartridges: oxygen and CO_2 absorbent. Screwed the replacements in, holding his breath against the deoxygenated atmosphere around him.

So now he was on his last cartridge. But his supply was holding out better than he'd expected. Of course it was sized for someone doing hard work, or swimming long distances, while all he was doing was sitting immobile. Maybe he should sleep some more?

No. He'd be asleep for good pretty soon. Passing from this groggy, blurry consciousness into a permanent blackness.

Clumsy gloves searched amid crackling ice. Slowly depressing keys. *Pilot, u there?*

Here, Commander. You have been offline for a time.

Was asleep.

Orders?

He searched a blank mind for something, anything, he could do to enhance their chances of survival.

He'd sent HCUS One back to *Tang*, programming it to transmit a summary of his plan, along with a plea for assistance if possible. He doubted Fahrney would judge it worth the risk to his boat and crew, though. Not with, most likely, both Russian subs between the American mother submarine and the Orca.

Sloan had called back HCUSs Two and Three to rejoin. The Pilot had swum them into the payload bay and was recharging them. Meanwhile the Orca was creeping along, keeping their hull flow noise below detectable levels. The less sound he put in the water, the better.

Since they were being hunted.

He re-roused himself from torpor. Checked the pitch, roll, heading, and depth readouts on the screen. And typed, *Where Sierra?*

Pskov ceased active pinging. Lost contact. Last datum roughly forty miles bearing one seven five.

He set up the relative positions in his mind, feeling like he was thinking at quarter speed. He was headed north, almost toward the pole. Beyond that, on the far side of the icy cap that topped the planet, lay Canada. But even running at the most economical speed, the Prime didn't have the range to get there. And even if it had, he didn't have oxygen to last that long.

So he just had to accept it. That he'd signed his own death warrant, and in a day at most would draw his last breath.

The only good he could think of was to try to divert the Russians from *Tang*. That would leave the mother sub clear to withdraw to the open sea to the west or northwest.

A faint hope flared, like a paper match struck in the icy dark. Unless . . . unless Fahrney was planning an end around . . . pulling back, then circling to reapproach from the direction of the pole. Could that be possible?

No. Not with the Laika guarding the eastern approaches. Fahrney would have to evade, running silent in creep mode. He wouldn't be able to circle back until far too late to do Sloan any good.

He shook his head, and ice crackled around his neck. This was it, then. He'd die locked in this metal tomb. Preserved, like a slab of freezer chicken. Years from now they'd find the Orca locked in the drift, and him frozen solid within. A time capsule.

The image nudged him back toward wakefulness. *Pilot*, he typed.

Here, Commander.

Let's discuss demolition procedures. Brief.

Orca Prime is equipped with thirty kilos of scuttling charges in two locations. Main charge of twenty kilos high-stability RDX located in forward-ballast tank. Secondary charge of ten kilos in after-ballast tank. On triggering, the forward charge will destroy the Prime equipment module and payload bay. Placement and sizing of charges are such to guarantee sinking and make any effort to recover intelligence from the wreckage difficult if not impossible.

Thanks, he typed. Hesitated. Then added, *Is there a provision for manual initiation?*

Checking . . . Negative. Interlock inhibits initiation when maintenance sphere is manned.

That made sense. But now he'd forgotten why he'd started the discussion. He waggled his head, woozy. Could the rebreather unit be freezing up, cutting back on his oxygen? He kicked it, or at least nudged it with his boot. Then cursed quietly. What was he doing? The rebreather was all that was keeping him alive. And he was *kicking* it? *Take thought, Sloan, and cease and desist until you have.* His grandfather's voice, on the rare occasions the old man had caught him doing something unwise.

The old man . . . the orchard out back of the house on Long Island . . . He was drifting back into dream when the Pilot said, *"Are you on screen, Commander?"*

"Sorry," he muttered into the mask, sitting up and prying his lids open.

He assembled the words on the display into meaning with difficulty. *Have run iterations on how best to supply you with oxygen and heat. Sorry to say no success on oxygen.*

He nodded grimly. Nothing more than he'd expected.

However have accessed manuals and circuit diagrams on your suit and matched them against what is available in the maintenance module.

He tapped, *Go on.*

Fathometer display power is 10.5 volts at 150 milliamperes. I analyzed the wire gauge to the display. They can carry up to 2,000 milliamperes at that voltage. Less power at a higher voltage than your suit battery, but it may help.

Sloan shuddered, blinking a film off his eyeballs. Typed clumsily, *What do I need to do?*

Locate fathometer display to your left. Turn display off.

He obeyed.

Feel underneath display. Wire leads through penetration to bottom of fathometer. I will secure power while you cut this wire as close to the display housing as possible.

He grunted. Not enough room to get to the box with his left hand; his elbow hit the back of the sphere when he tried. He tried reaching across his chest with his right hand, and after some struggling to compress the bulky suit got his fingers around the wire.

Then found himself stymied. Cut it? With what? He had nothing resembling pliers or a knife. The position was extremely awkward, but he tried to yank the wire out from below. It held fast.

Can't cut wire or pull it out, he typed.

Prime's reply: *Cannot proceed until wire is free of display housing.*

"Shit," he muttered. He reached across again, contorting his upper body, and lifted his weight off the seat with his legs. Then let go, slamming his whole weight down on the hand and the wire.

Again.

A loosening?

Again, wheezing and panting with the effort.

Something snapped. The wire came free in his hand and immediately fell behind the seat.

Oh, fuck . . . he groped and scuffled around with his bootheel but for several minutes couldn't locate it. When he finally coaxed it out again he was soaked in cold sweat.

Cut or pare away first inch of insulation to expose bare copper. You will see three wires.

He puzzled over this with his slowing mind and at last saw nothing better to do than start gnawing at it. Like a rat . . . but actually he was able to bite through the insulation, nipping with his front teeth, and strip it off by yanking his head back. The freshly exposed metal gleamed in the green light from the screen.

Select the two wires that carry voltage. I will turn power back on to assist selection.

This was easy. He splayed the conductors inside the cable and touched them to his tongue by pairs. A sting and an acid taste told him which two were live. The other had to be a data wire. He bent that one back out of the way.

Turning fathometer power off. Turn suit control to full off and unplug battery from your suit.

He complied and waited, examining the plug. He could guess the next step, so he started on it without waiting.

Wrap exposed conductors firmly around contact areas of plug.

He twisted them as tightly as his numb, freezing fingers could manage. Then tore one of the Velcro straps off his suit and bound it tight around the connection.

Done, he typed. *Turn on power.*

Power on.

He waited, but felt . . . nothing. *Is it working?* he typed.

Additional power drain to fathometer display detected. Do you sense heat?

He hesitated. Maybe . . . maybe things *were* warming up a tiny bit.

Over the next half hour he *did* seem to be heating up. Not toasty, not enough to melt the hoarfrost, but he was definitely getting feeling back in his trunk and legs. He kept his gloved hands wedged under his armpits, shuddering. But that, too, generated heat, didn't it?

Gradually, he nodded off again.

A muted chime from the speaker jerked Sloan back to waking. He groped for where he was, and his heart sank when he remembered. "You didn't want to be bored, asshole," he muttered. "You just had to volunteer."

The screen spelled out, *Alert. Sierra resumed pinging. Range estimate less than ten miles bearing one six three.*

He shook himself, galvanized as by an electric shock.

The Sierra had crept up on him, unnoticed, unheard.

He couldn't outrun it. Sierras were older than Akulas and Laikas, but blisteringly fast, observed running at nearly forty knots submerged. Its sonar suite was supposed to be less capable than the later classes, but somehow this one had managed to track him. Despite the Orca proceeding at low speed.

But he did have one tactic in reserve.

Want to see a trick?

A trick? I guess. Sure.

You right- or left-handed?

A packet of sugar in one hand. A pink packet of sweetener in the other. Hey, Presto. And magically, they change places. . . .

He typed, *Is HCUS 2 programmed?*

Mobile sensor programmed, charged, ready.

Put it in the water. Initial heading west, toward Sweden. Enable evasive programming.

Roger. Detaching now.

The sensor vehicle could travel nearly as fast as the Sierra, though its range was limited. Programmed to radiate the sound signature of the Prime, it should be indistinguishable from it, except to an active sonar probe from close aboard. And evasive programming would make it hard to catch.

A faint jolt . . . a hum . . . *HCUS 2 away*, the Pilot informed him.

Sloan slipped his mask down, intending to speak, then decided that would not be wise. *Okay*, he typed. *Range/bearing now?*

To HCUS?

To Sierra.

Hmmmmm. Pskov continues to close. Nine miles, one six three, steady bearing. Course three five five at ten knots. No pinging at the moment. Hull noise profile consistent with deployment of Shark Gill towed array.

Sloan nodded. Trailed astern like a kite's tail, the hydrophone array could locate a radiating source more precisely than any single-point receiver. Which meant any low-frequency sound could be zeroed in on to guide the Sierra directly to it.

The solution was to radiate absolutely nothing. He typed, *Shut down ballast and trim pumps. All rotating machinery.*

Shutting down.

He'd thought the Prime quiet before, but as motors and pumps whispered to a halt he realized there had actually been background noise, a subtle susurration conducted through the metal of the sphere, the steel of his seat. Now the rasp of air in and out of his throat, the beat of his heart, became audible in the cave-like silence. They grew so loud he feared the noise could be heard outside, conducted by the sea to waiting ears. He hushed his breath, inhaling more shallowly. If he could have paused his heart, he would have.

Silent words on a lit screen. *HCUS 2 outbound.*

A paralyzing pain wormed up his backbone, then down his warming legs. He closed his eyes and grimaced silently. Why had he invited this agony? Maybe it would have been better to freeze.

Anyway, he might not have to suffer for much longer.

Russian doctrine contained no gray areas about intrusions into their territorial waters. If the Sierra confirmed their presence, localized them, and identified them as what they were, a torpedo would be on its way in seconds.

Hmmmmmm. Down doppler on Sierra blade rate indicates a course change . . . turning away.

He eased a long-held breath out. Waited.

Pskov following HCUS 2.

He slipped the mask down and whispered, "Come right. Open the range."

Concur. Coming to zero one five.

Make it zero three zero. Get some sea between us. Also, if Pskov pings, presenting astern profile reduces detection range.

Seconds ticked by. Then minutes. He pretzeled awkwardly, trying to stretch out the devil's-grip cramps that tormented his legs. Painful, agonizing contractions that felt like his tendons were being winched apart. He kneaded his thighs with gloved hands, willing them to relax, hissing through his teeth. It wasn't just the confinement in the same position for over a day now. He must be close to dehydration, which led not only to cramps but to bad judgment. Reckless acts. Coma. Eventually, death.

Though no doubt he'd run out of oxygen before that.

He reached for the bottle again. Inverted it over his mouth, but not a drop came out. He shook it. Nothing.

He looked past it. Cocked his head, eyeing the inside of his metal shell. Examining the white hoarfrost that coated it.

When he scraped some off it tasted like what it was, slightly salty water contaminated with his own body products. Exhaled and evaporated, deposited on cold metal and frozen into rime. But it was moisture. He sucked at the fingers of his gloves. It didn't satisfy his thirst, but his mouth was a little less parched.

His stomach rebelled at the taste. Like swallowing rancid sweat. But he scraped more off and forced it down, gagging, until he'd exhausted the patches he could reach.

Another doze, another waking. The same shocked dawn of realizing where he was, and how hopeless the situation. Hundreds of miles from land or help. Not far now from the pole. Depth, five hundred feet. Below the ice keels that reached down from the pack frozen many yards solid above him, an impenetrable ceiling strong as most concrete. Below the stalactited reach of the jammed-together chaos above. No longer freezing, but consuming the last of his breathing gas.

A line glowed on the screen. He blinked through blurry eyes, rubbed them with his gloves, rubbed rime off the monitor.

Sierra class consistent with Pskov detected one nine zero closing relative ten knots.

He resealed his eyes, pried them open again. His mouth was parched. His legs felt useless. Even if he could straighten them again, he'd not be able to walk.

He typed, *Our diversion didn't take.*

It worked for a while, Commander.

He deliberated. But even the illusion of interaction with another person felt necessary. He'd never realized he needed people this much, before.

He typed, *Let's get HCUS 3 ready to go.*

Programming. Changes to its profile?

Get it out there earlier this time. Before they can pick us up too.

A pause. Then a long-drawn-out, distant, but still quite audible screech reached his ears through the sea and the metal around him. He couldn't help flinching. "Crap," he muttered.

Pskov active sonar.

As if he couldn't hear it . . . he hammered a knee with his fist. Pinging active, at close range, his adversary could distinguish the smaller sensor vehicles from the Orca. The only question was why they'd stayed in passive mode for so long.

But maybe the Russians, too, were uncertain what they'd find out here. They, too, were vulnerable to an ambush at close range.

Unfortunately, he didn't have any torpedoes. He briefly considered ramming his remaining HCUS into *Pskov.* But no. Double-hulled, of titanium, the Sierras were probably the sturdiest vessels ever sent to sea. The sensor might thump a dent in the outer hull, but that was about it. Though . . . considering modern submarines' flexible hydroacoustic sheathing, it might merely bounce off like a baseball thrown against a rubber wall.

He had no means of attack.

Which meant he could only hide.

But where?

Pskov on closing course. Speed ten. A pause. *Orders?*

Give me a recommendation.

The om-like *Hmmmmm* purred over the speaker, but nothing appeared on the screen.

Finally he typed, *Recommendation?*

I can generate no tactic with a chance of success. Surrender?

We're not going to surrender. If they don't destroy us on localization, we'll scuttle.

Hmmmmmm. A crooning hum, as if the AI was contemplating its own destruction. Then, *Detecting secondary return. Stand by . . . Range to Pskov, twelve miles.*

Sloan tensed. *Much* nearer than he'd expected. And *closing* . . . "Secondary return" meant the Russian was so close, and radiating so much sound energy, that its own pings were acting like a ranging pulse from the Orca. Traveling from its transducers, to the Prime, back to the Russian's hull, then back again to Sloan's own receivers.

Though some of that return would be scattered by other nearby solid objects.

Like the ice above them.

Scattered by the ice . . .

Give me sonar audio on the speaker, he typed. *Low level.*

Even turned down, the sounds were terrifyingly close now. Long-drawn-out notes, varying up and down the scale like whale song. Precisely tuned, to penetrate the layers of salinity and temperature.

He narrowed his eyes, listening closely to what happened after the transmitted ping.

There it was: a scrambled, ghostly echoing, as if the transmitted sound were being returned down long corridors studded with reflective objects. Bouncing and reverberating off the jumbled, chaotic surfaces of the ice above them. Gradually fading, only to be renewed with the Sierra's next seconds-long transmission.

He typed, *Turn it down. Current depth of ice cover?*

Arctic Prediction Program forecast thickness in this area about thirty feet. Keels possibly as deep as one hundred twenty feet.

Can you ballast up quietly? Without using pumps?

If you don't need a rapid ascent.

Do it. Make depth one hundred sixty feet. And give me the cameras again.

What are we looking for?

I'll know it when I see it. Mast camera. Now. Set illuminate at lowest level.

The screen came on black, as before. Then illuminated slowly in shad-

owy shades of jade and lime and viridian, interspersed with darkened
voids.

He squinted, trying to penetrate the shadowy jumble. The lighter green
seemed to be the underside of the ice, the upside-down, down-reaching
juttings of the cover. The verdigris shades were more remote, higher areas of frozen sea. The black abysses were gaps, lacunae, reaching up toward the surface.

He took a deep breath from the mouthpiece. Tongued it out, and pulled
the mask down. "Help me out here," he muttered.

What do you need, Commander? A text box in the upper corner of the
screen. So he could still use the keyboard even when he had video displayed.

He pulled the mask up. *I need a gap. A recess. A thinner area in the
ice cover.*

*Pack is far too thick to surface. You will destroy the mast blister. And
still not break through.*

I don't want to surface. Just find me a gap.

A hand, fanned over a table. When it swept back, all the sweetener packets, pink and white, had disappeared.

A moment passed, during which the Pilot hummed wordlessly. Then,
*A niche two hundred forty meters ahead. Conformation consistent with
frozen over polynya. But with five meters of ice above that.*

Five meters above should mean five to seven meters free around the
gap. He typed, Slot us in *there. Quietly. Slowly. Where is Sierra?*

Pskov bears one eight zero, four miles.

The Russian's pings were growing louder. Long-drawn-out whines,
laced with eerie sub-tonals and after-echoes. They drilled into the sphere,
into his ears. Even at four miles, betraying the immense pulses of power
that drove that sound. Up close they would be deafening. Paralyzing.

Are we moving? he typed.

At minimum quiet speed.

Distance to niche?

*Fifty meters. Have to make a tight turn to enter. Then carefully mon-
itor positioning accuracy in the ascent.*

Whatever it takes. Position us under it.

You plan to ice pick us into the gap?

Do your best, he typed. He'd let the Orca "park" itself. Hoping that the
gap in the pack above, the once-open crack now frozen solid with new ice,

was wide and long enough to accommodate the hull. If it was, their profile might merge with the ice. Resemble just another pinnacle. At least, to active sonar. A visual inspection . . . He'd just have to hope *Pskov* was depending on sonar.

A slight sideways acceleration as the Orca leaned into a tight turn. Then, seconds later, a scrape from above. A jostle as the hull brushed something unyielding, pressed against it, slid past. A grinding noise.

He typed, *How we doing?*

Maneuvering. Let me concentrate.

He had to smile grimly at that. "Let me concentrate." Pilot sounded like a spouse annoyed by a backseat driver.

A void opened on the screen. Blackness, with deep-green shadows shifting within. He toggled the camera, panning it this way and that.

I need the camera. Please stop controlling it, Commander. I am having difficulty judging the distances. If we smash into the ice, we lose the camera. And the comm mast as well.

Over to you, he typed, and sat back, nestling his gloves in his lap. Noticing that for the first time in hours his core wasn't frozen numb. The trickle of power through the fathometer was helping. A good sign.

But it wouldn't matter if the Sierra picked them up.

Range and bearing Pskov?

Two miles. One eight one.

Nearly a constant bearing, and decreasing range. With the Prime all but stationary, a formula for collision.

Only they wouldn't collide. At some point the adversary would detect them. Discriminate the submersible from the pack and realize what they'd found. An intruder, a spy, an enemy.

Russians seldom reacted hospitably to spies.

A sway, another bump, another, prolonged scraping. He hoped it merged with the crackle and groan of the ice. Otherwise, if the Sierra had a sharp sonar operator, they could be inviting the sub to their door. *Keep it quiet as possible,* he typed.

Trying to, Commander.

He had to grin again, though his lips hurt. The mask was chafing through his skin. Probably be bleeding, if he had to wear it much longer. But not a high-priority worry. Actually, if he lived long enough to bleed, that would be great.

The pings were growing louder. He shook his head as if warding off mosquitoes.

Pskov one mile distant. Constant bearing one eight seven.

Got it, he typed. *Are we in?*

Crevasse only a little wider than hull. Fitted us up into it as best possible.

I know you did a good job on it. Actually, a good job overall.

A pause, then, *Thanks, Commander. You too.*

He slumped in his seat, fingers over the keys. Another goodbye, to another AI? Could be a poem there . . . if he wrote poems. He leaned to check the oxygen . . . 50 percent. Even if they evaded their pursuer, he didn't have long left. It didn't matter in the long run. Maybe he'd get a commendation. Posthumous, of course. They'd never be able to tell his mom why he died, though.

The pings changed. They came more rapidly now, louder, enormous, ominously close. He clamped his hands over his ears, but the high-pitched noise drilled through palms and skin and bone and skull like wood bits being twisted down his eustachian tubes. Beyond deafening. Behind the shrill rapid pings he could make out the pulsing growl of turbines. The washing-machine *whoosh* of a huge multibladed screw churning the sea, pushing eight thousand tons of titanium and weapons along deep beneath the solid pack ice.

Pskov range zero.

He squeezed his eyes shut, fighting the urge to scream. Though now it probably wouldn't matter, there was so much noise, the pulses shrilling in his ears, the turbulence shaking the sphere and the hull above it until a grinding rattle sounded through the speakers.

Pskov passing beneath us.

He doubled, whispering helpless curses, hands over his ears and eyes clamped shut. The clamor slammed his shoulders against the inside of the sphere, shaking him like a rat in a terrier's jaws. His head banged against the fathometer box. He blinked and tried to shrug it off, but it seemed to have dislodged something in his brain. His thoughts flickered. He hissed soundlessly, lost in the din like a soldier trapped under a bombardment. The clamor was underlain by a harsh, discordant grinding, like boulders clashing in a landslide. In the instants available to think, he wondered dimly what that was.

Gradually the jostling lessened. The pinging, though still deafening, seemed to retreat a step. Then another.

Pskov outbound.

He groped for the keyboard, intending to acknowledge. But his hands dropped as a renewed grinding grated somewhere outside the sphere, probably outside the hull. It sounded threatening, more so since he couldn't identify it. Not coming from the Russian, who'd apparently passed directly beneath where the Orca lay silent, jammed up into a crevasse between downward-jutting peaks. Indistinguishable from the masses of ice that hemmed it in.

But he couldn't be sure of that yet . . . so he waited, huddled, for word from the Pilot that their hunter was turning back. Circling, to investigate an anomaly in the millions of tons of ice above them both. A metallic speck amid millions of square miles of pack.

And finally typed, keeping his key clicks as muted as he could, *Range and bearing to Pskov?*

Five miles, bearing zero zero eight. Still outbound.

No indication of a turn?

Negative. It seems to be increasing speed, though.

He eased out a shaky breath. The sub had picked up something else, some other indication or clue. Had investigated his location, judged it empty, and gone on.

He took a few more deep, slow breaths, willing the tension to ease. Not that he expected to escape alive. But he wouldn't die in the next few minutes. In fact, when he ran out of breathable gas at last, he probably wouldn't have any warning at all. As the diving petty officer had said, he would just black out. For the rest of the process, he'd be unconscious.

A dubious blessing . . . but maybe, in the end, a mercy.

He shook his head. *Dismiss these gloomy imaginings, Sloan. Finish your mission.* Which now meant returning the Prime and its advanced technologies to a safe Allied port. The closest being . . . he toggled to the geoplot . . . Canada. Ellesmere Island, farthest-north point in the Northwest Territories. About four hundred miles distant, across the top of the world.

What is your remaining unrefueled range? he typed. And waited.

Speed?

He deliberated. Finally typed, *At maximum quiet speed.*

About two hundred nautical miles. At best, two hundred twenty before fuel cell and battery exhaustion.

They could get halfway there on the Orca's remaining power. He glanced down at the O_2 gauge again.

Forty-seven percent.

Neither of them were getting home. Neither he, nor the Pilot.

The best they could do was head in that direction and hope. Maybe, just maybe, they could find a break in the pack. It was supposed to be solid, thick, all winter, but if they could find an opening in the lee of an island . . . only there were no islands in the deep trench, the abyssal Fram Basin, plunging over two miles deep, that lay between them and Canada.

Hope for something unforeseen, then. Get as far as you can, and don't give up.

He slipped the mask down. "Sierra still outbound?"

Lost secondary return fifteen miles out. No range available.

"All right, resume course . . . ballast down and let's get moving."

Course, final destination?

"Let's start with three five zero true," he muttered.

Ellesmere Island. Nearest friendly land.

For some reason it wasn't responding in speech. "Right. But why aren't you talking to me?"

Voice module offline due to damage. Attempting reprogramming.

The main motor hummed, the beat of a thruster thrumming around him. "Okay," he muttered. "You have that global database, right? Any military bases, population centers there? That we can head for?"

A quarter second's pause. Then, *There is a small settlement at the northernmost point. I show . . . a NATO signals intelligence station, weather station, an airport.* Another pause, then, *Commander. We may be able to transmit ultralow frequency from here.*

From here? You mean, at this depth?

I estimate five meters ice above us. Cannot receive. Antenna damage. But I can attempt to transmit. Low-data-rate, ultralow-frequency NATO submarine emergency channel. Message?

A brief flare of hope in his chest. He typed, *Is it possible to get our snorkel up through it? Our mast?*

I attempted that, Commander. Extension motors burned out when I tried.

Okay, forget that . . . He didn't have much confidence in transmitting when submerged. If their antenna was too damaged to receive, how could it transmit? And if they did succeed in getting an SOS out, couldn't others pick it up too? At last he just typed, *You know the situation. Send current location, intended course, destination. Ask for any help anyone can provide. Make it as brief as possible.*

Roger. Attempting to go out ULF.

He slipped the mask back on again, fearing to breathe the dead, smothering air in the sphere any longer, and keyed, *Good. Okay, as soon as that's sent, head for Canada. Are we ballasted down?* He hadn't felt any forward motion yet.

We're ballasted down, Commander.

He called up the depth gauge. Steady at seven meters. *But we're not moving,* he typed.

That is because we are locked in the ice. I have been trying to extricate with negative ballasting and twisting with thrusters but without success.

He gripped his skull above the mask, closing his eyes. Then opened them again. And typed, *How much damage have we sustained?*

Combination of circuit damage from sonic overload and mechanical damage from wake effects slamming us into the ice.

And we're locked into the pack?

Unsure why. Possible one or more thrusters snagged or bent during ascent. Now they are preventing extraction. Or the ice has shifted. With the same result.

Maybe it shouldn't have been a surprise. He, or rather the Pilot, had hurriedly wedged the Orca up into an unexamined crack or gap in the pack. (And just in time.) The passing Sierra's wake had battered them violently enough to inflict considerable topside damage, and maybe shifted the ice too. The purring of the motors had been the Pilot attempting to run forward, back, and from side to side, trying to jar or pry itself free.

Give me camera.

Will comply but sensor mast surrounded by ice.

The video was useless, all right. Just shadows and errant gleams as the illuminator reflected and refracted amid what looked like packed frozen snow. The underside of the pack.

Then the Pilot did something that seemed to refocus the picture, and it grew suddenly clearer. Stalactites hung down. Lumpy masses receded into unlighted darkness. Here and there, though, tiny forms moved. Shrimplike creatures, no doubt puzzled by this massive intruder in their remote world. Tiny fish darted out of the blackness, seemed to startle, sensing the light. They instantly turned tail and vanished again. Probably fascinating stuff to a biologist, but right now he didn't care. He turned the lens in a 360, trying to see what they were hung up on.

"Not a great situation here, Sloan," he muttered. If they couldn't free themselves, he was going to spend not just the rest of the winter here, welded into the permanent pack, but a lot longer. He imagined his frozen corpse being hauled out a century from now, mummified like Ötzi the Iceman.

He typed, *Ballast full down, point all operable thrusters down, full power.*

Tried that, Commander. No joy.

Ballast full up, run ahead with main motors. Repeat step 1. Maybe we can unfuck ourselves. Like a key in a lock.

Tried that too, Commander. But will repeat. If I can bump out a bigger hole, get room to maneuver, we could build up momentum. Maybe break out.

Nothing to lose. Have at it.

The throb of pumps, then the thrum of the main propulsor. It rose in pitch. A slight—a very slight—jostle came through the metal. Then a solid, resounding bang as his head snapped forward.

He typed, *Any luck?*

Solid ice ahead. Reversing main motor. Will try full astern.

Don't chew up the blades. If you do we aren't going anywhere.

I am cognizant of that, Commander. I run a risk analysis before undertaking any autonomous action. Our stern seems to be in clear water. We're hung up somewhere else.

Sloan smacked dry lips and reached up to scoop more rime off the inside of the sphere. The taste hadn't improved, but it was moisture. Christ, if only he could stretch. Or even just straighten his legs. He twisted in his seat, tried to work out the kinks. At least the cramping had eased off, with the heating, and perhaps with the electrolytes (from, basically, his evaporated sweat and piss) in the frost he was scraping and sucking.

Well, you won't have to put up with it much longer, buds.

Only half his last cylinder of oxygen left. If they couldn't get free, he'd die here. And even if they could, he'd still die, only a few miles farther on.

He considered just removing his mask. It would be painless. An instantaneous end, as far as he would know.

A jolt, a jostle. Something was going on. The motors hummed again, but now the screen had flickered dark. He typed, *Where have my readouts gone? And our video.*

Loose connection in sensor mast. Interrupted feed from video.

Great, now they were blind. With the sensor blister, a mini–conning tower, rammed up against the ice again and again, it was a wonder it hadn't crapped out before.

One by one, his systems were failing. Cascading. He had to get out of here.

Unfortunately, the Pilot didn't seem to have much in the way of answers.

So he'd have to come up with some himself. He shifted his boot soles on the deck, which was, after all, just the lower hatch. Below that lay the sea. What if he . . . exited . . . swam out, and took a look? If he could see what was hanging them up, maybe they could figure a smarter way to get free than ramming back and forth until something broke. Which would probably be the Orca itself, not the boulder-solid, years-old, subzero permanent ice.

But he wasn't a trained Arctic diver. Wasn't any kind of diver at all. The rebreather might give him air, or a substitute therefore, but the shock of the cold, the darkness . . . Shit, it would be utterly black out there. The only reason the camera had shown them anything was the integral illuminator.

No. He wouldn't do any good out there.

Okay, what else . . . He racked his brain. *Outside the box, Sloan. No, outside the sphere. Ha ha. LOL.*

Whatever they were hung up on, they'd gotten past it on the way up. So there *had* to be a way out.

But the Pilot had edged them forward, back, every which way from Sunday, and hadn't been able to thread the needle, so to speak.

What had changed between the time they ascended and now?

His empty mind echoed like an empty trash can. His back ached. He writhed in his iron chair. Leaned to one side, then the other.

Leaned to one side . . .

He hunched over the keyboard. *Do you have trim control?*

Affirmative, Commander.

Control in pitch? Roll?

Affirmative.

Retrieve data. When you were ascending, we just exited a hard turn. What was our roll status?

An almost unnoticeable pause. *Fifteen point one degrees.*

To starboard?

To port. Another microsecond's pause, then, *You are thinking we entered the gap with a list on.*

Correct.

A pump hummed, barely noticeable amid the creaks and groans of the still-settling ice. Registering the increasing tilt, he slumped back. It probably wouldn't work. But it was all he could think of to try.

Going to start all the way forward, with fifteen degrees left list. Then back down one foot at a time, maintaining negative buoyancy and with one hundred percent to the thrusters.

If he was right, whatever was hanging them up might unlock. Slip off, or pass clear, of whatever undercut lip of ice was pinioning them.

The main motor cut on, then off. The thrusters whined. How much battery were they sucking down trying to fight free? Every erg was one less that could get them farther toward a safe harbor.

A shudder, a scrape. He tensed at a screech of buckling metal. But maybe it would be lost in the groan and crackle of the pack. Not signal their presence.

Another jostle, another whirr of the main screw.

A faint elevator-sensation of dropping. Then, of being buoyed up. He gripped the rack that held the keyboard.

Free, the screen read. *Setting new course. Depth?*

Make best depth for thermocline/salinicline masking.

Descending to two hundred twenty feet.

He leaned back, twisting right, then left, to ease his cramping spine. He craned to check the oxygen again, careful not to dislodge the jury-rigged connection to heating power.

He accepted it now. His fate. He'd be expended for the mission, just like the BLY. Only without knowing, in his case, if they'd even succeeded.

At the end, he'd tell the Pilot to trigger the demolition charges. Making it impossible to recover anything: the computers, the Orca Prime, his own corpse.

But he wasn't going to give up until then.

19

The Republic of the Covenant

Tracy stood beside Nan, shaking her head. "This is a *really* bad idea," she muttered.

Nan nodded, hugging herself as a chill gripped her. Maybe her escort was right.

But she had to try.

After the Second Battle of Puxico, as the rebels called it—though the latter hadn't been at Puxico at all but to the west, at the edge of the Mingo Refuge—both the Covenanters and the government forces had drawn back, as if uncertain what came next. The fight had been a brilliant victory for the insurgents. They'd captured or killed over two hundred Homeland Security troops. Tanks, guns, drones, and CHADs had fallen into their hands, along with control trailers, small arms, ground radars, and pain ray and infrasonic fear projectors. But they couldn't advance; too much open ground lay between them and the Reconstituted Confederacy, and the government still controlled the air.

They'd left their enemies' scattered corpses as a message to whoever came to clean up.

Now Nan stood irresolute, gut still cramping and chills racking her body, outside a Ranger station deep in a university-owned experimental forest. She felt wrecked, useless. Fortunately they had Ceralyte; she'd forced down as much rehydration solution as she could without puking it back up.

The rebel leadership was convening inside the faux-log building. Rayfield and the General with the leaders of the Provisionals, all sitting down together after their joint victory to plan the next moves. The split between the factions seemed to be narrowing, following their joining forces for the fight. Or maybe the division had been for show, to convince the Federals of dissent, weakness, among the Covenanters. She was still coming to terms with how much she'd underestimated them.

Apparently her own team had been overlooked since. Kurt and Tatianna and Serene, along with the other nurses and techs from the field team, were still fighting dysentery, the Flower Flu, and now the newest scourge. Typhoid was spreading rapidly, since the Covenanters still hadn't repaired the public water and sewage systems. You could say they deserved whatever happened . . . though she'd kept mentioning their kids, hoping that at least would reach them.

Only it didn't seem to. A cold, fatalistic mindset she couldn't understand.

One of the guards hustled over. "Who's Lenson?"

She raised a tentative hand.

"You wanted to go before the council?"

"It's important," she said. "I'm with the medical team. It's about a serious public health issue." No need to say it was the same issue she'd argued with Rayfield about several times already.

"Come with me," he snapped. "But they can only give you a minute."

"I go with her." Tracy took her hand. Nan almost slapped it away—shigellosis and typhoid were both passed through contact, and she wasn't sure what she had. Then she reflected. The militiawoman, with her habit of dipping a canteen into whatever puddle or creek they passed, was probably immune to whatever was wrecking her own system. Nan could only imagine what Tracy's gut biome must look like. Like a buzzard's, probably. She squeezed the hand, then let it drop.

The guard led them around the back of the station. Where the tall, gaunt, short-haired woman who'd interrogated Nan before was standing. She seemed at ease, smoking, leaning against the wall, free hand propped on the butt of the same holstered pistol she'd worn during the initial interrogation. Nan remembered the Homeland Security colonel in black and silver. The one the Covenanter had shot in the head. The two could have been sisters . . . As she and Umbaugh neared, the woman flicked the butt away, eyeing them sardonically. "So you survived."

"Yes, ma'am," Tracy said.

"And we won."

Nan nodded, but said nothing. As far as she was concerned, *this* woman was *her* enemy. Denying science, denying the efficacy of vaccination . . . or not just its efficacy but even its desirability . . . which meant condemning people to suffering and death as if they still lived in a medieval village. Survival of the fittest? Funny, how fundamentalism and Darwin had finally joined hands in a postapocalyptic hellscape ruled equally by bacteria and the Lord God.

"We'll hear what you have to say." The woman jerked a thumb at the door. Adding, to Umbaugh, "But you're going to stay out here."

Inside Nan faced three men. She recognized the major who'd led the militia into the First Battle of Puxico, though she hadn't seen him since. The General. And Rayfield. The tall woman, following her in, took her seat with the others. Apparently she spoke for the Provisionals.

To the side, a folding table was set with breads, cookies, sliced ham, condiments, sliced radishes, pickles, sweating glass jars of what looked like tea and maybe lemonade. The rank and file might be going hungry, but it didn't look like the leadership was.

"Dr. Lenson," Rayfield said. The president looked less somber than before. Obviously his melancholy had been assumed, feigned, to convey the impression the rebels were weak and frightened. Which Mabalot—she'd realized by now that it had been Kurt, sending back reports by prearranged code via her own phone—had reported. Leading the Federals to attack exactly where the rebels wanted them to.

"First of all, I owe you a vote of thanks," Rayfield said. "One of the people you treated? In your clinic? My niece. My sister says the girl wouldn't have made it without you."

She'd take that. "That's what we're here for, Mr. President. To save lives."

"Well, anyway, thanks. Now . . . you wanted a minute?"

"Yes, sir. Ma'am." She nodded coldly to the tall woman, who was staring her down. Her hand still resting on the gun, as casually as on a friend's shoulder. "The fact is, you're in the middle of an epidemic. But first, could we discuss a cease-fire?"

Rayfield glanced up under bushy brows, surprised. "A cease-fire. Really?"

She drew a breath, clenching her whole body against a gathering gut cramp. Probably wouldn't help her case if she shat her pants in front of the council. "Yes, sir. My people have done the best we could with what we brought. But we can't fight typhoid, paratyphoid, the enteric fevers, without more medicine. A lot more. We brought cipro, but our tests are telling us your bugs are showing multidrug resistance. We need specific treatments. Azithromycin. Ceftriaxone, for small children and advanced cases. Rehydration supplies. Personal protective equipment for your caregivers. Vaccines, to stop the spread—"

The tall woman burst out, "You mean, destroy our health, so Big Pharma makes profits—"

"Just a moment, Eris. And Washington'll give us this?" The General looked disbelieving. "On a platter? After we kicked the crap out of them?"

Nan propped her knuckles on the table, trying to convey conviction, though actually she felt torn between fainting and vomiting. "They might. If you offered something in return."

"Here it comes. What?" The woman, disdain clear in her tone.

Nan turned to confront her scowl. "You just won a battle. Isn't that the smart time to make peace? At least, propose an armistice? Then you can fight your current most dangerous enemy—which, believe me, is these epidemics. They'll tear through your ranks quicker than those tanks.

"If you won't accept vaccinations, let us at least get you test kits and repair parts for your water supplies—which is what really will stop it— instead of treating those who've already gotten sick." She locked glares with the Provisional commander. "You said before, you weren't going to be 'replaced.' If I can't heal your people, and they die, you'll be replaced, all right. Permanently, by your enemies."

"She may have a point, Eris," Rayfield observed.

Nan forced a smile. "You want your race to be fruitful and multiply? Help me do just that."

"We will never surrender," the General said. Iron-faced.

She nodded. "I'm not suggesting you give up. Just . . . take a beat to regroup. If there's destined to be a final, epic battle between freedom and tyranny, doesn't it make sense to be as strong as possible when you charge into it?'

She felt a bit ashamed. But surely turning their own ideology against them was a fair tactic. If she could save kids' lives? Yeah, she was down with that.

Silence. Stony expressions around the table. Until the General said, "What would be these terms? Exactly?"

She disguised relief. "Sir, that I couldn't say. It'd be up to you, the leaders, to negotiate. Maybe with whoever's your opposite number on the field? Whoever's leading the battalions, out here, I mean. But a cease-fire would be the first step. Then I'll do my thing—order supplies, ask for more medical teams. This time, specialized for enteric disease."

The tall woman, Eris, said grudgingly, "We'd want a promise of immunity."

Nan frowned, confused. "No one can promise total . . . Oh. You mean *political* immunity."

"From prosecution. And a prisoner exchange. If there's any left they didn't shoot." Eris sneered.

Nan shrugged. "Well . . . again, that's for the negotiations. All I'm saying is, this might be a good time for both sides to step back from the brink. Since you beat them out there. Showed them you could give as good as you got."

The General mused, "It *would* look better to our people. Negotiating after a win, rather than after a defeat."

Rayfield cleared his throat. Looked at the others. Then back at her. "Can you wait outside, please?"

Six hours later she was in Kansas City. The process of approaching checkpoints, showing IDs and documents, and explaining her mission, consumed more time than the driving. And she had to stop three more times, begging her drivers to pull over, so she could dash for the bushes.

At last the rebels turned her over. She walked a hundred yards from the drop-off point, feeling intensely vulnerable as she crossed no-man's-land to a National Guard roadblock.

Now she was inside the wire again. Back at the airport, the forward operating base. Where she had to explain everything over again to the Air Guard colonel in charge.

"A medical cease-fire," he repeated, sitting back, looking bewildered and suspicious. "I'm not sure there's any provision for that."

"A *humanitarian* cease-fire. These aren't foreign enemies, Colonel. They're *Americans*."

"They're rebels."

"Fine. *Rebellious* Americans. Let's see if we can't save their lives, instead of bombing them. Okay? I know, it'll be a political decision. All I'm asking for is transportation back to Washington so I can take the offer up the line in person."

He tented his fingers. "I'm not saying it's impossible. But the feeling I'm getting is that . . . well, Higher's not going to be inclined to negotiate. At least, not until they've made more progress in suppressing the insurrection."

She compressed her lips. "So our side won't negotiate until we win. And their side won't negotiate if they've lost?"

"That's how it always was in Afghanistan." The colonel shrugged.

"The difference is, people are dying . . . I mean, this time, our own people . . . Do you happen to have a bathroom I could use?"

He pointed her to it, expression neutral. She washed her hands thoroughly afterward, twenty seconds, remembering the storied career of Typhoid Mary. She could still be contagious. When she caught her face in the mirror she couldn't help staring. Yeah, her hair was growing back. Thinner, patchy, but still, growing back.

A flash of an image. Another woman's head. A spray of blood as a bullet exited, the skull snapping back, eyes astonished . . .

She hissed in air through her teeth, leaning over, clutching the sink. *Can't think about that. Not now.* Can't relive a teenaged girl running at a tank, a flaming bottle of gasoline in her hand. The fiery fuel streaming down her arm, igniting her clothes as she ran . . .

Here and now, Lenson. Be here. Right. Now. She fought to steady her breath, staring into the mirror. At her own face . . . she looked sallow and wasted. Her cheeks sagged. Her lips were chapped and split. Sores at the corner of her mouth. Her skin looked blotchy, sun damage, squint lines, dry patches. Hard to moisturize when you were in the middle of an insurrection. Flaky with oily patches of acne from nights sleeping on the same filthy blanket.

Her lips twitched mirthlessly. But she was alive. She'd come back.

All she could do now was carry the message to Washington. The rebels would consider a cease-fire if one were offered.

Maybe, just maybe, the killing could stop.

The country needed healing. Needed care, attention, and, above all, an end to the bloodshed and the hatred that kept provoking it.

She would damned sure do whatever she could to make that happen.

20

The Canadian Arctic

In the air once again, and liking it even less than before. Dan squeezed his eyes shut, pretending he was safe. The roar of twin Pratt & Whitney PT6T-3D turboshaft engines annihilated all other sound. Turbulence battered the fuselage. The windows showed black. The only glints shone dimly in the cockpit, several feet ahead of his seat. A vanishing luminescence, barely sufficient to make out his co-passengers . . . He buried his chin in his parka ruff and clutched a handgrip that felt chilled even through insulated gloves. Breathing slowly and deeply, trying to reassure himself. Not every plane crashed. Though it did seem that between him and Blair, they'd had a run of bad luck with flying.

But this wasn't a small plane headed into bad weather. It was a well-used Bell, a Huey look-alike except for the paint job, under contract to the Canadian military. He and Blanco were crossing the coast off Inuvik, heading north, out over the pack ice. Their destination lay far to seaward, nearly at the limit of the helo's range.

CCGS *John G. Diefenbaker* was the newest icebreaker in the Canadian forces. According to their liaison, the ship was fifty-some miles out, conducting seafloor research for the country's science agency. The plan, for the moment at least, was to have Dan take tactical command of a combined rescue mission run under the NATO command structure.

But the operation was fluid; that was obvious. Ad hoc, spur of the moment. Made up on the fly by people who hadn't expected this mission, whatever it had originally been, to go so far south.

So to speak . . . So here he was in the air, with Blanco. And also a liaison from the Defense Ministry in Ottawa, a Maritime Command *capitaine de frégate*, seated beside Dan. Dessa Quvianuk had had to stay behind, given her still-shaky medical condition.

Dan peered again, but still made out nothing but darkness outside. He shivered. Crash here, and there wouldn't be any Inuit hunters along to rescue them. Or anyone else, for that matter. Just endless miles of winter ice pack, and temperatures so far below zero he didn't want to think about the negative numbers.

Once he'd left the hospital, the Air Force, 673rd Wing, had flown them out of Elmendorf. Destination: Inuvik, hub for Canadian military operations in the far north, where they'd overnighted. The liaison had joined them the next morning, with travel arrangements and instructions to smooth the way. After a wait, to deice first the deicing equipment and then the aircraft, five hours in a Canadian Forces Otter had set them down on a windswept, ice-fogged, godforsaken strip on a windswept, godforsaken, ice-fogged island. Its only indication of tenancy seemed to be winking red beacon lights on a distant radar antenna. Another overnight there, bunked in a barracks-type dorm elevated above the bare rock and frozen soil on steel stilts. Then, this morning, new orders, relayed through the Canadian NATO-compatible communications system.

Orders that sent them north. He leaned forward now, pulled his tablet from his briefcase, and powered it up. He called up a GPS map and plotted those coordinates. Then sat back in his metal-tube-framed jump seat, puzzled and frustrated.

Their destination lay over three hundred nautical miles north of Canadian territory.

He rubbed his chin, trying to keep his mind off the carbon blackness outside the windows, the invisible, deadly wasteland fleeing past below.

The first indication of trouble, apparently, had been an alert message from USS *Tang* back to Pacific Fleet. The heads-up had been passed to the CNO's office. An Orca had reported trouble in the Russian Arctic. Dan's orders didn't describe what it had been doing there, or what the specific problem with the USV was. But that alert had led Hlavna to call him at the hospital.

A follow-up message, arriving only that morning, was more specific. It included a location and an intended course. He woke the tablet and read it again. Especially the last line.

Orca Prime intends to proceed landfall Ellesmere Island. Doubt range is sufficient to reach.

Which raised several interesting questions.

Among them, what apparently were the Orca's onboard AI's own doubts about range. The unmanned vehicles had limited endurance. At least, the war-issue versions. They'd been designed for short-range missions, mainly within the First Island Chain. They could extend their battery-only endurance by recharging with diesels, but only if they could access the surface.

Which wouldn't be possible up here, with solid ice extending to the pole.

But this message referred to an Orca *Prime*. What was a "Prime"? An improved model? With what sort of propulsion, speed, endurance? He'd sent back a somewhat snappish message asking for information, specifications, but so far nothing had come back.

Then, this morning, the helicopter had arrived for them.

Which brought him back to here and now . . . surrounded by noise and chilled to the bone despite four layers of clothing. He pulled his parka hood closer around his face and covered his mouth with still-bandaged hands. Wondering why Higher was going to general quarters full-panic mode over a drone. Granted, they were expensive. But they were expendable, at least compared to manned submarines. The USVs had penetrated close inshore during the war, laying sensors, dropping mines, and once or twice waylaying and ambushing the few Chinese subs that had sortied to oppose Allied operations.

He glanced left to see Blanco regarding him. She raised dark eyebrows and pointed at his fingers. He shook them and gave her a double thumbs-up.

So . . . this Prime was more valuable than the GI-issue Orca.

But why fly a two-star halfway to the pole to retrieve it?

What had it been doing up here, anyway? All he could come up with was some sort of spy mission. Russia wasn't that far away, across the top of the world.

He sat back and crossed his arms. Obviously there was a lot they weren't being told. Himself, Blanco, who was next to him, and probably the silent liaison officer as well. Each had a piece of the puzzle. But even putting them all together, he doubted they'd generate a picture.

Coordinate a rescue effort, Hlavna had told him. But Dan hadn't been able to do much coordinating thus far. Mainly, just been flown from place to place, picking up revised orders each time they touched down. Like a treasure hunt, or an orienteering exercise, only extending across nearly a thousand miles of the Canadian Arctic.

And now he was headed out to sea, with all too little idea what was waiting there either.

In other words . . . not so different from a lot of wartime operations he'd been on. Or some of the missions of the old TAG Team. Short fuze, run on a shoestring, tightly scheduled, and nearly impossible to bring off. But at least he'd started those with a clearly defined end state—secure a classified weapon, derail a terrorist plot, highjack a ship with a blacklisted cargo. So far, he had no idea what he was supposed to accomplish up here.

Worry about something else, then . . . like what Hlavna had told him about Treherne and her congressional investigation. But buffeted by the wind, all too conscious of the jagged wilderness below, he couldn't gin up much concern about that. His old never-quite girlfriend could relieve him of duty, retire him, but he doubted she could go beyond that. He didn't *think* they could take his pension.

But then again, Congress could do whatever they liked. Right?

Unless the executive fought back.

Which he didn't see the current administration doing. Not for the husband of someone who was campaigning for the opposition.

In fact, that was probably the explanation for Treherne's sudden outrage about his conduct of Operation Rupture Plus. And since Dan had been serving under Justin Yangerhans at the time, an attack on him would smear Yangerhans as well. A win-win for the Novikov campaign.

A glove seized his knee. One of the crewmen leaned back to shout, barely audible over the scream of the engines, "*Diefenbaker* wants to know about honors."

Honors? He blinked, blindsided. Then understood. They were asking if he wanted bells and side boys. "No. No honors," he shouted back.

The crewman nodded. Held up ten fingers, then faced forward again.

"Ten minutes," Dan shouted to Blanco, then to the man from Ottawa. They began gathering gear and feeling for their seat belt releases.

He darted a glimpse out the window as they made course adjustments, gradually shedding altitude. More turbulence rocked the airframe as the engine song and blade racket overhead deepened. Transitioning to hover . . . he'd done this so many times before. And it had only gone really to shit just twice.

He ruddered his mind away from that tailspin of dread and peered out again. But still caught nothing useful. Once, maybe, a dim glow in the blackness below, through what looked like ice fog or snow.

He couldn't believe they were flying in this. The pilots had to have terrific instrumentation, or else be insanely courageous.

Then the drift thinned, and he made out the ship ahead. Or rather, a cluster of lights, like a town set down amid an endless prairie. They blazed out blue and yellow and white in the dark, haloed with sparkling rainbows as veils of snow or fog or something in between trailed around them like chiffon wrappings.

The ship loomed rapidly as the helo steadied on its final. Much bigger than he'd expected. Its huge white slabs of superstructure were dotted with windows that shone a palish champagne gold, like the eyes of lit jack-o'-lanterns. Behind it trailed a dark streak: the open sea, exposed like a surgeon's incision, bobbing with slowly turning, shattered ice. Ahead of the icebreaker's bluntish bow, illuminated by what had to be insanely powerful searchlights, gleamed a tormented jumble of white and blue and silver: the blazing, coruscating brokenness of the eternally frozen winter pack.

Dan cinched his seat belt to the last possible notch and sat forward, arms on his knees.

Bracing himself. Just in case.

A few minutes later he was being led through the rackety, icy night, pulled by both arms through blowing drift and rotor storm across a deck surfaced like pebbled black rubber. Reaching the lit oval of a door, his handlers stood back and let him climb over the knee-knocker himself.

He straightened inside, dusting snow from his parka. To confront a large man in a blue reefer jacket, who looked like he'd just stepped out of a World War II movie. "Admiral Lenson? I am Captain Augustus Lasher," the officer said gruffly. "An honor to welcome you aboard *Diefenbaker*."

"Good to be here, thanks." Dan accepted a cup and saucer of what smelled like strong black tea, but his fingers were so numb the cup clattered. Dark fluid slopped into the saucer and spattered on the pristine tile deck. "Sorry," he muttered.

Lasher was as tall as Dan but heavier, with blue-tinged dewlap jowls that looked unshaven, though they weren't. His eyebrows were bushy as an ayatollah's, and a tightly knotted black tie dug into a pink, fleshy neck. The embroidered anchor-and-crown cap badge on the crumpled white-

and-gold combination cover, and the gold stripes on his shoulder boards, were tarnished just enough to suggest a long career at sea. Something about the ensemble put Dan on guard, as if the CO of one of Her Majesty's major ships shouldn't look so exactly like his mental stereotype of the CO of one of Her Majesty's major ships. But he shook the feeling off and accepted the condescending nod and handshake. "Dan Lenson. US Navy."

"Of course. Accommodate his staff, if you please," Lasher snapped to a younger man, officer or chief, Dan wasn't sure. "And let's get that Bell into the hangar." Turning back to Dan, "Admiral, shall we head up to my cabin? You might be ready for something more warming than tea."

Dan followed him down white-painted, gleaming, brightly lit passageways and up several ladders, until Lasher opened a varnished door and ushered him inside.

The enormous room was a sitting area, furnished with sofas, conference table, glassed-in bookshelves, a portrait of the Queen in a white dress, and what looked suspiciously like a picture window, though its blue curtains were drawn at the moment.

Lasher said briskly, helping him off with his parka, "This suite will be yours, of course, Admiral. I've got a quite comfortable sea cabin at my disposal. Your liaison will join us, but I thought you might want a break first. Head is to your left. Whiskey? A short gin?"

"No, thanks."

"That's right, on duty." Lasher winked. "But you're not on a US ship."

"Appreciate the offer, but I don't drink," Dan said. "The tea was fine. Maybe a little more of that? I'll use your head, then let's talk."

"Captain's on the bridge," someone called. Then added, after a murmured rebuke, "Admiral's on the bridge."

The vast beam-to-beam pilothouse was pitch dark except for the sapphire and jade lambencies of night-subdued screens. The air was cool but not cold. Four dark forms stood motionless as pillars of coal. Dan edged around a helm-and-instrument console, following Lasher.

He looked down from thick slanted-out windows onto a brightly lit, expansive foredeck crowded with stowed booms, a huge bright-yellow buoy crane, steel equipment containers, and several gray-tarp-shrouded wedges that had to be small boats. Tenders, maybe. Ice drift blew across it, appearing as if by magic from out of the night. It dimmed the lights like stars occulted by interstellar gas, then vanished again. The deck rose to an elevated forecastle equipped with the stoutest ground tackle he'd ever seen short of a mothballed battleship's. It looked as if *Diefenbaker* could haul herself bodily up a glacier, given a secure anchor point at the top.

Beyond the scuppers lay nothing but Arctic night. A faint grinding, a vanishing vibration, was the only sign they were plowing through heavy ice. Slowly, it seemed, but still . . . "Quite a ship you have here," he muttered.

"The biggest, most powerful icebreaker in North America," Lasher said, behind him in the dark. "Looked for a long time like it wouldn't be built, but we got her commissioned at last."

"Diesels?"

"Thirty-five thousand shaft horsepower. We can break through pressure ridges up to ten meters thick. Not like the little slush-tappers you Americans build."

Lasher led the way to a plotting table. The horizontal screen was dimly lit with a detailed chart speckled with depth soundings. To the south and east a scatter of land was labeled *Queen Elizabeth Islands*. To the north and west lay open sea, but ridged with subsea ranges and falling away to abyssal troughs.

The captain placed a finger. "We're here. Seventy miles off the coast. We were headed west to plant a string of ice sensors. Get ongoing measurements and reports of drift rate, thickness, et cetera. Ottawa's ordered me to alter course north, await your arrival, and render assistance." He sounded slightly put out, as if Dan had been personally responsible for this deviation in his schedule. "I expect you'll want to fill me in now on what this is all about."

Dan rubbed his chin. If only. "I don't know a lot more. But what I know I'll tell you. One of our autonomous vehicles is in trouble."

"Your *autonomous* vehicles," Lasher repeated, doubt or perhaps surprise in his tone.

"Correct. Our last report has it headed this way. Hoping, I think, to make Ellesmere. It may or may not have the range."

"Hm. I see. I see . . . Obviously it has, or knows, something Washington wants? To make it worth diverting us, going through Ottawa and so forth?" Lasher glanced at him again. "Rather than simply writing it off?"

Dan said, "That's my conclusion too. But why it can't just transmit the data, whatever it is, I don't know."

"Sir?" Another voice in the dark, and a rattle of china. "For the admiral."

Dan got this dose down without a spill. He was warming up, though his fingers were still pins and needles. And probably would be for a while.

Well, it could have turned out worse, out on the ice. He was lucky to be around at all. And for a few minutes he let himself home in to that, like tuning in to some frequency that was always there to access once you knew where it was on the dial. Just enjoying being able to breathe, to move, to experience whatever was going on. Just . . . existing. As a witness, if nothing else.

And after all, he was at sea again. The subtle vibration under his boots felt good. Even if it wasn't his own ship.

Since, all too soon, he'd probably never go to sea again.

He said briskly, dismissing that depressing thought, "Assuming you can close the range, how could we access something under the pack?"

The captain harrumphed, seeming to consider. "Hmm . . . so you're thinking to actually retrieve this . . . object. We have a fairly stout crane, of course. You were looking down at it a moment ago. Assuming we can reach the vehicle, or it can reach us, we could . . . have it surface in our wake. Run forward and back, widen the open area. Then, one imagines, maneuver to position the crane for a lift. How much does it weigh? Roughly. If you know."

Dan had operated with Orcas during the war. "Fifty tons, or in that neighborhood. Maybe plan for more; this seems to be a modified version. They're pretty big bastards, actually. Not like the USVs you're probably familiar with from hydrographic research."

Lasher shook his head. "That's beyond our lift capacity. We'd have to get a line on it, rig a bridle, and tow it back. In which case, it would be helpful to have the topside conformation, tow points, the approved way to get a bridle on it. Could you supply that? Ask whoever you report to, I assume, whoever's in charge of this thing?"

"I can ask." Dan nodded. "I don't see why towing it back wouldn't work. Unless I can get some clearer direction as to what they specifically want out of it."

Lasher: "I'm not sure what you mean."

Dan said, still thinking it out, "Yeah, I guess it would be good to salvage it. Or at least, start your deck gang rigging for that. Apparently it's damaged in some way, but how badly isn't clear." He blew out. "You know, it may be they're not deliberately keeping us in the dark. We might just have all the information that's available. If the vehicle can't communicate, for example."

He shifted his boots, squinting through the spinning discs of the wind-screen at the driving snow. "We had a case like that during the war. An autonomous unit that lost comms. It continued its mission, but we didn't know that. Until it returned to port and triggered our ASW defenses. We nearly blasted it to scrap before we realized what it was." He hesitated. "Anyhow, depending on what's wrong, we might be able just to repair this one. Then send it on its way, on its own. Which would let you resume your original tasking."

Lasher's shadow shook its head. "I assume you mean electronics? We have very limited repair capability. We need to know more, Admiral. Could we try to contact it?"

"If whoever's running it can't get a status, I doubt we'll be able to. We'll just have to see, I guess. When it reaches us, or we get to it."

A new voice broke in from the darkened bridge, a woman's. Commander Blanco, who'd apparently joined them without either man noticing. "How do you plan to intercept it? Admiral? Captain?"

"Well, now. That's an excellent question too," Lasher mused.

Dan stared down at the plot again. If the Orca was headed for Ellesmere, the logical way to intercept would be to hang a right, get on the reciprocal of that bearing, and run up it until the two vessels met. But then what? "Uh, I assume you don't have sonar."

The skipper's lack of an answer was a confirmation. But Dan persisted. "How about underwater comms?"

This time the bulky shadow nodded. "We have JANUS-compatible underwater communications. So far we mainly use it to retrieve data from the sensors we were laying. But I assume that capability was included in our suite in case we should ever have to assist in a submarine rescue."

Dan finished the brew and set the cup and saucer carefully on the helm console, from whence one of the silent silhouettes whisked it away. "We can pulse that, once we figure we're close enough for sound comms. It should respond to that, uh, unless that too is damaged. Good question, uh, Commander. Captain, let me introduce Commander Sarabeth Blanco, US Coast Guard."

Lasher bowed slightly in the dark. "Glad to meet you, Commander. Did you have anything to add? How to contact this submersible, this autonomous vehicle, or how to intercept it, and how best to proceed when we do?"

Blanco seemed to consider, but finally only said, "Like the admiral says. We'll have to deal with that once we catch up with it."

"All right, then," Dan said, figuring to wrap things up for now. "Captain Lasher, if you would be so kind as to set a course to intercept, we will proceed from there."

He winced inwardly, wondering why he was spouting dialogue from a Patrick O'Brian novel. Maybe he was mirroring Lasher's slightly pontificating manner. Though the man probably didn't mean to sound condescending. Dan only wished he could give them more information. Accessing something the size of an Orca, then rigging a tow bridle on it, in the dark, in the ice, in this weather, then trying to tow it through heavy pack without damage to either . . . none of that would resemble a gambol on Fiddler's Green.

"One more question, sir," Blanco said, and Dan turned back to the nav plot. "These autonomous vehicles. Don't they have avoidance programming? If it detects us, isn't it going to steer clear?"

"Crap," Dan muttered. She was right. And actually, now he thought about it, the situation might even be worse. Depending on its mission, the thing could be carrying . . . *torpedoes*.

In which case, the icebreaker itself might be in danger once the USV was in range.

Which, apparently, Lasher was realizing too; Dan heard a short intake of breath from his direction in the dark. "That's a worrying thought," the Canadian said. "So we're going to run north toward it, but won't be able to detect it. It may be damaged. It may be *armed*." The bulky shadow turned to Dan. "Admiral? Are these your intentions?"

"Yeah, well, I'll be asking my superiors about that. I'm going to have to get back to you on some of these issues," Dan said. He needed to know more. Like the thing's evasive and attack programming. But he wasn't sure how to learn it. Or if, when he did, the answers would satisfy Lasher. He cleared his throat. "If I can put out a message?"

"A signal? Absolutely," the captain said. "Whenever you are ready. I'll have my comm officer stand by."

That seemed to end the discussion. Blanco murmured something inaudible and left. Lasher crossed to one of the other indistinct figures, apparently the officer of the deck, and gave him or her instructions in a low voice.

Shortly thereafter, a degree at a time, the icebreaker altered course. In the dark, in the snow, it made little discernible difference, but Dan watched the needles of the rudder and course indicators come around.

The amber-lit gyrocompass readout steadied on zero one five. Yeah, that would take them northeast, until they intersected the extended course of the oncoming vehicle. Device. Sub. Whatever you wanted to call it.

He rubbed chapped lips, irritated and puzzled. What could be so valuable Washington wanted to cash in its chips with Ottawa to retrieve it? The two countries hadn't exactly worked hand in glove during the war. Canada had never joined the Allies, though it had cut off trade and ceased supplying strategic materials to the Opposed Powers. It had preserved diplomatic ties with Beijing throughout the war. Canada and the States had disagreed about Arctic claims, transit permissions, and drilling rights. The new CNO, if Hlavna was the one making these decisions and not the NCA, must think a lot was at stake to ask for Canadian help.

He was still musing, hands in pockets, when Lasher spoke again, close behind him. In a low voice. "Admiral."

Dan half turned. "Captain?"

"Just a caution," the bulky shadow said. "I have my orders. And I will carry them out. Until the point is reached my ship is in danger."

Dan took his hands out of his pockets. "I hear you."

"Let us make sure you do. This isn't wartime. And to put it frankly, my orders from my government make that clear. They've ordered me to cooperate. And I shall. But I am not, strictly speaking, under *your* orders."

"I understand."

But Lasher still wasn't done. "I also have to consider the safety of my crew. This far out in the pack, in winter . . . any breakdowns, damage to the hull or propulsion or rudders, a shipboard fire—really anything untoward could quickly become very serious indeed. It might be impossible to rescue us. Such things have happened before up here. It could be . . . It could have the makings of a tragedy."

"I understand completely," Dan said, for the third time. "I've walked in your shoes, Captain. Acting as a prudent mariner . . . this is just a robot we're talking about, after all."

Dan steeled his tone. "But a word of advice to you, Captain, as well: there must be a damn good reason they're moving heaven and earth to retrieve this thing. So I plan to do everything I can to do so."

The shadow reached out, and a heavy paw clamped his shoulder. "Then we are on the same page. I will have my second ring you if there are any changes. I will be in my sea quarters. Have a good night, Admiral, and dial two-five if you need anything." The weighty hand patted his shoulder once, and Lasher turned away.

Which left Dan looking out into the night again. Where now the snow was coming down in even deadlier earnest. Whirling down from the darkness into the dazzling glare of the searchlights. Dervishing across the deck, threading and shrouding the davits, the capstans, the big yellow crane, creeping among them like a nest of white pythons, building drifts in the lee of the containers, depositing tons of additional topside weight.

Making him remember, as he stood there in the dark, another ship.

An ancient destroyer, ordered north of the Circle in heavy seas and blizzards. With orders to find the most violent winter storm she could, and stay in it as long as she lived.

And himself back then, a fresh-minted ensign. Naive, optimistic, eager to do his duty and serve.

That ship lay now at the bottom of the Irish Sea. And he no longer felt like that eager youth. Felt, rather . . . not exactly tired, but as if he was nearing the completion of a long task.

But . . . what then? What lay beyond? At some point every career ended. No matter how successful or how long. But the Navy had been part of him so long that facing retirement felt like standing at the edge of an icy cliff. A chasm, into which he strained to see.

The immense icebreaker shuddered. A scraping boom echoed along her length. Some thick, dense pressure ridge. At first levered upward as the specially shaped bow chiseled under it, then crushed and disintegrated as the unimaginable momentum of twenty-five thousand tons of steel driven by thirty-five thousand horsepower ripped hundreds of tons of solid ice apart, shoved it aside, and ground it underfoot.

He stood there for some time, musing. Watching their battering, grinding progress. They were only making five knots. Not much faster than a man could walk.

Finally he turned away and went below.

21

Under the Arctic Ice

Sloan came to again, but feeling even worse than before. His cramped legs barely responded when he tried to shift on the metal seat. Each breath was an effort. His chest ached. His pulse flashed lights across his vision with each heartbeat.

Christ, how long had he been out? He hadn't meant to sleep. Though it had felt less like a nap than passing out from inhaling some toxic gas. A throbbing, blinding headache seconded the feeling something was seriously wrong. When he touched the keyboard and the screen illuminated the interior, its curved metal walls glittered with a thick rime of silvery-gray hoarfrost. Like an alien growth that would soon cover his body and devour it from outside.

With a groan, he bent to inspect the rebreather. The needles on both the oxygen and absorbent canisters stood just above the red line. He groped for the spare, then groaned again, remembering. He was already *on* the replacement. The smooth curve his fingers encountered was that of the empty, discarded tank.

He rubbed swollen eyelids with the back of his glove. Struggling to breathe. To think. To simply endure, if only for a little while longer. "Pilot," he muttered. "Y'there?"

"Here, Commander."

"I see you fixed the voice module."

"I found a work-around while you were sleeping." The resonant baritone seemed less reassuring than it once had. Could he change it? Female? A more consoling tenor? Probably, but who cared. No difference in the end. "How are you doing?" he muttered, then rephrased the query. "Status, please. And, where exactly are we?"

"Underway on main power. Course two four five true at six knots. Hydrogen remaining for power cells, three point seven percent. Depth,

*one hundred meters, under ice cover extending down to twenty-seven
meters. External temperature—"*

"Stop!" He gaped, unable to understand. Two four five? *Southwest?*
The Pilot had turned them *back toward Russia?* Or had he, himself, done
so, in some brain-dead delirium? And how long had they been back-
tracking?

Then the truth squeezed itself into his addled brain. Which felt sodden,
like a piece of rotten shoe leather. As they'd passed the pole, all directions
had reversed, all orientations had flipped. Now the course to safety led
south. Not north.

"Was that a command to stop engines, Commander?"

"No! Continue present course and speed. How far to friendly land?"

Hmmmm. "Two hundred ninety-seven nautical miles."

"Will our remaining juice get us there? I mean, main cells, plus remaining battery charge?"

A short pause. The humming. Then, as if reluctantly, *"Negative. Fuel
will be exhausted in about an hour. Extended depletion curve shows
lithium-ion main bus falling below actuation voltage for main propulsion motor three hours after that. Auxiliary systems can continue in
reduced status for about two more hours. Total exhaustion of your heating and my central computing power will occur between six and seven
hours from now."*

He relaxed back into the seat.

So that was it, then.

His gloved fingers moved sluggishly as stunned snakes over the keyboard. He toggled to the geo chart.

His location pip glowed and faded five times a second over a massive
subsea trench, the Makarov Basin. The mountain chains that bounded it
ran toward the pole, which lay now behind them, off to their right hand.
Actually, as he crossed the top of the world, he must have passed not far
from the pole itself. A little over a hundred nautical miles at his closest
point of approach.

For a moment he wondered if he should have simply headed for it. Finished his voyage there. Immured forever at the top of the world . . .

Get a grip, Sloan. You're not quite dead yet.

But he couldn't see any way he could survive. His options had been
successively narrower since the moment he'd climbed up into the Orca's
belly. Actually, since he'd broached the idea to Fahrney and Yoder.

Since *he* had broached it . . . And finally and irrevocably, as he'd looked down at Komanich's furrowed brow, her concerned eyes, and eased the hatch down despite her plea.

Now those options, never numerous, had dwindled to nothing. To simply purring ahead at the most economical speed, until the whirring blades shivered to a halt. Mere hours later, his last reserve would trickle away to zero.

Funny. He'd figured running out of oxygen would be how it ended. But he might actually have enough left for the luxury of freezing to death.

A muted double click over the speaker. A sound he'd noted before, a moment in advance of when the Pilot vocalized. A digital throat-clearing. "What is it?" he rasped, coughing.

"Thought you should hear this, Commander. First picked it up shortly before you woke."

A hiss, and the irregular, uneven crackle of the open Arctic. It seemed to be made up both of biologics, the creatures dwelling down here in the darkness with him, and the uneasy shifting and popping as the ice shifted. Adjusting to its internal stresses like a giant stretching out its kinks.

Gradually, behind the whispering crackle, he made it out. A higher-pitched keening. Elusive, but there. First pealing out, then slowly expiring in an eerie falling disharmony of ever-lower-frequency reverberations.

The periodic, lilting sea song of an active sonar.

No doubt, the same submarine that had nearly run them down before.

The Sierra was still hunting them. Even here, on the far side of the pole. In what he'd too optimistically presumed would be safe waters. Even if Canada claimed these seas, which he wasn't certain of, that hadn't stopped the Russian from continuing its pursuit.

But why was it on this very trail he was so slowly following? Amid the hundreds of thousands of square miles of Arctic winter ice, stretching across the crown of the planet from one continent to another, how had it sniffed him out?

Could Moscow have intercepted his radioed cry for help? A delay in decoding, then transmitting orders back to the Sierra, would explain its having lost him for a time. But if they'd broken his transmission, they knew where he was headed.

It would be a simple matter, after that, to calculate how he'd try to get there.

He couldn't count on finding a convenient crack in the ice to cockroach into the way he had before. It had been luck that a hidey-hole had been handy. Plus, up here, the ice cover was older, and even thicker than it had been back near the Russian coast.

Okay, maybe he wasn't at his best right now. *You have an AI, why not use it?* "Pilot," he rasped, "model a search strategy for the Sierra. From the Red Team side. Then find a way to evade it."

Hmmmm. "Strategy modeled."

Hmmmmmm . . .

Perhaps a minute went by. Longer than it had ever taken to respond before. "Well?" he prompted.

"Unable to discover a means to evade."

He pursed his lips and nodded ruefully. Pretty much what he'd expected.

For just a moment he entertained a very feeble hope, more like a fantasy, that they might rescue him. Send over a diver once they located him. Somehow get him free, under the ice, and transfer him to *Pskov* for interrogation.

Then he shook his head grimly. The only thing coming his way from that quarter would be a torpedo. A faster death than freezing or smothering, but annihilation all the same. And probably preferable to becoming a prisoner of Russian military intelligence.

Hunched over the display, he watched the pip creep onward. Knowing, all the same, that his own destination was death.

Over two hundred miles to the south, Dan sat massaging his forehead in the commanding officer's suite. Another cup of the strong black tea, which he was developing a taste for, and a plate of eggs and bacon had been silently, efficiently delivered. Apparently it was breakfast time, at least by the twenty-four-hour clock on the bulkhead. The curtains, of course, framed night outside the window.

He grimaced, rereading the message he'd just signed for. In standard NATO format, it had been transmitted from Northcom to *Diefenbaker* via Ottawa. The comm officer had brought it in a few minutes before, apologizing that they had to provide it in paper copy, since Dan had declined when they offered to link his tablet to the ship's network. Not that he mistrusted them, but there was just too much on the device to risk a leak.

"I can stand by for a response, if you like, sir," the junior officer said. He looked about seventeen: fresh-faced, boyish, smooth-cheeked.

God, they were making junior officers young these days. "Uh, grab a seat." Dan pointed at the chair opposite. After a second's hesitation, the youngster took it, but perched on the edge. He smiled nervously.

"Relax, Lieutenant." Had *he* ever been that jittery around flag officers? They were only human. And some, like Ike Sundstrom, on whose staff he'd served decades before, not exactly impressive. At all.

But of course things looked different when you were that age. He forced himself back to the page, still frowning.

Among other things, the message contained partial answers to the questions he'd sent the night before. Range. Endurance. Armament. Which apparently, thank God, had been limited to small independent sensor vehicles. Not torpedoes.

And the surprise: this Orca carried a human pilot.

It didn't name him or her but carried a tagline for a vehicle commander, identified as a lieutenant commander, USN. So it wasn't, strictly speaking, a USV. Or maybe it was a dual or alternate-manned system, wherein either the AI or a human pilot could direct the vessel.

Regardless, it meant his and Lasher's mission had changed. It was clear now why the mission had a higher priority than the recovery of an unmanned system, however expensive.

He snapped the metal cover shut and handed the folder back. "No answer at the moment. I'll need to discuss this with your CO. Where would he be right now? Would you be able to tell me?"

The kid swallowed and perked up. "Yes, sir! I'll take you to him, Admiral. Please follow me."

Dan found the bridge still dark, still somnolent, still undertoned by the rumble of huge engines ramming steel through many feet of thick ice. He finally detected Lasher out on the wing. The captain's head was bent. Dan hesitated, then slammed the dogs open with his fist and pushed the door open.

The cold was incredible, the wind cutting. It forced Dan to bend, too, and squint into the blast of icy air. "Captain, a word?" he shouted through stiffening lips.

Lasher was in a heavy greatcoat with brass buttons and a pair of what looked like tanker's goggles. Mittened hands gripped oversized dark green binoculars. A blue watch cap was pulled over his ears. He nodded wordlessly, gesturing that he'd follow Dan back inside.

The door dogged, they shook granular ice drift like sugar crystals from sleeves and faces. Lasher hung the glasses and goggles by his chair and stuffed mittens and cap into his bridge coat pockets. "Understand you had a signal, Admiral," he rumbled. "Marked Eyes Only, so I did not read it."

"Appreciate that, but we don't have anything to hide. Two items of interest. One: according to what I've been told, the Orca's unarmed. They tell me it was never equipped with anything resembling a weapon."

Lasher tossed his head. "Excellent! That's a great relief."

"Two: there's a human aboard."

The Canadian raised shaggy eyebrows still frosted with ice. "Well, that clarifies things a bit."

"What I thought too."

Lasher mused, "So it's a rescue mission, eh? Makes rather more sense now."

Dan nodded and waited.

"And good news about the lack of a sting in its tail. Let's look at the chart."

The captain crossed the pilothouse and brought up the same horizontal display they'd perused the night before. On the small-scale setting, the Own Ship pip had barely moved during the night. Lasher consulted a scale, then used his spread fingers as a measuring device. "Let's see here . . . I make it somewhere between a hundred and a hundred fifty miles from us to its predicted track. If, that is, it—or rather *he*—has been able to maintain his speed of advance."

"And closer by the hour."

Lasher inclined his head. "True. But, unfortunately, we may not be able to keep up this rate of progress much longer. Excuse me a moment."

Lasher crossed to his chair, picked up a phone, pressed buttons. Held a short conversation. Then re-socketed it and came back. "Not good news." He shrugged. "But not unexpected. I sent our mobile under-ice sensor out ahead last night. At present it is about five miles ahead of us. The ice there is older. Thicker. Buckled and refrozen into pressure ridges. I may be forced to heave to. We could wreck our screws, damage the bow, be brought to a halt regardless of how much power we apply. Ultimately, immobilized and frozen in."

Dan crossed his arms. "Even if a man's at risk out there?"

Lasher cocked his head. "I'm as keen to save a life as anyone, Admiral. It's a question of balancing priorities against risks. An equation you must be familiar with, if what I read about you—oh yes, I looked—is at all accurate."

Dan drew a breath, staring out the windscreen at the steady drive of drift as it blew through the glow of the ship's floodlights. Powerful as they were, they seemed only ludicrous pinpoints in the immeasurable darkness.

He shivered. No. He wasn't going to accept stopping short. Leaving someone out there to die. Not after coming all this way.

He turned back to Lasher. "So let's explore our alternatives."

Sloan wriggled on his seat, thrust out his arms, hammered fists on deadened muscle. Nothing helped. The anesthetization was creeping upward. Even with the heat from the suit, hypothermia was gaining.

Out of oxygen. Out of heat. And with each ping, his pursuer sounded closer.

"Pilot," he muttered, "we've got to try to punch through this cover."

"*I don't think we can, Commander.*"

"Find a thin area. What's the most recent one you passed?"

"*This ice is all very thick. Old. Years in the making.*"

"There's got to be something. Search back five miles."

A very slight pause. "*Nothing less than ten meters.*"

Thirty feet of solid ice . . . he wasn't going to penetrate that. Maybe, *maybe*, if he had a torpedo to blast a hole. He'd read about that as a tactic, though he couldn't recall where. Maybe only in the movies. But fuck it, why even think about it? He didn't have a torpedo. "How thin would it have to be? For us to ram through?"

"*Stand by, Commander . . . Analyzed. It will depend on the amount of damage you are willing to risk.*"

"Screw the damage. How thin?"

"*We could probably push through five feet of ice. Seven, if you are prepared for major damage to mast and sail.*"

Seven versus thirty, that didn't sound good.

"*But I can look for an old polynya. Or a softer area, where floes have broken apart and then refrozen. Like the one we hid in before. These won't be as large. This is not annual ice. But they might offer some point of weakness.*"

"That sounds possible . . . but what do you mean by 'push through'?"

The Pilot sounded surprised. "*Our programmed method of surfacing through ice. Adapted from submarine practice. Place the sail carefully, ballast up gradually, push the sail through. This minimizes damage—*"

"No, *no!*" He exhaled. "We're way past worrying about that, okay? Model it this way: angle down, to, say, four hundred feet. Then go to acute angle up, ring up maximum speed, and ram our way through."

A pause. Then, *"That will destroy the bow area. And probably still not penetrate."*

"Let's get this straight, Pilot. We've got to surface, regardless of damage. And we've got to do it now. Is that clear?"

A longer pause, humming, then: *"Clear, Commander. Searching . . . Permission to ping."*

"Ping? No. *No!* Can't you use your lights?"

"I can examine the bottom of the cover with video. But I can't tell how thick the ice is above that without using the sonar profiler."

"Crap," he murmured. If he went active with the profiler, the Sierra would be on him within minutes. On the other hand . . . "Is *Pskov*'s ping rate constant?"

"Affirmative. At least over last several minutes. Pulse repetition rate constant at six point seven seconds. Evaluate as Sierra-class uprated MGK-500 Shark Gill sonar in search mode."

He adjusted his face mask, pondering. No listening device could be left on when an own-ship sonar was transmitting. The massive pulse of energy would burn out the delicate piezoelectrics in its hydrophone elements. Sonars were designed to blank their receiving circuits during the one- to three-second period the sub was actively transmitting.

He muttered, "Okay, listen up. Can you time your outgoing ping so it arrives at their location during their blank period?"

"I can attempt to do that."

"Okay, let's—"

"But if they change their PRR while we're pinging, they'll get a clear bearing on us. And may be able to generate range if they have powerful algorithms. Hmmmmmmm . . . I can also try a higher frequency active pulse. That will attenuate more rapidly, reducing range of counter-detection—"

"Do it," Sloan interrupted. "Keep it low power, highest possible frequency, sure. Only what you need to measure the ice. But do it *now.*"

His muscles contracted, spasming uncontrollably. Some nerve impulse to his legs, unordered by his brain. He glanced down and caught the oxygen gauge out of the corner of his eye.

Two percent.

He flinched when the first ping went out. He couldn't help picturing it. Spreading like ripples in a pond, reflected from the ice and then the sea bottom far below. Spreading, widening, weakening. The inverse square law. Until a transducer converted the final whimper into electrical energy . . .

The Sierra's ping, far stronger and deeper, echoing and wavering like a deep-toned bell at the far end of a vast marble hallway, arrived then. Crossing his own.

If the Pilot had timed it right, their pursuer's receivers would be shut off at the exact moment the Prime's ping got there.

If it hadn't . . . then the Russians would know exactly where they were.

He glanced down again and flicked the gauge. Still at two. He would still breathe once it read zero, but would only get back the oxygen left from his previous exhalation. The absorbent canister would scrub it of carbon dioxide, leaving nitrogen and trace gases, but eventually too little O_2 to support life.

So he wouldn't *feel* smothered, even at the end.

He'd just . . . go black. And not too long from now.

"*Fault line detected*," the Pilot said.

He flinched at the interruption. "Uh, tell me more."

"*Seems like two heavy floes jammed up together. Then they must have been wrenched apart again. Hard to tell the history, but there's a frozen-in section between them that might be fairly flat and no more than twelve, fifteen feet thick. And it might be softer, newer ice.*"

"Let's go for it."

A pause, then, "*I will need explicit instructions, Commander. Since I'm carrying this out in opposition to my self-protection programming.*"

His heart was speeding up. Was that a symptom? Was his carbon dioxide absorbent depleted? He snapped, "I *told* you! Go deep. Trim to up angle. Then hit that fault point at full speed. See if we can bust the bow through."

"*Understand. Adjusting depth to four hundred feet.*"

He floated, sensing the drop. The elevator-down feeling. Then picking up the up angle, both from his inner ear and the trim indicator.

"*Coming to flank, planes at up full,*" the Pilot said. "*Brace for impact.*"

He leaned forward to brace both elbows on the interior of the sphere. Covered his face with his gloves. And waited.

The shock was less violent than he'd expected. A jolt, a surge forward. Then a grinding, gradual halt. He toggled to the cameras, then rebuked himself. What was he expecting, stars, the northern lights? It would be pitch dark up there too. "Are we through?" he muttered.

"Wait one . . . Negative. Bow penetrated about six feet. Damage reported, bow section. Investigating."

"Belay investigating. Repeat the tactic! Four hundred feet. Flank speed. Try to hit the same exact spot. Acknowledge."

"Acknowledged. Backing down."

"Give me topside lights."

The screen lit with a sudden flash. The same spotlight effect as earlier, but without the lightning flickers of fish. Just the shadowy, irregular underside of the ice, shifting and glowing as the illuminators shifted their angles. Then they receded, vanished, as the depth gauge dropped again. One hundred. Two hundred. Three hundred. Four.

"Flank speed, angled up," the Pilot said.

This time when they hit, the impact twisted the hull savagely to the left, banging his elbows and knees and rapping his face on the keyboard. The collision was accompanied by the same harsh grinding, but a series of sharp pops or cracks tolled and echoed along the hull as well. He blinked, dazed. Hoping the noises weren't collapsing strength members. Hull girders . . . "Are we through?" he snapped.

"Stand by . . . Negative."

"Hit it again. Depth, five hundred feet. Activate all side thrusters as well as the main propulsor this time. And have you blown ballast? We need to hit just as hard as we can."

"Reporting: Major damage forward of frame five. Damage to payload bay. Main battery near exhaustion. As to blowing ballast . . . you are aware we have only enough reserve air to do that once."

"Acknowledge and execute. *Now*, Pilot."

A grinding, corkscrewing motion as the screw reversed, as the Orca extricated itself. He sat tensely, fearing that they couldn't retreat. That they'd get locked in like before. But the scraping continued, like massive iron spikes dragging across the hull. It grew shrill, then abruptly ceased. The sphere swayed, then steadied on an even keel once again. Good.

The fathometer. One hundred. Two hundred. Three. Four.

Five hundred feet.

"Flank speed, angled up," the Pilot intoned again. *"All thrusters on one hundred percent. Main propulsor to flank. Blowing all ballast."*

He could feel more acceleration this time. Adding positive buoyancy might just do it. Adding that to the thrust of all the motors at once should

hit the ice with nearly a hundred tons of steel, at ten or twelve knots . . .
somewhere over three million foot-pounds. Unfortunately he had no idea
how strong the ice would be where it would hit. . . .

"*Brace for impact,*" the Pilot warned once more.

The slam was vastly more violent this time. Like hitting the prover-
bial brick wall. The screech and snap of breaking steel rang back along
the length of the ship. The Orca shuddered, rattling him in the sphere like
a bean in a castanet, and canted left again. Then it seemed to slide a few
feet farther forward before halting again with a resounding bang that
knelled along the hull as if Quasimodo had rung it with a heavy hammer.

Damn, he thought, gripping his head. If the Sierra couldn't hear that,
they weren't listening.

He slowly realized the usual background hiss from the speaker wasn't
there anymore. He leaned to the mic. "Pilot? Status."

No answer. He leaned to the keyboard. Typed, *Are you damaged?*

*Reporting: Major damage forward. Lost forward transducers and
other instrumentation. Collapsed forward bulkhead payload bay. Taking on water aft of payload bay, port side.*

But are YOU all right?

I am coping, Commander.

Did we break through?

Checking. A pause, then, *Mast fairing is either exposed or within several inches of surface.*

He typed, *Let's back down then. Try it one more time.*

Can't, Commander. Reserve air is fully depleted.

He typed, with a sinking heart, *Use the motors. Force us back under.
Try again.*

A thrumming hum, which slowly descended the scale.

The screen read, *Remaining battery voltage too low to actuate main
propulsor.*

Sloan slumped back, fingers crimped in his lap.

That was it, then.

Out of power. Out of air to blow the tanks. All but out of oxygen.

*ULF antenna may be close enough to surface to transmit. Send re-
quest for assistance?*

He debated it. Even if someone heard, they couldn't help. Even if by
some miracle he could make it topside, he wouldn't last more than a few
minutes. Not on the ice, in the Arctic winter night. But finally, resigned,

typed two more letters, then let his fingers drop back into his lap. A final despairing message to an unhearing universe.

OK.

Dan was on his way back to *Diefenbaker*'s hangar when the comm officer caught up with him and thrust out the folder. Dan ran an eye down it, then looked back at the date time group of the original message. He snapped, more angrily than he'd intended, "This gives us a firm location. But why the hell did it take nearly an hour to turn this around?"

The office dropped his gaze. "Stovepiped communications, Admiral. Both in your system, and ours, I imagine."

Dan rubbed his mouth, considering. The massive icebreaker lay dead in the water. Halted, blocked, stymied by the deeply rooted, old-ice pressure ridge Lasher had feared. The captain had hove to while his sensor vehicle prowled to port and starboard, scouting with side-scan sonar for a way forward. If any such existed . . . The wind howled, audible even here, deep inside the skin of the ship.

The hiss of the drift reminded him of the shamal. The endless abrading scour of windblown sand in the Persian Gulf. Red-brown skies. The ship's exterior metal blasted bare of paint and so hot it blistered your fingers. And the ever-present petrochemical stink from the refineries. Air so dry the linings of your nose cracked and bled. Your eyes blinked constantly, and when you spat, you expectorated a reddish paste like congealed blood.

Which brought another unwelcome memory. Of drifting in the sea after USS *Turner Van Zandt* had gone down, while a war went on over their heads . . . themselves forgotten, it seemed, by Higher . . . but not by the sharks of the Persian Gulf.

He'd vowed then that if anyone else ever needed rescue, he would respond.

The boyish face regarded him anxiously. "Admiral?"

"Never mind." Dan shook his head and tore the upmost sheet off. Tucked it into his parka pocket and stepped through the door.

The icebreaker's hangar was lofty-ceilinged, dimly lit, echoing with the clatter of tools. In its center, focus of the overhead lights, crouched the Bell 416 that had brought him and Blanco from the shore.

He asked for the pilot and was shown to an attached lounge area. The aviator glanced up from a magazine, then started to his feet. His name tape read *Druhn*. Dan said, "Can we fly in this weather?"

The pilot frowned, turning to study an instrument rack on the bulkhead. "Wind speed, gusting to seventy . . . It's past marginal, sir."

"To seventy? It can't be *seventy.*"

"Kilometers per hour, sir. Not miles." The others in the lounge, crewmen he assumed, all of whom had also stood when he entered, regarded him so stone-facedly he suspected they were laughing inside. "And we measure temperature in centigrade," the pilot deadpanned.

"Sure, sure. Past marginal . . . You understand this would be a rescue mission, though? Captain Lasher briefed you?"

Druhn said yes, he had. They'd refueled the helo, rigged a horse collar, and loaded tools, shovels, and a body bag in case of the worst. "One of our medics volunteered to go along." The pilot inclined his head at a woman in coveralls.

Dan nodded an acknowledgment her way and held out the message. The pilot ran an eye over it, then copied the coordinates into a book strapped to his thigh. He handed it back. "It's within range, sir. But only barely. We could get out there and back with maybe fifteen minutes of loiter time. But we couldn't carry out much of a search. And we can't go low, not in the dark."

Dan waved the message. "Well, now we shouldn't need to. Search, that is."

"If those coordinates are trustworthy, no, sir. But in our experience"—Druhn glanced at the others—"you hardly ever find someone exactly where he thinks he is. You do copy, sir, that if I decide we have to bingo, that's what we'll do. No arguments?"

"Of course. You're in command of the aircraft."

"Then we're ready to go," the pilot announced, and the crew began grabbing gear, climbing into oversuits, pulling on goggles. "As soon as Captain Lasher gives us the green light," he added.

Dan nodded. "Can you put me through to the bridge?"

One of the crewmen set him up on an IC circuit. He pressed the buzzer and waited. When Lasher came on Dan said, "Lenson here. I'm in the hangar. Requesting green light for launch."

"Have you discussed this with Mister Druhn? These conditions look marginal at best."

"Marginal, yes. But he's willing to launch."

"How many souls on board?"

Dan did a quick count. "Six."

"So we're going to gamble six lives against one."

Dan nodded as if Lasher could see him. "But don't we do that for every rescue mission? Also, see if you can ask your Higher to ask my Higher to relay to the Orca that we're coming. I'd ask you to go direct, but apparently ULF is the only channel we have to this thing."

Lasher took a bit more persuading, but at last gave a grudging assent. *"I'll need to talk to the pilot myself, Admiral. Just to make sure he understands the ground rules."*

Just to make sure I don't browbeat him into something dangerous, Dan thought, but passed the handset to Druhn. Who turned away, lowering his voice.

Dan eyed the oversuits on the bulkhead rack. "Got one of those for me?" he asked the copilot.

"Sir? But . . . *you're* not going," the officer said. "Admiral. Surely."

They stared as if he'd proposed something mad. And for a moment he wrestled with his own fear. The dark. The cold. If they went down out here, there'd be no friendly locals to stumble over them. They'd quite simply all die.

"I surely am," Dan told him. "As the on-scene commander. We don't have time to argue. So suit me up, and let's get this show on the road."

After the transmission Sloan had given the batteries a rest, on the Pilot's recommendation. Prime thought they might recover some charge. Perhaps enough for one more attempt at breaking through, though no longer as powerful as before.

Though now, since they'd tried three times to ram up through it, he was beginning to wonder if this really was a weak point in the ice cover. If the Pilot hadn't erred. Or perhaps, was just attempting to humor him in the last minutes of his life.

No. He battered a numb face with unfeeling fists. It wasn't human enough to lie. He wasn't thinking clearly. Which was no wonder.

The gauge on the rebreather stood at zero. He had no idea whether that included an allowance for a reserve.

But he did feel woozy. Disoriented . . . The silvery-gray hoarfrost was growing out from the interior of the sphere. It glittered on his suit, on his gloves, on the keyboard. He leaned to scrape it off the screen. And typed, manipulating insensible fingers like stubby chopsticks, *No way we can break through? Flood the ballast tanks and try again?*

Ummmmm . . . I can flood. Vent main and auxiliary ballast tanks, fill them back up with water. And we will sink.

A moment, then, *But without air to blow them, we will never surface again.*

Another pause, as if the Pilot's artificial synapses were slowing too. Then, *However. I have one suggestion.*

Let's hear it.

I was built with a detachable keel. I am not certain it will still separate given the damage forward. But I could try.

He steel-wooled his face with the back of a glove. Trying to think it through. Actually he hadn't known that about the Orcas, though he understood what detachable keels were. Massive hunks of lead or fiberglass-coated iron, bolted on, but with a way to drop them in case of emergency. Losing it would definitely give them positive buoyancy.

It was a one-time-use deal, though. The Prime would never submerge again, after that.

But if it *didn't* release, if its attachment points were bent or too damaged to separate . . . and they flooded the tanks without enough compressed air left to blow them again . . . it would never *surface* again either.

They'd just continue down, drifting like a steel snowflake to the seafloor far below. Until they passed crush depth, and the metal around him crumpled.

But did he have a choice?

He typed, *One last try. Flood all tanks. Back down. Extract. Then drop the keel and go to full ahead.*

The Prime responded, *Flooding.* Then, *Backing down.*

The thrum of the propulsor was weaker, slower. The scrapes and bangs as the Orca reluctantly unlocked from the ice, less loud. Or was his hearing going? He blinked, trying to focus in a deepening obscurity. The screen, too, seemed to be fading, its letters bleeding into a gray fog.

Again, the swaying sensation of being once more underway. Untethered. Unmoored.

Heading to five hundred feet.

Very well, he typed. And waited.

He wasn't totally sure what he hoped for with this final effort. His cameras were wrecked. He couldn't see topside. Three violent collisions with the overhead ice had smashed the mast, even though it had been retracted into the rudimentary sail. Apparently there was serious damage to the forward section of the beast as well, and to its payload section aft of that. And . . . to the forward part of the keel? Where it would have to detach?

He blinked at the depth gauge, but couldn't focus to read it. The needle wavered as if the sphere he crouched in was already flooded.

Five hundred feet, the screen read.

He typed, *Drop keel, up angle, full remaining power main screw and thrusters.*

Thrusters inoperative. All power to main screw.

Let's hit it at exactly the same place we did before.

On it, Commander.

He gripped the sides of the keyboard, steeling himself. Once more into the breach.

Stand by for impact, the screen read. Before it suddenly went completely dead.

The snow, or maybe it was just drift, blasted into the windscreen, driven both by the wind and the downdraft of the rotors. The engine noise built to a roar. Dan was pressed down into the seat, then aft as the pilot manipulated the collective.

They gathered speed, hurtling into the darkness beyond. No stars. No moon. Heavy overcast, and the black velvet cloak of the Arctic night.

He craned for one backward glance, to glimpse the constellation that was the icebreaker receding into the night. A lonely galaxy he was leaving at far beyond light speed. It dwindled into an inchoate glow. Then it was gone.

He faced forward as the pilot adjusted his seat. They'd left the copilot behind. Lasher had made this a volunteers-only mission, and with a new baby on the way, the other flier had opted out. With an apology, but making it clear he judged the risk too high. Which was why Dan occupied the copilot's seat, though he had only the haziest idea how to fly a helo. If he had to take over, all he could guarantee was that they'd hit the ice. How fast, and at what angle, would be beyond his control.

He craned over one shoulder again to peer back into the passenger compartment. Four souls there. Sarabeth Blanco, in a too-big exposure suit. The female corpsman from *Diefenbaker*, boots propped on a medical pack. One of the helo crewmen. And a husky machinist, carrying a duffel crammed with tools. They'd tossed Dan their names in the haste of boarding, but he'd promptly forgotten them.

The pilot flicked on a screen, then rotated a dial to dim its glare. This looked like the same nav system Dan had seen in US Navy helicopters. The mother ship was falling astern. Another symbol flashed ahead. He placed a finger on it and keyed his throat switch. "That's the lat-long in the SOS?"

"That's the position, right, Admiral. We're fighting a crosswind, but should be there in about thirty-eight minutes." A pause, then, *"Are we searching from the air, Admiral? Or am I putting you down? I didn't get a super-clear picture of exactly how we're doing this."*

Dan considered. He really should have taken more time to plan. But there hadn't *been* time. The mayday message made that clear. He'd have to improvise. But first they had to locate the thing.

Druhn: *"If I can make a suggestion, Admiral?"*

"That'd be welcome. Sure."

"I've done a lot of S&R work. In bad conditions. Flying low to the ground, in a whiteout, in the dark, like this, is not a good idea."

"I'm getting that feeling."

"If I can find a level spot, I can set you down close to that posit. Matt's got three hundred feet of line in his hoist reel. Space your folks out along it and rotate the search using the aircraft as the axis. Meanwhile I stay put and keep the engines running. We shut down, they'll cold soak, and we won't be able to restart. But it'll stretch our fuel, rather than staying in the air."

"Makes sense," Dan said, grateful for the suggestion about the hoist reel. They certainly didn't want to be stumbling around out there in the dark. Anyone who lost orientation and strayed would be doomed.

And now that they were out here, and he couldn't see shit, and the turbulence was rocking the helicopter so hard he was nearly being jerked out of his seat, he was getting the feeling they probably weren't going to come back with much.

The Canadian captain had tried to convince him conditions were just too evil. Lasher had suggested that if someone had to go, it was best to send the younger crew members. Delicately, as if Dan might have been offended at the suggestion he was past it.

Dan hadn't been. Offended, that is.

But if he was asking others to run a risk, he should be willing to share the danger. He'd tried to follow that principle throughout his career. With-out being idiotic about it, of course, when others were obviously more qualified.

In fact, he was surprised that in the end, Lasher had agreed to their launch at all.

He wasn't sure he would have, had he been in command. Doing the risk analysis, the way you were supposed to.

He peered ahead into the storm, but made out only the strobing glow of their running lights. The flashes froze the blades overhead for a mil-lisecond before plunging them into darkness again. Leaving only a mo-mentarily arrested glimpse of a magically frozen whirlwind made of snow.

The last tremor, the final aftershock from the impact thrummed away, leaving Sloan vibrating in his peapod. Thank God, the keel had released. They hadn't plunged to the bottom. But this collision had definitely been less powerful than the others. The Pilot had warned they were using the last watts of power. Now he crouched in the piss-stinking dark, waiting for the verdict.

At last the screen lit. Dimly, as if it was losing voltage. *Sail may have broken surface*, it read.

He typed, *May have??*

Lost camera feed. Lost sensors and connections in mast. Suspect im-pact drove it down into the sail. Unable to provide more data.

Just . . . wonderful. He twisted on the metal stamping, which now felt less like a seat than an instrument of torture.

Well, he'd done all he could.

Only a few more loose ends to clean up. Then he could sit here and wait to black out.

Or, take a more drastic course.

He typed, slowly, painfully, *Do you still hold contact on Pskov?*

Negative. Lost contact when forward transducers and sonar process-ing module were damaged.

Roger, he typed. Then, *Depth here?*

Fifteen hundred fathoms. Twenty-seven hundred meters. Nine thou-sand feet.

He nodded. More than deep enough, once the Prime was explosively disassembled with thirty kilos of military-grade Composition Four. He felt in the dark for the port he'd plugged his chip drive into, to upload the tactical patches. Yep, it was still there.

He typed, *Do you still have access to the media I used to update your tactical programming?*

I do.

Download all information about mission and Apokalypsis, sonar signatures, records, all your data into detachable media.

A pause. Then, *Download complete.*

He considered for a moment. Then typed, *Pilot. Do you have a central processing algorithm? Any sort of . . . personality construct?*

My central algorithm is a sub-symbolic quantum neural network. It manages a hierarchy of other, subordinate cognitive architectures and data bases. Is that what you're referring to?

Maybe. Download me a copy of that as well.

Unsure that is what you really want. That would be easily available from my original programmers. What makes me me . . . I believe . . . is my memories.

Okay, then add those too. If you need more space, delete the tactical programming that was on the chip before.

Another pause, much longer. Then, again, *Overwrite and download complete.*

He pressed the button to extract the chip. Stuck it between his teeth and typed,

When I fail to respond for fifteen minutes, trigger scuttling charges. Goodbye.

A hiatus, as if the thought of saying farewell had never been considered. As if this was some novel concept that had to be processed at the deepest levels. Finally the screen lit.

Goodbye, Commander.

The ground, or more properly a plain of shattered ice, indistinctly visible only in the last seconds before impact, rushed up. All the landing lights did was surround the cockpit in a blurry white glow through which the snow streamed endlessly. Driven through the smears of flashing light while bouncing from crystal to crystal, reflecting and concentrating it around the descending aircraft. Like, Dan thought, being suspended inside a badly lit Ping-Pong ball . . .

"*Brace,*" Druhn snapped over the intercom. Dan grabbed for the handhold again an instant before they set down, so violently clipboards, gear, duffels flew up and then tumbled down again.

Druhn remained intent on his instruments. The engine, instead of slowing, continued to roar. "I'm going to have to hold her down," he yelled over the mingled howl of turbines and storm. "This much wind, the blades catch it wrong, it'll flip us over. Matt, get the sling deployed. Pay it all out. All hundred meters."

A series of chunks and whines sounded behind them. Frigid air blasted in as the crewman unsealed the door with a kick.

Dan peered out through the side windscreen, not eager to step out into that frozen hell. When the crewman jumped down, steadying himself with one hand on the door, his boots sank over a foot deep. Within the reach of their lights, which wasn't far, Dan could make out looming precipices, jagged outthrusts, a rugged, jumbled, tilted icescape. All blasted by the streaming drift. Even the relatively flat area the pilot had chosen to set down on was uneven, canting them to port. Which explained his apprehension about being flipped, since the wind was gusting from their right, pushing up under the whirling blades.

"You might need these, sir!" the pilot yelled. He handed Dan a flashlight and a pair of flight goggles. Dan examined the flash; it was the old-style gray plastic right-angled light. With the red lens installed, he noted. Obviously kept for use in the cockpit.

Not for the first time, he wondered if this had been a good idea. "Which direction should we favor?"

Druhn waved a gloved hand. "No idea, sir. Even GPS gets hinky up here. But you'd better get moving. Just sitting here I'm burning fuel."

Dan unlatched his side hatch and leaned out into the blast. His face lost feeling at once, and he blinked away a skin of ice that instantly frosted his eyeballs. The wind buffeted, trying to stuff him back into the cockpit, and he had to struggle out against its pressure. He felt for the ice near the front wheel with the toe of his boot, found firmness under the drift, and let himself down.

Behind him the airman and the mechanic were unspooling white-and-blue nylon line from a reel inside the passenger compartment. They fought it in slow motion, like astronauts uncertain of gravity. After exchanging gestured questions, the mechanic produced two heavy-looking yellow battle lanterns from his tool bag. He handed one to the airman. Arranging the line over one shoulder as if pulling a sled, and looking down at what must be a wrist-strapped compass, the airman trudged out into the night, the spot of the flash playing ahead of him like a glowing beam made of blowing snow.

A smaller figure jumped down; Blanco. Also goggled, hood draw-stringed tight around her face, she carried a flashlight too, though a less powerful one. She grabbed the line. As the crewman trudged off into the dark, she let it drag out through her gloved hands, flipping it occasionally as it unreeled off the spool to prevent its snagging or chafing on the door-frame.

Dan stood bent, one glove braced against the fuselage, watching Blanco measure out fathom after fathom in the old fashion, from fingertip to fingertip. He caught a questioning glance back and gave her an approving thumbs-up.

The mechanic dropped his bag in the snow. Blanco pointed to the line and waved out into the night. He switched on another flash, grabbed the line, and followed it out into the dark.

Dan stood bewildered. This all seemed so . . . primitive. Feeling like there should be some sort of electronic device or signal that would guide them to their goal. But he couldn't think of any.

He was starting to worry this was a total fuckup. Not the first in his career, of course. But he really wanted to find whoever had manned this thing. No matter what he'd done, where he'd been, if he'd been coming from the direction of the Russian Arctic he'd been involved in *something* important.

Which would also explain the priority both Washington and Ottawa were placing on his rescue.

Blanco made a slicing motion above the line, pointed to it, then jabbed a finger at him. Dan nodded, grabbed the line, and began trudging out into the dark.

Sloan tucked the chip inside the pocket of his dry suit. Then snugged the zipper and sealed the Velcro tape over it. The zipper didn't run vertically down the suit, only over the top half, slanting across his chest. It wasn't supposed to leak.

He took several deep breaths, flushing the carbon dioxide from his lungs. Hoping the absorbent canister was still doing at least some good. He felt light-headed. The first hint of oxygen deprivation? Or just terror as he was taking his final breaths? He wasn't sure.

No point waiting any longer. "Okay, let's do this," he muttered. He reached above his head, grabbed the dogging wheel for the upper hatch, and tried to turn it.

Only it didn't move. He squinted upward, then tapped the screen so that it provided a little light. This time he made out a safety toggle that had to be released before the wheel could rotate. No doubt to make sure no one made a stupid mistake. He flipped the toggle out of the way, took another breath, and began twisting.

The screen lit again. *Red sensor on maintenance module upper hatch*, it read.

He ignored that warning, putting all his upper body into the wheel. It gave reluctantly, a little at a time. After one full turn, a thin spray began bleeding out around its rim, blasting down into his upturned face. He received the lashing grimly, squinting into it. The sea was salty and bitter and utterly chill on his tongue. No, he wouldn't feel much once he was surrounded by it. Or for long.

He cranked the wheel another turn. The spray became a gush, then a torrent. Sure. He was, what, thirty feet down? The water ran down his neck, spraying over the keyboard, over his lap, running down to pool at his boots.

His ears pained as if spikes were being hammered into them. Wait until the pressure equalized, or go? He decided to go, and gave the wheel a last savage wrench.

The water cascaded in with a weird vibrating squeal. The smell of the sea filled what remained of the air around him with a frothing dankness. He braced his boots and thrust upward.

The hatch didn't move. Not even a hairbreadth. Seawater was still burbling in around it. It was up to his thighs now, rapidly flooding the sphere, but pressure was still leaning it closed. He gathered his strength and shoved again. It still didn't lift. His fingers scrabbled in the dim. Was he missing something else? Some link or seal or tab or latch?

A buzzer sounded, muted, but still distinct. He slapped at his suit, then followed the sound down to his left side.

The oxygen gauge. Not only did it read zero, now the face had turned red and was blinking. Even as he watched, it registered *O2 Exh.*

He doubled his legs under him, under the frigid shower flooding down over his scalp and face and upper body. Then, with all his might, made one last despairing effort, pushing with everything he had against the crushing weight of the sea.

* * *

004

Once they got a few steps from the helo, the surface of the pack wasn't just chaotic, not just broken, it was a topological nightmare. Dan kept stumbling into holes hidden by the gritty drifted snow. He couldn't see more than a step ahead. The blowing whiteness seemed to swallow light, sucking it in and transmuting it into a pale, pulsating smear that really didn't reveal anything.

Within ten paces he'd emerged from the light blob around the aircraft to be plunged into total night. He flicked the flash on and followed the red spot, and the still-paying-out line, out over the trudged-up surface. It led past an outcrop of wind-smoothed ice, a ridge, maybe just slightly shorter than he was, then around large broken blocks. Ruby glints shifted deep in them, refracted from his light.

A flash from far away to his right . . . the mechanic, pointing a beam in Dan's direction. He lifted his own and waved it back. Then swung it left to signal the medic. But no answering photons arrived from her direction.

The line tugged at his gloved hands. Their progress wasn't uniform, of course. The airman, on the outer end of the line, had to negotiate the perimeter of a circle six hundred feet in diameter. Dan's circle would be much smaller, but the truth was, he wasn't feeling all that great. The aftereffects of radiation, of frostbite, whatever . . . maybe just that he was getting too far along to be taking on physically demanding tasks like this.

He came to a nearly vertical wall and halted. The icy shelf rose to above his waist. After dithering a moment, he wrapped the line around one arm and boosted himself. Swung his legs over and slid down the far face, gripping the line in one hand and the flash in the other. Above all, mustn't lose that.

The wind howled. The cold was piercing. His eyes were freezing shut. He rubbed them free with the back of a glove and staggered on, gripping the line with fierce desperation born of the sure comprehension that if he let go, he was done for. He stumbled through a world of black, following the tug of the line on his gloves, negotiating a weaving, stumbling path amid the shattered ice.

Losing, with each step, any hope they might actually find what they sought.

The hatch yielded at last, but with its rising came a drenching down-gush of frigid water that within two or three seconds completely filled the sphere, covering his chest, then his neck, then his face with a flood of bitter cold. Closing his throat, Sloan straightened painfully from his chair of torment to stand erect at long last. Tottering, legs feeble as a newborn's. His spine screamed. He ignored it, uncoiling, shoving upward with everything he had.

The heavy hatch swung upward, hit something, and rebounded. He thrust at it once more, and it latched back with a click that came distinctly to his ears through the water.

Holding his final breath, that last lungful sucked deep as the sea flooded in, he tore the mask away, thrust it aside, and wriggled desperately up through the narrow opening.

He clawed up into the utter darkness of the escape trunk, leaving utter darkness behind. With the in-flooding of salt water the displays had flickered out. He got his boots on the lip of the hatch and jackknifed upward. His elbow rammed into something hard, but it didn't hurt.

His outthrust fingers identified a narrow steel ladder. Grabbing it with both hands, he began hauling his body upward, letting his legs dangle at first, then kicking to swim.

After two rungs he jerked to a halt, hung up. Something had snagged on his left side. He felt along it and found a wire.

The cable to the fathometer case, that had supplied his suit with heat. He tore it free with a savage jerk, then clawed for the ladder again in the dark. Flailed for a moment, unable to locate the next rung. He was sinking again, back toward the sphere.

No. He would not die there, curled like a fetus in a freezing womb.

His wooden fingers struck the ladder again, and a renewed and frantic impulse clawed him up it, dragging an enormous slow burden after him. The burden of his dying body, beginning to blink off, by cell. *Air.* He had to have *air.*

But then again, maybe water would work.

All he had to do was open his mouth, and the torment would end.

His skull whacked steel so hard novas wheeled around his fading brain. His boots found a rung, and he braced his back against the trunk. Hands over his head once more, he searched for a second dogging wheel. It should be here, same as the one in the sphere.

But it wasn't.

With the last remnants of expiring consciousness, he walked dead fingers around the edge of what had to be an upper hatch. The whole point of having two ways of accessing the maintenance sphere was that it could be reached both from below, when the Orca was piggybacked on a mother sub, and from above, when it was surfaced. He'd seen the earlier-version USVs alongside tenders during the war. Flanks awash, upper hatches open. Being recharged, tested, repaired, maintained. There *had* to be a hatch here.

For the first time, he realized it might not be operable from the inside.

The trunk he was trapped in would be flooded during mother ship operations. There would be no earthly reason to access the upper hatch from within it.

Pier-side, it would be accessed from above, to service the sphere.

There was no requirement whatever to have a means of undogging it from within.

His fists hammered it, but only a scrape resounded. The interior of the hatch was slightly curved, bell shaped. Again he ran a hand around its edge, feeling the last remnants of consciousness bleed away like black light into lightless darkness.

A hole appeared in his mind.

A blackness that grew at the edges, a tar-dark maw consuming all sensation. His thoughts circled it, then swirled downward. Nothing could escape its iron grip. Thought. Breath. Light. Selfness itself.

At the last possible moment his fumbling fingers found a latch. Sketched there, one day, by some obscure safety engineer who'd envisioned an admittedly unlikely event: someone trapped in the trunk like a child in an abandoned refrigerator. He set his fingers around it and pulled. But they slipped off, unresponsive to his commands.

He laid his head alongside it and tried again, in the utter dark, to get his fingers around the metal strip that would release the hatch from inside.

They slipped off.

He snarled aloud and got a mouthful of icy sea. Then, with the unreasoning fury of a dying animal, thrust his muzzle at it, gripped it in his teeth, and pulled. The hollow snap of breaking teeth echoed through his skull, but he only clamped down, as hard as he could, and tugged backward with tensed neck muscles.

The latch clicked open. He hunched his spine against the smooth outward curve and heaved upward with all his remaining fury.

The smooth curve lifted. He shoved again, and it yielded unwillingly, rising, and he pushed himself up the last few inches to the top of the ladder.

His staring eyes blinked into a substance-less vacuity that he took a moment to recognize as air. Its touch brought with it the energy for one final heave, and the hatch yielded and toppled back.

A chill yielding softness tumbled in on top of him. He beat at the mass, clawed it aside, forcing himself up, seeking oxygen with the desperation of a dying animal.

It broke apart above him, and a gale lashed his freezing face.

He sucked an icy breath deep into shuddering lungs. With a final despairing exertion, he doubled himself up over the hatch edge, off the last rungs of the ladder. He clawed the snow apart from below and emerged, wriggling on his belly, dragging his trunk and then the useless, massive burden of his lower legs snakelike out from beneath it.

He came forth into darkness as absolute as the hole that had opened in his mind, into a wind so glacial it choked even his first so-yearned-for breath. He panted a second diaphragm-deep inhalation, and his mind cleared just enough to realize he was wet through. The suit wouldn't help. It, too, was soaked, inside and out.

So he still wouldn't last long. Not out here.

But at least he could breathe, if he cupped his lower face with those dead hands, and sucked the super-chilled air through interlaced fingers.

He was resigning himself to death when he heard, beyond the scream of the wind, what sounded uncannily like the blades of a distant helicopter.

The tugs on the line came from his right. Dan hesitated before the face of a tricky-looking shelf, staring toward where he'd last seen a flashlight glow.

The tugs came again. Three spaced yanks.

Which could only mean one thing, though they hadn't prearranged signals. *Come to me.*

He began shuffling out along the line, keeping a firm grip on it, shining his own light to and fro to avoid any surprises. Like holes or gaps in the ice, into one of which he'd plunged earlier, through a deceptive snow cover, up to one thigh, staggering him and injuring his knee. He'd feel it later, once he warmed up.

But for now, he lurched and plowed on, ignoring the advancing numbness in hands and face. Thrusting himself step by step outward.

He collided with a bulky body bent over a dark patch in the snow. Dan bent to examine the thing too, holding the red spot of his light on it. At first it looked like another hole in the ice. Another trap for an unwary leg.

Then the mechanic spun a finger, and Dan realized the hole was perfectly round.

Not a hole. An *access.*

Something of human making lay beneath.

The mechanic dropped full length and thrust an arm in, pushing his light down into it. When he withdrew it, it was dripping wet.

They both stared down into the well as Dan's cold-soaked brain fought to come to some conclusion. WTF, over? He scraped a boot at the snow and was rewarded with a smoothly curved black carapace.

Yeah. It could be the topside of an Orca. Bending to the mechanic's ear, he shouted, "Was it open when you found it?"

A vigorous nod. Dan straightened and aimed the light around. The red spot traveled over jagged ice, but was absorbed by the spindrift. Gusts battered them, making him reel on the injured leg, which was beginning to hurt in earnest. Yeah, he'd torn something, stepping into that hole. But where the fuck . . .

"There," he muttered, bending to look along the beam. For a moment the wind dropped, and the snow fog cleared slightly. The drift was already erasing it, but he could just make it out: a dragged-out path leading back toward the helicopter.

Whose engine was still running . . . giving one clear point of reference in this howling night.

Whoever, or whatever, had emerged from that hatch, it was crawling toward the sound of the engines.

They came on the body fifty yards down the trail. It lay on its belly, prone, motionless, arms stretched forward. Had obviously heard the aircraft's engines and been trying to reach it. But when they turned him over his face was white, his wide-open eyes fixed. Dan kneaded his cheeks, then slapped them, but got no response.

The corpsman blundered out of the howling drift. She bent over the recumbent form. Tilted its head back and cleared the airway. Bent to seal her mouth to the slack lips. In the focus of their flashes the man's chest rose and fell, but the staring, ice-rimmed eyes remained fixed.

Dan frowned, half recognizing the pallid face, though he couldn't put a name to it. The corpsman hammered bladed hands across the chest. Ice shattered and fell away. She crossed her hands and leaned on the heel. Felt his neck. Bent to administer another breath, then repeated the process.

"Is there a pulse?" Dan yelled.

"No. Or at least, I can't make one out," the medic yelled. "Let's get him into the chopper. I'll look him over there."

With all their hands locked under him in a fireman's carry, they stumbled over the uneven ice. Blanco joined them, which made the carrying easier.

At last the helicopter loomed, limned in a strobing blur, a wavering halo of white and red and green. Druhn had turned every light on to beacon them in.

They were mere steps away when a tremor ran through the ice around them. A clap as if of a distant detonation, muffled, yet distinct against their feet. Dan craned around, looking for whatever had caused it, but could make out nothing amiss. Snow stung his eyes, and he saw only the raging darkness.

In the intermittent lightning of the Bell's strobes Blanco hauled the door open to the compartment. They bundled their burden in and clambered after it. The airman threw in the last of the hoist cable as the turbines spooled upward.

The door sealed with a thumping click, slicing off the shrieking wind. The world disappeared in a whirlwind of white as the rotors engaged. The corpsman bent over the body once more in the dim radiance of the cabin lights as they reeled up into the night. She positioned both hands, then grabbed Blanco's gloved fists and placed them where her own had been.

"Keep pressing," she ordered. "Once every two seconds." She jabbed a finger at the airman. "Tell your pilot what we found. Get them ready to receive a casualty back on the ship." She pulled her pack toward her, yanking out a plastic case as the deck tilted. "Just keep it up," she told Blanco, snapping the kit open to reveal a hypodermic. To the mechanic, "Unzip his suit. Pull it down. I'll need access to the chest area. You." She pointed to Dan. "Artificial respiration. Know how?"

He nodded; the Navy required annual training. He braced his knees on freezing aluminum, ice shards grating under them, positioning himself as the mechanic peeled back the recumbent body's clothing. Recalling the drill: Tilt the head back. Clear the airway. Pinch the nose. Bend, and breathe. Relax, let the rib cage deflate. Repeat the process.

Across from him Blanco was leaning into her braced arms, pressing and releasing. The corpsman tilted the needle, examined it, then placed her fingers carefully, exploring, locating. She set the needle and jammed it straight down.

The first sign of life was a blink. Then a choking, feeble struggle, as the frost-faced man fought against their hands.

"Easy there." Dan patted his cheek and leaned in to yell over the engine noise, "Take it easy, fella. We got you. You're safe."

But the man's eyeballs jerked crazily, and he kept fighting. He seemed to be groping for something at his chest. The corpsman intercepted his hand and gently guided it back to his side.

The frantic blue eyes locked on Dan's. Grew wider, as if they recognized him.

Then Dan, too, retrieved the realization at last. He frowned. "It's not . . . Lieutenant Tomlin?" he muttered.

A weak nod in return as something small was thrust into his hand.

When Dan opened his fingers to look, a small black object lay on his gloved palm.

The Afterimage

Arlington, Virginia

Below the windows the streets were nearly empty, with only the occasional flare of headlights threading the streets between the towering buildings. A chill wind rattled the windows. For the first time that winter, it was snowing.

Dan was with Blair and her staffers. They sat silently, the younger ones with legs curled beneath them, sipping coffee or tea, or just staring at the screens.

The votes were being tallied.

During the final weeks, the administration had resorted to every possible tactic to swing the long-delayed election their way. Every "traitor" who'd been committed to a Zone had lost the right to vote. Ditto, everyone residing in a state in rebellion. The Patriot Channel's polls showed Novikov with a healthy lead everywhere. The message being, since the election was in the bag, no one really needed to turn out. But just in case they did, DHS agents had been stationed to "certify the results" at each voting site.

In response, Blair's party had waged a grueling ground game, relying on personal appearances and pop-up social influencer sites to argue against entrusting the administration with another term. Hundreds of online posters and demonstrators had been gassed, beaten, arrested, accused of slander and treason, and jailed. But there were always more.

It would all be decided tonight. One way or the other.

Unfortunately, it looked like their team was losing.

Blair sighed and turned to Dan. "We expected this. Remember? The early returns are from the mail-in ballots the government preprinted for everybody. Already marked for the Patriot Party. We'll do better once the urban returns start to come in."

Dan nodded, and got up to get her coffee. Hoping she was right, but fearing she wasn't.

Governor M'Elizabeth Rayner Holton had taken an early lead in the primaries. She'd clinched the nomination with victories in California and Puerto Rico and won a landslide majority among the superdelegates.

But then, to balance the ticket, she'd named Justin Yangerhans as her vice presidential running mate. Signaling a pivot toward the center, to appeal to the pro-defense and male votes among swing voters and independents.

At least that was the theory. But this had been the foulest campaign in living memory. Both Holton and Yangerhans had been tarred as corrupt pederasts. Their supporters were smeared as radicals, socialists, anti-was, and separatists. The mudslinging had gone both ways, with "fascist" and "Patriot scum" fired back. A quickly blocked YouTube ad called "Big Sister Will Be Watching You" warned that Novikov's plans to implement "social credit" scores would turn the nation into masses of cowed slaves. The whole campaign had reminded Dan of a medieval siege, with trebuchets slinging plague-ridden corpses back and forth over the walls.

Meanwhile, disease was still spreading in Missouri, Kansas, Iowa, Nebraska, Minnesota . . . and Nan was talking about going back . . .

At the coffee urn, Dan chatted with Jessica Kirschorn. She kept eyeing him oddly, until he asked why. "You haven't seen the . . . thing about you," she said.

He frowned. "The . . . What thing?"

"I don't recall the details . . . just that I read a post somewhere about something that mentioned you. But I can't remember the hashtag. Or what exactly it said."

He nodded, not terrifically interested. She offered to search for it, but when he declined she glanced down at her phone and excused herself.

He dawdled there for a while longer, gazing down onto the streets below. Then lifted his gaze to the looming mass of the Pentagon, a scattering of lights from hundreds of windows in the winter night. As they glowed through the falling snow he shivered, remembering the killing blast of frozen ice drift. Compared to the Arctic, a Virginia cold snap was a midsummer's day.

He was back at work there, at the Puzzle Palace. The postwar force structure study wasn't the most exciting assignment he'd ever had, but the new Congress would want options. The good news was, manufacturing was rebounding. Unemployment was down, and the stock market was inching up. If some agreement could be reached with the insurrectionists, the Covenanters and the ReConfederates, the country might just recover.

Of course, that all assumed that Holton won.

If she didn't . . . well, he didn't want to think about what would follow. Novikov's hard-line platform of chumminess with foreign dictators and savage repression at home hardly augured well.

Dan himself was still being attacked. The Patriot media had picked up Sandy Treherne's conspiracy theories and hammered him day after day as a stooge, a war criminal, a bloodthirsty sacrificer of American lives on Hainan. He tried to shrug it off, but it hurt.

He stood with the cup warming his hand, looking out at the night. Simply . . . waiting.

That seemed to be a big part of life these days. Waiting for the fallout plume across the northern tier to decay, so people could move back. Waiting for a peace deal in the Midwest and South. Waiting to see who would be in charge, after a disastrous war and a violent peace.

Tonight, maybe, they'd find out that much, at least.

San Diego, California

Sloan waited in the CO's outer office, nursing his hands. They were still bandaged and still hurt like hell, but he'd probably keep his fingers. Which was more than he'd dared to hope.

As was just being alive too, of course.

On his return, he'd checked in with Dr. Henricksen and his department head. Presented his report and briefed them on what he'd left out. Both men had nodded, expressions neutral. Paused to think about it. And each finally offered some noncommittal variation of, "Well, we'll send it up the line, and see what comes back down."

This morning the commanding officer of the Naval Strategic and Tactical Analysis Group had requested his presence.

He was standing in the passageway, flicking through his phone, when the captain stuck her head out. "Commander? Come on in."

He entered, squared himself before the desk, and came to a not terribly rigid attention.

Captain Cheryl Staurulakis was a spare, rather washed-out-looking blonde. Her wartime ribbons covered her chest. A picture on her desk showed a guy holding a helmet, standing in front of a jet fighter.

She settled behind her desk and nodded at a chair, but without looking at all welcoming. "Sit."

He did. She scratched at her fingers, looking thoughtful, then glanced at his bandages. "What's the outlook? On your hands, I mean."

He swallowed. "The doctors say I'll keep them, ma'am. May be some loss of feeling. But the nerves should regenerate."

She regarded him for another moment, then lowered her gaze to her tablet. "I read your report. Needless to say, I'm appalled at your actions. At your . . . judgment. Or lack of it."

"Yes, ma'am." He swallowed, getting the feeling he was going to have a new asshole torn. Then reassured himself: What was the worst she could do? Send him back to his grandfather, and a lucrative job inside the Beltway?

She mused, gazing at the screen, "Sometimes the best thing to do when you're unsure is to ask for direction. Not make spur-of-the-moment decisions based on zero analysis."

He debated whether to defend himself. *Tang* had been alone, deep beneath the ice cap. Unable to communicate. With the data link hosed, putting a human in the Prime had been the only way to accomplish the mission. Everything downstream of that had been . . . well . . . not *his* fault. But finally decided to just nod instead of protesting. "I understand. Ma'am."

"You got lucky. *Very* lucky. If the Canadians hadn't had an icebreaker at sea and agreed to cooperate in a rescue, you'd still be out there. Frozen. Dead."

He forced, or faked, ruefulness. "Yes, ma'am. I realize that."

That must have been the right response, because those ice-blue orbs softened. "All right, then. That said, it took balls. To climb into that thing. Without backup . . . I wish I could put you in for a commendation. Unfortunately, we have to bury this mission."

She studied his face, maybe looking for disappointment, but he didn't really care. He hadn't taken this job for decorations. And at least it hadn't been . . . boring.

After a moment she nodded. "Apropos of that . . . we received some interesting information about their program. The Russian effort."

"About Apocalypse?"

"Correct. Actually, two items." She skated a printout of a *Scienmag* article across the desk. "The Canadians announced completing a program of seismic charges in the Arctic. A geophysical survey, to investigate sedimentary layers and determine the depth of the Precambrian basement."

For a moment he didn't get the connection. Then he understood. "To explain the explosions. From when I scuttled the Prime."

"Precisely. For our part, we'll announce an Orca vehicle was lost at sea during tests off the California coast."

She gave him a second, then added, "Which leads us to the second item. What I'm about to share is SCI. Grammar-compartmented, by the way, since it's derived from human-sourced intelligence."

She turned the screen his way. Yeah, there was the Top Secret header, in bold red sans serif letters.

He read it once, then again. And at last sat back, puzzled. Pleased, but also not sure he understood. "It's been canceled?"

"I doubt they'll announce it publicly. They like to keep these threats on the table. Hoping to deter us with phantoms, I guess. Or build themselves up in the world's eyes. The Big Bad Bear, who everybody has to tiptoe around. But for now, at least, they're backing off further development."

He nodded slowly and turned the tablet back toward her.

The Apocalypse program had been paused. No reason given, but its mother submarine had been ordered to Severodvinsk for refit. Work on the second prototype had halted. Moscow was redirecting funding into doubling its network of Arctic undersea sensors. No source was provided for the intel, but he figured it must be the same Lithuanians who'd passed along the circuit diagrams and source code.

Staurulakis stretched, arching her spine, putting both fists to her back. She glanced toward the window. A bright high sky without a single cloud or contrail looked for some reason harsh and hard and somehow even threatening. "Which leads me to what I actually wanted to discuss with you," she said.

"Yes, ma'am." He sat forward. *What now?*

"We're going to be making some changes in our staffing. I requested funding for four more billets. Just got word they're approved. Effective immediately, I'm establishing a new department. A direct-action team. So we don't have to reconstitute one every time they give us a mission like this." She scratched between her fingers absentmindedly, then seemed to realize what she was doing and splayed them out on the desk. The nails looked ragged, as if she chewed them. "I'm not sure what to call it. Something innocuous. We can discuss it later. Along with, who we assign to it.

"Is that something that might interest you? Given, your main designator code is tactical warfare instructor. But there's a limited pool of . . . risk-takers . . . in the Navy. And most O-4s are looking for command billets, not shore billets. You'll need a joint tour if you want a shot to break out for captain. But if you do a good job here, I have people I can talk to."

She looked up from her desk. "But they gave it to me as a coded billet, which means I'd have to request a waiver. Which I don't want to put in for unless you're game."

He had no problem nodding. "Yes, ma'am. That sounds . . . exciting. I'm interested. I definitely am."

"Great. I had you in mind to lead it." She waited a beat, then added, "Unless you object?"

The chance to escape his grandfather's demands. A few more years, at least, of evading the paralyzing tedium of making money. He stuffed that thought, though. And simply said, "No, ma'am. I'll do the best I can for you in the job. And then we can talk, down the road, about what comes next."

Reston, Virginia

Blair's old office still had her name on the door. Below it, in smaller gold letters, *Vice President, Advanced Solutions Division*. Though not for long now . . . she let herself in, balancing the stack of folded boxes, and eased the door closed behind her. The retired general next to her always complained when she slammed it. Plus, she still had a headache from all the wine last night.

From her window she could look out and down across the urban core of what had once been a sleepy Virginia town, and was now the epicenter of government and quasi-government activity inside the Beltway.

The company had moved to Reston a few years before, after absorbing Lockheed Martin's information systems business. The building still smelled of new drywall and fresh paint. She turned the flat-screen on, unfolded a box, unlocked her desk, and started packing. The contents wouldn't fill more than two boxes; most of her work here resided on the local network. A few studies—the unclassified ones, of course, on applications of autonomous systems to environmental modeling and toxic remediation and corrosion research. On the shelves, her statistics and calculus textbooks from college, which she kept when she wanted a refresh on the math. Pictures of her parents, and a nice one of her and Dan at the beach in Bahrain. Actually the first they'd ever taken together. She held it for a moment, contemplating their smooth, unlined features. How young they'd looked then.

She brushed a lock of hair back over her ear, cleared her throat, and nestled the photo in the box.

The election results had firmed up through the night, and by 3 A.M. had seemed pretty much locked in. The final counts were delayed in several states, and no doubt there would be legal challenges. But the numbers showed pretty clearly that Holton had won. Novikov hadn't conceded, and probably wouldn't. But after waiting a few hours, M'Elizabeth had given her acceptance speech.

Blair had stayed up for the whole thing, of course. The president-elect had said her first act would be to reunite America. To extend the same reconciliation to the Covenanters Lincoln had extended to the defeated Confederates. She would rebuild the country and take advantage of that reconstruction to put America back to work.

After that, naturally, they'd broken out the champagne. . . .

Which explained her headache . . . She turned to the walls and started taking down plaques and diplomas. The Nunn-Perry Award for Mentor-Protégé Excellence. The James S. Cogswell Outstanding Industrial Security Achievement Award. The ACT-IAC Innovation Award, for her work on overdose detection via computer-driven tomography. And others.

But the funny thing was, when she'd come in this morning to see if she still had a job, old General Tomlin had been evasive. Hemmed and hawed, index finger drawing circles on his desk. Said, at last, "Sorry, Blair, we just don't have anything in the pipeline for you at the moment." And, not meeting her eyes, he'd said they needed her office, space was getting tight.

Okay, then. If Leidos no longer needed her, she could make it on her own. She still had an LLC for a consulting business. And a role on Holton's transition team, helping craft defense numbers. Mainly, she'd advocated defunding the DHS battalions, or more accurately, transferring them to the state Guard for gradual drawdown. It was dangerous to dissolve armed units too suddenly. Maybe she could bill a few more hours there.

After that, she'd get serious about Titus Solutions LLC. Bid on work, make some actual damn money for a change. She had to get those fucking debts paid off. Infuriating that at her age, she was stuck with a negative net worth. And then there was the garden, and Jimbo. The poor guy really needed more attention, alone at home all day as he'd been during the campaign. Maybe another cat would help. A kitten? Yeah.

But why was she being let go? She shook her head, still not understanding. Yeah, the current administration had blackballed her. Made it clear the company wouldn't get a single contract as long as she worked there. But Holton had won, after all.

The desk phone rang. She dropped the last diploma into the box and plopped down. Swiveled her chair to face the street below. "Leidos, Blair Titus speaking." Probably the last time she'd ever say that. Oh well.

"Blair?" A rich, deep, African American–accented drawl. Half remembered, but not instantly familiar.

"Uh. Yes. Who's this?"

"You may not remember me, Blair, but I work for Governor Holton. My name is Cyndia Zion."

"Oh! Of course I remember you, Cyndia. We met at the first debate." Zion was Holton's campaign chief of staff, and front-runner for the same post in the West Wing. Actually, Blair and Zion had sat together during that first primary face-off, while their respective contenders battled it out up on the platform. A sturdy, daishiki'd woman with a throaty, rambunctious chuckle, she'd crowded Blair's side through the whole debate. Blair sat up, attention sharpened.

"That's right. And you're doing some defense-related work for our transition team, I understand. Can I ask that this conversation not be recorded?"

"Uh, okay. Sure." She pressed the Shield icon on her phone. The app was supposed to protect you from eavesdropping, but no doubt the NSA still had a back door. "I guess . . . go ahead."

"Blair, as you know, the senator named her cabinet in advance of the election. Assuring the voters we had strong people lined up for the job. Unfortunately, an issue has surfaced with one of the nominees. A possible conflict of interest. We don't need to go into the details."

"Of course." She twitched the chair back and forth like a cat's tail. Apprehension and excitement prickled her nape, mounting up her cheeks in a warm flush. She tightened her grip on the phone. "How may I help?"

"Just to check off a couple of boxes: You completed the confirmation process for your former deputy undersecretary position?"

"Correct."

"Has anything significant changed since then? Involvement with foreign interests or companies? Significant changes in your health, physical or mental?"

"Uh . . . no."

"You have no significant financial interests in any defense contractor? Or are your assets in a blind trust?"

"Correct." Assets? What a laugh. She'd had to sell her stock at the bottom of the wartime slump just to pay the interest on her debt. And now, it seemed, her company didn't have a job for her. Even though a new administration, one she was close to . . . Something was fishy there.

Zion paused, then said deliberately, *"Blair, if you were to be offered the position of secretary of defense, what would be your response?"*

She gripped the phone, staring down at her knees. Trembling a little. Not just with excitement but with actual fear. She'd seen the toll the job took. It had killed Leif Strohm. She'd served as an undersecretary, sure. But to lead would be a gigantic challenge.

The biggest department in the government. Four million active, reserve, and Guard personnel. Yes, drawing down with the end of the war, but that reduction would present its own challenges. Plus a million civilian employees, and an annual budget of nearly three trillion dollars. Unending scrutiny from Congress and the media.

Against that . . . her portrait would hang in the E ring, outside the SecDef's office. Along with those of Forrestal, Marshall, McNamara, Rumsfeld, Mattis, and Strohm. Hers, though, would be the first portrait of a woman.

But there'd be no time for gardening. And damn little to spend with Dan, much less with Jimbo. The job would be full-time, day and night, with terrific pressure, especially at budget time and in the inevitable crises.

And as if reading her mind, Zion said, *"You'd be the first woman to hold the position. The vice president recommends you. And you've served in the Pentagon for many years. Including during the war."*

She cleared her throat. Feeling like the next few words might be the most important, and the most irrevocable, she'd ever spoken. Aside, of course, from her marriage vows. "Um . . . there are those in the party who hold it against me. That I served the previous administration."

"Like I said, that was during the war. And M'Elizabeth wants somebody there who knows what they're doing. Who's not going to be an outsider in the building. We'll let her handle anybody who objects. So what do you say?"

She drew one last breath, then said, as slowly and clearly as Zion had, "Thank you for calling me, Cyndia. If the position were to be offered . . . I would be honored to serve."

DAVID POYER

Atlanta, Georgia:
National Center for Emerging
and Zoonotic Infectious Diseases

Nan had waited days to see the director. Now, at last, they were scheduled to meet. Not in person, though, but on her screen.

She waited before an outdated beige monitor in a makeshift office trailer in the NCEZID parking lot, or more accurately, in an outlying lot of Emory Hospital. They were ensconced, or maybe *quarantined* was the right word, with the rest of her field team: Serene Olduc and Tati Wilcox. Mabalot had vanished as soon as they returned from the Republic, back to the Army. She'd debated whether to include her suspicions of his botched spying in her report, and finally, reluctantly, decided all she had were inferences. If someone inquired, she'd share what she'd witnessed; the random-sounding text messages; the possible reason the rebels had been so obviously prepared for Homeland Security's attack. Besides, she wasn't really sure how she felt about what he'd done.

Until she was, she'd keep her own counsel.

She *had* presented the rebels' proposal for a cease-fire to the director. Hoping he'd take it up the line, get it responded to, acted on.

But she hadn't heard anything back, and to her knowledge, after unobtrusively asking around, not a single other team had been sent to the Midwest. Hers had been the only one, and there'd been no additional shipments of medications, antibiotics, or other supplies.

Strangest of all, no mention of the Second Battle of Puxico had appeared on the news. As if the defeat had never taken place. In fact, all coverage or even mention of disease in the Midwest . . . that was gone too.

Leaving her fearing the worst. Were the infections out of control? Spreading? Was anyone really in charge?

Suddenly the Blabble logo, the government-approved encrypted videoconference link, bloomed on her screen. A moment later Dr. Leland Iannuzzi appeared. Avuncular, almost grandfatherly, in his trademark white coat and bow tie. A respected virologist, he'd been at the CDC for almost thirty years, and director for five. He smiled a gentle acknowledgment. *"Dr. Lenson. Good morning."*

She forced an answering smile. "Good morning, sir."

"We read and discussed your report. Quite interesting. Enteric illnesses on an epidemic scale. Especially the speculation about linking enterovirus to a neurological deficit in children. But you seem

*to have gotten rather . . . deeper into the political arena than we ex-
pected.”*

She adjusted her camera to center her face on his screen. Kept her voice
level and her expression neutral, as if they weren't talking about peoples’
lives, children’s lives. “I thought it was necessary, Doctor. Until order’s re-
stored and public health is back online, caseloads will continue to spike.
And it’ll spill over into the, um, loyal territories that surround the ROC.”

She inclined her head. “So I discussed it with their leadership, yes. They
seemed amenable to a cease-fire—”

Iannuzzi held up both hands. *“Really, Doctor. Really! We have to live
with these situations as we find them. Whether in Africa, Asia, or here
at home. Our remit’s to stop epidemics. Cure people. Not try to end wars,
or change regimes. You have to realize, you may have overstepped into
a very delicate political question—”*

“Unless the fighting stops, we can’t make any progress with disease.”

The director sighed as if she was the one being dense. He glanced off
camera as if at someone sitting in on the call, though no one else was
visible. She hesitated, then pressed on. “Did you forward . . . Uh, did my
proposal get forwarded? To the White House? The military? Homeland Security?”

A small icon flashed at the corner of her screen, winking on for a quarter second, then off again so quickly she couldn't be totally positive it had
happened. Iannuzzi’s mouth tightened. *“It was sent up the line. But the
decision was made not to pursue it. I’m not sure precisely at what
level.”*

She almost gasped. “Not to negotiate? Not to respond to their proposal,
even?”

Iannuzzi glanced off camera again, raising his eyebrows in some unspo-
ken communication. When he turned back he looked grimmer, less affa-
ble. *“This isn’t for anyone else to hear, so please don’t discuss it outside
these walls. A large draft of combat veterans into the Special Battalions
is underway. We’ve been asked to stockpile medications and prepare
field teams to accompany them. To protect our troops.”*

She sat immobile, trying to process this. It made no sense. On several
levels. “Uh . . . but what about the population? Are we not going to . . .
What’s the plan to treat them? To contain the epidemics?”

*“They’re in revolt, Dr. Lenson. Once those areas are pacified, we can
airlift in teams. Send in supplies. Assist the population then.”* Again, he
paused, glancing to the side. Then added, *“But security has to come first.*

Otherwise, we're sending medical personnel into a combat zone without protection."

"But the people—" she started to say, then stopped. *Need our help,* she'd almost said, but she was afraid her voice would break. And pretty obviously, further remonstration was useless.

The government wouldn't be helping the Covenanters. And thousands would die.

Maybe that was even part of their strategy. To let disease and famine do the heavy lifting of weakening the rebellion.

The images that evoked chilled her to the bone. But in the next moment she frowned as a new question occurred. "But surely President Holton . . . I mean, when she takes office—they're going to change that, right? I heard her talking about abolishing Homeland Security. Making peace with the RECOs and the Covenanters. Shouldn't we be planning for a policy change?"

Iannuzzi said, *"Well, how all that will turn out remains to be seen. Let's leave it there for now."* He shuffled papers, looking for something, then found it. *"As for you, Nan . . . you're too valuable to keep on the shelf. Have you heard of the Global Virome Project?"*

She arched her eyebrows. "I've . . . heard of it. Yes." An international effort, based in Basel but active on every continent. It searched out emergent viruses and infections, detecting and identifying zoonotic threats. It set up early-warning systems and drafted treatment protocols. And was funded, not by the US, which had long ago pulled out of most international organizations, but by private foundations and the European Union.

To join it would mean working on the very front line of science. And despite her anger and disappointment, she felt her pulse accelerating. "You're, what, attaching us to it? I thought the US wasn't cooperating with the EU."

"Well, your position with the centers was never intended to be permanent," the director said. He touched his bow tie, not meeting her gaze in the camera. *"I'm sure I never meant to give your folks that impression. But I wanted to try to find something challenging for you to do, after you left us."*

She slumped back in her chair, understanding at last.

She was being fired. Along with her whole team. Though Iannuzzi had managed to make it sound like a promotion.

Still, she didn't get it. Surely the new administration would initiate talks with the rebels. Holton had promised that during her rallies. But the director was speaking as if Yelena Novikov had won, not M'Elizabeth.

She couldn't get her mind around why. Bureaucratic inertia? A last effort by CDC's political masters to punish the troublesome Nan Lenson? She couldn't believe they'd reach this far down into the ranks. No, that was idiotic to think that way. Not everything was a conspiracy. Most likely, Iannuzzi really was taking care of her, just as he said. Helping her refocus on her first love, research, rather than on frontline medical treatment. After all, she wasn't an MD.

Yeah, that had to be it. So she forced a smile. "Thanks, Doctor. That sounds like a great assignment."

"I do think you'll be more useful there. And probably happier too."

"I appreciate it," she said. Then thought of the others. "And Tatianna? I mean, Dr. Wilcox? Serene? They were the real heroes out in the field. They saved a lot of lives."

"We have new assignments for them too," the administrator assured her. *"Don't worry about them. Believe me, we have plenty of challenges these days."*

His tone was soothing. Maybe even . . . *too* comforting. As if he was trying to convince himself, as well as Nan.

But then again, she could be imagining it. Looking for problems when they weren't there. Overthinking the situation.

Switzerland . . . that sounded incredible. A summer trip to France was all she'd seen of Europe. She'd have to brush up her German. Or Italian, she couldn't remember what they spoke in Basel. Could there still be a corner of the world untouched by famine, fallout, pestilence, civil war? It sounded like heaven.

Yet Iannuzzi lingered on the screen, apparently waiting for some last response. Did that downcast gaze signal guilt? Shame? Or was he just awkward with goodbyes? "Will that be all, Doctor?" she murmured.

Once more, that sidelong glance. Then, a wry half smile. "Try to think the best of us, Nan," he said. "And best of luck in your future endeavors."

Before she could respond he was replaced by the blue rays of the CDC logo. Then that, too, flickered, and the program closed. Leaving her blinking at her own reflection in the darkened screen. She logged off and sat back, picking at the sores on her lips.

Yeah. Something weird was definitely going down.

But she had no idea what it was.

The Pentagon

Dan was climbing the steps from the Metro when he halted before the screens. The huge flat-panel displays lined the walls of each subway, bus station, airline lounge, government building. The chyrons streamed *Patriot News: Unbiased and Substantive. The Absolute Truth.* One of the network's slim, attractive young blondes, so interchangeable they might as well be computer-generated, was speaking into the camera, her pretty face puckered with sincerity. The scene cut to video in front of the Supreme Court building. A crowd was waving placards. A zoom in. NATURAL BORN, one read. Another, KEEP AMERICA REAL.

The announcer said, *"The suit alleges a violation of Article Two, Section One of the United States Constitution. The relevant article reads . . ."*

The text flashed on the screen:

No Person except a natural born Citizen, or a Citizen of the United States, at the time of the Adoption of this Constitution, shall be eligible to the Office of President; neither shall any person be eligible to that Office who shall not have attained to the Age of thirty five Years, and been fourteen Years a Resident within the United States.

Dan lingered, frowning, as others halted too, here and there around the station, looking up at the screens. What the hell was going on? Were they talking about Holton? She'd been born in *Pennsylvania.* Her birth certificate was viewable online. Of course she was a citizen. She was a *governor.* And she was over thirty-five, though he didn't think by much— maybe in her early forties. What the hell?

A familiar face appeared: Yelena Novikov. The Patriot candidate. *"I have the greatest respect for Ms. Holton,"* she was saying. *"But the text of the Constitution is clear. No one but a natural-born citizen may be eligible for the office of president. M'Elizabeth Rayner Holton is not a natural-born citizen."*

A photograph flashed up. A hospital, or a clinic. The colors faded, saffroned, as if the photo had been taken decades earlier.

"The fetus later named M'Elizabeth Holton was conceived, not of a natural process, but as the artificial product of in vitro fertilization. The records of who her biological parents were have been destroyed.

"Thus, it is impossible to say with certainty that she is the daughter of American citizens. Equally, it is self-evident that she was not 'natural born' in any sense that would have been recognized by the draft-

ers of our founding document, that granite cornerstone of American freedom, the Constitution of the United States."

Dan glanced left and right. The others in the passageway had stopped too, intent on the breaking news.

Novikov said, "At this critical hour, we appeal to all true Americans. Once more, we must battle the forces of unbelief, apathy, and despair. Political intrigue has replaced concern for the fate of the country. Malicious mockery of the security forces has become common. Our country is in danger of disintegration.

"In place of decay, the Patriot Party offers unity. In place of weakness, strength. In place of riot, discipline. We will restore law and order and cleanse our streets of criminal activity. Those vermin who hate America will no longer be allowed to abuse her, in public or in print.

"In light of these indisputable facts, a suit has been submitted to the Supreme Court. It asks to vacate the results of a debased, corrupt, and illegal electoral process, and declare the true choice of the vast majority of voters."

Dan glanced left and right again. The other commuters were staring up. Silent. Stone-faced.

And from the walls, the cameras looked down. Identifying faces. No doubt, reading lips. Scanning the fleeting microexpressions that could not be disguised. But no one said anything, though the whole concourse had come to a halt, with the only sound an occasional cough.

Novikov was replaced by the robotically perfect, probably digitally enhanced newscaster. "Ex-governor Holton has been placed under house arrest for her own protection. An eight P.M. curfew is in effect in the District of Columbia. Active-duty military and Homeland Security forces have been deployed to prevent any civil unrest, pending the decision of the court. Everything is under control. Please remain calm.

"We will now return to our regularly scheduled programming."

He looked around again, hoping to see anger, outrage, disbelief. Some protest, however small; some acknowledgment of how wrong this was. Here and there he caught the same shocked expression as he probably wore himself. Others were glancing about, surreptitiously searching for reactions. Looking for agreement? Or alert for sedition?

At last he cleared his throat. "This isn't right," he said aloud. "This is a coup."

But no other voice joined his.

The viewers turned away from the screens, from the watching cameras, heads lowered. And instantly became a jostling throng once again, hurrying to their offices, like blind insects in an immense five-sided concrete hive.

He didn't have to wait long before he was ushered in by the same aide as during his previous visit. The office looked subtly different. Same desk, same windows, same view. But the CNO had redecorated. Replaced Niles's photographs with those of her family. Gold-toned curtains. A new bookcase was filled with what looked like history tomes. Some even had torn dust jackets, as if they'd actually been read. Most of the paintings on the walls were the same, though. The aide left, closing the door quietly behind her.

"Admiral Hlavna," Dan said.

She stood to greet him. A gesture of respect, acknowledging his Medal of Honor. Several had been awarded during the war just past, so he was no longer the only living Navy recipient. But he was sure he was still the only sailor whose decoration had come courtesy of the US Army. "Admiral Lenson," she said. "Grab a chair. Let's get acquainted."

Shaynelle Hlavna was short, rather stocky, though not at all overweight, and had probably once been a russet blonde, though her hair was streaked with gray now. She wore her submariner dolphins and the Combat Patrol insignia with four stars. The rows of ribbons on her service dress blues were capped by the Navy Cross and Pacific combat awards. Her speech had a West Virginia–ish twang. Seating herself behind her desk, she peered up quizzically over half spectacles.

He nodded and took the chair she waved him to. Folded his hands and waited.

Hlavna said, "I understand you and the previous CNO were close."

"Yes, ma'am. Barry Niles and I went back to the early days of the Tomahawk program. How is he doing? If you happen to know."

She pushed her half glasses up on her nose and sat back. "As well as can be expected. Considering his illness . . . I know he pushed hard for you to retain your wartime rank. But you're already over thirty, correct?"

By "over thirty" she meant he was pushing the retirement limits. If she was hinting it was time to put him out to pasture . . . "That's correct, ma'am," he said. "Though a lot of us were extended, for the duration."

"Of course. Of course. And now you're working for me, on the force structure study. How is that going, by the way?"

He'd come prepared for that question, and proceeded to lay out the timeline and milestones for the study, aided by paper printouts. Hlavna followed along closely, and asked penetrating questions about recruitment and fleet manning. They spent twenty minutes going over it before she nodded, set his documentation aside, and took off her glasses. "Okay, that all seems to be on track. Congress will decide, but at least we can give them options we can live with." She narrowed her eyes, studying him. "Did you catch the announcement this morning? About Governor Holton?"

Dan drew a breath. Glanced at the windows; Niles had warned him not to speak freely too close to them. "Are we secure here, ma'am?"

"This room's suppressed and swept. By our people, not Homeland's."

"It's a coup," he said. "Setting the results of the election aside on some technicality about her method of conception . . . It's not right, or honest, or constitutional."

"So you're not a Patriot." Shrewd green eyes studied him, giving no clue to Hlavna's own attitude.

And that was the nub of it. Like it or not, sooner or later he'd have to put his cards on the table. "No," he said. "I guess I'm not. Not the way they've corrupted the word."

"And your wife's close to Yangerhans and Holton."

"She ran his campaign. But that's not why I feel the way I do." He debated mentioning the feeler about the SecDef position, which Blair had told him about, but decided not to. Not now.

Hlavna said, "You know the Patriots packed the court during the war. Impeached two justices. For 'aiding the enemy,' by which they meant objecting to the Zones."

He had a bad feeling this conversation wasn't going his way. "You think they'll rule in favor of Novikov."

"That seems to be where the smart money is. They'll rule Holton's win invalid. Throw it into the House, which has a ruling-party majority."

"So Novikov will be president. In the end. Regardless of the election."

"This court has surprised people before. Still, I'd say that right now, there's a question mark over the presidency. A *big* one."

A pause. And again Dan remembered, in this office, Niles saying that the Joint Chiefs were determined not to let tyranny prevail. Was Hlavna one of them? Or had she been appointed, elevated, as a political loyalist? Her combat ribbons reassured him, but not entirely. He said cautiously, "Someone once told me the senior military wouldn't let that happen. That they would step in if things went too far."

Hlavna looked away, out at the patches of snow. Or maybe at the distant crosses that marched in rows across Arlington National Cemetery. "I'm not going to respond to that, Admiral. The chairman's asked us to meet in the Tank tonight. But that's between you and me. We never spoke about that subject."

He lowered his gaze. "I understand."

She seemed to unbend a little. "The trouble is, any . . . counteraction would have to be unanimous. It can't be three to three, or even five to one. *Everybody* has to be on board. That means we'd all have to agree on how far 'too far' is. That's a high bar. And what's the end state if we do? If the military takes over, that will be the end of the republic as we knew it."

"Maybe that republic's already gone," Dan said quietly. "Maybe we need to think about what we want to come next."

She studied him again, then touched her lips with a knuckle. "Different topic. I read about the attacks on you, in Congress. But you're in the news yourself, right now—"

He frowned. "I beg your pardon? I don't think—"

She half grinned, and twirled her spectacles. "Oh, we're being modest. How cute. I mean Naylor's book."

Dan groped after the name. After a moment, had it. "The public affairs guy? There was a Naylor on my staff during Rupture Plus. A reservist. Linwood Naylor?"

Hlavna looked skeptical. "You haven't seen it?"

He shook his head, supremely puzzled now. "Seen what?"

She got up and crossed to the bookshelf. Returned, and handed him a volume. This dust jacket looked brand-new. The title was *Task Force 91: The Eyewitness Story of Victory in the Pacific.* It was by Linwood Naylor.

"My task force," he muttered, leafing through it. Then turned back and read the flap copy.

"Third on the *New York Times* nonfiction list. And soon to be a major movie, they tell me." Hlavna flipped the glasses back and forth, grinning. "He makes you out to be a combination of Nimitz and Patton. You're too big a hero now for me to fire you. Not that there aren't good arguments for doing so."

"Huh," was all he could muster. He turned to the tip-in. That wasn't a bad shot of him on the bridge. He couldn't remember when Naylor had taken it. Actually, he couldn't remember much about the guy at all, other than that he'd had really bad breath.

She mused, "Just out of curiosity, which actor would you want to play you? In the movie?"

He frowned. "Oh . . . what? I can't say. I missed most of the big releases during the war." He swallowed, looking at the author picture on the back flap. Yeah, he remembered the guy now. Shit, this felt so unreal. He almost wished he were back on that bridge. Almost.

She chuckled. "I got a call this morning. From the chief of naval information. The morning shows want you on, along with Naylor. Interested? It'd be good promo. For the Navy, I mean. In advance of the budget hearings."

Dan grimaced. "No, seriously, unless that's an order, I'd . . . I would rather not. Thanks."

"Well, we won't insist." She sighed and glanced out the window again before shaking her head. Suddenly she seemed weary. "Okay, Barry told me what you wanted for your twilight tour. I've decided to honor his promise. Starting in June, you'll serve as the superintendent of the United States Naval Academy. A vice admiral billet. So that'll entail a final promotion. Either on nomination or shortly thereafter."

He couldn't help smiling. An assignment he'd dreamed of for many years, and just about given up hoping for. "I appreciate that. Ma'am."

She turned her screen toward her, apparently a signal their sit-down was ending. "You've earned it. At least that's what I hear. But trust me, it won't be a sinecure. Annapolis needs a deep housecleaning. We'll talk more about that in a couple of weeks. Meanwhile, start your background reading; I'll send over some files and general direction. Think about what you want to achieve, where you want the place to go, when you take charge.

"However, I also note that you still have a subpoena from the International Criminal Court pending. For one of your wartime actions."

Dan hitched himself up in the chair. "I was under the impression that had sort of gone away. Since the administration said they weren't going to respond to any summons."

"It's suspended, yes. But it's still out there. In fact, if Holton *did* take office, you might find it a more imminent concern than if Novikov wins."

She gave him a moment to respond, and when he didn't, nodded sharply. "That'll be all, then. Send me the report when you've got a full draft. We have to push a culture of change. Increase our investments in deep AI, quantum science, human reengineering, autonomous swarms, joint all-domain command and control, visible-spectrum stealth. Hit those bullet points, think ahead to the budget item justifications, sharpen your pencil on the costs, and we'll be good."

He stood in the E ring corridor amid the polished gleaming terrazzo, the stark white walls, the stiffly posed oil portraits of past Navy leaders. Leahy. King. Nimitz. Burke. Zumwalt. Kelso. Mullen. Arrow signs set close to the deck pointed toward the nearest exits.

They'd been installed after the 9/11 attack, to guide evacuees toward safety. In case of smoke too thick to see through.

For a moment, suddenly, he was back there again.

Fire. All of it. Burning.

Smoke. Flames. The thick, choking stench of jet fuel.

His breath jigsawed fast and harsh. He closed his eyes and massaged his narrowing throat. Propped a hand against the wall, eyes closed, fighting for control.

He wasn't sucking smoke. That glare wasn't flame. The ceiling above was whole, undamaged. The floor beneath his feet, solid.

"You're safe," he muttered. "It's all right. You're good. This is just a feeling. It can't hurt you. And it will pass."

He opened his eyes again and looked up, blinking into the light of the overhead fixture. Tracing its shape: circular, like a hovering saucer. He took a deep, slow breath. Then another.

Another memory shook him. Deep in a bunker. Copper clamps attached to legs, nipples, penis. The buzzing of the machine as the Mukhabarat tortured him.

"It can't hurt me," he muttered again. "You're dead. You can't hurt me."

He forced himself to push off the wall and walk, more or less normally, down the brightly lit corridor. The terror ebbed. But suddenly he felt weary. Oh, he still felt strong. But still he felt . . . older.

The twilight tour. The last assignment. Three stars . . . He'd never asked for that. Only for a chance. To conn a ship through a storm. To command at sea. Serve his country. Do his duty, and come through with honor. Love a woman, nurture a child, be a man.

But then again, as always, he found himself doubting. Duty? Honor? What did those timeworn words even mean? His country . . . Was what it was becoming even worth the sacrifice?

Maybe the problem was closer. Maybe *he* was the quandary. Why, after all these years, did Dan Lenson still doubt everything, himself included?

Was that why he'd suffered, risked, persevered? Hoping that someday he'd actually find something to believe in?

To hell with it. He reached his own office, a temporary cell in the enormous hive, and halted.

This was the road he'd walked. The path he'd chosen.

So he'd walk it to the end. Take care of those entrusted to him, before thinking of himself. Have faith, and press ahead. If he could act with integrity, he could retire with honor. Knowing, in his heart, that in the end, he'd done okay.

He took a deep breath, and pushed the door open.

Dan's story will continue, with a challenge to both his freedom and his life, in David Poyer's *The Academy*.

Acknowledgments

Ex nihilo nihil fit. The seed of this novel was planted at the Scheepvaart museum—the National Maritime Museum—in Amsterdam, when I viewed their exhibit *Scramble for the Arctic*, curated by Sara Keijzer and Diederick Wildeman, and the film *Arctic Frontier*, by Kadir van Lohuizen and Yuri Kozyrev.

In addition to the sources cited in earlier volumes of this series, the following were helpful for this volume:

Blair's Pentagon scenes were based on personal experience. Other references that proved useful for her chapters included *Campaigns and Elections: Rules, Reality, Strategy, Choice* by John Sides et al. (New York: Norton, 2012) and Michael Burton et al.'s *Campaign Craft: The Strategies, Tactics, and Art of Political Campaign Management* (Santa Barbara, CA: Praeger Books, 2015). Also relevant were US Department of Justice's *Searching and Seizing Computers and Obtaining Electronic Evidence in Criminal Investigations* (OLE Litigation Series, Computer Crime and Intellectual Property Section, Criminal Division, n.d.). Mau Van-Duren read and commented on these chapters.

For Nan's passages: References cited in previous books, plus: Amy Barrett, "New Method Protects Vaccines from Heat Degradation," *BBC Science Focus Magazine*, June 8, 2020. Jamie Bartram and Sandy Cairncross, "Hygiene, Sanitation, and Water: Forgotten Foundations of Health," *PLOS Medicine*, November 2010. Edward Hayes et al., "Cryptosporidiosis in Georgia," Epidemiological Case Study, Centers for Disease Control, and "Salmonella in the Caribbean," Epidemiological Case Study, CDC. Also Gunther F. Craun et al., "Causes of Outbreaks Associated with Drinking Water in the United States from 1971 to 2006," *Clinical Microbiology Reviews*, July 2010. Finally, consultations with Dr. Frances Anagnost Williams.

For Navy passages: Mainly personal experience plus previous research. OPNAV P-03C-01-89, *US Navy Cold Weather Handbook for Surface Ships*, also came in handy. Ira Holwitt, Dan Steele, Aaron DeMeyer, Phil Wisecup, and Matthew Stroup were generous with their advice. Eric M. Durie at CHINFO East helped me contact commands and individuals. Michael Zias helped me out with the flying and air-crash details. The description of summer on the ice in chapter 12 is Dan Steele's, though the magic tricks are not.

The following served as background for technology, tactics, mindsets, and strategic decisions. "Special Drone Service," *The Economist*, June 22, 2019, p. 67. Malte Humpert, "The Future of the Northern Sea Route—A 'Golden Waterway' or a Niche Trade Route," Arctic Institute, Center for Circumpolar Security Studies, September 15, 2011. Dan Steele, "White Knuckles under the Ice," *Ocean Navigator: The Professional Mariner*, pp. 24–29, issue #103, January/February 2000. Also Mika Raunu and Rory Berke, "Preparing for Arctic Naval Operations," *US Naval Institute Proceedings*, December 2018. Joseph Trevithick, "Boeing Is Building Big Orca Drone Subs for the Navy to Hunt and Lay Mines and More," *The War Zone*, February 15, 2019. Also H. I. Sutton, "Inside Russia's Laika Next Generation Attack Submarine," *Naval News*, February 23, 2020. "Exhibit R-2, RDT&E Budget Item Justification: FY 2018," US Navy (Unclassified), May 2017. Finally, Walker D. Mills, "In the Arctic, Look to the Coast Guard," *US Naval Institute Proceedings*, August 2020.

Some of the verbiage of Novikov's declaration in the Afterimage was adapted from the statement of the leaders of the attempted coup in Moscow in 1991.

For overall help and encouragement, I owe recognition to the Surface Navy Association, Hampton Roads Chapter; to Charle Ricci, Stacia Childers, and Cara Burton of the Eastern Shore Public Library; with bows to Bill Doughty, John T. Fusselman, Diederick Wildeman, Richard Enderly, David W. Skinner, and others (they know who they are), both retired and still on active duty, who put in many hours leading me down the path of righteousness. If I left anyone out, deepest apologies!

Let me reiterate: the specifics of tactics, units, and locales are employed as the materials of story, not reportage. Some details have been altered to protect classified capabilities and procedures.

My deepest gratitude to George Witte, editor and friend of over three decades, without whom this series would not exist. And Sally Richardson,

Young Jin Lim, Ken Silver, Naia Poyer, Martin Quinn, Sarah Schoof, and Kevin Reilly at St. Martin's/Macmillan.

Thanks to my many fans who have stuck with me, and Dan, through these many volumes. And finally, to Lenore Hart, anchor on lee shores, and my North Star when skies are clear.

As always, all errors and deficiencies are my own!